"Every ph~~ ~~
sparkles wi~~~~ wit and charm." —*Romantic Times*

Praise for
The Devil's Delilah

"It is a rare pleasure indeed to savor the myriad pleasures of an author as talented as the Regency genre's newest superstar, Loretta Chase. . . . Truly reminiscent of the incomparable Georgette Heyer."
—*Romantic Times*

Praise for the novels
of Loretta Chase

"Poignant, beautifully written." —Mary Jo Putney

"Well-matched, appealing protagonists, a lively, witty writing style, and excellent dialogue . . . compelling."
—*Library Journal*

"Witty banter . . . terrific scenes . . . sparks fly . . . sensual." —*The Denver Post*

"The dialogue and witty writing are a delight and the characters are lovingly created."
—*The Atlanta Journal-Constitution*

"Great reading." —Pamela Morsi

"A formidable talent, indeed a dazzling diamond of the first water." —*Rave Reviews*

Viscount Vagabond

AND

The Devil's Delilah

Loretta Chase

A SIGNET BOOK

SIGNET
Published by New American Library, a division of Penguin Group (USA)
Inc., 375 Hudson Street, New York, New York 10014, U.S.A.
Penguin Books Ltd, 80 Strand, London WC2R 0RL, England
Penguin Books Australia Ltd, 250 Camberwell Road,
Camberwell, Victoria 3124, Australia
Penguin Books Canada Ltd, 10 Alcorn Avenue,
Toronto, Ontario, Canada M4V 3B2
Penguin Books (N.Z.) Ltd, Cnr Rosedale and Airborne Roads,
Albany, Auckland 1310, New Zealand

Penguin Books Ltd, Registered Offices:
80 Strand, London WC2R 0RL, England

Published by Signet, an imprint of New American Library, a division of
Penguin Group (USA) Inc. *Viscount Vagabond* was previously published
by Walker & Company and by Avon Books, a division of HarperCollins
Publishers. *The Devil's Delilah* was previously published by Walker & Company and by Fawcett Crest, a division of Random House Inc.

First Signet Printing, June 2004
10 9 8 7 6 5 4 3 2 1

Viscount Vagabond copyright © Loretta Chekani, 1988
The Devil's Delilah copyright © Loretta Chekani, 1989
Excerpt from *Miss Wonderful* copyright © Loretta Chekani, 2004
All rights reserved

 REGISTERED TRADEMARK—MARCA REGISTRADA

Printed in the United States of America

PUBLISHER'S NOTE
These are works of fiction. Names, characters, places, and incidents either
are the product of the author's imagination or are used fictitiously, and any
resemblance to actual persons, living or dead, business establishments,
events, or locales is entirely coincidental.

Viscount
Vagabond

= 1 =

CATHERINE PELLISTON HAD never beheld a naked man before. She had never, in fact, observed a man in any state of undress, unless one counted the draped figures in Great-Aunt Eustacia's collection of classical statuary. Those, however, had been carved stone, not at all like the large, all-too-animate male who was breathing alcoholic fumes into the stuffy room. Even Miss Pelliston's ramshackle papa, so careless of all else when in the latter stages of inebriation, remained properly—if not neatly—attired in her presence.

The figure floundering near the door, on the other hand, had already torn off his coat and neck-cloth and flung them to the floor. At the moment, he seemed to be trying to strangle himself with his shirt.

Miss Pelliston was possessed of an enquiring mind. This must explain why, despite the extreme gravity of her present situation and the natural modesty of a gently bred woman, she gaped in fascination at the broad, muscular shoulders and equally muscular chest now exposed to her view. Her analytical mind automatically began pondering several biological puzzles. Was it usual for the masculine chest to be covered with fine, light hair? If usual, what possible purpose could such growth serve?

As she posed these questions to herself, the object of her analysis yanked his shirt over his head and tossed it into a corner.

"Gad, what a curst business," he muttered. "Makes a man wish he was a Red Indian. A few hides to throw on and off and none of these infernal buttons."

Apparently in search of the buttons, he bent to peer owlishly at the waistband of his pantaloons—and over-turned himself in the process. He fell face forward with a loud thud.

"Deuce take it!"

Not at all disconcerted, the stranger struggled clumsily to his feet again. He squinted into the flickering shadows of the room, his gaze flitting confusedly from one object to the next before finally fixing on her.

"Ah, there you are," he said, staggering with the effort to remain focused on one spot. "Give a chap a hand, will you?"

To bring her mind from abstract theory to disagreeable actuality required a moment. In that brief time the man suc-ceeded in locating a trouser flap button and commenced a mighty struggle with it. The implications of this contest were not lost upon the stunned Miss Pelliston, who prompt-ly found her voice.

"Help you," she repeated at a somewhat higher than nor-mal pitch. "I should think not. In fact, I am certain it would be best for all concerned if you did not proceed further with—with your present activity. I fear, sir, you are labour-ing under a gross misapprehension—and no doubt strong drink as well," she finished primly.

"What the devil did y' say?"

To her relief, he stopped what he was doing to stare at her.

Relief swiftly gave way to apprehension as she realised what he was gawking at. The dreadful old harridan who'd abducted her had taken Catherine's clothes, providing in their place one tawdry, nearly transparent saffron gown with a neckline that drooped below all bounds of propriety. Her cheeks vermilion, Catherine hastily jerked the dingy coverlet up to her chin.

To her dismay, the great, drunken creature burst into laughter. His laugh was deep and resonant, and in other circumstances Catherine might have appreciated its tonal qualities. In the present case, the sound made her blood run

2

cold. His laughter seemed to fill the entire room. *He* seemed to fill the room. He was so large and overpowering, so male—and so very drunk.

God help me, she thought. Then she recollected that Providence helped those who helped themselves.

Gathering the coverlet more tightly about her as though it were the courage she felt fast ebbing away, she spoke. "In your current state of intoxication, a great many matters are bound to strike you as inexpressibly amusing. Nonetheless, I assure you, sir, that your guffaws are hardly appropriate to the present situation. I am not a—a—what I seem to be. I am here against my will."

Many people have nervous habits which grow more pronounced in times of agitation. Miss Pelliston tended to become preachy and pedantic when she was agitated. Her papa found this characteristic so unappealing that he had been known to toss the occasional bottle or mug in her direction. Since he was usually three parts disguised in these cases, he never struck her. He didn't particularly want to strike her. He only wanted her to go away.

Catherine cringed, half expecting something to be thrown at her as soon as the words were out of her mouth. When no object came flying past, she glanced up.

The man smiled—a crooked, drunken smile displaying a set of perfect, white teeth that made him look like a lunatic wolf—and advanced upon her. For a moment he swayed uncertainly over the bed upon which she seemed to be riveted. Then he dropped heavily onto it, raising a cloud of what she hoped was merely dust, and making the frame creak alarmingly.

"Of course you are, darling. They're always here against their will, to feed their poor starving infants or buy medicine for their aged grandmothers or some such tragedy. But enough of this game. You're here against your will and I haven't any, which puts us all square—and friendly, I hope."

He reached out to dislodge her fingers from the coverlet. She pulled back and leapt from the bed. Unfortunately, he

3

was now sitting on a corner of the coverlet. She could retreat only a few feet unless she chose to relinquish her makeshift cloak.

"Now where did you think you'd go?" he asked, having watched this exercise with some amusement. "What's gotten into you, dashing about to make a man's poor, tired head spin? Come, sweetheart." He patted the mattress. "Let's be comfortable."

"Good grief! Don't you understand?"

"No," came the cheerful reply. "I didn't come here to understand—or to talk. You're making me impatient, and I ain't even patient to begin with. Oh, all right. I'll chase you if you like." He started to get up, changed his mind, and slumped back against the pillow in a half-recumbent position. "Only it's such a bother."

Miss Pelliston realised that getting this drunken creature to understand her predicament and provide assistance was an unpromising endeavour at best. On the other hand, she could not afford to wait for another potential rescuer. Even if she got this one to leave—which was more than likely, if he was the impatient sort—what sordid species of humanity could she expect to darken the door next?

Catherine took a deep breath and spoke. "I have been brought here against my will. I was most foully deceived and abducted."

"Ah, abduction," said the man, nodding sleepily.

"It's quite true. Shortly after I disembarked at the coaching inn, a thief made off with my reticule. Mrs. Grendle, who was nearby, appeared to take pity on me. She seemed so kindly and motherly when she offered to take me to my destination that I foolishly accepted. We stopped for tea. I remember nothing that happened after, until I woke up in this very room to find all my belongings gone and that odious woman telling me how she meant to employ me."

"Oh, yes." His eyes were closed.

"Will you help me?" Catherine asked.

"What would you have me do, sweeting mine?"

She moved a tad closer to the bed. "Just help me get out

4

of this place. I can't do it on my own. Heaven knows I've tried, but they've kept the door locked, and you can see there are no windows. Moreover, before you came she promised unpleasant consequences if I made a fuss."

One unpleasant consequence was a burly fellow named Cholly, whom Mrs. Grendle had assured her was eager to teach Catherine her new trade if the young lady was unwilling to learn through trial and error on her own. Miss Pelliston preferred not to speak of that. Instead, she watched her visitor's face. She wondered if he'd gone to sleep, because he didn't answer or even open his eyes for the longest time.

So long a time was it that she began to wonder if she was going mad. Perhaps she'd never said a word and had only imagined herself speaking, as so often happened in nightmares. Perhaps, she thought, her heart sinking, *he* believed she was mad. A choking sob welled up in her throat. In the next instant she gasped in surprise as she found herself gazing into the bluest eyes she'd ever seen.

They were deep blue, the color of the late night summer sky, and framed with thick, dark lashes. Once more her analytical mind began running on its own as she wondered what on earth such a fine-looking young man was doing in this low place. Surely he had no need to *pay* for his sport. As she thought it, she blushed.

"Just escort you out the door, is that all?" he asked.

Catherine nodded.

"May a chap ask where you propose to go, with no clothes and, I take it, no money?"

Oh, heavens—he might actually help her! The words spilled out in a rush. "Why—why, you could lend me your coat, you see, and take me to the authorities, so we may report this dreadful business. I'm sure they will see justice done, and at least my belongings will be returned and I can go on as I'd intended—to find my, my friend, you know, with whom I was to visit."

Her sensible plan of proceeding seemed to leave him unimpressed—or perhaps was beyond his limited intellectual capacity—because he looked blank. Just as she was about to repeat the information in simpler terms, he spoke.

"You're serious, aren't you?" he asked.

"Oh, yes. Of course I am." Noting a suspicious twitch at the corner of his mouth, she drew herself up and continued with more dignity. "This is hardly a joking matter."

The piercing blue gaze travelled from the fuzzy light brown curls that formed a faery cloud about her head down to the bare toes that poked out from the frayed border of the coverlet. After another interminable silence, the man got up from the bed, yawned, stretched, and yawned again.

"Oh, very well," he said.

Mrs. Grendle was a plump woman of uncertain age and below-average stature. The inches Nature had denied her were compensated in part by an enormous mass of rigid curls, dyed apparently with shoe blacking and heaped upon her head like so many unappetizing sausages. Her lips and cheeks were carmine, and when she smiled, as she did now in her effort to understand just what her customer was proposing, the paint on her face cracked, loosening flakes of white powder which fluttered down upon her enormous, creased, and also thickly painted bosom. As she finally comprehended her client's request, the smile twisted into a ferocious scowl, showering more flakes onto the eroded white mountainside.

"Cholly!" she cried. "Jos!"

Two burly minions came running at the summons.

"Put him out," the brothel keeper commanded. "He's mad. He wants to steal one of the girls."

Cholly and Jos obediently laid their greasy hands on the client's shirtsleeves. The client looked down in a puzzled way at first one filthy paw, then the other. As his gaze rose to the faces of his assailants, his fist did also. He cracked Cholly on the nose, and Cholly staggered back. The customer then grasped Jos by the neck, lifted him off the floor, and threw him onto a large piece of obscene statuary. Jos and the statue crashed against the wall. The statue

6

crumbled into fragments and Jos sank unconscious to the floor. Cholly, his nose bleeding, advanced once more. The stranger's fist shot out again with force enough to hurl Cholly back against a door frame. There was a sickening crack, and Cholly also sank to the floor.

Mrs. Grendle had not survived in a hard world by fighting lost causes. She studied the wreckage briefly. Like any experienced commander, she must have decided that a change of tactic was required because, when she turned to her guest, her painted face was sorrowful.

"Here's a beastly mess you've made, sir, and me a poor helpless female only trying to earn my bread. A sick mother I have as well. Now there'll be the surgeon's fees for these two, and that fine statue which my late husband brought all the way from Italy, not replaceable at any price." She shook her head, setting the sausages atremble. "And when I think of the time and money spent on this ungrateful young person, I could weep."

"Yes, yes," the tall customer agreed impatiently. "How much to cover your costs and hurt feelings?" He drew out his purse.

The purse seemed a heavy one.

"Two hundred pounds," said the bawd, her voice brisk again. "One hundred for the girl and another for expenses."

Catherine, who'd shrunk into a corner to avoid the flying bodies, now ran forward to clutch her rescuer's arm. "Oh, no. Good heavens—pay her? Reward her for what she's done? It's—it's obscene."

"Don't scold, darlin'," he answered, pushing her behind him before returning his attention to Mrs. Grendle. "Two hundred pounds is a tad steep, ma'am. That ugly piece of plaster must have driven scores of customers away. It certainly scared the daylights out of me. Those chaps would be wanting an undertaker if I weren't in such a jolly mood, so there's more bother I've saved you. As to the girl—"

"A fine, healthy girl," the procuress interrupted.

The man glanced at Catherine, who flushed and clasped his coat more tightly about her.

"She doesn't look so healthy to me," he said. "She's awfully skinny—and I suspect she's bruised as well."

"If you wanted a plump armful, why didn't you say so?"

"Twenty pounds, ma'am."

"How dare you! She's cost me that much in food and drink alone. Not to mention her gown. Not to mention she hasn't earned a farthing."

"Then I expect you'll be glad to see the back of her. Thirty pounds, then."

"Two hundred."

"On the other hand," said the client as though he hadn't heard, "I could just take her away without this tiresome haggling. I 'magine you wouldn't like to bother the Watch about it."

Mrs. Grendle accepted the sum with much vivid description of her customer's want of human feeling and diverse anatomical inadequacies. He only grinned as he counted out the money into her hand.

The much-tried madam's forbearance was further tested when Catherine shrilly demanded the return of two bandboxes.

It took another twenty pounds to jog Mrs. Grendle's memory on this matter, but at length all the money was paid, the boxes collected, and Catherine, having hastily thrust her naked feet into her half boots, followed her rescuer out into the night.

"Where are we going?" Catherine asked, as she hurried after her gallant knight, who was zigzagging briskly down the filthy street.

"My lodgings." He threw this over his shoulder.

She stopped short. "But the authorities—I thought we were going to report that odious woman."

"It's much too late. Authorities are always cross if you bother them in the middle of the night. Besides, you got your things, didn't you?" He stopped to glance impatiently at her. "Are you coming or not?"

"I most certainly cannot come to your lodgings. It isn't proper."

The young man stood and surveyed her for a moment. The crooked smile broke out upon his face. "Silly girl. Where else do you 'spect to go dressed in my coat and little else?"

A large tear rolled down the young lady's thin nose.

"Oh, drat," he muttered.

Another tear slid down her cheek.

He heaved a sigh. Then he strode towards her, picked her up, flung her over his shoulder, and continued on his way.

"There you are," he announced as he deposited her in a chair. "Rescued."

"Yes," Catherine answered a trifle breathlessly. "Thank you."

She looked about her. The room was very dingy, dingier than that she'd recently escaped and in a far worse state of disorder. Her rescuer was increasing the disorder as he searched for a drink. The quest apparently required a great deal of thrashing about, the flinging of innocent objects onto the floor, and the opening and crashing shut of what sounded like dozens of drawers and cabinet doors.

At last he found the bottle he sought. With more bangs, bumps, and oaths, he succeeded in opening it, and broke only one glass in the complicated process of pouring the wine. After filling another none-too-clean tumbler for Catherine, he sat down at the opposite end of the cluttered table and proceeded to stare her out of countenance while he drank.

"You seemed nearly sober only a short time ago," Catherine finally managed to say. "I wish you would try to remain so, because I need your help."

"Had to be sober then. Business, you know. It wasn't easy, either, arguing with what looked like half a dozen old tarts at once. Those nasty black things on her head. Damme if I didn't think I'd cast up my accounts then and there."

"Which should indicate to you that you've had a sufficiency of intoxicating beverages, I would hope," Catherine retorted disapprovingly.

As soon as she spoke, she winced, expecting a volley of missiles. None came. The blue eyes only widened in befuddlement.

"How you scold, Miss—Miss—why, I'm hanged if we've even been introduced."

He jerked himself to his feet and made a sweeping bow that nearly sent him and the table crashing to the floor. At the very last instant he regained his balance.

"Curst floor won't stay put," he muttered. "Where was I? Oh, yes. Introductions. Max, you know. Max Demowery, at your service." This time he managed his bow with more grace. "And you, ma'am?"

"Catherine. Pe-Pettigrew," she stammered.

"Catherine," he repeated. "Cat. Nice. You look rather like a cat my sister once had—leastways when it was a kitten. All fluffy and big eyes. Only the little beast's eyes were green and yours—" He leaned forward to peer intently into her face, causing Catherine's heart to thump frantically. "Hazel!" he cried in triumph. "Odd color, but no matter. It's time we went to bed."

"To—to bed?" she echoed faintly.

"Y-yes," he mimicked. "More comfortable, y' know."

She looked about her again. As far as she could ascertain, his shabby lodgings comprised two rooms. There was no bed in this one. Her face grew warm. "Well, then, good night," she said politely.

Mr. Demowery considered this briefly. "I'm foxed, darlin', so maybe I'm not hearing straight—but that sounded om'nously like a dismissal."

"You expressed intentions of retiring."

"And you ain't 'retiring' with me?"

"Good heavens, I should hope not. I should not be in your lodgings in the first place. It's most improper."

"Sweetheart, I can't decide," he began slowly, after he'd mulled over these remarks as well, "whether you're insane

10

or horribly ungrateful. Didn't I just pay fifty quid for you?"

Her face flushed, this time with indignation. "You have preserved me from a fate reputed to be worse than death. I asked you to do so. It's completely illogical that I should express gratitude by doing exactly what I wished to avoid in the first place."

As he stood gazing at her, his puzzled expression gave way to a rueful smile. "Very complicated reasoning, m'love. Too complicated for me." He lifted her out of the chair, and, oblivious to her startled protests or the two small fists pounding on his chest, carried her to the bedroom and dropped her onto the bed.

"I will not cooperate," she gasped.

"No, of course you won't. It's just my luck, ain't it, this night of all the rest?" He turned and left the room.

Catherine lay upon the mattress, frozen with apprehension. Less than an hour before, her main concern had been escaping a place that could have been one of Dante's Circles of Hell. Now, evidently, she'd leapt out of the pan into the flames. She'd left home for excellent reasons with a logical plan. Now she could not believe she'd been so naive, so horribly misguided. She had fled what promised to be a life of wretchedness and rushed headlong into what had speedily become the most horrid two—or three or four, she hardly knew—days of her existence.

Despite his drunkenness and apparent penchant for squalor she had believed that her benefactor was not entirely sunk to the depths of depravity. Yet, instead of taking her directly to the authorities, he'd carried her over his shoulder like a sack of corn to his lodgings and clearly expressed intentions of bedding her.

Perhaps he too meant to drug her. Mayhap even now he was preparing some foul concoction and would come back to force it down her throat. Catherine scrambled out of the bed and ran to open the window. It was stuck shut. Furthermore, there were three floors between herself and the ground and no visible means of descent.

Her panicked gaze darted about the room. She dashed to

11

grab the basin from the washstand. Let him try, she told herself. Just let him try.

And if she did somehow miraculously succeed in overpowering a man nearly twice her size, what then? Where would she go, alone, in the middle of the night in this alien, hostile city? One crisis at a time, she counselled herself, as she crept to the door. She tried to close it quietly, but it would not shut altogether. Frustrated, she looked for a position from which she might take her attacker unawares.

At that moment she heard from the room beyond the terrifying noises by means of which primitive man once warned away the creatures skulking near his cave at night. She crept closer to the door and listened. It was true. Mr. Demowery was snoring.

For all that the sound might have in bygone days frightened away wild beasts, Miss Pelliston found it reassuring. She would wait another quarter hour to be absolutely certain he was asleep for the night. Papa was known to lose consciousness over his dinner—apparently dead to the world—then suddenly start up again minutes later, quarrelling with her as if he'd been awake the whole time.

Catherine was very weary, and the steady rhythm of that snoring made her drowsy. She looked longingly at the bed. She would lie down just for a few minutes and think what to do next. The few minutes stretched into half an hour, at the end of which Miss Pelliston too was fast asleep.

= 2 =

THE SUN, WHICH had risen many hours earlier, strove in vain to penetrate the grimy window as Clarence Arthur Maximilian Demowery awoke. He was not at all surprised at the great whacking and thundering inside his head, since he had awakened in this state nearly every day of the past six months. He was very much surprised, however, to find himself sprawled face down on a tattered piece of carpet in front of the sooty fireplace. Gingerly, he turned over on his side. A pair of shabby bandboxes blocked his view.

"Now where in blazes did you come from?" he asked. Though he spoke aloud, he was startled to hear a faint moan in reply. Had he moaned? From what seemed a great distance he heard a cough. Then he remembered.

He'd gone to Granny Grendle's to enjoy one last night of nonrespectablility. There he'd found a curiosity and had brought it—or her, rather—back with him. Though he was not at the moment certain why he'd done so, he was hardly surprised. As a child he'd regularly carried home curiosities of various sorts: insects, reptiles, and rodents, primarily. He wondered how his father would respond to this particular trophy. At eight and twenty, Max was too old and much too large to be spanked. Anyhow, there was no reason to enlighten his father regarding this or any other of the past six months' adventures.

A second faint moan from the bedroom dragged Mr. Demowery to his feet. Not only his head but his muscles ached, jogging his memory regarding several other details.

He'd gotten into a brawl in a low brothel, after which he'd also parted with fifty pounds for the privilege of hearing a bit of muslin show her gratitude by politely denying him the favours he'd so extravagantly paid for.

He hauled his weary body to the partially open bedroom door and glared at the frail form entangled in the bedclothes. A cloud of light brown hair billowed over the pillow, veiling what seemed to be a very small face, out of which poked a straight, narrow little nose. Gad, he thought in sudden self-disgust—she's only a child.

At that moment the object of his scrutiny opened her eyes, and his heart sank. They were wide, innocent hazel eyes whose expression changed from childlike wonder to fear in the instant it took her to recall where she was.

"How old *are* you?" he asked abruptly, feeling unaccountably frightened himself and therefore more annoyed.

"One and twenty," she gasped.

"Hah!" He marched away from the door and threw himself into a chair.

Steadfastly he ignored the sounds that issued from the bedroom—the rustle of bedclothes, the splash of water, more rustling, and some thumps. He pretended not to see her creep out to grab her bandboxes and scurry back to the room again, pushing the stubborn door half-closed behind her.

When she finally emerged, he thrust past her into the bedroom and took an abnormally long time about his own washing up. Was *that* what he'd brought home? Dressed in a sober grey frock, with all that glorious hair yanked back into a vicious little knot, she seemed neither the curious baggage he'd taken her for last night nor the child he'd believed was swaddled in his bedclothes.

Yet the frock and bun matched what he recalled of her conversation. She had sounded like a schoolmistress last night, and that in combination with the personal charms he'd briefly glimpsed had appealed to his sense of humour—or maybe his sense of the absurd was more like it. Such a creature was not at all what one expected to find in an establishment such as Granny Grendle's.

Max Demowery was no wet-behind-the-ears schoolboy. He'd had considerable experience with the frail sorority in England and abroad, in the course of which he'd heard any number of pathetic tales. He'd not actually believed her story, but had taken her away because she amused him. Purchasing her from the old bawd had seemed a fitting conclusion to his six-month orgy of dissipation.

Not until the young woman had declined to reward him as he'd expected had he, drunk as he was, begun to wonder whether her tale was true. Besides, he'd never yet forced himself upon a woman.

That was as far as he'd been able to reason at the time. Today, in the clear, too-bright light of early afternoon, he found a deal more to puzzle and distress him. A common strumpet he could put back upon the streets without a second thought, assuming confidently that she must be able to survive there or she would never have reached the advanced age of one and twenty. Suppose, however, she wasn't street goods?

Suppose nothing, he told himself as he savagely scoured his face with the towel. If he had a sense of impending doom, that was because he was hungry and out of sorts. He'd give her some money and send her on her way.

He was debating whether to shave now or after breakfast when he heard the door to the hall creak. Flinging away the towel, he hurried out of the room to find the young woman attempting to close the door behind her without dropping her bandboxes.

He ought to have breathed a sigh of relief and cried good riddance, but he caught a glimpse of her face and found himself asking instead, "What the devil d'you think you're doing?"

Her guilty start caused her to drop one of her boxes. "Oh. I was leaving. That is, I should never have abused your hospitality in the first place. I mean, I should never have fallen asleep—"

"Ah, you meant to leave in the dead of night."

"Yes. No." She reached up to push back under her dowdy bonnet a wispy curl that had broken loose from its moorings.

Part of his brain was wondering why she'd made herself so deuced unattractive, while the other part watched, fascinated, as she struggled not to look frightened. Each step in the process of composing herself was evident in her face, and most especially in her large, expressive eyes.

"What I mean is, this is a very awkward situation. Moreover, I have put you out dreadfully, and therefore it seemed best to go away and leave you in peace. I'm sure you must have a great deal to do."

"You might have said good-bye first. It's usually done in the best circles."

"Oh, yes. I'm so sorry. I never meant to be rude." She picked up the bandbox. "Good-bye, then," she said. "No, that's not all. Thank you for all you've done. I will repay you—the fifty pounds, I mean. I'll send it here, shall I?"

Though Mr. Demowery didn't know what he'd expected, he was sure it wasn't this. He was also certain that, even if she were not a child, she might as well be, so frail was she and so utterly naive and so very lost—like some faery sprite that had wandered too far from its woodland home.

This fanciful notion irritated him, making him speak more harshly than he intended. "You'll do no such thing. What you will do is leave hold of those ridiculous boxes and sit yourself down and eat some breakfast."

"*Sit*," he repeated when she began backing towards the stairs. "If you won't on your own, I'll help you."

She bit her lip. "Thank you, but I'd much rather you didn't." She reentered, dropped the bandboxes, marched to a chair, and sat down. "I've been flung about quite enough," she added in a low voice, her narrow face mutinous.

"Beg your pardon, ma'am—Miss Pettigrew, if I remember aright—but you picked an uncommon careless and impatient chap as your rescuer. Right now I'm impatient for my breakfast. It'll take a while, I'm afraid, because my landlady is the slowest, stupidest slattern alive. While I'm gone, I hope you don't get any mad notions about sneaking away. You're in the middle of St. Giles's. If you don't know what that means, I suggest you think about Cholly and Jos and imagine several hundred of their most intimate acquaintance upon the streets. That should give you a notion, though a rosy one, of the neighbourhood."

Catherine's host returned some twenty minutes later bearing a tray containing a pot of coffee and plates piled with slabs of bread, butter, and cheese.

They ate in silence for the most part, Mr. Demowery being preoccupied with assuaging his ravenous hunger, and Miss Pettigrew (née Pelliston) being unable to form any coherent sentence out of the muddle of worries besetting her. Only when he was certain no crumbs remained did Max turn his attention again to his guest.

Now that his stomach was full and his head relatively clear, he wondered anew what had come over him last night. She was not at all in his style. He was a tall, powerfully built man and preferred women who weren't in peril of breaking if he touched them. Full-bosomed Amazons were his type—lusty, willing women who didn't mind if a man's head was clouded with liquor and his manners a tad rough and tumble, so long as his purse was a large and open one.

He was amazed that, after taking one look at this stray, he had not stormed back to Granny Grendle to demand a more reasonable facsimile of a female. Miss Pettigrew appeared woefully undernourished, so much so that he'd thought her smaller than she actually was. In fact, she was so scrawny that he wondered just what had seemed so intriguing last night. This, however, troubled him less than the realisation that he'd come so close to forcing his great, clumsy person upon this young waif.

He'd never had a taste for the children who walked the streets of London by night and populated its brothels, though he knew of many fine fellows who did. Had six months' wallowing through every sort of low life in a last, desperate attempt to enjoy something like freedom finally rotted his character and corrupted his mind?

Still, he dismally reminded himself, there would be no more such excursions into London's seamier locales. If he sought feminine company in the future, he'd be obliged to do so in the accepted way. He would go through the tiresome negotiations required to set up some Fashionable Impure as his mistress. Even the assuaging of simple carnal needs would be complicated by some infernally convoluted etiquette. He refused to think about the greater complications he could expect when he acquired a wife—and the passel of heirs his father impatiently awaited.

Mr. Demowery glowered at the elf—or whatever she was—and was further annoyed at the fear that leapt into her eyes. "Oh, I ain't going to eat you," he snapped. "Already had my breakfast."

"Yes," she answered stiffly. "I'm amazed you had the stomach for it. My f—that is, some people are quite unfit for taking any sustenance after a night of overindulgence."

She winced—no, actually, she ducked. Dimly he recalled seeing that nervous movement before. He wondered if it were a tic.

"Oh, I'm so sorry. You were very kind to share your breakfast with me. Thank you." She stood up. "I should not keep you any longer. I've put you out quite enough, I expect." After a brief hesitation, she put out her hand. "Goodbye, Mr. Demowery."

Remembering his manners, he rose to accept the proffered handshake. What a small white hand it was, he thought as his own large tanned paw swallowed it up. That realisation also annoyed him, and he was about to hurry her on her way when he glanced at her face. Her expressive hazel eyes gave the lie to the rigid composure of her countenance. Her eyes said distinctly, "I am utterly lost, utterly frantic."

Mr. Demowery's own face assumed an expression of resignation. "I don't suppose you have any idea where you're going?"

"Of course I do. My friend—the friend I had intended to visit—"

"I can't imagine what sort of friend would let an ignorant young miss find her own way from a coaching inn through a strange city, but I suppose that's none of my business. Still, I ain't ignorant, and I know that if you were foolish enough to be cozened by that old strumpet, you'll never make it to this friend of yours on your own. If you'll give me a few minutes to change into something I haven't slept in, I'll take you."

"Oh—that's very kind of you, but not at all necessary. I can find my way in broad daylight, I'm sure."

"Not in this neighbourhood, sweetheart. Night or day is all the same to the rogues about here."

She paused. Obviously, she was weighing the perils of the squalid streets against the dangers of accepting his protection. She must have concluded that he was the lesser of two evils, because she soon managed a squeaky thanks, then began an intensive survey of the ragged corner of carpet on which she stood.

Max Demowery did not consider himself a Beau of Society. The process of shaving and changing was therefore accomplished in short order. A few fierce strokes with his brush were enough to subdue his tangle of golden hair, and with scarcely a glance into the stained mirror he strode out to rejoin his guest.

Not until they had nearly reached their destination—Miss Collingwood's Academy for Young Ladies—did the sense of impending doom return to settle upon Mr. Demowery's brow. A school?

He stole a glance at the young woman beside him. She looked like a schoolteacher, certainly, and her air and manners, not to mention her speech, bespoke education and good breeding. It was as he had feared: She was respectable and her story had been true and though all that had been evident by the time they'd left his lodgings, only now did the implications occur to him. Any respectable woman

19

who'd spent two nights as she had just done was ruined—if, that is, anyone learned of the matter.

He halted abruptly and grabbed Miss Pettigrew's arm. "I say, you'd better not tell anyone where you've been, you know. That is," he went on, feeling vaguely ashamed as the hazel eyes searched his face, "you may not have considered the consequences."

"Good grief, do you think I've considered aught else? I shall have to tell a falsehood and pray I'm not asked for many details. I shall say I was delayed and pretend that my message to that effect must have gone astray. It must be simple," she explained, "because I'm not at all adept at lying."

This being a perfectly sensible conclusion, Mr. Demowery had no reason to be sharp with her, but he answered before he stopped to reason. "Good," he snapped. "I'm relieved you don't have any hard feelings. I did, after all, take you to my lodgings in opposition to your expressed wishes. Another woman would have exacted the penalty."

"I collect you mean she would insist that you marry her," was the thoughtful response. "Well, that would be most unjust. In the first place, though you arrived at erroneous conclusions about my character, the evidence against me was most compelling. Second, you must have reconsidered, since I am quite—unharmed. Finally," she continued, as though she were helping him with a problem in geometry, "it is hardly in my best interests to wed a man I met in a house of ill repute, even if I had any notion how to force a man to marry me, which I assure you I have not."

"No idea at all?" he asked, curious in spite of himself.

"No, nor is it a skill I should be desirous of cultivating. An adult should not be forced into marriage as a child is forced to eat his peas. Peas are only part of a meal. Marriage is a life's work."

"I stand corrected, Miss Pettigrew," he replied gravely. "In fact, I feel I should be writing your words upon my slate one hundred times."

She coloured. "I do beg your pardon. You were most kind to consider my situation, and I ought not have lectured."

Whatever irritation he'd felt was washed away by a new set of emotions, too jumbled to be identified. He brushed away her apology with some smiling comment about being so used to lectures that he grew lonely when deprived of them.

They had reached the square in which Miss Collingwood's Academy was located.

"Shall I wait for you?" he asked, hoping she'd decline and at the same time inexplicably dismayed at the prospect of never seeing her again.

He had at least a dozen questions he wished she'd answer, such as why and how she'd come to London and where she'd come from and who or what she was, really. Yet, it was better not to know, because knowing was bound to complicate matters.

"Oh, no! That is, you've already gone so far out of your way, and there is no need. I'll be all right now." She took from him the bandboxes he'd been carrying. "Thank you again," she said. "That sounds so little, after all you've done for me, but I can't think how else—"

"Never mind. Good-bye, Miss Pettigrew."

He bowed and walked away. A minute later he stopped and turned in time to see her being admitted into the building. He grew uneasy. "Oh, damnation," he muttered, then moved down to the corner of the street and leaned against a lamppost to wait.

"Oh, dear," said Miss Collingwood. "This is most awkward." Her fluttering, blue-veined hand flew up to fidget with the lace of her cap. "I sent your letter along to Miss Fletcher—that is, Mrs. Brown, now, of course. Did she not write you?"

Without waiting for an answer, the elderly lady continued, "No, I would expect not. I am sure she had not another thought in this world but of *him*, and what a pity that is. She was the most conscientious instructor I have had since I founded this school, and the girls doted upon her. Naturally, I was compelled to discharge him. I have never held with these odd conventions that it is always the woman's fault. Men are such wicked deceivers. If even Miss Fletcher could be overcome, what hope is there for weaker vessels, I ask you? To be sure, he was a most charming man. Ten years with us and always most correct in his behaviour, though the girls *will* become infatuated with the music master."

Catherine barely heard the headmistress. Miss Fletcher, that paragon of propriety, had run off with the music master? No wonder she hadn't answered Catherine's last letter. By the time that epistle reached the school, Miss Pelliston's former governess had already become Mrs. Brown and departed with her new husband for Ireland.

"I'm so sorry you have come out of your way for naught," Miss Collingwood continued. "I feel responsible. I should have counselled Miss Fletcher: marry in haste, repent at leisure." ·

"I'm sure you did all you could," was the faint reply. "I should have waited until I heard from her . . . though it was inconceivable that she should not be here. She last wrote me but two months ago and only mentioned Mr. Brown in passing. Still, I was at fault."

Greatly at fault, Catherine's conscience reminded. She had let her hateful passions rule her and was now reaping the reward.

"No doubt," Catherine went on, pinning what she hoped was a convincing smile on her face, "Miss Fletcher's reply is at home awaiting me."

After assuring Miss Collingwood that the trip would not be a total loss, and concocting some plausible story about doing a bit more shopping (that explained the bandboxes) with the aunt who'd supposedly travelled with her and was now visiting friends, Catherine took her leave.

She made her way slowly down the street, not only because she did not know where to go, but because her conscience was plaguing her dreadfully and she must argue with it.

She would not be in this predicament if she hadn't run away from home, but she wouldn't have run away if her papa had only stopped now and then to think what he was doing. However, he never thought—not about her certainly. His cronies, his hounds, his wenching and drinking were much more important.

Papa should have arranged for her to have a Season. Even Miss Fletcher had believed he would, or she'd never have accepted the post in London three years ago. Instead, he had sent Catherine to live with Great-Aunt Eustacia. If that elderly lady had not died a year and a half later, Catherine would be there yet. She would have endured those endless monologues on religion and genealogy day after day until she dwindled into a lonely spinster like Aunt Deborah, who'd been the old lady's companion for some thirty years before Catherine came.

She had no illusions about her attractions. Her sole assets were her lineage and her father's wealth. She knew she had no chance of attracting a husband unless she entered an environment where suitable bachelors abounded. That meant the London Marriage Mart.

Yet, even after the family's mourning period, had Papa troubled himself about his daughter's Season? Of course not, she thought, staring morosely at her trudging feet. He thought only of himself. He went off to Bath and found himself a handsome young widow. Upon his return, he'd announced his own and his daughter's wedding plans simultaneously.

Lord Browdie, of all people, was to be her mate. He was more slovenly, crude, and dissolute than Papa. The man was ignorant, moody, and repulsive. Catherine had never expected a Prince Charming—she was no Incomparable herself—but to live the rest of her days with that middle-aged boor! She had borne much in the name of filial obedience, but Lord Browdie was past all enduring.

Now she knew better. Now she knew what it was to be utterly helpless, utterly without protection, and virtually without hope. She had no idea how to get home, dreadful as that homecoming would be. She had not a farthing to her name, and Mr. Demowery must be miles away by now.

=== 3 ===

HER EYES SWAM with tears, and Catherine scarcely noticed where she walked. She would have stumbled into the path of an oncoming carriage if a hand had not shot out to grab her elbow and drag her back to the curb.

"Damme if you ain't an accident waiting to happen," said a familiar voice.

Still immersed in her misery, Catherine looked up into a lean, handsome face. As she had the previous night, she caught her breath, as though the piercing blue of his eyes had stabbed her to the heart.

"You ought to be carried about in a bandbox yourself." He took her baggage from her.

"Mr. Demowery, how—what are you doing here?"

"Protecting my investment. I wasn't about to watch fifty quid trampled into a puddle. Not to mention how it mucks up the streets, don't you know?" With that, he strode swiftly away from the square, and she, seeing no alternative, followed him. They had not gone many yards before he located a hackney. Not until her luggage was stowed away and she had been hustled into the musty-smelling vehicle did Catherine venture to ask where they were going.

"That's what I'm trying to figure out," was the abstracted answer.

"Oh, no. I mean, there isn't anything to figure out. I shall have to go back now."

"Back where? Granny Grendle's?"

"Good heavens, no! I shall have to return h-home."

24

Though her voice broke at the last, Catherine squeezed back the tears that had welled up as soon as she'd thought what she'd be returning to.

"Is it as bad as all that?"

The sympathy she heard in his voice nearly undid her. So unused was she to sympathy of any kind that it rather frightened her, in fact. "Oh, no. I've made a dreadful mistake. I see that now, and it has been a lesson to me—not to let my passions rule me, I mean," she explained, just as though he had been Miss Fletcher and had asked her to examine her conscience.

"What passions are those, Miss Pettigrew?"

"Resentment, certainly. And pride. And—oh, everything opposed to reason and good sense. If I'd stayed and done what I was told, none of these horrid things would have happened to me—"

"What were you told?" he interrupted.

Subterfuge was alien to Miss Pelliston's character. She was, as she had admitted, an inept liar. The fibs she'd told Miss Collingwood had cost Catherine agonies of guilt. Besides, she could conceive of no more unworthy return for his unexpected kindness than to lie to him.

She told him the truth, though she eliminated the more sensational elements in order to present the matter with dry objectivity. She did not enlighten him regarding her true identity, either, and named no other names. Though that was not precisely objective, she had rather keep her disgrace as private as possible.

"So you ran away because you couldn't stomach marrying the old fellow your father chose for you?"

"I never stopped to consider what I could endure, Mr. Demowery. I'm afraid I did not weigh the matter as carefully as I ought," she said, gazing earnestly into his handsome face. "I just took offence—"

"And took off." He smiled—not the crooked, drunken grin of last night but a friendly, open smile. "Yes, I see now what a passion-driven creature you are. Oh, don't go all red on me again. The colour's too bright and you must think of

25

my poor head. I ain't fully recovered, you know."

She drew herself up. "Actually, I am seldom ruled by emotion. This is the first time I can remember ever behaving so—so unsensibly."

"Sounds sensible enough to me. As you said before, people shouldn't be forced to marry. M' sister felt the same. Bolted, when m' father tried to shackle her to some rich old prig. They tried to get me to fetch her back, but I wouldn't. You wouldn't either, if you knew Cousin Agatha. That's who Louisa went to. That's what you need, Miss Pettigrew—a Cousin Agatha to terrify your papa into submission."

"Well, all I had was Miss Fletcher and she doesn't terrify anyone, and now she's gone," Catherine answered ruefully.

"What, no old dragon ladies in the family to scorch your papa's whiskers for him?"

Catherine shook her head.

"Then I think," said Mr. Demowery, turning his blue gaze to the greasy window, "you had better meet Louisa."

"Bolted?" Lord Browdie exclaimed. "Well, if that don't beat all."

He ran his thick fingers over the rough, reddish stubble on his chin. Probably should have shaved, he thought, though that seemed a deal of trouble to go to merely on Catherine's account.

Miss Deborah Pelliston left off snuffling into her black-bordered handkerchief long enough to offer a weak protest. "Oh, don't say it," she moaned. "I cannot believe Catherine would do such a thing. Surely there is a misunderstanding. She may have met with an accident or, heaven help us, foul play."

"And left a note? That don't make sense."

The glass of Madeira at his elbow did, however, make sense to his lordship. Therefore, he turned his attention to that while nodding absently at his hostess's stream of incoherent complaint.

Should have married the little shrew right off, he thought sourly. She'd be broken to harness now. Instead there was going to be a deal of bother and no one but himself to deal with it.

The whole business ought to have been simple enough. James Pelliston had decided to marry a handsome widow from Bath. The widow didn't think a house required two mistresses and had dropped a hint to her future husband. Pelliston, as usual, had confided the problem to his crony: what was to be done with Catherine?

The crony had considered the matter over a bottle of brandy. He considered the property Catherine's great-aunt had left her and found that agreeable. He considered Catherine's appearance and decided he'd seen worse, especially now she was out of that hideous mourning. He considered that he himself had long been in need of an heir and therefore a wife, which in any other case would require a lot of tedious courtship. Catherine's like or dislike of himself he considered not a jot.

"I'll take her off your hands," he'd charitably offered.

By the time the gentlemen emptied another bottle, the dowry had been settled and an agreement reached whereby the two households would take Aunt Deborah by turns, until such time as neither could put up any longer with her whimpering and she might be packed off to quarters in nearby Bath.

The two men had toasted each other into a state of cheerful oblivion after settling matters to their satisfaction. Since that time, over two months ago, Lord Browdie had spoken to Catherine once, at her father's wedding. Their conversation had consisted of Lord Browdie's jovially informing his betrothed that she was too pale and skinny and should eat more. Like the other wedding guests, Lord Browdie then proceeded to drink himself into a stupor. He never noticed his fiancee's disappearance. He had enough trouble remembering she existed at all.

Yesterday, the engagement ring he'd ordered in a fit of magnanimity had arrived. He'd come this afternoon to present it to his affianced bride. The trouble was, she'd fled three days ago during the wedding celebration, and this sniffling, whining, moaning creature sitting on the other side of the room had been too busy having megrims and palpitations to report the matter to him immediately. By now Catherine might be anywhere, her trail so cold he doubted that even his well-trained hounds could track her down.

"Wish you'd told me right off," his lordship grumbled when there was a break in the snuffling and sobbing.

"Oh, dear, I'm sure I meant to. That is, I wasn't sure if I ought. I never missed her that night because I'd gone to bed so early with a terrible headache. Then, when I found that dreadful note next day, I had such fearful palpitations and was so ill I couldn't think at all, and with James away . . . Well, one cannot trust the servants, because they will talk and the scandal would kill me, I know it. So I kept to my room. But who could have imagined she would do such a shameful thing? Such a good, biddable girl she has always been."

"Never thought she had the pluck," said Lord Browdie, half to himself. "Anyhow, where's the scandal in it?" he asked his hostess. "Ain't no fine Society hereabouts to be shocked. Just let on she's sick."

"But the servants—"

"Will keep their tongues in their heads if they know what's good for them. I'll talk to them," Lord Browdie assured her as he dragged his gangly body up from the chair.

"You are too kind. You make me quite ashamed that I did not confide this trouble to you immediately—"

"Yes, yes. Just calm yourself, ma'am. Important to behave as though nothing's happened out of the ordinary."

"But surely James must be told—"

"No sense interrupting his bridal trip. By the time he's back we'll have Cathy home safe and sound, and no one the wiser." He had no difficulty speaking with more confidence than he felt. Lord Browdie was accustomed to swagger.

Miss Deborah sighed. "It is such a relief to have a man take charge. I cannot tell you how beset I've been, not knowing where to turn or what to do. Why, I'm frightened half to death each time the post is delivered, not knowing what news it will bring—though she did say she would be perfectly safe. But will not her friends wonder when she doesn't answer their letters?"

As far as Lord Browdie knew, Catherine hadn't any friends. He pointed this out to his hostess.

In response, and with much fussing and flustering, the lady drew out a letter from her workbasket. "It's from Ireland," she explained, handing it to Lord Browdie. "I did not like to leave it lying about, because the servants—" She gasped as he tore the letter open. "Oh, my—I don't think— it is *hers*, after all."

He ignored her twittering as he scanned the fine, precise handwriting. Then he folded the letter and stuffed it into the tail pocket of his coat. "Good enough," he said. "Won't be no wild-goose chase after all. She's gone to London."

"Dear heaven!" The spinster sank back in her seat, fumbling for her smelling salts.

"Now, now, don't fuss yourself," Lord Browdie said irritably. "There's only the one place she can go, so there'll be no trouble finding her. No trouble at all."

Miss Collingwood's Academy had been squeezed into a tidy corner of a neighbourhood best described as shabbily genteel. Miss Collingwood catered to bourgeois families that did not yet aspire to the glory of housing governesses, but did wish to improve their daughters' chances of upward mobility by means of a not-too-taxing course of education. While the training would not make a butcher's daughter a lady, it might subdue the more blatant signs of her origins.

The streets the hackney coach now traversed bespoke an entirely different social level. Here were trees enclosed in tidy squares upon which the sparkling windows of elegant townhouses bent their complacent gazes. These streets were wider, cleaner, and a good deal quieter, their peace broken only by the rumble of elegant carriages and the clip-clop of high-stepping thoroughbreds. A gentleman stood at one doorway drawing on his gloves as his tiger soothed the restless, high-strung horses impatiently waiting. On the sidewalk, a neatly dressed female servant hastened along, basket in hand.

Catherine surveyed the passing vista with confusion at first, then growing anxiety as her companion replied that, yes, they had long since left the City proper and were now in Mayfair. She shrank deeper into her corner of the coach and wished there had been room in her bandboxes for an enormous poke bonnet. This was precisely the sort of neighbourhood in which one could expect to meet Papa's friends. Lord Pelliston never came to Town, but his cronies did. How would she explain her presence here if one of them recognised her?

The hackney finally halted before a splendid townhouse of classical design and proportions. Catherine concluded that Mr. Demowery's sister must have married very well indeed, even if she had rejected the "rich old toad" her parents had initially selected for her.

So preoccupied was Miss Pelliston with her wonderings and worries that she scarcely attended to her companion's conversation with the butler. Only when she was ushered into the sumptuous drawing-room and beheld her hostess did the words belatedly register.

The butler had addressed Mr. Demowery as "my lord," and was not corrected. Now Catherine heard distinctly the sigh of exasperation her benefactor uttered when the butler announced, "Lord Rand to see you, My Lady." Miss Pelliston's face grew hot and her heart began pounding so hard that she believed it must burst from her bosom.

"Ah, Max," said the lady. "Am I the first to behold the prodigal's return?" She gave her brother a peck on the cheek before glancing enquiringly at Catherine.

"Louisa, may I present Miss Catherine Pettigrew. Miss Pettigrew, Lady Andover—m' sister, that is."

The ersatz Miss Pettigrew sank into a graceful curtsey, and wished she might sink through the floor. Her benefactor's sister was the Countess of Andover! Her benefactor himself was a nobleman. Demowery, indeed—

he probably had a dozen names besides.

When Catherine rose she found Lord Rand staring at her in that puzzled way he'd done several times before. She gave him one reproachful look, then turned to his sister, who was expressing rather subdued pleasure at the acquaintance while dropping a quizzical glance at Miss Pettigrew's frock.

In her ladyship's place, Catherine would have been hard put to express any sort of pleasure at all. What must the countess be thinking? Catherine looked like a betweenstairs servant. She had carefully designed a wardrobe that would convey that impression. To dress as befitted her station would have aroused speculation and, probably, trouble during her travels. Her present costume, however, was bound to provoke another sort of speculation in these surroundings.

Still, for all that Lord Pelliston was an arrant scapegrace, his title went back to the eleventh century at least, and his daughter had been scrupulously trained. She returned the countess's greeting in her politest manner, apologised for intruding, made another curtsey then turned to leave the room.

Lord Rand's none-too-gentle grip on her elbow prevented her. "Dash it, Miss Pettigrew, don't be such a coward. It's only Louisa, you know. She won't bite you."

"Not, certainly, on such short acquaintance," Lady Andover observed. She gestured towards a chair. "Won't you be seated? I'll order some refreshment."

Miss Pettigrew murmured more gratitude and apologies along with a firm expression of her intentions to leave.

"Oh, sit down," said her benefactor. "You haven't anywhere to go, you know, and wouldn't have the first idea how to get there if you did. Besides which, Louisa's all afever to know why you're here and who you are, only she's too dashed well-bred to show it. Ain't that so, Louisa?"

"I am curious why Miss Pettigrew looked so stunned when Jeffers announced you, Max. Have you been running about under false colours all these months?"

Without waiting for a reply, she bade her brother ring for a servant. That personage appeared instantly—not at all, Catherine thought, like those at home, who pretended to be deaf, and then if they did heed a summons were prodigiously offended. This one appeared, vanished, and reappeared in minutes, a scrupulously polite and efficient wraith.

In the interim Lord Rand's sister kept up a light flow of amusing conversation, unaided by her two visitors and all about the weather. The tea arrived along with coffee for her brother, who gave one affronted look at the cup offered him and marched to a table upon which stood several decanters.

"Max," said the countess.

He stopped in the act of lifting a decanter.

"You require coffee, My Lord."

"Dash it, Louisa," he muttered, putting the bottle back. "It's well past noon."

"So it is. Still, I suspect you have some explaining to do not only to me, but to Miss Pettigrew, and you are cryptic enough when sober."

"Nothing to explain," his lordship answered as he studied the sparkling crystal containers wistfully. "I found Miss Pettigrew in a spot of trouble and hadn't time to discuss genealogy. Not that she's been very forthcoming herself."

The sister returned her attention to her oddly attired guest. "Sugar, Miss Pettigrew?"

Catherine, who'd been staring at the vagabond who'd so abruptly turned into a member of the nobility, dragged her gaze back to her hostess, and then wondered how one could have possibly ignored, even for an instant, this magnificent woman.

The Countess of Andover was as fair-haired as her brother and quite tall as well, but his lean, chiselled features found a softer counterpart in her lovely countenance. Clad in an aqua gown that seemed to have been poured upon her perfect form, Lady Andover was the most beautiful woman Catherine had ever seen. Though not *au courant* with the latest modes, Miss Pelliston was sure that the countess's gown must be the first stare of fashion, the handiwork of the finest of *couturieres*.

Nearly blinded by her hostess's brilliance, Catherine grew agonizingly conscious of her own drab appearance. A guilty conscience, which in recent hours had developed all the vicious attributes of a swarm of outraged wasps, did not improve her poise. All she could manage was a nod.

"What sort of trouble?"

Though Lady Andover's voice was kindly enough, the suspicious glance she sent in her brother's direction brought two bright spots of color to Catherine's cheeks. Luckily, Miss Pelliston was spared from replying when Lord Rand favoured his sister with an answering scowl.

"You needn't look as though it were *my* doing, Louisa. Leastways, to start off with it wasn't." He wrenched himself away from the tempting array of decanters and took a seat by her ladyship.

He seemed, Catherine thought, suddenly very uncomfortable, though she could not be sure she wasn't investing him with her own feelings. She, after all, was fervently wishing she might melt quietly into the Aubusson carpet and thus be relieved of having her outrageous behaviour and its gruesome consequences called to this lady's attention.

"Then what have you done, Max?"

"Oh, please," Catherine interrupted. "Mr.—his lordship has been everything that is kind, and it is all my fault, really."

"It *ain't* your fault, and I can't think what bloody idiot's filled your head with that sort of nonsense that you've got to be beggin' everyone's pardon for doing what any woman in her right mind would do. Dash it, Louisa, you'd think it was the Dark Ages still in this curst country."

"I must admit that at present your subject is rather dark to me," his sister replied. "Perhaps Miss Pettigrew can be more enlightening."

Miss Pettigrew had thus far managed to endure any number of indignities without weeping. Now, at being accused of nonsensicality, she gave way. Her chest heaved, and the tears she struggled in vain to keep back made it rather difficult to understand the shameful words she blurted out.

"Ran away?" Lady Andover repeated, after her brother had translated. "I don't understand. Surely Miss Pettigrew is not an apprentice."

"Of course not. What are you thinking, Louisa?"

"If she is not a runaway apprentice, why does she weep? I shall have to consult Edgar, of course, but as I understand, it is runaway apprentices who are subject to legal action. It may be a fine or imprisonment—"

"She ran away from home because her father's making her marry some old dotard." Lord Rand went on to explain about the stolen reticule and the elopement of Miss Fletcher. Catherine was relieved to note (between sobs) that he tactfully left out certain other adventures and described the events as having occurred but a few hours ago.

When he'd finished his summary and answered one or two of his sister's questions, that lady directed her gaze to her guest, who had regained a semblance of composure.

"I see," said the countess. "Max has brought you here in order that I may enact the role of Cousin Agatha."

"Oh, no! I told him I meant to go home. That is—" Catherine's colour deepened, but she swallowed her pride and went on. "I'm afraid I will need the loan of a few shillings for coach fare."

"Now if that ain't the most cowardly thing—"

"Max," Lady Andover said quietly.

"But she can't—"

"If Miss Pettigrew wishes to return, I can hardly keep her prisoner, can I?"

"Dash it all, Louisa—"

The countess turned her back upon her brother. "All the same, Miss Pettigrew," she said, "you are too overset at present for travel. You will pardon my saying so, but your colour is not good. If I were to allow you to depart now, my conscience would plague me so, *I* would become ill."

"Really, I'm quite well," Catherine protested. "I've never had good colour."

"My conscience refuses to believe you. I do apologise, my dear, but mine is a very fierce conscience. Molly will convey you to a guest chamber and bring you a fresh cup of tea—you've scarcely touched yours and it is grown cold, I'm afraid." Lady Andover's tones became commanding. "Tonight you will remain here. We will reserve further discussion until tomorrow when you are rested."

"Might as well do as she says," Lord Rand suggested, taking his cue. "M' sister's got a stubborn conscience. No use arguing."

In other circumstances, no amount of cajolery or command would have kept Catherine in Andover House. She was still in London, and every step she'd taken since coming here had hurled her into disaster. She wanted only to flee.

She knew she should press harder for the small loan that would allow her to go home immediately without having to answer embarrassing questions. By the time she'd met Lady Andover, however, Catherine was on the brink of hysteria. Miss Fletcher's elopement had been the *coup de grace* of a series of stunning calamities. A clean, comfortable bed, a maid to look after her, and a hot cup of tea to consume in private was more temptation than Catherine could withstand.

She made the feeblest of protests, to which Lady Andover proved quite deaf. Moments later, Molly was leading the unexpected guest upstairs.

= 4 =

Now that his charge was in capable hands, Max was eager to get away. He was not permitted to do so. Fortunately, Lady Andover not only ordered him to remain where he was, but invited him to sample the contents of the alluring decanters. After filling a glass and taking a long swallow, Max ambled over to the fireplace and commenced a rapt contemplation of the marble.

His sister studied him for a few moments before she spoke. "Well, dear," she said, "this is a very interesting homecoming present you've brought me. Only I'd thought it would be you welcomed back with fatted calves and such—though she isn't very fatted, is she?"

"I didn't know what else to do with her, damn it. I could hardly send her off in a coach on her own, and I couldn't go with her—bound to cause trouble with her curst father."

"Who is she, Max? Not a schoolmistress, despite that quiz of a dress. Not your mistress either, I'll wager. Wild and unconventional as you like to appear, even you have your limits. Besides, if that girl ever had a depraved thought in her life, I'll eat my new bonnet."

"What a lot of strong opinions you've acquired, considering you hardly let her open her mouth."

"I observed." The countess settled herself comfortably upon the sofa. "I don't think you'd have brought her here if you had not sensed that she is—how shall I phrase it? Out of the common way? Not what she appears or wishes to appear? Her curtsey was quite elegant. Her manners are

36

refined—though that is not at all unusual in a governess or teacher. However, since I did not perceive the usual submissive attitude of the class, I concluded that she was gently bred. I may be mistaken, of course. She may be a radical. That is not impossible, though most unlikely."

There was relief in the countenance Lord Rand turned to his sister. "Then I did the right thing?"

"Oh, Max, you never do the right thing. Only you would take up a stray female as though she were one of those abandoned kittens you were forever bringing me. This is a bit different, I'm afraid. One cannot banish her to the kitchen to make Cook's life a misery."

"Don't tell me you mean to send her back?"

"I never know what I mean until Edgar explains it to me, dear, and he will not be home until just before dinner. I confess I am curious why you're so set against her going back. You're not in love with Miss Pettigrew, are you?"

Her brother stared at her in horror. "Gad, Louisa—a scrawny little girl like that who sermons at the drop of a hat? You ain't heard her yet. I daresay she was overawed by your magnificence, but give her half a chance and she'll be preaching at you. It was all I could do to keep a straight face . . ." He trailed off, realising he could not very well repeat to his sister the lectures he'd heard in the brothel or his lodgings.

"Then what is it to you if she returns to marry this person her papa has selected for her?"

"It's against my principles, and I won't be a party to it, any more than I was when the old man tried to shackle you to that birdwitted old troll. It's against her principles as well. I know, because she gave me scold on that too before she ever admitted it was her own trouble."

"Principles," her ladyship repeated. "I see. Still, I must consult with Edgar. If he feels we must return her to her family, we must."

"Now, Louisa—"

"Surely you don't doubt his judgement? Was it not Edgar persuaded Papa to allow you six months to finish sowing your wild oats? And was that not because Edgar convinced Papa that you are a far better horseman that Percy and therefore much less liable to get your neck broken in the interim? That Papa has not troubled you once in these six months is all Edgar's doing, I can assure you. Between answering Prinny's every petty summons and keeping Papa in temper, poor Edgar has had not a moment to himself."

"Don't try to make me feel guilty. Andover's only had to pamper the Old Man these six months. I'll be doing that and everything else from now on. I suppose he's got my bride picked out?"

"Actually, he's picked out half a dozen. Not, I'm sure, that you'll want any of them, as Papa well knows, but he does like to feel he's doing something, poor dear."

Max groaned. "Half a dozen. And the blasted house?"

"I've taken care of that. Not a trace of Percy. I'm sure you'll be pleased."

"Oh, I wasn't afraid he'd haunt the place, if that's what you mean. Old Percy hadn't the gumption. Wouldn't have gotten himself killed if he had. Curse him, that horse could have taken the stream."

"Yes, dear, and you'd told him often enough to put more trust in his beast. Poor Percy—he never had much spirit, did he? He should have been the younger son. He might have gone quietly into orders then, and Papa would have accepted it."

"And I'd still be in the same blasted predicament. Oh, well." His lordship finished his wine and deposited the glass on the mantel. "Might as well get used to it. I'll go see the Old Man later today. But if Edgar wants to send the girl back, you must promise to tell me straightaway."

"Why?"

Lord Rand bent to kiss his sister's forehead. As he straightened he said, "Because I've half a mind to go back with her anyhow. Maybe I've a choice word or two for her papa."

Catherine fretted over her dilemma while she sipped her

tea. By dinnertime her host and hostess would be sure to ask unnerving questions. What on earth could she tell them?

To run away from home and travel unchaperoned was enough to soil a young lady's reputation. To have spent one night in a brothel and another in a bachelor's lodgings was utter ruin.

She would earn no credit for having managed to preserve her virtue. Appearances alone would make her an outcast, a disgrace to her family—unless, as Lord Rand had advised, no one learned of the matter. At present he was the only other person who did know. Since she was merely Miss Pettigrew to him, the Pelliston name was still unsullied. She had rather keep it that way. Her homecoming would be painful enough as it was.

Besides, if she admitted her true identity, Lord and Lady Andover would never let her return home unaccompanied, and Catherine did not intend to bring witnesses to the humiliating scene with which she was certain to be greeted, especially if Papa had been summoned home from his bridal trip. He had no self-control at all, and if he was drunk, as he was bound to be —oh, there was no point thinking about that. Papa was sure to carry on in the most mortifying way.

"There, Miss," said Molly, jolting Catherine from her unhappy reverie. "You just lie down now and have a nice long nap, and I won't bother you none 'til it comes close on dinnertime. I'll clean up your dress for you and press it," the abigail added, her gaze flickering disappointedly over the grey frock draped upon a chair. "You'll be fine as fivepence and all rested too."

"Oh, no. That is hardly appropriate for dinner," was the embarrassed response. "The peach muslin will do far better."

"Beg pardon, Miss, but there weren't no peach muslin I could find, and I unpacked everything you brought. Just a brown frock and underthings and such." The maid's round, rosy face plainly expressed her bafflement at this paltry wardrobe.

Catherine had been too agitated earlier in the day to take inventory of her belongings. Now, with a faint stirring of anger, she realised that the brothelkeeper must have stolen her one good gown.

"Oh, dear," she said quickly. "I packed in such haste that I must have forgotten it. How stupid of me. Yes, I suppose the grey frock will have to do."

Molly tiptoed from the room as Catherine crawled into bed. She did not expect to sleep, not with her mind churning so, but a few hours' rest would help her think more clearly, as she should have done two months ago.

She hadn't been able to think because the hot temper she'd inherited from her papa had made her wild and blind. Though she hadn't shown it, she'd become completely irrational, just as he always had, incapable of considering consequences. At the very least she should have prepared for every eventuality. She'd had weeks to reconsider, to at least think ahead.

No wonder Lord Rand thought her an ignorant young miss. Now he thought even less of her. He'd called her a coward and a nonsensical one at that, which was no surprise considering the disgusting display of weakness she'd provided him. Twice at least she'd wept in front of him—she who abhorred tears. Was not weeping maudlin self-indulgence when done privately and a bid for pity when done in public? Aunt Deborah burst into tears at every fancied slight, which enraged Papa and filled even Catherine with exasperation.

Lord Rand must have been mightily relieved to have her off his hands. The thought set off an inner flutter of pain, and her eyes began to sting. Oh, for heaven's sake! Of all the excellent reasons she had to weep, why must the mere thought of her rescuer be the one to set her off?

Firmly she banished Lord Rand's image from her mind to concentrate instead on her hostess. The Andover name was so familiar. Was the family connected to hers? That would hardly be surprising, when half England's, even Europe's, aristocracy was related to the other. Perhaps, though, the earl's family had simply been the topic of one of Great-Aunt Eustacia's rambling dissertations on genealogy. The old lady knew her Debrett's as intimately as she knew her Bible. As Catherine recalled the long monologues in those dim, cluttered rooms, exhaustion crept over her.

Genealogy. "Hadn't time to discuss genealogy," he'd told his sister in that abrupt way of his. Actually, it was rather funny, in the circumstances.

What an odd man he was, Catherine thought vaguely as her eyelids grew too heavy to keep open. Lost, of course, with his drinking and wenching, like Papa, but young . . . and handsome . . . and so strong. He'd lifted her up as easily as if she'd been one of her bandboxes.

He must have been shocked, when he had sobered himself, to realise what he'd brought home with him. Perhaps that would teach him to exercise moderation in future. With this pious thought, Catherine drifted off to sleep.

"Now who in blazes are you?" Lord Rand demanded, surveying the small, slim man before him.

His lordship had already had two nasty surprises. The first was a butler even taller than himself, whose accents hinted an intimate acquaintance with the bells of St. Mary Le Bow: a Cockney butler named Gidgeon, of all things. The second was a chef who spoke not a word of English, thereby forcing Lord Rand to rake the recesses of his mind for the French he'd determined to bury there forever along with Greek and Latin.

In front of him at present stood a mournful creature who'd been dogging the viscount's footsteps all the way down the long hall.

"Hill, My Lord," said the little man sadly.

"Hill," Lord Rand repeated. "And what do *you* do?"

"Your secretary, My Lord."

"What the devil do I want a secretary for? Ain't there enough here as it is? The bloody place is crawling with servants. I'll wager there ain't been such a crowd in one place since Prinny married that fat cousin of his."

"Yes, My Lord. A tragic business, that," Hill gloomily agreed.

"You don't know the half of it," his lordship grumbled. "Well, what is it you do, exactly?"

"Her ladyship—Lady Andover, that is—indicated that you required assistance in managing your paperwork, My Lord. Now that you are in residence there will be a daily supply of invitations requiring responses."

"I ain't going to any of those fusty affairs."

"Very good, My Lord. You are aware, I trust, that you are engaged to dine this evening with Lord and Lady St. Denys?"

"Tonight? Already? Plague take him. The Old Man don't give me a minute to catch my breath. How the devil did he know I was back?"

"It is a regrettable fact, My Lord, that servants' gossip travels at an alarming rate," said Mr. Hill in dismal tones. "His lordship's summons arrived an hour ago. I am afraid the invitation is indeed for this evening."

"Of course it is. They can't wait to clap the irons on me." The viscount muttered something unintelligible, then said more distinctly, "Very well. Might as well get it over with."

Considering the matter closed, he was about to continue on his way, but the secretary seemed to be in melancholy expectation of something more.

"Is that all?" the master asked impatiently.

"Her ladyship also mentioned that there would be numerous matters claiming your attention, though scarcely worthy of it. She indicated that I was, insofar as possible, to relieve you of the more trivial."

'Lord Rand sighed. "Such as?"

"Your valet, My Lord."

"Don't want a valet. Can't stand someone poking about my things."

"Quite so, My Lord. Therefore I have screened the applicants in advance and reduced their number to three, in hopes of sparing you some trouble in seeking one worthy of your employ."

"Didn't I just tell you I don't want a valet?"

"Yes, indeed, My Lord. So I will explain to the man you select."

"I don't want to select anybody, damn it. I can dress myself. I ain't a baby."

"Very good, My Lord." The secretary stared dolefully at his master's scuffed boots. "I suppose, then, one of the lower servants will attend to your footwear? In that case, I will ask Mr. Gidgeon whether such a person might be spared from the present staff."

Lord Rand fought back a wild urge to bash either his own or his secretary's head against the door frame. "Where are these prodigies? I suppose they are here or you wouldn't be badgering me about it."

"In the hall outside your lordship's study. If you will be so kind as to ring when you're prepared, I shall send the first candidate in."

"No," snapped the employer as he stormed down the hall. "I'll see 'em all at once."

Half an hour later, the disagreeable task was done, the viscount having quickly settled on the one candidate whose serene countenance promised intermittent relief from the lugubrious Hill. Lord Rand was further heartened some hours later when Blackwood (for such was the name of this gentleman's gentleman), having accompanied his master to the latter's private chambers, volunteered the information that he'd recently been invalided home.

"A soldier," said Lord Rand, breaking into a smile for the first time since he'd entered the house. "Where?"

"Peninsula, My Lord. I caught a ball in my leg, and being of no further military use, had to take up my old work."

So it happened that amid the exchange of stories, the one talking of the Old World and the other of the New, Lord Rand forgot most of his objections to having someone poking about his belongings and gave utterance to only one mild oath when the valet laid out dinner clothes.

"Confound it," his lordship muttered. "I'd almost forgotten the kind of rigout I'd be stuffed into for dinner. With the Old Man, no less. You could stand a regiment on his neck-cloth and the blasted thing wouldn't so much as crease. Wouldn't dare."

"Likes everything in order, does he, My Lord?" the valet asked as he gathered up his employer's scattered belongings.

"And can't for the life of him figure out how he sired such a disorderly brute of a son."

"If you'll pardon my free speech, My Lord, I must disagree with that assessment. It's a pleasure to a man of simple tastes like myself to attend to a gentleman who wants neither padding nor corsets nor any sort of artifice to look as he should."

=== 5 ===

THAT HE LOOKED as he should, and better than he had ever done in his life before, was of small comfort to the Viscount Rand some time later when he endured his mother's effusive welcome and his father's frigid greeting.

Lord Rand's neck-cloth began to grow rather snug, in fact, as the dinner conversation turned to his domestic responsibilities and, in particular, his need for a wife.

"Lady Julia is very sweet," his mother told him. "Raleforth's youngest girl, you know."

"Simpers," said Lord St. Denys.

"Miss Millbanke does not simper, Frederick. Very clever, too, they say."

"Blue-stocking. Worse, she's a prig. From what I hear, the family wants to shackle her to that one with the bad foot that fancies himself a poet."

Lord Rand fought down his annoyance, though he could not keep the challenge from his tone when he spoke. "I daresay, m'lord, you've someone particular in mind."

"No," the earl replied without looking up from his plate.

"No?" the son echoed in some astonishment.

"But Frederick, what about Miss—?"

"No," the earl repeated. "It's none of our affair, Letitia. The lad is perfectly capable of finding his own wife."

"Why, yes, of course," Lady St. Denys agreed as she turned apologetically to her son. "I never meant to imply, dear, that you were not. Only that you go about so little in Society—"

"Doesn't go about at all," her husband interrupted.

"Why, yes, dear, and that is just the point. If he does not go about in Society, how is he to find a suitable girl?"

"Perhaps, Mother, I ought to advertise, and ask my secretary to screen the applicants for the position. Worked well enough for finding a valet."

"Oh, Max," the countess gasped.

"Got a valet, have you? I thought you appeared more presentable than usual."

"But, Frederick, he can hardly advertise for a wife as one does for a servant. What would people think?"

"How should I know? None of our set's ever done it before."

"Oh, Frederick, I believe you're roasting me. And you too, Max. You wicked creatures." The countess smiled indulgently and returned her attention to her dinner.

Baffled by his father's uncharacteristic behaviour, the viscount had trouble concentrating on his meal. Never in Max Demowery's twenty-eight years had his parent shown any confidence whatsoever in his younger son's judgement.

The father had the same tall, strong Demowery physique. However, his features were haughtier, more aquiline and forbidding, and maturity had added distinguished grey to his thick hair. That and the extra stone or so of girth made him a formidable figure—one, in fact, of a man accustomed to command. The Earl of St. Denys was indeed so accustomed, having inherited his title at a very early age. His voice rang out in the Lords as he enumerated with sonorous regularity his colleagues' errors. That same voice resounded with equal force through his household. The Old Man, Max often complained, had never noticed that his children had graduated from leading strings.

Lord St. Denys had not permitted his eldest son to take orders, though that was what Percy wanted and what everyone knew him best fitted for. The earl had also tried to choose his daughter's husband. Fortunately, unlike Percy, Louisa had not inherited her mother's meekness. She'd refused. Threatened with being locked in her room

46

until she could work herself into a compliant frame of mind, she bolted, dragging a reluctant abigail with her, to take refuge with the one human being her papa could not command—his formidable Cousin Agatha.

In this Louisa had followed the example of her younger brother, who'd been running away from everyone and everything since his little legs were strong enough to carry him. Max had run away from home innumerable times. At the age of ten he'd fled Eton and would certainly have found other ways to make himself unwelcome there after being dragged back had not a young, perceptive master taken the restless boy under his wing and found work to challenge him.

Max had managed his Oxford career with a few scrapes, but without disgrace. Immediately upon quitting that institution he'd enlisted under a false name as a common soldier. The earl had eventually tracked him down and gotten him discharged. Less than a year later, Max smuggled himself on board a ship bound for the New World.

There he'd have contentedly remained had Percy not met with the riding accident. Rebellious as Max was, even he was no match for the claims of eight centuries of Demowerys. Even he could not ignore this one great duty, especially after the earl had effectively sundered the one tie that might have kept his new heir in that raw, wild, young country. The place had suited Max. It appealed to his restless nature, his impatience with convention. He had learned there that he could make his own way. He could achieve success without depending upon either his social station or his father's largess.

Max returned from his sojourn in the wilderness with a fortune of his own. That was some consolation for having to embark upon a life he'd always detested among people whose narrow-mindedness, rigid rules of behaviour, and arrant hypocrisy made him seethe with frustration. He might have to accept the responsibilities of an heir, but at least he need not beg his managing father for money. He owed the earl nothing.

So the heir had meant to assert as soon as Lord St. Denys embarked upon the hated topic of marriage and producing heirs—several, preferably. After all, as Percy's accident had demonstrated, a nobleman could never be certain he wouldn't require spares.

Now the viscount felt the wind had been taken out of his sails. He'd looked forward to another blowup with his father. The heir's townhouse, with its army of servants and its spotless, tasteful furnishings, had seemed so cool and proper and polite that it suffocated him. The prospect of living there as the lone master oppressed his spirits.

In the past when he'd felt stifled, he'd always run away. Since he couldn't do that now, he wanted to take out his frustration on the Old Man. Lord Rand wanted, as well, distraction from the odd female whose eyes and voice persistently intruded upon his thoughts. A quarrel about the future viscountess was just the thing—only it seemed he was to be forestalled in that too.

Refusing to give up hope altogether, the viscount raised the subject again after his mother had left the two men to their port.

"I confess I'm puzzled, My Lord. Louisa told me today that you had half a dozen suitable brides picked out for me—but just a while ago you claimed you hadn't any."

"Oh, I do," said the earl. "Five, actually."

Max's blue eyes gleamed, and he felt a rush of exaltation as the old animosity blazed up within him.

"Only five?"

"Yes, but I'm not going to tell you who they are."

The son put down the glass he'd just raised to his lips. "I beg your pardon?"

"I said I won't tell you. What sort of fool do you take me for? As soon as I breathe a young woman's name you'll take her in dislike, sight unseen, simply because *I* suggested it. No, as I see it, the only way my opinions stand a chance is to keep them to myself."

"Do you mean to say that you think I'll approve one of these five?"

"I'm not saying anything, as I just told you. It's your affair, and if I come poking in with my opinions, you're bound to go contrary on me, as you always do, Max. Since the day you were born, I think."

Lord St. Denys took an appreciative sip from his refilled glass. "Still, you're no longer a child, as my son-in-law has pointed out repeatedly," he went on while absently turning the goblet in his hands. "Edgar claimed you'd be back at the end of your six months, ready to do your duty. So you are, punctual to the minute. I have no doubt you'll do your duty in the matter of finding a bride. More than that a parent has no right to ask."

Had Lord Rand not been staring perplexedly into his own glass, he might have caught the suspicious twinkle that lit his father's eyes. As it was, the viscount was aware only of a surging frustration—and a resultant need to find some topic on which the two might loudly disagree.

"Except, I suppose, that I do this duty at the earliest opportunity," the son suggested.

"Whenever," was the provoking answer. "Plenty of time, plenty of fish in the sea. If you never do get around to it before you reach your dotage, there's always your Cousin Roland. Serena—his wife, you know—just produced their fifth, I hear. No danger of the title dying with you."

Max ground his teeth. He detested his sanctimonious Cousin Roland and suspected his father did as well. The idea of Roland or one of his puling brats becoming Earl of St. Denys was more than one could stomach, even if one didn't give a damn about titles and thought the whole business of primogeniture a poisonous carryover from barbaric times and the aristocracy itself a cancer on the body politic.

"I thought you'd rather see the line die out than have it carried on by Roland and that stupid cow he married," he could not help reminding.

"Won't matter to me, will it, when I'm six feet beneath the earth?"

This altogether unsatisfactory conversation ended shortly thereafter when the gentlemen rose to join Lady St.

Denys in the drawing-room.

Consequently, as soon as he'd taken leave of his parents, Lord Rand marched himself directly to White's, confident that he would be denied entrance to that bastion of Torydom and might, in response, instigate a riot in St. James's.

Lord Rand had reckoned without Mr. George Brummell. That gentleman, upon learning of a brewing altercation upon the club's outer steps, and finding himself holding a singularly poor hand, put down his cards and strolled to his usual place at the famous Bow Window to join his colleagues in watching the scene.

"Who is that tall, noble-looking fellow?" he enquired of his neighbour.

"Wh-why—L-Lord Rand, sir," stammered Sir Matthew Melbrook, his poise knocked to pieces at being addressed by the Great Beau. "A r-radical—and a great r-ruffian."

"Ah, yes. Viscount Vagabond. His neck-cloth is a work of art," said Society's arbiter of fashion. He turned away and sauntered back to the card table.

In less than a minute his pronouncement had made its way out to St. James's Street. A gentleman who'd been endeavouring to lay his hands upon that same neck-cloth—apparently intending to throttle his adversary with it—backed away, and Lord Rand, to his astonishment, was invited to enter the club.

"I ain't a member," he challenged loudly as he stomped inside.

"'Fraid you are," drawled Lord Alvanley while he surveyed the newcomer with appreciative amusement. "Have been this twelvemonth. Andover sponsored you and the decision was unanimous. Apparently some of our lads forgot that small matter. I would have spoken up sooner myself, but I hated to spoil the entertainment you were so kind to offer us."

"Confound it," the viscount complained as Lord Alvanley ambled away. "Has everyone in Town taken leave of his senses?"

"If you mean the warm welcome," came a voice behind him, "it must be they suddenly remembered what a dull old stick Percy was. Either that or the fact that Brummell admired your cravat." The voice's owner, a good-looking young man with dreamy grey eyes and rumpled brown hair, moved to Lord Rand's side. "Don't you remember me, Max? Langdon. We were at Oxford together."

"So we were, Jack," said the viscount, a smile finally breaking through his clouded countenance. "Only how was I to know you without a book in front of your nose? Damme if I didn't think they grew there."

"Oh, these suspicious fellows won't let me read when we're at cards. They claim I keep a spare deck between the pages. But come. As your brother-in-law isn't here to do the honours, let me introduce you around."

His humour partially restored by the presence of his old school chum, Max submitted with good grace. Whatever remained of his rage soon evaporated in the convivial atmosphere of gambling, drinking, and increasingly raucous conversation as the night wore on. So convivial was the company that Lord Rand had to be carried out to a hackney shortly before dawn, from which vehicle he was removed by a brace of footmen, who carried him to his bedroom. There Blackwood succeeded to the honours of attending to his happily unconscious lordship.

While Lord Rand had been trying to ascertain whether an alien spirit had taken possession of his father's body, Miss Pelliston had been having an equally baffling evening with her host and hostess. Catherine had expected an interrogation. When that did not occur during a dinner she was far too agitated to eat, she anxiously awaited it later, when Lord Andover, after a quarter hour alone with his port, rejoined his wife and guest.

No attempt was made, however, to ascertain just what exactly this odd young woman was doing in the Earl of Andover's noble townhouse. Catherine was sure her pristinely elegant host must think her odd, given the occasional pained glance he dropped upon her grey frock.

Whatever he thought, he was scrupulously polite and thoroughly charming. Conversation through dinner focused on politics, and after dinner on books, the earl having quickly discerned his guest's keen appetite for literature.

While she inwardly cursed her cowardice, Catherine could not bring herself to open the subject so courteously ignored, though she did wince every time her host addressed her as "Miss Pettigrew."

It must be as the countess had said, Catherine told herself later, while Molly brushed her hair. The matter was reserved for discussion on the morrow. She did wish she might have some peace and quiet in the meantime, so that she could decide at last what to do. Unfortunately, Molly talked incessantly from the time she entered the bedchamber until the time she left.

The abigail's main subject was Lord Rand, with whom she unblushingly admitted she was infatuated.

"Not but what I knows, of course, that he'd never notice me—or should, either. Still, a cat may look at a king," she paraphrased in response to Catherine's startled expression. "Once when her ladyship took me with her to a picture gallery I fell in love with a picture of a foreign gent what had on no clothes to speak of, just a bit of cloth. And so long as he was only paint on a bit of cloth himself there's no harm in it. Same with him—My Lord Rand, I mean—like a great handsome statue, because *he* wouldn't be pinching a girl, either, no more than the statue would. Not like some I could mention, who if you so much as smile the least bit they grows another dozen hands all at once, I declare."

Catherine's attempts to distract Molly from discussion of the roving hands of males of all classes only led to further enlightenment about the idol. He had not returned to England, according to Molly, until eighteen months after his brother's death.

"It weren't so long a voyage as all that, Miss, either, but that he didn't want to come back on any account, as he already had a sweetheart there and was planning to marry her and stay there forever, living among the wild Indians."

"I collect," Catherine faintly responded, "the lady changed her mind."

"Say Lord St. Denys changed it for her, rather. Mum's been with Lady St. Denys since afore her ladyship married and she was at the house when Mr. Max come back. Mum said he was arguing so loud with his papa you could hear it down at the stables. She says everyone in the house heard him yelling that his papa had sent the girl money to break it off. Not but it wasn't the right thing, you know, her being a nobody and a foreigner at that. Mr. Max—his lordship, I mean—couldn't hardly bring back some poor farmer girl and take her to meet the Queen, now could he?"

From what Miss Pelliston knew of his lordship, she was convinced that he could very well introduce a farmer's daughter at court—and in pattens, no less. Had he not introduced to the Countess of Andover a girl he'd found in a brothel?

"I suppose that would be rather awkward," said Catherine. "Especially when our two nations are at war."

Molly, who knew nothing of international politics and who believed the United States was located somewhere in China or Africa, wisely ignored this remark.

"Anyhow, I know he never did get over it," she went on. "He hasn't spoke a word to Lord St. Denys six months now—nor anyone else, either. Until today, that is. Why, you could have knocked me over with a feather when I come into the drawing-room and seen him sitting there, chatting with her ladyship just as easy as if he'd been here every day, and her ladyship no more amazed than if he had been."

Having doggedly brushed Catherine's hair the required two hundred strokes—Catherine had kept count as a means of steadying her nerves—the abigail stood back to admire the results. "What splendid hair you have, Miss. I declare when I first saw it I was sure I was in for a long night of it—curly hair do tangle so—but yours is soft as a baby's. Such a handsome colour too. There's folks'd pay a pretty penny for it."

Miss Pelliston had been contemplating, in spite of herself, Lord Rand's tribulations. Now she came abruptly to attention. "Pay?" she asked. "Not money, surely? Or did you simply mean that some would be envious?"

"Brown hair is common enough, but not light and soft and curly as yours. Oh, I'd expect plenty would like to have it, Miss."

"You mean for wigs? But surely those have been out of fashion for years."

"That don't mean a hairpiece don't come in handy for some folks. Monsoor Franzwuz, what does her ladyship's hair, could tell you stories about that. Nor I don't mean *her*," the maid hastily explained. "Every bit of what's on her head is her own, and no curlpapers, neither. Now then, Miss, shall I bring you a nice warm cup of milk?"

This Catherine politely declined.

"Really, I think you should, Miss. Tom says you never touched your dinner hardly and if you'll pardon my saying so, you'll be all hair and eyes if you keep on at this rate."

Touched by this concern, Catherine acquiesced, though when the milk arrived she found it difficult to swallow enough to satisfy the well-meaning abigail. Miss Pelliston was too excited about the alternative that had suddenly presented itself to care about nourishment, and the prospect of becoming all hair and eyes did not alarm her in the least.

"Well, Edgar," said the countess as her husband settled himself among the pillows and took his book from the nightstand, "what do you recommend we do about her?"

"Burn that dress," he replied. "It frightened me out of my wits. And do something about her hair. That knot is a crime against nature."

"Then you believe we should take her in?"

"Have to," said his lordship as he opened his book. "Pelliston's chit."

Her ladyship, who'd also snuggled comfortably against her pillows, bolted upright. "What? Who?"

54

"How many times have I told you, Louisa, not to make sudden movements? You've made me lose my place."

"Stop teasing, you wretched man. Are you telling me you know her?"

"Not personally. I believe her mama was my mother's second or third cousin." He returned his attention to the Bard.

"Edgar!"

"Yes, my precious?"

Lady Andover jerked the book from her husband's hands. "If you do not explain this instant, I shall tear the curst thing to pieces."

The earl breathed a sigh. "Ten years, and I have never been able to teach you patience. Still, what's a mere decade to centuries of impatient Demowerys? I see you intend to beat me over the head with poor Will's work if I cannot satisfy your all-consuming curiosity." He gazed sadly at the bedclothes.

"Well, then?"

"I met her some months before that blissful day when we two were united—"

"Edgar!"

"Ten years ago. Our families have never been close, but Pelliston is known for his hounds and I meant to make a gift of a pair to your papa."

"And you recognised her after all these years?"

"She closely resembles her mama, especially in the eyes—most unusual, very like Eleanor's."

"No wonder you never questioned her. I expected to see you work your subtle arts upon her, extracting information without her ever realising. Still, I'm surprised she didn't recognise you," the countess added fondly as she admired her husband's wavy black hair and classically sculpted features.

"Her father had a crowd of his cronies rampaging about the place. To her I think we were all one noisy, unwanted crowd. Besides, she kept her eyes on her papa. I found her intriguing. She behaved as she did tonight, stiffly proper

55

and courteous, but with that wild, pent-up look in her eyes. I was waiting for her to explode. She never did, though her papa was provoking enough."

"Apparently, he has provoked her at last."

"Yes. I'm not surprised he wants to marry her to one of his loutish friends, if his behaviour that day was typical. Still, I know little enough about them. In fact, it's only because my dear mama pointed out Pelliston's wedding announcement in the paper that I made the connection. He and his doings were already in my mind when I met the girl tonight."

"If her papa is the ogre he sounds, I can understand the false name," said Louisa, "but then why is she so adamant about returning home?"

"We needn't understand everything this minute. Tomorrow you can tactfully explain that we know all. I'll write her father."

"To say what?"

"Why, that you wish to bring my cousin out. Since fate— or your brother, actually—has dropped her upon our doorstep, we might as well keep her. I am not blind, Louisa. You are itching to get your hands on the girl. Potential there, you think?"

"Oh, yes. How convenient that she's a relation, however distant. My motives will seem of the purest. How considerate of Max, don't you think, darling?"

<h1 align="center">= 6 =</h1>

LORD RAND EYED with distaste the murky liquid in the glass his valet offered him. "What's that filthy mess? You don't mean me to drink it?"

"I highly recommend it, My Lord. Guaranteed to eliminate the aftereffects."

Either the aftereffects or the cure would kill him, the viscount was certain. He groped for the glass, brought it to his lips, held his nose, and drank.

"Ugh," he croaked. "That's the vilest-tasting stuff I ever swallowed in my life."

"Yes, My Lord, I'm afraid so. However, I thought you would require a prompt-acting restorative, as the Countess of Andover has sent a message requesting your immediate attendance."

"She can go to blazes," his lordship groaned, sinking back onto his pillow.

"She sent this," the valet said, holding up a note.

Lord Rand shut his eyes. "Tell me what it says."

Blackwood unfolded the sheet of paper and read aloud: " 'The cat has bolted. Please come at once.' "

The viscount let loose a stream of colourful oaths while his valet busied himself with arranging shaving materials.

"Yes, indeed, sir," Blackwood agreed, when his master stopped to catch his breath. "Your bath is ready, and I have laid out the brown coat and fawn pantaloons."

Not long after, Lord Rand stormed unannounced into the

breakfast room of Andover House, where the earl and countess sat, their heads bent close together as they perused what appeared to be a very long epistle.

"There you are, Max," Lord Andover said, looking up with a faint frown. "Seems our guest has fled. Apparently," he went on calmly, oblivious to the thunderclouds gathering upon his brother-in-law's brow, "she slipped out shortly after Jeffers unlocked the doors—before the rest of the household was up."

"Then why the devil ain't you out looking for her?"

"Because we were waiting for you," Lady Andover answered. "Edgar has already dispatched nearly all the menservants to comb the streets, so there is no need to stand there scowling. Do sit down, Max. Perhaps you can help. We were rereading her note in hopes of discovering some clue as to where she's gone."

Lord Rand snatched up the letter and read it. "Oh, the bloody little fool," he muttered when he'd finished.

"I do wish you'd speak more respectfully of my relations," said the earl. " 'Poor, misguided creature' would be rather more like it, I should think."

"Relations? What the devil are you talking about?"

"My cousin—at least I believe she is the daughter of my mama's second or third cousin—but you will have to ask Mama about that. By the time it gets to second cousins and times removed I lose all ability to concentrate."

Lord Rand sat down abruptly.

"Her name," said Louisa, "is Catherine Pelliston—not Pettigrew. Her papa, according to Edgar, is the Baron Pelliston of Wilberstone."

"Why that deceitful little b—"

"If you persist in insulting my cousin, Max, I shall be forced to call you out, and that will be a great pity, as you are the better shot and Louisa has grown rather accustomed to me, I think."

"Your cousin can go to the devil," Lord Rand retorted. "How dare she pretend to be a poor little schoolmistress, playing me for a fool—"

"As easily as you pretended to be some lowborn lout, I suppose," his sister interrupted.

"Perhaps," said the earl, "she suspected that you might hold her for ransom if she admitted her identity. You did not, I understand, admit yours, and Pelliston's rich as Croesus. At any rate, I was intending to question Molly as soon as she recovered from her hysterics. Care to join me, Max?"

Lord Rand maintained crossly that he didn't give a damn what became of a spoiled debutante and an ingrate at that, not to mention she was an ignorant little prig. His brother-in-law took no heed of these or any of the other contradictory animadversions which followed regarding the young lady's character, motives, and eventual dismal and well-deserved end. When the viscount had finished raving, Lord Andover merely nodded politely, then rose and left the room. Grumbling, Lord Rand followed him.

The Viscount Rand was too restless a man to be much given to introspection. All the same he was not stupid, as his Eton master or Oxford tutors would have, though some of them grudgingly, admitted. He was therefore vaguely aware that his invectives upon Miss Pelliston were a tad irrational.

Although she'd had no reason to trust him with her true identity—just as Edgar said—Lord Rand felt she'd betrayed him somehow, which was very odd. His chosen course of life had resulted in what he called "a tough hide." Even Jenny's defection had not penetrated his cynical armor—he was too used to having careers and friends bought off by his interfering father. He'd had a wonderful row with the Old Man about it, of course, but inwardly he'd felt nothing more than a twinge of disappointment in his American friend.

Though he told himself he had far less reason to be disturbed about Miss Pelliston, the viscount was disturbed all the same. He was worried about her—she was far too naive—and he hated being worried, so he was furious with her.

Unfortunately for his temper, Molly was worse than useless. When asked about her conversations with the young houseguest, the loquacious abigail became mute. She was not about to admit having discussed Lord Rand's private life in vivid detail, and was so conscious of her indiscretion in doing so that she could remember nothing else she'd said.

"She gave no hint of her intentions?" the earl asked patiently. "Did she seem distraught or frightened?"

"Oh, no," said Molly. "She didn't say much of anything. Shy-like, My Lord. Even when I admired her hair she acted like she didn't believe me, poor thing," the abigail added as tears welled up in her eyes. "It weren't no flattery, either. Curly and soft it was, like a baby's, and as easy to brush as if it was silk."

"You needn't carry on as if she was dead," Max snapped, agitated anew by the tears streaming down the maid's round, rosy cheeks.

The earl quickly intervened. "Very well, Molly. Thank you," he said, patting the girl's shoulder. "Now do go wash your face and compose yourself. You will not wish to distress her ladyship, I am sure."

Molly dutifully wiped her eyes with her apron and, without daring another peek at her idol, curtsied and hurried from the study.

"That," said Lord Rand, "was a complete waste of time. I'm going to the coaching inns."

"She can't board a coach without money, Max."

"I know that and you know that, but she's just ignorant enough to throw herself on the mercy of the coachmen. The little idiot trusts everyone."

With that, he stomped out.

The little idiot was at the moment trying to understand how she'd lost her way twenty times in one morning. A milliner had given her clear directions to Monsieur Francois's establishment. At least they'd seemed clear at the time. The trouble was, there were so many turns, so many lanes and ways and roads and streets bearing similar names, and so many other people contradicting each previous set of instructions that by now she had no idea whether she was any closer to her destination than when she'd started.

Catherine was tired, hungry, and miserable, and wished she could sit down—but a lady could not plunk herself down upon a cobbler's doorstep. She had been able to reduce her luggage to one bandbox, thanks to the stolen peach muslin and a few other missing items. Now she transferred the box to her other hand and tried to straighten her stiff shoulders.

"Got a penny, Miss?" a childish voice enquired from behind her.

She looked around. A very untidy boy was studying her gravely.

"No," she said. "Not a farthing."

The boy shrugged and turned to a nearby lamppost, which he gave a savage kick.

"I don't suppose," Catherine said, "you know where Monsieur Francois's shop is?"

"I don't know nuffink." He scowled and kicked the lamppost again.

"Don't know anything," Catherine corrected automatically, half to herself. "Is there anyone in this wretched city who can speak without murdering the King's English?" Dispirited, she stared about her. Where on earth was the horrid hairdresser's shop?

The urchin followed her gaze. "You ain't batty, 'er you?"

Catherine met his scrutiny and sighed. "Not yet, though it is likely I will soon descend to that state. No one," she went on wearily, "knows anything. Or if they do, they will only vouchsafe the information in the most esoteric formula possible. Or else they may as well be speaking Turkish for all one can comprehend of their dialects and cant."

The urchin nodded wisely, though Catherine was certain that her words had been Turkish to him. "I thought you wuz batty on account of you wuz talkin' to yourself. SHE talks to herself. Only SHE says it's on account of Aggeration."

"I hope that is not your mother to whom you refer so disrespectfully," she said.

"Me mum's dead."

"Oh, dear, I am so sorry."

"I ain't sorry," was the shocking response. "Beat me sumfin' fierce she did—when she could cotch me."

"Good heavens!"

"Well, she don't any more, as 'at Blue Ruin killed her."

"Oh, my! And have you no papa?"

"No. Only HER."

This odd conversation was bringing her no nearer her destination. There was nothing for it but to continue walking. Catherine turned the corner. To her surprise, the boy followed. Evidently, having begun to talk, he had no inclination to leave off, but chattered amiably as he accompanied her down the street.

SHE, it turned out, was Missus, who kept a shop where she made clothes for the gentry. This morning, according to the boy, Missus was in a state of Aggeration on account of someone named Annie.

Since Missus was not a hairdresser, she was certainly not going to be any help. Catherine's throat began to ache. She would very much like to sit down on the curb and cry her heart out. It must be past noon by now. If she didn't make her transaction soon, she'd miss the coach that could take her home before dark.

"Are you sure you don't know where Monsieur Francois's shop is?" she asked in desperation. "A hairdresser? I was told he would buy my hair—and I do need the money."

The boy frowned as he studied her drab bonnet. "Oh, you mean 'at wig man. Won't do you no good. Gone to do a wedding. I got"—he bent to stick one grimy finger into a shoe a full size too large for his foot—"tuppence. What SHE give me to go away and not Aggerate her. We could get a meat pie."

Catherine needed a moment to understand that the scruffy child was offering to share his worldly wealth with her. When she did grasp his import, she was touched almost to tears. "Oh, dear, how very generous of you, but one pie will scarcely feed a strong, growing boy like yourself."

"Oh, SHE'll give me suffink arter she's done Aggeratin' herself. I knows a place," he added with a conspiratorial wink that required the cooperation of all the muscles of his face and made him look like a goblin. "Pies as big as my head."

"Come along," the urchin said impatiently, as his invited guest hesitated. "Ain't you hungry?"

Catherine was very hungry and she could not remember when she had ever felt so desolate. She gazed down at the round face and smiled ruefully.

"Yes," she said. "I am very hungry."

The boy nodded, satisfied, then took her by the hand to lead her to the establishment where one might find a meat pie as big as his head.

While they ate he grew more confiding. He introduced himself as Jemmy, and explained that Missus had taken him in after his mother's death—the *modiste* being, Catherine guessed, a charitable soul who had some employment for the child which might keep him from the rookeries and flash houses with which he appeared to be appallingly familiar.

Jemmy ran his mistress's errands and swept the floors, but was primarily left to educate and amuse himself, which he did by wandering about the city streets.

Even as she wondered at this unchildlike existence, Catherine found herself confiding her own tale, reduced to the essentials of stolen reticule and absent friend.

At this the lad shook his head and looked as wise as it is possible for a boy of eight or nine years to do. He told her that she must be a "green 'un" not to keep better watch on her belongings.

"Yes," Catherine ruefully agreed. "I fear I am very green indeed."

"Why, 'em knucklers and buzmen ken fence a handkercher easier wot you ken wipe yer nose. Wonder is you still got yer box 'n' all."

Catherine glanced at the bandbox beside her and considered. If a handkershief was of such value to these persons Jemmy spoke of, surely she must have something she could pawn for her coach fare. While she meditated, she could not help but note the longing with which her young host eyed a large fruit pastry being served to a fat gentleman at the next table.

She opened the bandbox and rummaged in it. "I wonder, Jemmy," she said finally, holding up a peach-coloured ribbon, "whether this would buy us one of those pastries."

The boy's eyes widened. "Oh, I'd say, Miss—" Then he subdued himself. "But you hadn't orter."

"Oh, yes I ought. You take this ribbon to your cook friend and ask if she will accept it in trade."

The boy dashed off with his treasure to the shop's owner, whereupon a discussion ensued, nothing of which Catherine could hear over the loud voices and clatter about her. When she saw the cook look questioningly at her, Miss Pelliston responded with a smile and a nod. The cook shrugged, turned away briefly, then presented Jemmy with a plate upon which reposed two plump, mouth-watering fruit tarts.

"She says," Jemmy explained as he deposited the feast upon the rough table, "as she'll only hold it some 'til you can pay her."

Jemmy's companion tasted only a bit of her dessert before declaring she was too full to enjoy it. She insisted that he not let it go to waste. As he disposed of her portion, Jemmy's round face grew thoughtful.

Catherine waited until he was done before asking if he would direct her to the nearest pawnshop.

"What for?" he demanded.

"I need money," she bluntly explained. "That seems to be the only way left to get some."

Unfortunately, Jemmy didn't know nuffink about pawnshops, except perhaps those around Petticoat Lane, an area he was quick to explain was no place for green females. He volunteered instead to take his new acquaintance to Missus, who could answer her questions better than he could.

64

* * *

Missus's Aggerations must have dissipated somewhat, because when Jemmy returned to the shop he was clasped in a welcoming hug, then grasped by the shoulders and shaken affectionately as the plump *modiste* demanded to know what mischief he'd been up to, worrying her sick all this time. Only after she had done scolding the boy and telling him what a naughty little wretch he was did she take notice of the young woman in the dowdy grey frock who stood by the door.

As Catherine stepped forward to introduce herself and make her enquiry regarding pawnshops, she was startled to hear Jemmy announce, "I told her as how Annie took a fever and you wanted a girl and she wants a job, and so I brung her."

=== 7 ===

Missus, it turned out, was Madame Germaine, a woman of strong sentiments and changeable mood. Though her temperament might be considered Gallic, her only claim to the nationality was her late husband's name. Madame was no more French than Miss Pelliston—less, in fact, for the former's ancestors had not entered England with the Conqueror.

The *modiste* wanted but a moment to study Catherine's pale, thin face before her susceptible heart softened. This was hardly surprising in a woman who had taken in a budding delinquent the instant she'd learned of his plight from a beadle's wife.

Still, Madame would never have achieved her current prosperity if she had not been an astute businesswoman. She discerned at once that the despised grey frock was extremely well cut, neatly sewn, and altogether modestly becoming in a respectable working woman. That she wanted desperately to see a respectable working woman may have urged the dressmaker to her speedy resolution. Whatever the cause, she led Catherine to her office, plied the young woman with tea and biscuits, and immediately embarked upon an interview to which Miss Pelliston, oddly enough, responded just as though she had been seeking a position.

She too had made a speedy decision. There was nothing but misery for her at home. Aunt Deborah would never let her forget how she'd disgraced them all, and Papa would make certain his daughter lived to regret her rebellious act—

if, that is, he didn't drive her from the house with a horse-whip.

On the other hand, here was an opportunity to begin a new life under a new identity. When her conscience insisted she deserved the punishment awaiting her at home, she answered that working was more productive penance than passive submission to endless reproaches and abuse. Providence, after all, "judgeth according to every man's work," she told herself as she accepted Madame's offer.

Catherine Pelliston—now Pennyman—would earn her own way in the world, enduring the hardships of her lot as other less privileged women did. She was thankful that she had done the rather dreary duties of the lady of the manor, taking supplies to ailing villagers and sewing endlessly for the needy. All those hours of sewing would provide her means of survival from now on.

She wondered anew at the little boy who'd led her to this momentous decision. He'd apparently taken to her immediately, and he'd never heard of the Baron Pelliston. To Jemmy she was another waif like himself, in need of useful work and shelter.

Shelter. Good heavens. Where would she live?

"Madame Germaine," she began hesitantly, "I wonder if, before I begin working, you might direct me to the nearest pawnshop."

When Catherine explained to the startled *modiste* that she required funds in order to obtain lodgings, and went on to admit that she had no idea where to find said lodgings, Jemmy cut in.

"Din't I tell you wot a green 'un she is? You orter put her upstairs wif Betty, Missus."

"Oh, no," Catherine cried, seeing the doubts writ plain on the dressmaker's face. "I would never impose in such a way."

Jemmy's dire predictions regarding what would happen to Miz Kaffy if she were let loose upon the streets combined with the new employee's dignified refusal of charity to erase Madame's doubts. With an empty bed in the housemaid

Betty's attic chamber, there was no reason Miss Pennyman could not be accommodated until she'd received her wages and might seek proper lodgings.

After lengthy debate and many direr predictions from Jemmy, Catherine acquiesced—on condition, she said, that she might repay the favour. Her eyes on the little boy, she proposed to tutor Jemmy in the rudiments of reading and writing.

Madame snatched at the suggestion as though Miss Pennyman had showered gold upon her.

"Why, that's just the thing! What a clever, kind girl you are to think of it. You can see for yourself what an ignorant creature he is. I cannot trust him to go to school as he should— nor spare the time to teach him myself. And though I do my best to keep him tidy, he is such a restless little devil, always into something, that in half an hour one would think he never saw soap or water in his life. How he manages to tear his clothes to ribbons in such a short space of time I shall never know. I would need half a dozen more girls just to keep him patched. Isn't that so, you young ruffian?" she asked, pulling Jemmy to her for yet another fierce embrace.

"Wot's she going to do to me?" Jemmy asked, scowling at the hug, though he otherwise bore it manfully.

"Why, teach you the alphabet, you ignorant child. Do you know what that is?"

Jemmy didn't know nuffink and didn't want to know nuffink, especially if it had to do with soap and water. The *modiste's* excited monologue had led him to conclude that reading and writing were somehow connected with bathing.

Catherine hastened to explain, pointing out the advantages of being able to read signs and shopkeepers' bills without assistance. She was not certain how much the boy understood, but he seemed to trust her and eventually agreed to "try it some and see as he liked it."

A just Providence must look favourably upon efforts to lead this young soul out of the darkness of illiteracy, Catherine assured herself later as she sat working with the other seamstresses. Surely that must compensate in part for the disobedient act to which she'd been driven.

She was far less easy in her mind concerning the family she'd run away from this morning. She had written a long letter of apology, though, hadn't she? Besides, Lord and Lady Andover had more important concerns than the fate of the lowly member of the working classes they must have taken her for. They'd probably decided, just as Lord Rand had remarked the other night, that Catherine was either insane or horribly ungrateful. By now they'd all ceased thinking about her altogether. She only wished she could stop thinking about *him*.

Well, strong personalities were very difficult to ignore— look at Papa—and whatever one thought of Lord Rand's unfortunate habits, one must admit he had an overwhelming sort of presence. When he was in the same room one became oblivious to everything else. He was also mind-numbingly handsome. His deep blue eyes alone were enough to stop one's brain dead in its tracks. Add to that a face and physique like a Greek god and a mop of wavy golden hair . . . yes, indeed, he was just as Molly had said, like a great handsome statue. Any person of any aesthetic sensitivity must be impressed.

Handsome is as handsome does, Catherine reminded herself as she threaded a needle. She would never see the man again, and that was fortunate, because he was evidently embarked upon the same dissolute courses as Papa, and in a few years those godlike features would degenerate. In time Lord Rand's face would match his character, a conclusion she had rather not witness. She sighed softly. What a terrible waste.

The search for Miss Pelliston was not brought to the speedy conclusion Lord Rand had hoped for. He'd expected to find her the same afternoon, cowering in a corner of the inn yard, or else—as he imagined in a more lighthearted moment—delivering one of her scolds to a giant, red-faced coachman.

Three days later he was still seeking her. When enquiries at coaching inns proved futile, he had, sick at heart, descended into the seamier environs in which he'd first found her. He'd even stormed Miss Grendle's establishment, where he was met with mocking assurances that the "ungrateful young person" was warming the bed of some rich nob.

The viscount learned no more in London's underworld than he had at the inns. The only news he acquired in those three days was from a tavern keeper. The man had not seen the young lady, but had heard her described by another "gentry cove." The description of this man—a tall, thin, middle-aged redhead—bore no resemblance to anyone with whom Max or Lord Andover was acquainted.

"The fellow's not her father," Lord Rand confided to his valet. It was daybreak of the fourth day since Miss Pelliston had run away, and his lordship had made another of his brief visits home for a bath, an hour's rest, and a change of clothes. "Andover says the old brute's short and shaped like a pear. Besides which he's in the Lake District on his bridal trip. Must be the confounded fiancé."

"That tells us the young lady has not returned to her family," Blackwood replied.

"I wish she *had*, damn her. At least then we'd know she was safe and could forget about her, the stupid chit."

Blackwood, who'd learned somewhat more about the missing lady than his master had intended to relate, had begun to have some ideas of his own. While his employer lay down for a short nap, the valet noiselessly exited the chamber, donned his hat and gloves, and departed for Andover House.

In the same quietly efficient manner in which he'd taken charge of his employer, Blackwood insinuated his way into the heart of the Andover household, eliciting from Jeffers, the earl's butler, an invitation to stop belowstairs to "take a bite of breakfast" with the others.

As Blackwood had hoped, the very same Molly his employer had characterised (though in more vivid terms) as incapable of intelligent speech was enjoying an early repast with her colleagues. The valet's openly appreciative

70

gaze won him a place at her side and a scowl from Tom, the footman. Mr. Blackwood's charm did the rest. Lord Rand would have been amazed to find what an entertaining fellow his inscrutable valet could be. That was because his lordship did not know what Blackwood quickly learned: that added to his own winning personality was the considerable advantage of personal attendance upon Molly's idol.

Molly's infatuation with Lord Rand was a household joke, and a grim provocation to Tom, who was equally besotted with the rosy-cheeked abigail.

"Why, all he had to do was look at her or anywhere's near her an' she busts out bawling. Didn't you, then?" he accused his beloved. "An' wasn't no help at all, an' his lordship's cousin lost now an' his lordship up all hours looking for her."

"I'm sure Miss Jones faithfully reported all she could," said Mr. Blackwood, bestowing a compassionate smile on the maid. "Though it must have been very trying indeed having to answer two gentlemen's questions at once."

"Oh, don't you know it, Mr. Blackwood. Here was my master asking me a hundred things and Mr. Max—his lordship, I mean—frowning and grumbling like I stole her myself. And all I ever did was explain about his lordship being away all that time and tell her what nice hair she had. As even you said yourself, Tom Fetters, and was carrying on so about her eyes as made a body wonder what *you* was thinking of."

Blackwood smoothly stepped in to prevent the angry retort forming on Tom's lips. "Ah, yes," Lord Rand's gentleman said, "even ladies of quality do not object to being reminded of their assets from time to time."

"Well, I don't know about that," Molly said frankly. "She looked like she didn't believe a word of it—as if I was the kind to flatter in hopes of getting something by it," she added scornfully.

"You strike me," said Blackwood, "as the soul of honesty. She ought to have believed you."

71

"I should say so. Don't I know that Lady Littlewaite's paid as much for a set of curls like that as she did for a ball gown? Nor they didn't match properly neither, but was the best Monsoor Franzwuz could do on short notice, when the other one fell into the turtle soup. Which it never would have done, he says, if she wasn't always flirting and tossing her head like she was a girl of eighteen instead of a grandmama."

Blackwood listened carefully, his precise mind examining, selecting, and discarding as Molly continued talking. He had come because he knew Lord Andover's servants would speak more freely to one of their own kind than to their masters. In their less guarded speech might be a clue to Miss Pelliston's whereabouts. A remembered word or phrase might offer some inkling of her plans.

Now he sorted out two facts that appeared significant. Miss Pelliston had come to Andover House penniless, and, according to his master, desperate to go home. Molly had talked to her of the buying and selling of hair. This, perhaps, was the clue he wanted.

"Sold her hair?" Max repeated, aghast, when the valet presented his report. "That glorious—" He stopped short, equally horrified at what he'd been about to say. "That's ridiculous," he snapped. "If she'd done it, then why ain't she home? Why didn't anyone remember her at the coaching inns?"

"A confused mind is a vacillating mind, My Lord. Perhaps she changed her mind about returning. If she managed to acquire money, she may have sought temporary shelter in London."

"Or maybe someone changed her mind for her," was the angry response. "Confound the woman! Why couldn't she stay put? Did you ever hear of such a henwit?"

Blackwood wisely refrained from responding to this. Silently he handed a snowy white length of linen to his employer.

"Damn it, man, I haven't time to fool with that thing. Takes me half a dozen to do it right, and I'm in no mood to bear those pained looks you give me when I do it wrong, as though I'd just put a ball through your other leg. I'll wear one of the old ones that don't feel like such a noose about my neck."

"With the Bath superfine, My Lord?" the valet stoically enquired.

Lord Rand looked at his coat, then back at the neck-cloth the valet held. "I suppose," he said after a moment, "if we do meet up with the wretched girl, you think the combination will drive her off again."

"Rather excessive for a young lady's sensibilities, I do believe, sir."

"Very well," said the defeated employer. "The gibbet it is. Only you had better tie it, unless you mean to see your master garrote himself."

"Bit early in the day for this sort of thing, ain't it? Sun ain't even set, said Lord Browdie as his companion led him through the door into a red velvet-draped vestibule.

"Ah, you're getting old, Browdie. Time was you were ready for a bit of fun morning, noon, and night. Or is it you're afraid of being disappointed? No fear of that. Granny's gals'll tend to you, day or night—and cheaper than the kind you usually spend your money on."

On no account did Lord Browdie care to be reminded of his age. If his dark red hair had origins more pharmaceutical than natural, that was a secret between his manservant and himself, as were the yards of buckram padding that filled out his chest, shoulders, and calves. These features were no secret to a host of low females of his acquaintance, either, but he regarded their opinions no more than he regarded their sensibilities.

Might as well have a bit of fun, he thought, as he was led to meet his hostess. Damned tiresome business, this. He'd been in London four days and not a trace of his fiancee could he discover.

He had, moreover, met with a great deal of discourtesy.

The frigid crone at the school had disclaimed all knowledge of Miss Pelliston and had been notably unforthcoming regarding the blasted governess. A man-hater, that one. He'd had to bribe a maid to learn what little he now knew— that a young woman answering his description had come calling, but had stayed only a short time.

The maid, who'd been daydreaming out a window instead of attending to her work, had seen the young lady meet up with a tall gentleman, but no, she couldn't say who that was. The two had met up on the opposite side of the square, and that was too far away to see what the man looked like.

When Catherine turned out not to be where she was supposed to be, Lord Browdie was stymied. He hadn't the faintest idea how to find her. Thus he spent most of his time in diverse taverns and coffeehouses, occasionally remembered to enquire about the girl, and generally convinced himself he was diligently seeking her.

"—and this is Lynnette."

Lord Browdie looked up from his musings to behold a shapely brunette wearing a great deal of paint, cheap jewelry, and a bizarrely demure peach-colored gown from whose narrow bodice her ample bosom threatened to burst any minute. The woman seemed vaguely familiar.

"Don't I know you?" he asked a few minutes later as she led him upstairs.

"I don't think so, sir," she said, with a naughty grin. "I'd remember a handsome face like yours, I'm sure."

If Lynnette might have had what she wished, she would have wished for a younger patron who was a tad more considerate. Being ambitious, however, and not overly fastidious, she left wishes to dreamy idealists. She had risen from the Covent Garden alleys to this house. It was not the best sort of house but it wasn't the worst, either. At any rate, she would not remain longer than necessary. She meant to have an abode of her own, paid for by a wealthy gentleman, as would be the myriad gowns and jewels that normally accompanied such transactions.

Being an astute judge of character, she knew what her customer wanted and proceeded to fulfill his fantasies. Lord Browdie, who was not overly generous, was sufficiently moved by the experience to offer a bit extra compensation. He promised to see her again very soon.

"Thought you looked familiar," he said as she helped him on with his coat. "Now I know why. You're the gal of my dreams, ain't you, my lovely?"

Not until the next afternoon, in a rare interval of sobriety, did Lord Browdie realise that it hadn't been the female who was familiar, but the gown. The experience of remembering a woman's frock was so unusual that he actually puzzled over the matter for some minutes. Then his crony, Sir Reginald Aspinwal, appeared, the sober interval abruptly concluded, and Lord Browdie forgot all about frocks.

Catherine had adapted remarkably well to her new life, despite its obvious deficiencies. No one waited on her, willingly or otherwise. She dined simply in the workroom with either her fellow employees or Jemmy. She had neither fine clothes nor elegant accessories nor even the pin money to buy a single ribbon. On the other hand, she had not to cope with a drunken papa wreaking constant havoc with her attempts to keep the household in order, finding fault with everything she did and didn't do, and making her feel—despite what reason told her—that she was worthless, unlikable, and ought never to have been born.

The other seamstresses seemed to accept her as one of themselves. Though Madame was inclined to be emotional and easily provoked by demanding customers, she indulged her aggerations in the solitude of her office. She treated her employees kindly, realising that good health and even tempers were as critical to the creation of exquisite finery as were quality fabrics, well-lit work areas, and carefully maintained tools.

Yes, she had been most fortunate to meet up with Jemmy that day, Catherine thought, as she watched the little boy who sat with her at the worktable. At present he was stabbing viciously with his stubby pencil at a grimy piece of foolscap.

If she had not met him, she'd be home now and utterly wretched. She would never marry Lord Browdie. Now, being unable to provide a respectable accounting of her disappearance, she could never marry at all.

Perhaps Aunt Deborah was worried about her. Perhaps even Papa was concerned. If so, their concern was mainly pride. If they'd truly cared about her, she would never have gotten into this fix in the first place. How could they possibly have expected her to give her property and person into the keeping of that odious *roué*?

Good heavens, even her employer showed more compassion—and Jemmy seemed genuinely fond of her. He was so determined to please Miz Kaffy that he would drag out his foolscap and pencil the instant the other seamstresses rose to leave for the day. They were all gone now except Madame, who was in the showroom attempting to rid herself courteously of the inconsiderate customer who was staying well past closing time.

"No, dear," Catherine said as she gently extracted the pencil from her student's grasp. "You do not clutch it in your fist as though it were a weapon. You hold it thus, between your fingers." She demonstrated.

Jemmy complained that the pencil wriggled like a worm.

"You must show it who is master. You are a great, growing boy and this is only a small pencil. Here, I'll help you." She inserted the instrument between his grubby fingers and guided them with her own. "There. That is 'J.'"

"J," the boy repeated, gazing soberly at the mark he'd must made.

"Isn't that grand? I'll warrant none of the other boys you know can do that."

"No," he agreed. "To ing'rant."

Catherine stifled a smile. "You, on the other hand, are very clever. In just a few days you've made all the letters in the alphabet as far as 'J.' Do you realise that's nearly halfway?"

Jemmy groaned. "More still? Ain't 'ere never no end to 'em fings?"

"*Those things*—and 'ain't' is not a proper word. Sixteen more to go. Then," she quickly added, noting the expression of profound discouragement upon his round features, "you will have enough letters to make every word you ever heard of—even your own name. By this time next week you'll be writing your whole name all by yourself."

"Show me wot it looks like," Jemmy ordered, offering her the pencil.

Miss Pennyman agreed on condition he help her. Once more she placed the pencil between his fingers and guided them.

"Miss Pelliston, I presume?"

The "y" of "Jemmy" trailed off into a long crazy scrawl as Catherine dropped the child's hand.

At the sound of the familiar voice all the muscles in her neck stiffened. Slowly, painfully, she turned her head in the direction of the voice. In the same stiffly painful way, she became aware of gleaming boots, light-coloured trousers, a darker coat, and the blinding contrast of white linen as her gaze travelled up from the floor to his face, to be pinioned by the deep piercing blue of his eyes.

Blue . . . and angry. He had never seemed so tall and overpowering as he did now, his long, rugged form filling the narrow doorway.

= 8 =

JEMMY STARED AS well. As he took in his teacher's shocked white face, he waxed indignant. "Here now," he sharply informed the stranger, "you can't bust in here."

The stranger ignored him. "Miss Catherine Pelliston of Wilberstone, perhaps?"

Jemmy leapt from his chair to confront the aggravating visitor. "Din't I jest tell you you wuzn't allowed here? 'At ain't her name, neither, so you just be on yer way, sir, as you's had too much to drink nor what's good fer you." Apparently unaware that he was addressing the stranger's waistband, Jemmy endeavoured to turn the man around and push him on his way.

Lord Rand caught the child by the collar. "Settle down, boy," he said. "I've business with this young lady."

Jemmy did not settle down. He immediately began pounding the man with his fists and shouting threats, along with loud advice to Missus to call the Watch.

Lord Rand, whose short store of patience was quickly deserting him, gave the boy a light cuff on the shoulder and bade him be still. This adjuration proving ineffective, he picked the child up and slung him across his hip, in which position Jemmy, undaunted, flailed and kicked, mainly at empty air.

"Oh, do stop!" Catherine cried, rising from her chair. "Jemmy, you leave off that noise this instant and stop striking his lordship. And you, My Lord—how dare you bully that child!"

78

"The little beast is bullying me, in case you hadn't noticed." Nonetheless, Lord Rand released the boy, who ran back to shield his teacher. The urchin stood in front of her, scowling fearlessly at the giant. The teacher's great hazel eyes flashed fire.

"Is this your latest protector, ma'am? If so, I'd advise you not to stand too close. I daresay the wretch has lice."

In response, Miss Pelliston put her arm about the boy's shoulder and drew him closer to her. "I suppose, My Lord, you are provoked with me," she said stiffly. "I will not deny you may have reason. That is no excuse for picking on a helpless child."

"He's about as helpless as a rabid cur. Little beast *bit* me," Lord Rand grumbled.

"'N'll do it agin if you don't go away," Jemmy retorted.

"Very well," his lordship replied. "I do mean to go away— but not without your lady friend."

At this Jemmy set up a screeching that brought Madame to the workroom door. "Heavens, what is the child howling about?" she cried. "Jemmy, you stop that racket this minute, do you hear? Whatever will his lordship think? And poor Miss Pennyman—Miss Pelliston, I mean—you dreadful boy. Isn't she ill enough without your giving her the headache besides?"

Lord Rand moved aside to let the *modiste* enter the room.

"My dear," said Madame, taking Catherine's hand, "I had no notion. Such a shock it must be for you—but my poor brother had the same trouble. Knocked over by a farmer's cart and when he came to he didn't know who he was. Thought he was a farmer himself. It was two days before he came to his senses."

"I beg your pardon, but I am in full possession of my wits," said a baffled Catherine.

"Yes, dear, so he thought too. It's the amnesia, you know. If I hadn't been by to help him, he might have wandered off just as you did and none of us would ever have known what became of him."

"Amnesia?" Catherine faintly repeated.

"Yes," said the viscount as his face quickly assumed a mask of concern. "Apparently you tripped on the stairs the other morning and hit your head. Of course you don't remember, Miss Pelliston," he added, as she opened her mouth to contradict. "But I described to Madame the bandbox you'd packed with old clothes for the parish needy and she tells me you arrived carrying the very one."

The dressmaker nodded her agreement.

"Evidently you got muddled in your brain, ma'am, and thought it was your own luggage. Naturally, one understands how your confused mind perceived it."

Miss Pelliston's enormous eyes opened wider at this arrant falsehood. "My mind was—is—not in the least confused—"

"There, there," Madame comforted. "Just as my brother kept insisting. But his lordship is here to take you home now, and in a day or so you'll be right as a trivet. I shall miss you terribly, though. I never did see such fine, neat stitches as you make, dear, and never wasting a scrap of fabric."

Jemmy, who understood nothing but that his teacher was to be carried off by this evil giant, began objecting loudly. Catherine hastened to comfort him. She bent to embrace him and murmur soothing remarks, most to the effect that she would never desert him.

Jemmy was a child wise in the ways of the world. He knew that tall, fancy-dressed gentlemen always got exactly their way in that world, and most especially when they were addressed as "My Lord." He refused to be consoled.

Catherine gazed up pleadingly at her erstwhile rescuer. "My Lord, I am sure there is some misunderstanding. You've confused me with someone else—"

"It's you who's confused. I'm only getting a headache is what. Drat it—can't you stifle the little b—lad?"

"He doesn't understand what's happening. Oh, please go away. Don't you see?" she begged. "He needs me. Madame needs me as well, as she just said. Oh, do go away, please."

The viscount, who'd expected to be greeted with every

possible expression of gratitude, was confounded. An hour earlier, Blackwood had found a pastry cook who had not only seen the young lady the valet described, but was in possession of a length of ribbon belonging to her. The cook having volunteered directions to Jemmy's place of employment, Blackwood had hastened across the street to inform his master, who was questioning a chemist.

On the way to the dressmaker's, Blackwood had tactfully reminded his impetuous employer of the need for discretion if the young lady was found. After all, hadn't Lord Andover refused to call in Bow Street, fearing that a scandal would result? It was the valet who'd suggested the tale of amnesia.

Now there seemed to be prospects of precisely the to-do Lord Rand had promised to avoid. The boy's shrieking was loud enough to raise the Watch, if not the dead, and Miss Pelliston had got that mutinous expression on her thin face. Even the seamstress was beginning to look doubtful.

The valet, who'd been waiting in the showroom, now appeared. "There seems to be a difficulty, My Lord," he said in as low a voice as possible, given the noise the child was making.

"The brat's taking fits, and so she won't come," was the frustrated response.

"Indeed. If you'll permit me, My Lord?"

Lord Rand shrugged. Blackwood moved past him to approach Jemmy.

"Here, now, my lad. What's all this fuss?"

Forgetting all Miz Kaffy's lessons in grammar and elocution, Jemmy burst out with a stream of loud outrage and complaint in cant so thick that none of his listeners could comprehend a word he said. None, that is, but Blackwood.

"And is that what makes a great strong boy like yourself cry like a baby?"

"I ain't no baby," was the angry retort.

"In that case, perhaps you would express your objections calmly to his lordship—man to man, so to speak."

Jemmy considered this while Catherine wiped his nose

with her handkerchief.

" 'N' I will too," he said, looking round at the company. He marched up to Lord Rand, gave him a fierce glare, and spoke.

"Miz Kaffy is learnin' me to write all 'em hundred letters and now you come to take her away and we just got to 'J' and there's a pile more arter. 'N' who sez anyhow 'at's all wot you say?" the boy demanded. "How does we know you don't mean bad for her? She ain't one of 'em wicked ones, you know. Miz Kaffy's a lady and knows all 'em letters and eats wif her fork and all. 'N' she tole you to go away besides," the child summed up with his most unanswerable argument.

Lord Rand, as has been noted, was not a stupid man. He had been a bold, angry little boy himself once. He'd had precious scraps of treasure torn from him and burnt as trash, had been ordered to do and whipped for not doing a great many things without being given any comprehensible reason. Even as an adult, he'd had someone he cared for driven away from him. He knelt to look the urchin in the eye.

"Of course your friend is a lady," he answered. "That is why I've come to fetch her. You know, don't you, that ladies don't work for a living?"

Jemmy nodded grudgingly.

"I realise you'll miss her," his lordship went on, "but her relatives have been missing her several days now, and they've been very worried about her. They'll be most grateful to learn what good care you and Madame Germaine have taken of her in the meantime."

The boy's face grew very still, except for the tears that welled up in his eyes. "But 'ey'll—they'll—have her back and I won't see her no more . . . and we only got to 'J.' " His voice quavered.

"Yes, that is a problem." Lord Rand stood up, darting a glance at Miss Pelliston, whose own eyes were filling. Gad, but her eyes were extraordinary—a great, unfathomable world seemed to exist there.

Lord Rand made a hasty decision, precisely as he was accustomed to do. "Suppose then, Jemmy, you come back with us to see where Miss Pelliston's relations live, so you can be sure everything's right and respectable. You can ride with the coachman," he offered.

"The boy's eyes lit up. "Ken I?"

"Yes—if you assure Miss Pelliston that you won't raise any more fuss and will be as brave as you can. Maybe then she'll come by to visit you from time to time."

"You knew I had no choice but to come," Catherine accused as the carriage rattled down the street. "Nonetheless, I cannot condone your methods, My Lord. You bribed that poor child with the promise of a ride on a fancy coach."

"Miss Pelliston, you are the most contrary woman I've ever met. Did you honestly intend to work as a seamstress the rest of your days?"

"Yes. I was content—and it was honest work."

Max studied her narrow face. Was it his imagination or was her color better? Somehow she didn't seem as tired and drawn as before, yet she must have been working ten, eleven, twelve hours a day. What a mystifying creature she was.

Aloud he said, "I'll be sure to mention that to Louisa. Perhaps she'll set you to embroidering her gowns—or making your own. I suppose that would spare all those tiresome visits to dressmakers. She can boast that you're the only debutante in London who's made very stitch of her Season's wardrobe."

Miss Pelliston, who'd been staring dismally at her hands, looked up. "I am not, as you well know, My Lord, a debutante. I am engaged to be married—or I was. Perhaps he won't want me now," she added with a faint, rueful smile. "Then at least something good will have come of all this."

"Sorry to upset your happy fantasies, ma'am, but I don't think your fiance has anything to say in the matter. Louisa's determined to bring you out, and once Louisa's determined on something there's nothing and no one can stand in her way. Certainly not irate papas or broken-hearted bridegrooms."

"Bring me out? Where? Why? What on earth are you talking about?" She leaned forward eagerly in her seat only to find Lord Rand's blue-eyed gaze rather too close for rational thought. Abruptly she sat back, her heart thumping wildly.

"Oh," she said. "You're talking nonsense. I didn't think you were inebriated, but one can never be certain. I suppose you have a very hard head." She winced as soon as she'd finished speaking, realising that, as usual, she'd been quite tactless.

Lord Rand smiled. "Bless me if you don't have the oddest way of flattering a man. I can hardly wait to see the other fellows' reactions when you treat them to some of your compliments."

To his satisfaction, her face turned pink.

"Yes, I do have a hard head, Miss Pelliston, but the fact is I'm sober as a judge at the moment. Dash it, didn't the Andover name ring any bells with you? Probably not. Country's crawling with relations—who's going to keep track of a lot of third and fourth cousins?"

"Oh, dear," she said softly as she took his meaning. "They are relations. I was afraid of that."

"You weren't afraid of slaving your life away for a miserable handful of shillings a week. What's so terrifying about Andover?"

"I know it will sound cowardly to you," Catherine began reluctantly, "but I didn't want anyone to know who I was. People treat one so differently. . . . I mean, they would have felt obliged to go out of their way on my account and I'd be obliged to accept, even though it would make matters worse."

"With your family, you mean? But how? They don't come any more respectable than Andover. Even the Old Man— my father, that is—can't find fault with the fellow, though he's tried hard enough for ten years."

"I mean," Miss Pelliston said so softly that Lord Rand had

to bend closer to hear her, "I had rather face Papa alone—not before strangers."

Lord Rand began to think he understood. She must have expected a perfectly horrendous homecoming if she'd elected to work for the miserable wages of a seamstress instead. The rage and frustration that had been building in him for days abruptly dissipated. She was gallant in her way, wasn't she? He remembered the girl clutching a coverlet about her as she sought help from a wild, drunken vagabond. Brave then too.

"Miss Pelliston, I assure you I'm not the least foxed," he said more kindly. "Edgar and Louisa intended to tell you the very next morning, after you'd had time to recover from your—experiences. No," he added hastily in response to her horrified look. "They know nothing of Granny Grendle or how you spent that night and they'll never know of it, I promise you."

"Thank you," she whispered.

"Anyhow, my brother-in-law's no stranger, and no one intends to make you face your papa at all, because Louisa's set on keeping you with her in London. You don't know my sister, Miss Pelliston. She's got scads of energy and intelligence and no productive use for 'em. She wanted dozens of children and would have been happily employed domineering them, but she's been unlucky that way. She needs to take charge of someone. She took to you right off, and that's all the reason she needs. I do wish you'd give her half a chance—you'd be doing her more of a favour than you would yourself."

That last was a stroke of inspiration. Catherine might have persuaded herself that she did not deserve to be rewarded for undutiful, ungrateful behaviour with a Season. She was not proof, however, against a plea on another's behalf.

Lord Rand seemed to believe his sister needed her, and Catherine wanted badly to be needed. Though she was distressed to abandon Jemmy and Madame, and thought that they—Jemmy especially—being less privileged folk were more entitled to her help, she knew that she'd never be allowed to return to work. She was not certain she could possibly do the self-possessed, breathtakingly beautiful Lady Andover any good, but Lord Rand claimed she could.

"If matters are as you say, My Lord, I would be both ungrateful and un-Christian to object. I am deeply sorry now that I behaved so rashly."

"Oh, never mind that," his lordship answered generously. "I like a bit of rash behaviour now and again. Keeps things interesting, don't you think?"

Lord Pelliston had spent a most enjoyable fortnight touring the Lake District with his bride. So enjoyable was the experience that more often than not he forgot to have recourse to his usual several bottles of strong spirits per diem. He had no idea he was being managed and would have scoffed at anyone who had the temerity to advance such a ridiculous notion.

His new wife had helped him forget a great many things, actually, including his dismal sister and waspish daughter. Now he had a letter from the Earl of Andover and one from his sister, in both of which Catherine's name seemed to appear repeatedly. He was not altogether certain of this fact because he was too vain to wear the spectacles he needed or allow his new wife to see how far away from his face he must hold the epistles in order to peruse them.

He glanced at his helpmeet, who was tying the ribbons of a most fetching bonnet under her dimpled chin. She was a dashed handsome woman. Just as important, she understood a man and talked sense.

Lady Pelliston turned to meet his gaze.

"Why so thoughtful, my dear? You don't like the bonnet? Say so at once and I shall toss it on the fire."

"No, it's the da—dratted letters. Don't anyone know how to write legible any more?"

His wife smiled and held out her hand. "Let me see them,"

she offered. "I seem to have a knack for deciphering anything."

A few minutes later she looked up. "Well," she said. "Well, well."

"Can you make 'em out?"

"Yes, dear. How I wish you'd explained matters to me more fully. I might have talked to the girl . . . but there, it is no business of mine. Catherine is your daughter and I do not like to interfere."

"With what? What's Andover palavering on about?"

"My dear, I believe you need a glass of wine." Lady Pelliston knew he'd prefer a few bottles, after which he would become unpleasant. This was her idea of a compromise.

Not until after he'd been supplied with refreshment did she set to work. "Catherine is not a strong girl, I take it?"

"If you mean in will, she's obstinate as a mule. If you mean body strength, well, what does she expect? Plays with her food instead of eating it and then goes gadding about among a lot of whining peasants, poking her nose where it don't belong or else locked up in her room with her infernal books. Plagues the life out of me," the baron complained.

"I see." The baroness rapidly readjusted her previous estimation of her stepdaughter. "Apparently, these unfortunate habits resulted in unsettled nerves. She ran away on our wedding day and left a note for your sister saying she was driven to it because she could not abide Lord Browdie."

"Ran off! There now—didn't I just tell you what a stubborn, plaguey gal she was? Ran off where? As if she had any place to go, the little bedlamite." Lord Pelliston polished off his glass of wine, muttering to himself between gulps.

"Evidently, she did not get far. Lord and Lady Andover happened to run across her. He does not say where, but he does remark that Catherine was quite beside herself. Very ill, he says, and terrified half out of her mind. I hope, James, it was not Lord Browdie who terrified her. His rather brusque ways are liable to intimidate a delicate lady. Particularly one," she hastened to add, "accustomed to more refined treatment from her papa."

"That's ridiculous. Browdie tells me that if he so much as says a word to the gal she glares at him like she meant to turn him to stone."

"As a Pelliston, she would scorn to show her fear, whatever she felt within," the baroness flattered. "Dear me, I had no idea she objected so to the match. Though I daresay," she quickly corrected, "that was mere missishness. How I wish I had been her mama and might have talked to her—but I am not and it is none of my affair. What do you mean to do, James?"

"Fetch her back, curse her. She ain't back, is she?" he asked hopefully.

"No, she is in London with her cousin and his wife."

"Cousin—fah! Family's never had a word to say to me unless they wanted hounds. Sold Andover a fine pair too, years ago, and that was the last I heard of him. Why the devil didn't he take her home again? Now we must be traipsing off to London—filthy, stinking hole that it is. Where's that bottle, Clare?"

Lady Pelliston was a young woman, and she did not mean to waste her remaining youth buried in a remote country village. She had every intention of visiting London in the near future. She meant, in fact, to spend every Season there until she grew too decrepit to stand upright. Interrupting her bridal trip in order to drag an unwilling stepdaughter to the altar was not part of these plans.

The situation was bound to be unpleasant, and Lady Pelliston hated unpleasantness. Also, she knew that the action would not win her husband—and herself by association—the earl's esteem. She had taken into account the Andover connection as systematically as she had all Lord Pelliston's other assets, and meant to use it to her advantage. The baroness was a practical woman.

Lord Andover wrote of his wife's intention to bring Catherine out. That was very odd of them, to be sure, but the Earl and Countess of Andover must be indulged their eccentricities. Lady Pelliston was not about to permit her spouse to interfere with those plans and thus wreak havoc upon her own. Accordingly, she removed her bonnet, poured her husband another glass of wine, and set about the formidable task of making him see reason.

=== 9 ===

LORD BROWDIE FROWNED at the heavily embossed sheet of vellum in his hand. Old Reggie had procured him the invitation to Lady Littlewaite's ball, thinking to do his friend a favour. Reggie had been visiting the day Pelliston's note arrived, and Lord Browdie being at the time more drunk than discreet had shared its contents with his friend. A good thing too. He might have dropped into a sulk if he'd been alone.

Fortunately, Reggie had been there to rally him, repeating his red-haired crony's many complaints about the girl's sour disposition and physical inadequacies. She had told her papa she couldn't abide Lord Browdie. Well, she'd soon learn that no one could abide *her*, and in a few months her papa would be apologising again and begging Browdie to take the shrew back.

Lord Browdie thought this unlikely. Lady Pelliston must have engineered the betrothal's end, just as she had instigated its beginning. Pelliston, he told Reggie, had been henpecked before he ever reached the altar. Pitiful, it was.

"Don't waste your pity on him," Reggie had argued. "He'll be feeling sorry for himself soon enough. You're a free man again—in London in the Season—with a hundred pleasanter females ripe for the plucking. What better time and place to find a wife? They're all here, my boy, from the baby-faced misses fresh from the schoolroom to the lonely widows who know what they're missing."

Hence the invitation. The trouble was, Lord Browdie had

far rather spend his time with the accommodating Lynnette than at the tedious work of courting either innocent misses or less innocent widows. He was even beginning to think seriously of setting Lynnette up in a modest house in Town. Though that would be a deal more expensive than what he now paid for her company, he'd have that company whenever the mood seized him, instead of having to cool his heels in Granny Grendle's garish parlour while his ladybird entertained another fellow.

Lynnette was greatly in demand. If he did not remove her from the premises soon, some other chap might. Still, no reason a man mightn't eat his cake and have it too. He'd take a look at Lady Littlewaite's display of potential breeders. If nothing there appealed to him, he'd pay Lynnette a visit. Meanwhile, he'd better see about that house.

"What in blazes is that?" Lord Rand demanded, staring out the window.

Blackwood looked out as well. "Jemmy, My Lord."

"I know it's Jemmy. What the devil is he doing there?"

"Sweeping the steps, My Lord."

"May a man ask why he is sweeping my steps when I have a regiment of servants already stumbling over one another looking for something to do?"

"Gidgeon set him to it, My Lord. The boy's been haunting the neighbourhood this past week, and the footmen complain that they hardly dare step out the door for fear of tripping over him."

Lord Rand sighed. "Doesn't the brat have work enough at the dressmaker's? Why must he haunt my house?"

"Apparently, sir, he's spying on you."

"Oh, give me strength." The viscount ran his fingers through his golden hair.

"Indeed, sir. It seems Mr. Hill was endeavouring to chase the boy away a few days ago. Mr. Gidgeon, who doesn't care for interference in household matters, took the lad's part in consequence. They had rather a row about it, and what must Mr. Gidgeon do but call Jemmy in for a talking to and tell him we wouldn't have vagrants hanging about. Mr. Gidgeon handed the boy a broom. Mr. Hill was fit to be tied."

"No wonder Hill's been sulking. I was missing his funereal pronouncements. So Jemmy's watching me, is he? Does he thing I'm one of Buonaparte's spies?"

"No, My Lord. He wishes to assure himself that you do not attempt to spirit Miss Pelliston away to your domicile 'for no wicked biznez,' as he puts it."

The viscount decided it was high time to have a talk with young Jemmy.

When Lord Rand opened the door, he found Jemmy diligently cleaning the railings. "Don't the maids do it well enough for you?" his lordship asked.

"Me hand's smaller," was the sullen reply. "I ken get in 'em—them—those little places."

"Don't you have work to do for Madame Germaine?"

"Not in the arternoons. Besides, SHE'S in one of 'em Aggerations. Allus is now, wif Miz Kaffy gone and Annie still sick."

Jemmy threw the viscount a reproachful glance before returning to his work.

"I suppose you haven't seen your friend in some time now?"

"Not since you took her off."

"Would you like to see her today?"

The urchin nodded, though he kept his focus on the railing.

"Shall I take you, then?"

A pair of brown eyes squinted suspiciously at the viscount. "You don't mean 'at—that."

His lordship uttered a small sigh. "I'm afraid I do. Only I can't take you to my sister's looking like a dirty climbing boy. Go down to the kitchen and ask Girard to give you something to eat," he ordered, breaking into a grin as he envisioned Jemmy's confrontation with the temperamental Gallic cook. "I'll see whether Blackwood can find you a better rigout."

Despite his vociferous objections, Jemmy was given a bath by a pair of housemaids assisted by a footman. Following that ordeal, the boy was dressed by Lord Rand's own valet in a brand-new suit of clothes, and his brown hair was brushed until it shone. Jemmy's own mother, even if sober, wouldn't have known him. He endured these diverse insults to his person only because, according to his lordship, they were necessary sacrifices.

"Look at me," Lord Rand said. "D'you think I let Blackwood strangle me with this blasted neck-cloth because I *like* it? Ladies are very difficult to please," he explained.

Had he been so inclined, the vicount might have also mentioned that he'd like to take a look at Miz Kaffy himself. He'd not seen her since he'd removed her from the dressmaker's shop—more than ten days ago.

Miss Pelliston had been nowhere in View whenever he'd called, and his sister had refused to bring her into sight, claiming that Max would have to wait, as everyone else must, until Miss Pelliston was fully prepared for her entrance into Society. Lord Rand was not, however, inclined to explain this to Jemmy.

When their respective sartorial tortures finally ended, the two males marched bravely to Andover House and into the glittering presence of Lady Andover.

"I believe you've heard something of Jemmy," the viscount said to his sister.

"Oh, indeed I have." She smiled at the boy. "Catherine has told me all about you."

"Where is she?" Jemmy demanded, not at all intimidated by Lady Andover's grandeur, though he thought her very fine indeed.

"She'll be down in a moment," the countess said easily, making Max want to slap her. "Perhaps you'd like some biscuits and milk to sustain you while you wait."

Though Jemmy had been very well sustained at the viscount's establishment, he was not fully recovered from his recent ordeal. He was, moreover, a growing boy, and like others of the species hungry all the time. He nodded eagerly.

He had just plunged a third biscuit into his mouth when Catherine appeared. He nearly choked on it, so great was his astonishment. Lord Rand, who had not been eating biscuits, only blinked and wondered if he'd been drinking all day without realising the fact.

In place of the prim schoolteacher he'd expected was a delicate-featured young lady in a fashionable lavender gown. Her light brown hair was a confection of curls, some of which framed her face and softened its narrow features, while the others were held back in an airy cloud by a lavender ribbon.

He stared speechless at her as she made a graceful curtsey. She darted one nervous glance at his face, then hurried forward to clasp Jemmy in her arms.

"How happy I am to see you," she said. "And how fine you look."

"He made me do it," Jemmy answered, recovering quickly from his surprise. "Made me have a bath 'n' everything."

"Oh, my. Was that very dreadful, dear?"

"It wuz horrid. But I done it cuz he said he wouldn't bring me if I didn't *He* had to be strangled, he sez."

Lord Rand did strangle an oath before hurriedly explaining, "I was referring at the time to my neck-cloth. Blackwood claims it is a Mathematical. I call it a Pesticidal myself. Feel like a curst mummy."

"You look very well for all that," said his sister. "This Blackwood must be an extraordinary fellow from all I've heard—and seen," she added, eyeing her brother up and down.

"Yes. Drives me terribly. He has interesting notions about who is master. Just like the rest of the household. Not a one of them does anything but what he pleases. My butler drops his aitches and sets young vagrants to sweeping my steps. I'm hanged if there's one of them ever hears a word I say."

"If they listened to you, Max, the house would be a shambles and yourself the sad wreck you were but two weeks ago. Was he not a sad wreck, Catherine? Was he not falling to pieces before our very eyes, and that because he'd spent six months doing exactly as he pleased? Now that he does his duty instead, he's almost presentable, don't you think?"

Though Miss Pelliston had led Jemmy to the sofa in order to talk quietly with him, she had not missed any of the preceding discussion. She glanced at the viscount, then looked quickly down at her hands when she felt heat rushing to her cheeks.

She had never thought him a sad wreck, except perhaps morally, and now he was so tidy and elegant that one must have a very discerning eye indeed to detect the crumbling moral fiber within. One certainly could not detect it in his eyes, which were no longer shadowed and bloodshot. There had never been any lines of dissipation about his mouth, as there were about Papa's, nor was Lord Rand's long, straight nose webbed with red, spidery veins.

Still, Papa was past fifty and Lord Rand not even thirty . . . and it was perfectly absurd to sit here tongue-tied like a shy little rustic, she told herself angrily.

She raised her head to meet the viscount's unnerving blue gaze. His lips twitched. Was he laughing at her?

"His lordship and I are so recently acquainted that I have no basis for forming an opinion on that subject," she answered. "At any rate, I do believe some years of concentrated effort are needed for a healthy young man to reduce himself to a sad wreck. The human body is amazingly resilient." Then, in spite of herself, she winced.

Lord Rand's blue eyes gleamed. "Right you are, Miss Pelliston. I told my family six months wasn't nearly enough time. Some years, did you say? How many do you suggest?"

"I suggested nothing of the sort. Certainly I would never undertake to advise anyone upon methods of self-destruction."

"No? Well, that's a relief. I'd hate to have it get about that a young lady of one and twenty had to instruct me in dissipation. Most lowering, don't you think?"

"I should say so. I hope I know nothing whatever about it."

"Catherine, you must not take Max so seriously. He is bamming you."

"I was not. I thought for once I had someone on my side."

"You have your valet on your side, dear, and that is all a man requires, according to Edgar."

"Can't be. Miss Pelliston has neatly avoided answering your question about my presentability, so I can only suspect the blackguard has failed me."

"I beg your pardon, My Lord. I had no idea you sought reassurance," Catherine responded with a trace of irritation. "I assumed your glass must have told you that your appearance is altogether satisfactory."

"Is it? Kind of you to say so. Did your own glass tell you that you look like a spray of lilac?"

If this was more teasing, Catherine was at a complete loss how to respond. Her face grew hot.

"Here now," Jemmy cut in. "Wot's he about?"

Haven't the vaguest idea, Max answered inwardly. Aloud he said, "I was telling Miss Pelliston how lovely she is. Don't you agree?"

Jemmy gazed consideringly at his friend for a moment. Then he nodded. "Why'd you go all red, 'en?" he asked her.

"I was embarrassed," was the frank reply.

While Jemmy was deciding whether or not he approved this state of affairs, Lady Andover hastened to Catherine's rescue. "My dear, you must become accustomed to compliments. You will hear a deal more tomorrow at Lady Littlewaite's ball."

"Still, she might blush all she likes," said the provoking Max. "The chaps will love it."

"Since you know nothing whatever about how gentlemen behave at these affairs, I beg you keep your opinions to yourself," the countess retorted dampeningly.

"Being a chap myself, I expect I know more about it than you do," her brother rejoined before returning his attention to Miss Pelliston. "So that's to be your first foray into Society?"

"Yes. I did not wish to take any steps before we were certain Papa would not object. Lord Andover just received his letter a few days ago. Apparently, Papa has reconsidered—about Lord Browdie, I mean."

"Browdie. So that's the old goat's name. Never heard of him."

"You never heard of anybody higher in the social scale than a tapster, Max. The Baron Browdie is not precisely an old goat, as you so poetically put it, though he does have nearly three decades' advantage of Catherine. He is also reputed to lack refinement. According to Edgar's mama, Lord Browdie's company is not coveted by Society's hostesses, though he is tolerated."

"Better and better," said Max. "Means you're not likely to be running into him very often. That is, if he's in London at all."

"That we don't know," the countess answered, before Catherine could look up from her conversation with Jemmy. "Lord Pelliston wrote that Lord Browdie had come to Town looking for Catherine but would be receiving written notice that the engagement was off."

"There now, Miss Pelliston. Didn't I tell you to put your faith in Louisa?"

Miss Pelliston, who had not yet fully recovered from her previous exchange with his lordship, had much rather talk to Jemmy. She answered, a tad distractedly, "Oh, yes—certainly. Still, I can scarcely believe it. Even when Lord Andover let me read Papa's letter, I couldn't believe it. It was so unlike—I mean to say, I mustn't have expressed myself plainly enough—"

"Oh, of course," Lord Rand sweetly replied. "Never mind that Andover can talk the horns off a charging bull. Don't you know that's what they're always wanting him for at Whitehall? If he ain't persuading Prinny's ministers he must be persuading Prinny himself."

"I did not mean to discount Lord Andover's efforts. I agree that I should have listened to you in the first place, My Lord." Catherine's gaze dropped to the child sitting beside her. "Yet if I had, I would never have met Jemmy. I cannot be sorry for

97

that, whatever hundred other things I am sorry for."

Though much of the conversation was beyond his comprehension, this Jemmy grasped.

"So why don't you come see me?" the boy demanded.

"I will. Tomorrow afternoon when Lady Andover takes me to order the rest of my wardrobe from Madame," Catherine promised. "The dress I'm wearing had to be made up in rather a hurry, I'm afraid, along with a gown for tomorrow night, and I didn't want to impose on her, knowing how very busy she must be."

"Will you show me more letters when you come?"

"I will show you some now, if her ladyship and his lordship will excuse us," Catherine answered, so eagerly that Lord Rand frowned.

"Well, Max, you do look fine," said her ladyship after teacher and student had exited, "but you are no match for Jemmy's sartorial splendour."

"No, despite my fine feathers, Miss Pelliston knows I'm a bull in a china shop. Leastways she looks at me as if she thought any minute I might step on her or crash into her or I don't know what. Am I that clumsy, Louisa?"

Lady Andover studied her brother for a moment before answering quietly, "I don't think anyone's ever teased her before, Max. She is rather fragile in some ways."

"Bull in a china shop, just as I said. Well, then, as long as she's out of the room, why don't you tell me your plans for your innocent victim? Has she the least idea what she's in for?"

Some hours later, as he recalled his conversation with Miss Pelliston, Max grimaced. Like it or no, he seemed to be undergoing a transformation, and that annoyed him. In the first place, he thought, glaring into the cheval glass, there was his appearance. When he'd first returned to England, he'd let his sister coax him into ordering two new suits of clothing. These he'd promptly abandoned after the battle with his father and the truce allowing the heir six months' freedom.

Max had considered two new costumes sufficient, even when he assumed his rightful position in Society, since he most certainly had no intention of gadding about with a lot of dim-witted macaronis. Yet the day after he'd returned Miss Pelliston to his sister's care, he'd made a long visit to Mr. Weston. There and at the establishments of Mr. Hoby, the bootmaker; Mr. Lock, the hatter; and diverse others, Lord Rand had ordered enough masculine attire to fit out Lord Wellington's Peninsular Army for the next decade.

A person would think he was well on his way to becoming a damned fop, he mused scornfully.

In the second place, there was his behaviour. *A spray of lilac*. What the devil had he been thinking of? That was just the kind of trite gallantry that had always filled him with disgust and that was one of the reasons he avoided Fashionable Society. Young misses expected such treacle and one must be endlessly cudgelling one's brains for some effusive compliment or other, even if the miss had a squint and spots and interspersed her sentences with incessant Oh, la's.

It didn't matter that Miss Pelliston had neither squint nor spots and was perfectly capable of intelligent conversation. It was the principle of the thing, dash it!

That she'd left off her prim, buttoned-up, spinster costume was no reason to pour smarmy sludge upon her. Obviously his new *ensembles* had gone to his head. Because he looked like a fop, he'd tried to act like one. Clothes make the man.

Apparently, they made the woman as well. Perhaps he might not have taken leave of his wits if he hadn't been so very surprised at her transformation. The lavender gown and soft hairstyle had brought out a subtle, delicate beauty that no one but Louisa would have realised the girl possessed.

Idly he wondered whether other men would appreciate it, and if they did, what they would make of the curious character beneath. Not that most men would waste much time evaluating her appearance or personality when they learned who her papa was. She would be prey to fortune hunters, naturally, but Louisa and Edgar would protect her.

Miss Pelliston was in good hands. All the same, he might as well pop in briefly to Lady Littlewaite's "do" tomorrow night. If other fellows turned out to be slow to recognise Miss Pelliston's attributes, she would need a partner. Though Max had little taste for the convoluted intricacies that passed for dancing, he knew all the steps just the same. He would dance with her and appear captivated and Edgar would do the same and eventually some other chaps would notice.

The ball, of course, would be tedious, stuffy, and hot, as such affairs always were. Still, he had only to do his duty by the young lady, then take his leave.

It occurred to him that he hadn't addressed certain needs in nearly a month. About time he turned his mind to that issue. After he left the ball, he'd drop by the theater and see what the Green Room had to offer.

Lord Rand accosted his lugubrious secretary and ordered the startled Hill to convey his Lordship's acceptance of Lady Littlewaite's invitation.

"Excuse me, My Lord, but I sent your regrets, as you requested, three days ago."

"Then unsend 'em," came the imperious reply. "Apologise for the mistake or whatever. *She* ain't going to argue. They always want those affairs well-stocked with bachelors, don't they? Daresay she wouldn't turn a hair if I towed you along with me—or Jemmy, for that matter," the viscount added wickedly.

=10=

"THAT'S ALL THAT'S left," said Miss Pelliston, examining in some surprise the names scrawled upon her fan, "except for the waltzes, and I mayn't dance those until I receive permission from Almack's patronesses."

"You seem to be the belle of the ball," said Lord Rand.

"There seems to be a shortage of ladies, rather. Nearly everyone who attended Lady Shergood's musicale the other night is ill," she explained. "Fortunately, hers was a most select affair or I daresay this ballroom would be deserted."

"Don't be ridiculous. The house is crawling with females. You underestimate your attractions."

"Hardly that. It's my papa, you know. Though he's only a baron, the title is an old one. You see, his ancestor, named Palais D'Onne, arrived in England with the Conqueror. Thus we are quite ancient," the lady recited, precisely as her great-aunt had taught her. "People put much stock in such things, though one does wonder why. I had not noted that human beings were bred for speed or endurance as horses or hounds are. I suppose it is because ancient titles are so rare nowadays."

"Indeed," her attentive student soberly replied. "If Charles II had not been so generous to his illegitimate offspring, we would speak of the Upper Ten, rather than the Upper Ten Thousand. So you conclude that your rarity accounts for your popularity?" Lord Rand asked, sternly suppressing a smile.

"Not entirely. I'm sure Papa's money and the property I

101

inherited are considered as well."

As perhaps must the fact that she looked like a pink rose, Lord Rand thought. Her eyes sparkled with happiness, her cheeks were flushed, and her pink muslin gown with its delicate embroidery fit her to perfection. That much he'd noticed from halfway across the crowded ballroom.

Now it struck him that she appeared a deal healthier overall. She had gained some weight. He hadn't realised that yesterday. He decided the addition became her, and felt somewhat relieved that life with his domineering sister was proving agreeable—physically at least—for the young lady. What she wanted now was a tad more self-confidence. Ancient titles, bloodlines—she knew as well as he what rubbish that was!

"I mean to debate this issue with you, ma'am, at length," he answered. "But later, when your next partner is not bearing down on me. Will you save me the country dance and sit out one waltz?"

"Oh, you really needn't—," she began, but he'd turned and left, and her partner had come to claim her.

Really, he was too obliging, she thought as Sir Somebody led her to the dance floor. All the women in the room were ogling the viscount as though they were half-starved and he a holiday banquet. In his simple evening garb—black coat, dove grey unmentionables, and snowy white linen—he was more striking and handsome than ever.

How graceful he was. For all his great height and those broad shoulders, he was well-proportioned, as the perfect tailoring of his coat clearly demonstrated. Well, he was an active man, and such men seemed to have an inborn grace—the natural result of physical self-confidence. In plain point of fact, he was splendid, and certainly needn't waste a waltz on her when she couldn't even dance it and there were scores of beautiful women who could.

He had asked her, though, and did not seem drunk. He would probably fluster her—he already had—but that was because she was unused to the ways of elegant gentlemen. One could not avoid every new experience simply because it was new or one would never develop intellectually.

"Dash it, Mother, I ain't a baby to be hauled about by the ear," Lord Rand complained as Lady St. Denys clutched his arm.

"My dear, no one ever led you by the ear—at least I should hope not, or if they did it must have been because you were doing what you oughtn't, and no one would have done so at any rate when you were a baby and couldn't walk at all until you were nearly two years old and then it was run, run, run."

She paused to catch her breath and Max was about to order her to let go of his sleeve when he found himself confronting a statuesque blonde whose light blue eyes were nearly level with his own. Dimly he heard his mother rambling on at the fair goddess's mama and then babbling at the goddess herself. He shook out of his daze in time to hear the introductions. Lady Diana Glencove. She even had the name of a goddess.

He heard himself uttering all the inane imbecilities he despised, and couldn't stop them from dribbling off his tongue. The goddess seemed to accept them as her due. After she'd made some gracious reply, she asked, in throaty tones that made his brain whirl, what he had thought of North America.

At the moment, Max knew as little of the New World as Molly did. It seemed to exist, along with everything else but this fair Juno, in another galaxy. With a mighty effort he wrenched his mind back to answer as rationally as he could. Then at last—blessed relief—he had to talk no more, for she'd agreed to dance with him.

That, Catherine thought as she watched the two tall fair ones take their places in the set, was exactly as it should be. They matched perfectly, Lord Rand and the beautiful unknown, like a pair of Norse deities. If her own face had suddenly grown overwarm, that was because the way he looked at his partner could not be quite proper. Though

Catherine was unsophisticated, she was quite certain a gentleman ought not stare at a lady as though he were a famished horse and she a bucket of oats. Goodness, she was full of dietary similes this evening!

Catherine decided she was hungry. Lately her appetite astonished her. She, who normally picked wearily at her meals, had just this morning accepted Tom's offer of a second helping, and she blushed to recall how many of those delicious tiny sandwiches she'd consumed at tea. She would grow out of her new wardrobe before Madame had finished cutting the pattern pieces.

When the viscount came later to claim her for the country dance, Catherine forgot all about being famished. The steps were a tad too complicated—especially for one who'd just learned them—to permit concentration on much else, and the movements too energetic to permit witty repartee. She did miss a step when he told her she was in looks, but she reminded herself about intellectual development and managed a faint smile.

She returned to Lady Andover feeling rather pleased with herself and somewhat awed at the novel sensation. Catherine knew she was not, as Lord Rand had flattered, the belle of the ball. She had not expected to be.

Still, Papa's lineage and wealth counted for something, and she was grateful that they offered her a chance to find a more agreeable husband than Lord Browdie. None of the gentlemen she'd met so far appeared irritated or bored with her company, and she had managed to control her sharp tongue. She'd acquitted herself reasonably well, she thought, even with the one man who could unsettle her with a glance. London was not such a terrifying place after all.

Her new-won confidence and optimism helped her through the rather difficult few moments that ensued between Lord Rand's relinquishing her to Lady Andover and Mr. Langdon's appearance to claim Miss Pelliston for the next set. During these few minutes she found herself face to face with the hated Lord Browdie.

The shocked look that creature bestowed upon her gave Catherine some grim satisfaction. He had always made unpleasantly jocular remarks about her appearance. "Skinny as a broomstick" was not her idea of a witty compliment, any more than his blunt advice that she put some meat on her bones had ever sounded like affectionate concern. He had always spoken to her precisely as he spoke of his horses and hounds—except that he considered the beasts with far greater warmth. If he'd had his way he'd surely have put her in the care of a stableman who'd have made her eat her corn.

Now, though she found the way he leered at her bodice highly objectionable, she bore his clumsy compliments with frigid composure. Looking, she reminded herself, was all he'd ever be able to do.

She was delighted that she could decline his request for the next two dances without uttering any falsehood. Her pleasure would have been unalloyed had he not gone on to ask for the supper dance. She had hoped the somewhat absentminded Mr. Langdon would remember to ask her about that. He was very attractive, and his soft voice was so calming. Now she darted a pleading glance at Lady Andover, who promptly came to her rescue.

"So sorry, My Lord," the countess told Lord Browdie with a cold smile. "Another gentleman has won that honour."

Mr. Langdon appeared in time to hear this exchange. When he led Miss Pelliston out, he expressed his disappointment. He looked so forlorn that Catherine had to stifle a maternal urge to brush his hair back from his forehead and murmur something soothing. She too was disappointed. Mr. Langdon seemed so gentle and intelligent. She would have enjoyed talking quietly with him during supper. Now she would dine partnerless—though that was hardly a tragedy. Her cousin and his wife would be with her and they were both most entertaining—and had she not already achieved undreamed-of success?

Having dragged six debutantes about the dance floor,

Lord Rand decided he'd done his duty. In fact, he might be on his way to fulfilling the most unnerving duty of all.

He'd never expected to meet in elevated company a woman whose physical attributes so perfectly met his ideals. Not only was Lady Diana in no danger of breaking if one touched her, but she was generously formed and stunningly beautiful. Her throaty voice was a merciful relief from the usual high-pitched nasalities. She did not chatter endlessly about nothing and certainly didn't lecture about everything. Actually, she'd said very little, he now realised. Instead, she'd encouraged him to talk, and upon a subject she seemed to find as fascinating as he did.

The viscount's obligation to marry and get heirs began to seem less onerous. Tall, fair Junos were a rarity, even in the crowded London Marriage Mart. Courting Lady Diana would not be a punishment . . . still, he needn't make so weighty a decision this instant.

Nudging duty aside for the moment, Lord Rand headed for the card room. There he had the dubious honour of being introduced to Lord Browdie and the satisfaction of finding the brute as contemptible as he'd imagined. The viscount's enjoyment of the evening was further heightened when he proceeded to relieve Lord Browdie of a respectable sum of money, despite the rather paltry stakes.

Lord Browdie was a poor loser. Though he managed to put on a swaggering show of hilarity at the outcome, he decided he disliked Lord Rand. After the card game broke up and its participants filed out to supper, dislike grew into loathing. Lord Browdie watched the blond viscount saunter confidently up to the Earl and Countess of Andover, make some remark that caused the couple to smile, and offer his arm to Miss Pelliston.

Lord Browdie had expected to find Catherine languishing at the sidelines with the other antidotes. To discover her dancing her feet off the entire evening was a greater shock than her improved appearance. He felt he'd been villainously deceived and ill-used, and though his feelings for her were no more affectionate at present than they'd ever been, he remembered her property and dowry with every sort of tenderness. He recalled as well the numerous rebuffs he'd borne this evening from all those other females Reggie had claimed were panting to breed Browdie heirs.

How he'd like to wipe that insipid smile off her sharp little face, and how he'd love to put that grinning, yellow-haired Exquisite in his place. Much as he would have enjoyed these innocent diversions, Lord Browdie had no idea how to bring them about. He decided, therefore, to leave the party and get roaring drunk in more congenial surroundings.

"You see, Catherine?" Lady Andover was saying. "We spoke no falsehood to Lord Browdie. My instincts must have told me Max would forget to ask anyone to sup with him. Though that's hardly complimentary to you, perhaps he'll contrive to be entertaining enough to make you forget the insult." The countess took her husband's arm and they preceded Max and Catherine to the supper room.

"Never mind what she says," Max told his partner. "Browdie was deuced generous to confound all the other fellows' hopes for your company. Because of him, my own lack of virtue is rewarded. If I'd been playing the proper gentleman, I'd have to sup with someone else."

Miss Pelliston found herself more pleased than she wished to be with the way the supper issue had resolved itself. Self-annoyance made her face rather stiff as she answered, "Since taking a lady into supper is hardly a moral obligation, your argument is unsound. In the first place, you committed no crime. In the second, if you had, there are a number of ladies here whose company far better qualifies as 'rewarding.' Your argument for the rewards of wickedness is specious, sir," she concluded with satisfaction.

"I'm a Sophist, am I? Oh, don't look so amazed," he added as her wide hazel eyes opened wider. "I learnt philosophy as well as the next chap, I suppose. Which is how I know that your logic is shaky. You don't know a thing about those other ladies, yet you claim them more rewarding company than yourself. Shall we take a poll of the gentlemen, Miss Pelliston?"

"No, of course not. It was a pretty compliment. I would not have argued if you had not used it to defend an immoral philosophy—though I would be forced to admit that virtue is not always rewarded in this world and wickedness often is. But you see, you were merely forgetful, not wicked."

"Then you'll allow the pretty compliment to stand?"

She bit her lip. "I suppose I must, for you have twisted the issues so that . . . well, never mind. You are only trying to divert me, as her ladyship suggested, and I have no business scolding you for it."

"Of course not. You never scolded Jack Langdon, I'm sure. Why, he spent at least ten minutes raving about you. Then he forgot all about it and wandered off to find his book. I'm amazed he didn't have it with him when he danced with you. Often does, you know."

"Yes, Lady Andover mentioned that he was a tad eccentric. Still, I found his comments on the Medes and Persians most intriguing, though I'm afraid my ancient history is rather weak."

They'd reached the room where a very large number of very small tables had been set out to accommodate hungry guests. Lord Rand drew out a chair for Miss Pelliston. As she sat down, he leaned over her shoulder and said in a low voice, "I'm sure he was too busy talking himself and staring into your lovely eyes to notice your scholarly failings. Or if he did, he's far more levelheaded than he should be. You look like a pink rose."

Miss Pelliston turned pink enough. Lord Rand stared blankly at her for a moment before he remembered where he was and hastily took his seat beside her. Why had he uttered that revolting treacle?

He now wished he hadn't offered to sit out the waltz with her. That would not take place until sometime after supper and he wanted out of this confounded menagerie now, before every last vestige of his common sense was stifled by etiquette.

Meanwhile, if he didn't want her to get the wrong idea, he'd better bring the conversation into more impersonal channels.

"Miss Pelliston, you are behaving very badly," he lightly chided.

"Why, what have I done? This is the proper spoon, I'm sure," said Miss Pelliston, surveying her silverware in some alarm.

"You were supposed to make a clever retort to my compliment."

"I know—but I just couldn't think of a single thing," she confessed with chagrin.

"I'll think of it for you. You must warn me of your thorns."

She considered. "Thorns—that seems apt enough. And the part about my eyes?" she asked, focusing those brilliant orbs upon him.

He leaned a hairsbreadth closer. "Yes," he said, wondering why he felt as though he were in quicksand, "your eyes are lovely."

"That's what you told me," his disciple reminded patiently. "What must I answer?"

He hauled his attention back to his plate. "Why, that they're sharp enough to detect the wicked truths lurking behind honeyed words.

"That sounds rather like a scold."

"Not if you smile when you say it, and especially not if you contrive to blush at the same time. That will encourage the gentleman to declare his innocence."

Miss Pelliston sighed. "This is very complicated."

"Yes," his lordship concurred, more heartily than she could know. "Very complicated. Anyhow, you're thinking instead of eating and you'll need sustenance if you hope to dance until dawn. We'll talk of something less taxing, shall we? How long before I can expect Jemmy to begin lecturing me on the rise and fall of the Roman Empire?"

Relieved to turn the conversation from herself, Catherine responded with more of her usual poise, though her mind drifted elsewhere.

She thought she'd been handling his lordship's altogether unexpected attentions with reasonable composure—until he'd bent to whisper in her ear. Then she had become acutely aware of a faint scent—a mixture of soap and something woodsy and cheroots and wine.

Examined objectively, this should not be an aesthetically pleasing combination of aromas, the two latter ingredients being vivid reminders of masculine frailties. Lord Browdie always stank of tobacco and spirits and that, along with his other unfortunate personal habits, usually made her wish herself in another county when he was by.

Lord Rand aroused an altogether different response, a host of sensations so novel that she could not be certain what they were. She realised, however, that these feelings were not altogether objective. Turning gooseflesh all over and having to count to twenty to settle one's pulse back to normal rhythm was not her idea of aesthetic detachment.

Except for ruthless exposure to most of her father's vices, Catherine had lived a very sheltered, isolated life. She had never had a friend her own age. There was no room for sentiment or frivolity in her education. Had she not been such a voracious reader on her own, she might never have known that such a thing as flirtation existed. Any tender, silly sentiments she'd felt before had been summoned up by plays, poetry, and novels, and had always seemed to belong to a fantasy world completely unconnected with her own sober existence.

Now she began to understand—viscerally—Sophia Western's trembling when Tom Jones was near. This was troubling. One ought not be so susceptible to a few pleasing words. If she did not keep a careful lookout, she would imagine herself in love with every gentleman who flattered her.

Lord Rand merely did what was expected at these affairs, she reminded herself. His behaviour seemed out of character only because she'd never seen him in such an environment before. Obviously, he could not have intended that she take his remarks seriously or he would not have offered to teach her how to play the game. If, at the moment, the game seemed perilous to one's peace of mind, that was because new experiences were often unnerving. Once she mastered the necessary skills, she would go about the business as coolly as he did.

Not that she meant to become a coquette. Even if capable of so far lowering her standards, Catherine was incapable of playing the part. She'd only look ridiculous. She wished she could find some safe island between prudery and impropriety—but the Beau Monde offered no solid moral ground. Hypocrisy seemed to be the fashionable equivalent of propriety, discretion indistinguishable from morality, and the rules seemed to constantly shift on whim.

Still, that was the way of the world. If Lord Rand could navigate these treacherous waters with such skill, there was no reason an erudite young lady could not.

=== 11 ===

As LONG AS he'd already plunged into the turbulent waters of the Beau Monde, Lord Rand decided he might as well swim the distance. Dutifully he called the following day upon the young ladies with whom he'd danced. Among these was Lady Diana, whose mama beamed as the viscount entered her ornate drawing-room.

The young lady was fortunate, Max thought, to have been built to such generous proportions; otherwise she'd have been lost among the bric-a-brac. The room was large enough, but so thickly furnished with ancestral wealth that it seemed a museum whose collection had outgrown it. The walls suffocated under the weight of heavy tapestries and massive paintings, the latter encased in thickly carved gilded frames. Everywhere was gilt and ornate carving—chairs and tables so ponderous that any one would require a dozen strong men to lift it.

Lady Diana managed to hold her own among this gilded magnificence. She accepted with quiet graciousness his tribute of compliments and all the other nonsense he uttered about the pleasure of her company the previous evening. As he found himself speaking mainly with her mama, the disloyal thought occurred that perhaps gracious acceptance was the sum of Lady Diana's conversational talents.

Her mother must have had the same thought. Out of the corner of his eye Lord Rand noted the minatory glance Lady Glencove shot her daughter.

"My Lord, I am so glad you found a moment to stop with

us," Lady Diana obediently began. "I had been endeavouring without success to locate upon Papa's maps the town you described so beautifully last night. Is it part of the United States proper?"

Lord Rand ought to have been flattered that the young lady had exerted herself to examine maps. It did not occur to him to be flattered. Between his starched neck-cloth and the oppressive room he was certain he would be asphyxiated, and his mind was fixed on getting out to the street where he might loosen his cravat and breathe.

Not until he'd left the temple of the goddess and arrived at his sister's residence did the viscount realise he'd forgotten to invite Lady Diana to drive with him. Oh, time enough for that. He'd stop in again one day soon.

When he entered the saloon, he found Jack Langdon entertaining the ladies. At Max's entrance, Jack glanced at the clock and exclaimed, "Good grief, you sweet creatures have let me run on well past my time. Miss Pelliston, you must not ask such thorny questions about Herodotus when a fellow's allowed only a few minutes' visit," he gently chided, looking thoroughly embarrassed.

"I suppose you'd have answered well enough if I hadn't kept interrupting," said Miss Pelliston.

"If you hadn't, Jack wouldn't have let you get a word in edgeways," Lord Rand put in. "We once spent four hours debating Herodotus's explanation for the difference between the Persian and Egyptian skulls."

Miss Pelliston's obvious astonishment at this hint of his erudition would have put Max completely out of temper if her blank look had not immediately given way to one of dawning respect. He barely heard, therefore, Jack's overlong leave-taking, and scarcely noticed his exit. Max was too busy scrambling through the recesses of his mind for the section labelled Ancient Authors to even notice himself dropping into the chair nearest the young lady instead of that next his sister.

"What is your opinion, Miss Pelliston?" he asked. "You

113

have an abiding interest in hard heads, I recall. D'you think the Egyptians did have thicker skulls than the Persians, and that it was on account of shaving their scalps?"

"Really, Max, must we discuss such morbid topics?" said his sister with a ladylike shudder. "Skulls and scalps, indeed."

Catherine intervened. "Actually, I was curious about just that matter. Perhaps it is morbid of me—but that is not Lord Rand's fault."

"Oh, everything's my fault," he answered carelessly. "You aren't morbid at all, Miss Pelliston. Your interest is scientific. You seek wisdom."

"Then she seeks at the wrong fount," said her ladyship.

The viscount threw his sister a quelling glance which was utterly wasted.

"Louisa refuses to hear our speculations about the effects of exposure to the elements upon the human skull. We'll have to talk about the elements themselves, I'm afraid."

Miss Pelliston looked disappointed, but bravely took up the subject. "Very well. A lovely day, is it not? Rather warm for this time of year." She frowned. "That was not very scintillating, was it?"

"Of course not. How in blazes can talk of the weather be scintillating? Oh, you do it well enough, Louisa, but then you've scads of practice. M' sister," he explained to Miss Pelliston, "has had years to develop the art of making the dullest topics sound horribly scandalous. I suppose you'll learn all that in time, but I'd rather you studied it with some other fellow. Shall I take you driving, so that we can talk morbidly to our hearts' content without offending her delicate sensibilities?"

A pair of startled hazel eyes met his gaze. "Driving?" she echoed faintly.

"Max, you're impossible. Catherine can't just dash out of the house at your whim."

"Why? Have you got an appointment with another chap?"

"Oh, no, My Lord."

"She's expecting callers, you inconsiderate beast."

"I see." Of course she'd have more callers. Bound to, when she'd danced until the wee hours. He had no reason to wish the whole lot of capering jackanapes at the Devil.

"Then what about tomorrow?" he asked.

Tomorrow the two ladies were promised to the Dowager Countess of Andover.

"Then the next day," he suggested.

That would not do, either. They must meet with Mrs. Drummond-Burrell in order to satisfy that august personage as to Miss Pelliston's eligibility for vouchers to Almack's. After that, they had an appointment with Madame Germaine.

"Then the day after," Lord Rand persisted.

"Yes, I suppose that's all right, if, Catherine, you have no objections? Max is an excellent whip, so you need have no fear for your safety."

A rather stunned Miss Pelliston had no objections she could voice. A time was settled upon, and shortly thereafter the viscount took his leave.

"That was very obliging of him," said Catherine when he was gone. Frowning, she studied the lace at her wrists.

"Max is never obliging if he can help it, dear. I rather think he enjoys your conversation."

Miss Pelliston expressed disagreement and began to fuss with the lace.

"Well, at least you do not make him impatient," said the countess. "Not once during supper last night did I see that caged animal expression he normally wears in fine company."

Lady Andover's glance dropped from her protégée's face to the hand tugging nervously at the delicate fabric. "Obliging or not," she continued, "you must contrive not to look so thunderstruck when a gentleman seeks your company, my dear. It makes them conceited. At any rate, being seen with Max will do you considerable good—though of course I would not say so before him. People may call him Viscount Vagabond, but he's a great catch for all that. Your driving with him will arouse the competitive instincts of the other gentlemen."

Catherine had no opportunity to rebut, because at that moment the Duke of Argoyne was announced.

"Invited her for a drive?" Lord Andover repeated. "All on his own? You never had to drop a hint?"

The countess shook her head as she draped her dressing gown over a chair.

"Amazing," said her husband. "Should I demand his intentions, then? In loco parentis, I mean. As you told her, Max is an excellent catch . . . though I was certain he'd set his mind on that great gawk of a girl of Glencove's. She's the right altitude for him, certainly, even if she hasn't a thought in her head that wasn't put there by her mama first."

"Regardless her size, Lady Diana is a fair catch herself."

"Oh, I daresay. She has certainly developed well enough, and the Glencoves are prolific, are they not? Five sons and two daughters."

"You needn't be vulgar, Edgar. I know precisely why Lady Diana is one of Papa's half-dozen eligibles." Lady Andover climbed into bed and snuggled next to her husband. "I also know that she's a sweet girl. She will make an agreeable wife and a kind mama and would never give Max a moment's difficulty or disquiet.

"Now why didn't I think of that when I was looking for a wife?" his lordship asked.

The countess kindly proceeded to unravel this knotty problem for him.

At the moment Lord Rand was demanding his own intentions. How the deuce did he expect to make progress with the fair Juno when he was gallivanting about town with Miss Pelliston? She had been engaged today, and he should have let the matter drop. He'd only asked her on a whim because he'd rather talk of the Egyptians than the Americans. He'd been at the time sick to death of the

Americans. Lady Diana's mama evidently knew his hob-byhorse and had ordered the girl to humour him. He hated being humoured. It made him feel like a recalcitrant little boy.

An adult ought not be coaxed into courtship as a child is coaxed to eat his peas, he thought, unconsciously para-phrasing one of Miss Pelliston's remarks. Not until he reached the entrance to White's did he realise that he *had* paraphrased her. Really, wasn't it enough that the chit had forced him to chase all over town for her? Must she now formulate his thoughts for him as well?

Two glasses of wine were required to mollify him. Then Jack accosted him and undid all the good the spirits had done.

Jack Langdon might live in a jumbled dream world hap-hazardly composed of history and fiction. He might be con-sidered an eccentric. All the same, there was no denying he was a good-looking enough chap, with a more than respect-able income, not to mention clear prospects of a title. He might have been married long since if only he could have kept his mind fixed on the matter. Jack Langdon, however, rarely fastened on anything in the present for more than ten minutes at a time, doubtless because his brain was too crowded with historical trivia.

Now, unfortunately, he had battened his mind on Catherine Pelliston, and Lord Rand had consequently to en-dure an overlong soliloquy about that young lady's perfec-tions. Max was a man of action. He thought that if Jack was so very much taken with the female, he had much better set about taking her in fact—to the altar, if that's what he meant—instead of plaguing his friends with the young lady's views of Erasmus, Herodotus, and a lot of other fel-lows who'd been worm meat this last millennium.

Lord Rand shared this view with his friend.

Mr. Langdon's dreamy grey eyes grew wistful. "That's easy enough for you to say, Max. You've always been a dashing fellow. You can sweep women off their feet without even thinking about it."

"That's the secret, don't you see? Can't think about those things or you end up thinking and hesitating forever."

"Like Hamlet, you mean."

"Exactly. There he was meditating, waiting, and watching—and where does it get him? His sweetheart kills herself. Don't blame her. The chap wore out her patience."

Mr. Langdon considered this startling theory briefly, then objected to it on grounds that *Hamlet* was not first and foremost a love story. There was, after all, the matter of a father's murder to be avenged.

"On whose say-so?" Max argued. "A ghost. He had no business seeing ghosts. If he'd attended to the girl properly, he wouldn't have had time to see ghosts. If you want Miss Pelliston, my advice is to go and get her, and never mind palavering at me about it. While you're thinking, some other more enterprising chap's going to steal her out from under your nose."

Mr. Langdon stared. "Egad, you're right. There's that stuffy Argoyne and Pomprey's younger brother and Colonel—"

"Argoyne?" Max interrupted. "Lord Dryasdust? What the devil does he want with her?"

"He approves of her views on agriculture."

Jack stopped a waiter and ordered more wine before turning back to his friend. "I hear he had his face stuck in Debrett's all morning, rattling her ancestral closets for skeletons."

"Why, that pompous ass—" The viscount caught himself up short. "There you go, Jack. Three rivals already. No time to be wasted. Now, can we find ourselves a decent game in this mausoleum?"

Three days later, Catherine Pelliston was perched upon an exceedingly high vehicle pulled by two excessively high-strung horses. She was nervous, though that was the fault of neither carriage nor cattle. If the fault lay with the driver, that had less to do with his obvious skill in handling the delicate equipage than the nearness of a muscular thigh encased in snug trousers. The scent of herbs and soap, today unmixed with other aromas, seemed more overpoweringly masculine than ever. At least she hadn't to cope with the viscount's intense blue-eyed gaze as well, because he had to keep his eyes on the crammed pathway.

They had discussed Egyptian customs between the inevitable interruptions of stopping to greet acquaintances. These were short delays, Lord Rand having scant patience with the gentlemen who stopped them from time to time to pay their compliments to Miss Pelliston.

"Curse them," he muttered after the fifth interruption. "Can't they do their flirting at parties instead of holding up vehicles in both directions?"

"Oh, they weren't flirting." Catherine coloured slightly under Lord Rand's incredulous gaze. "Were they?"

"They meant to if given half a chance. Only I don't mean to give it them, inconsiderate clods. Good Lord, is all of London here?"

"It's past five o'clock, My Lord, and Lady Andover says everyone parades in Hyde Park at five o'clock."

"Like a pack of sheep."

"Very like," she agreed. "This is one of the places one comes to see and be seen. At least we are not at the theatre and they are not rudely ignoring the performance. Really, how provoking for the actors it must be to find their best efforts—their genius, even—utterly thrown away upon ninety percent of their audience."

"I'll wager you'd like to stand up and read them a lecture, Miss Pelliston."

"I should like, actually, to heave them all out at once. I'm sure my thoughts last night were as murderous as those of Lady Macbeth."

"Do you often have murderous thoughts, ma'am?"

"Yes." She stared at the toe of her shoe.

"Such as?"

"I'd rather not say."

"They must be quite wicked, then."

"Yes."

"Are they? That is very exciting. Do tell."

"You are teasing me," she reproached.

"Of course I am. I know you never had a truly wicked thought in your whole life. Not even a naughty one, I'll wager. You don't even know when a fellow's flirting with you. If that ain't innocence, I don't know what is."

"That is lack of sophistication."

"Then enlighten me, Madam Choplogic. What is wickedness?"

"You know perfectly well. Besides, I thought you considered it lowering to be instructed in wickedness by a girl of one and twenty."

"In dissipation, perhaps. But I won't tell if you won't. Come," he coaxed, "tell me a murderous, wicked thought."

She scowled at her shoe. "I have wanted to strangle my papa," she muttered.

"Egad! Patricide. Well, that's a relief," said he with a grin. "I thought I was the only one. Still, you probably had more provocation. My father at least never tried to force me to marry someone twice my age, and one who don't bathe regularly to boot. That Browdie is a revolting brute, I must say. I wonder you didn't run off the same day you got the happy news."

"I would have," she grimly confessed, "only I had no idea where to go and needed time to plan it out. I thought I had planned so carefully."

Max gazed at her in growing admiration as she went on with his encouragement to describe her elaborate arrangements—the governess's garments she'd sewn with her own hands, the route she'd planned that would get her to the coaching inn unremarked, the weary trudging through fields and little-used back lanes.

Had he been in her place, with her upbringing, he wondered where he'd have found the courage to embark upon so complicated and hazardous an enterprise. Why, Louisa had gone off with her maid in tow, in her own father's carriage, and only a few miles at that. This young woman had no adoring relative to hide with, only a prim governess who might send the girl right back to her papa.

"I never thought about what slaves to propriety women of the upper classes are," he admitted. "But there's really nothing you can do unchaperoned, is there? I can drive you in the park in an open carriage or take you to Gunther's for ices . . . and that's about the sum of it. Confound it, if I were a female, I'd want to strangle *everybody*."

"Fortunately, you are not. You may do and think what you like, for the most part. The world tolerates a great deal from a man."

"Oh, yes. We can drink ourselves blind, gamble away the family inheritance, beat our wives and cheat on 'em and no one turns a hair. Is that what you mean?"

She nodded.

"We live, Miss Pelliston, in a corrupt, unjust, hypocritical world. In the circumstances, you're justified in thinking murderous thoughts. If you didn't, I'd have to suspect your powers of reason."

He was at present suspecting his own. What did he know of injustice? He'd spent his life raging over what he now saw were a few paltry duties, minor irritations in a life of virtually uninterrupted freedom. She, on the other hand, had attempted one small rebellion—an act he'd engaged in repeatedly since childhood—and had very nearly been destroyed.

She'd never have survived Grendle's. Though she had the courage, she lacked the skill—because no gently bred female was allowed to acquire the necessary experience.

Now he wondered if she had the skill—sophistication, as she put it—to manage the petty treacheries of the Beau Monde. Not that her beaux weren't respectable. Andover would make sure of that. Still, she should not settle merely for respectability. She needed someone who'd not only allow her, but would teach her how to be free, how to find expression for the wild tumult always churning in her eyes.

He didn't realise he'd stopped the carriage and was staring fixedly into those eyes, because he was preoccupied with wondering what he saw there that made him feel he was whirling in a maelstrom.

"My Lord," she said somewhat breathlessly, "we've stopped."

She jerked her own gaze away to stare past him. Then her eyes widened in shock and her face paled and froze. Lord Rand looked in the same direction to discover Lord Browdie, in company with a female Miss Pelliston had better not know, bearing down upon them.

"Don't let on you see them," Max warned. "If the fool knows what's what, he won't dare acknowledge you—not with that demirep beside him." He urged the horses into motion.

Miss Pelliston lifted her chin and gazed straight ahead. Browdie and his barque of frailty clattered past, both of them staring boldly at the pair opposite.

"Now if that didn't look like a chariot from hell, with a couple of brazen demons in it," said Lord Rand when the vehicle had passed. "Him with his painted head and his trollop with her painted face. What a nerve the brute has to gawk at you—Miss Pelliston, are you ill?" he asked in sudden alarm. She'd gone very white indeed and was trembling.

"N-no," she gasped. "Please. Get me out of here."

═ 12 ═

THEY HAD REACHED the Hyde Park Corner gates. Lord Rand steered the horses through them and on to Green Park. The place was nearly deserted. He stopped the carriage by a stand of trees and turned to his companion.

"What is it?" he asked. "Are you ill? Or was it that disgusting fellow leering at you?"

"I know that woman. I thought I'd dreamed her, but there she was, real—and—dear heaven!—she was wearing my peach muslin dress! Oh, Lord," she cried. "I am undone. She knew me—I could see it. Didn't you see the way she smiled?"

Lord Rand saw at the moment only that Miss Pelliston was beside herself with grief. Since she was also beside him, he did what any gallant gentleman would do. He put his arms around her in a comforting, brotherly sort of way. He experienced a shock.

At that moment, Miss Pelliston looked up at him, her eyes very bright with unshed tears. His grip tightened slightly. His head bent and his lips touched hers. He experienced another shock as a wave of most unbrotherly feeling coursed through him.

Miss Pelliston made a tiny, strangled sound and pushed him away.

Lord Rand stared at her. She stared back. Her eyes were very wild indeed, he thought, as he resumed his grip on the reins and restored the horses to order. Perhaps she would knock him senseless. He wished she would. He had much rather be senseless at the moment. He did not like what he was feeling. Why the devil didn't she box his ears at least? He would settle for pain if insensibility was out of the question.

"I'm sorry," he made himself say, though he suspected he wasn't remotely sorry. "Something came over me."

"Oh, dear," said Miss Pelliston, turning away. She was also turning pink, and that at least was an improvement. "How very awkward."

"I'm sorry," he repeated stupidly. "I couldn't help it."

"How could you not help it?" she demanded. "What came over you?" She turned to look at him and he thought he saw in her eyes . . . was it fear?

"Miss Pelliston, you were in distress. I meant to comfort you, but I'm afraid my—my baser instincts got the better of me. As you know, I'm rather impetuous—drat it." He felt like a fool. What on earth had possessed him to kiss Catherine Pelliston of all people?

Her eyes were still distraught, though her voice sounded calmer. "My Lord, there are times when honesty is preferable to tact. I have come to think of you as a friend. I hope, therefore, you will be quite frank with me. Did I . . . did I do or say anything to—to encourage you?"

"No, of course not. It was all my own doing, I assure you," he answered with some pique.

Her face cleared. "Well, that's all right then."

Taken aback, he spoke without thinking. "Is it? Does that mean you wouldn't object if I did it again?" But he didn't mean to do it again, he told himself.

"Oh, I must object, of course."

" 'Must'? Only because you're supposed to?" he asked, though he wasn't at all sure he wanted to hear the answer.

She bit her lip. "My Lord, I asked you to be frank. I will return the favour. You are a very attractive man and I am completely inexperienced. No gentleman has ever kissed me before—at least no one who wasn't kin—and that was on the cheek. I think—I believe I'm . . . flattered. All the same, I am not *fast*," she added.

"Of course you're not."

"Therefore I had rather you didn't . . . flatter me again, My Lord. Right now I have enough on my mind without having to question my morals as well. In fact," she went on sadly, "it looks as though the whole world will be questioning my morals soon enough."

"There's nothing to fear," Max answered, firmly thrusting the image of a blonde Juno from his mind. "I'll marry you."

"What?" she gasped.

"Isn't it obvious? We should have done it at the outset. You can't expect to hang about in brothels and spend a night in my lodgings without some trouble coming of it. It's our duty to marry, Miss Pelliston."

Miss Pelliston's colour heightened. "With all due respect, My Lord, that is out of the question. It is perfectly ridiculous, in fact."

"With all due respect, it's you who's ridiculous. The tart is wearing your dress. She's with Browdie. If she's recognised you, she'll tell him, and since he's no gentleman, he'll carry the tale. The only way to spike his guns is to marry me. Then, if he so much as hints scandal, I'll call him out and put a bullet through his painted head. It's quite simple."

Catherine grew irritated. She had not escaped a drunken tyrant of a father in order to acquire an overbearing rakehell of a husband. She did not express her objections in precisely these terms, but object she did, and in detail. She treated the viscount to a lengthy discourse upon her views of marriage, in which suitability of temperament figured most prominently.

Lord Rand reacting to this sermon with blank indifference, she went on in some desperation to tear to pieces his rationale for proposing.

In the first place, she told him, perhaps that wasn't her dress after all, or if it was, very likely Granny Grendle had sold it to a secondhand dealer and that was how Lord Browdie's companion had come by it.

Second, Miss Pelliston could not be absolutely certain she

125

recognised the woman. With all that paint, fallen women tended to look alike. She'd barely glimpsed any other women besides Granny during her brief time in the brothel, having been drugged for most of that time.

Third, even if the woman knew her and did tell Lord Browdie, he likely wouldn't believe it. Or if he did, he was not so foolhardy as to carry so improbable a tale, especially when that might lead to a breach—or worse—with her Papa or Lord Andover. Either might challenge Lord Browdie to duel, and he was a great coward.

Max glared at her. "So you claim you're not in the least alarmed?"

"Not in the least," she answered spiritedly.

"Then why did you take a fit?"

"I did not take a fit. If I gave way for a moment that was because I was shocked. Possibly I overreacted."

"All the same, I've compromised you," he reminded. "Besides everything else, I just kissed you in a public park."

"Good heavens, you can't be serious. Surely you do not go about proposing marriage to every woman you kiss. In your case that would most assuredly lead to bigamy."

Catherine stared off into the distance, her spine ramrod straight and her chin high.

"I think you must be drunk," she continued. "Yes, I'm sure you are. It was your vices that entangled you in my difficulties in the first place, and though I am grateful you were there to rescue me I cannot but regret the reasons you *were* there. Just now, vice has nearly led you into a grievous error which you would have cause to regret all the rest of your days. Later, when you are sober, I hope you will consider the matter and learn from the experience. For the present, I wish you would take me home."

"There now," said Lynnette. "Didn't I tell you it was him?"

Her companion appeared not to hear her. He was sulking. Lord Browdie might not care where he found his entertainment, but he had rather keep that entertainment out of public view—unless, of course, the female at his side was

126

in great demand among Society's gentlemen and one might lord it over the competition.

Whatever degree of popularity Lynnette had achieved at Granny Grendle's, she was scarcely in the running with the Wilson sisters. She ought, therefore, to know her place and be content to abide quietly, awaiting her protector's pleasure in the modest house he'd rented for her. But no, she must be wheedling and whining at a fellow the livelong day for "a breath of fresh air." Wasn't any fresh air in London. And now Miss Prim and Proper and her uppity viscount had seen him in company with a common harlot.

"Didn't I tell you it was him?" she prodded.

"Him, who?" was the peevish response.

"The one that took the new girl off." Lynnette went on to describe the highly entertaining scene she'd unabashedly watched from the top of the stairs.

"That's how I got this dress," she said. "I saw the old witch take it from the box and made her give it me." Lynnette neglected to add that the dress was the compensation she'd demanded for having turned such a promising customer over to a mere beginner. Lynnette had deeply and loudly resented having to entertain an ugly, drunken sailor instead of a drunken Adonis.

"Fifty quid?" Lord Browdie repeated as she concluded her story. "You meant to say the fool paid fifty quid for a scrawny country servant?"

"I never got more than a glimpse of her, but she looked all skin and bones to me. Anyhow, it was thirty for her and twenty for her things—only they never did get all her things, as I said. Then the poor man is back two days later looking for her. The ignorant thing must have run off, thinking she could do better. Some girls have no common sense at all, I declare. A viscount you said he was?" Lynnette shook her head in regret, and perhaps not all of that emotion was reserved for the poor rustic who'd tossed away a golden opportunity.

The news that Granny Grendle had so easily cozened the aggravating viscount restored Lord Browdie to good humour. When he had a moment to himself he'd turn the matter over and see what could be made of it. Rand gulled by an old bawd and then the gal bolts after all. Oh, that was rich, it was.

Had Miss Pelliston been privy to the exchange between Lord Browdie and his light o'love, she would have had the unalloyed satisfaction of knowing she had acted aright in rejecting Lord Rand's offer. She had not heard that conversation, however, and was consequently most uneasy on two counts. One, whatever assurances she'd offered the viscount, she was certain that painted face was familiar; therefore Catherine was sure Lord Browdie knew her secret. Second, she did not believe he'd keep the tale to himself. He might not want to alienate her papa or Lord Andover and he might not want to be killed in a duel, but Lord Browdie was first and foremost a drunkard, and a loud, indiscreet, talkative one.

She could expect the rumour mills to begin grinding any day now, and after a short while they would grind her reputation to dust. Her poor unsuspecting cousin and his wife—they had no idea the scandal in store.

The worst was that she couldn't warn them. Of course Lord Andover would believe in her innocence. All the same, he'd make Lord Rand marry her. Even the viscount, for all his wild ways and impatience with convention, believed that was the only solution.

Catherine trudged slowly up the stairs to her bedchamber, followed by a prattling Molly, who could not say enough about Lord Rand's elegant carriage, prime cattle, and altogether stunning personal appearance. She declared that Miss Pelliston was the most fortunate woman in creation, having been honoured by a drive with the most splendid man in all of Christendom—and heathendom besides.

"Really, Miss, I always said as he was the handsomest man," she raved, "only that was in a rough sort of way, you know. I do think he never cared much how he looked. But, oh, when I seen the carriage come up and him sitting there like the prince in the fairy tale like the sun itself was only shining to shine on him—"

Catherine cut short this venture into the realms of poesy with the information that she was very tired and wanted a nap if she was to survive tonight's festivities in honour of Miss Gravistock's birthday.

Molly subsided. That is to say she left off talking and commenced to sighing. However, this evidence of the state of her feelings had only to be endured a quarter hour, at the end of which time she left her mistress to her "nap"—if one could call the torments of the damned a nap.

Catherine lay her head upon her pillow and immediately that head grew feverish.

He had kissed her. As kisses go, it was not much of a kiss, but Catherine knew little of how kisses went, as she'd told him. She now wished to learn no more. What had she told him? *Flattered*? She touched her lips, then jerked her fingers away. Her whole face burned, and in her mind, where there ought to be sober reason, there was only the chaos of jolting thoughts and alien, edgy sensations.

It was only a kiss, she told herself, and only the most fleeting contact at that—but somehow the sky had changed, and that was not how it should be, not with him. Good Lord, not with *him*.

In novels, heroines got kissed, but by the heroes they would marry, which made it acceptable, if not technically proper. This was not the same, and not acceptable for her. And she had liked it, which made no sense.

Had she not met him in a brothel? Hadn't he been utterly castaway at the time? Hadn't she heard Lord Andover's ironic sympathy for the gentlemen at White's with whom Lord Rand regularly gambled? Hadn't she heard as well from several others how Lord Rand had tried to start a brawl on the very steps of that club?

Besides, he was overbearing and hasty, just like Papa. Why, the viscount even affected the speech of common ruffians, full of oaths and bad grammar. That was hardly the stuff of which heroes were made.

Yet despite the ill she knew of him, she'd pushed him away only because she'd been so startled—and immediately she'd wished she hadn't made it stop.

Who was the Catherine who'd thrilled at the muscular strength of his arms, who even now lay shuddering as she remembered the soft, moist touch of his mouth, so light—only an instant—yet somehow hinting a warm promise that made her want . . . oh, *more.* There was the clean masculine scent of him, his face so close as his dark lashes veiled the deep blue of his eyes, the warmth of his hands on her back . . . only that. It was not so much. What had it done to her—and why *him?*

If she were a true lady, she would have recoiled at his polluted touch. She hadn't, and the reason was obvious: she'd inherited her papa's depravity.

Why not? She had inherited his temper. The only difference between them was that she took the trouble—and it was a deal of trouble—to keep hers in check. Now there was yet another demon to restrain . . . and a rakehell had released it.

Lord Rand had rather a knack, didn't he, of drawing out the worst in her. Good heavens—she'd even sat there blithely chattering away about wanting to murder her father and practically boasting about her scheme to run away.

Catherine turned angrily onto her stomach and buried her hot face in the pillow.

The man was dangerous. He seemed reassuring even as he was turning the world upside down. He was already making a shambles of her neat system of values. What would he do, given the opportunity, to her morals? What would he do if he knew how easily he conjured up those demons? He could turn her into a monster of passion—like Papa—wild, angry, driven. Lord—marry him! She'd as soon plunge into a tidal wave. Never. Her reputation was precious, but so was her sanity. If the reputation needed saving, she must save it herself.

* * *

In his own way, Lord Rand was as troubled as Miss Pelliston. The fact that he'd kissed her filled him with every species of astonishment. The fact that he'd liked kissing her filled him with horror. The fact that he'd proposed to her was so utterly bizarre that he could think of no expression suitable to characterise it.

He was not, however, given to prolonged introspection. He'd taken leave of his senses, which was not at all unusual, and had behaved rashly, which was even less unusual. That was all the explanation he needed.

Regardless what had driven him to commit this afternoon's atrocities, they'd pointed out, just as Miss Pelliston had noted, that he had become entangled in her affairs. If he wanted to make progress with the blonde Juno, he'd better get himself unentangled very soon. The way to do that was to eliminate Miss Pelliston's problem.

Lord Browdie, possessed of information certain to make the blond viscount the laughingstock of the clubs, lost no time in relaying this news to his friend, Sir Reggie. The baronet's reaction was not what he'd hoped for.

"Oh, yes," said Reggie. "Heard about that from one of those fellows—Jos, I think it was. Imagine. Him and Cholly both no match for Rand—and them twice his weight and him foxed in the bargain. Broke Cholly's nose, you know."

Reggie, it turned out, was full of admiration for the viscount's prowess and thought fifty quid a cheap price for such a marvelous mill. If Granny had kept back a few of the girl's rags and trinkets, what was that to St. Denys's heir? If he wanted, he could have decked the wench like a queen and never noticed the cost.

"But the gal run away after all," Lord Browdie reminded in desperation. "Joke's on him, don't you see?"

"Joke's on her, rather. Where's she now? Probably haunting Drury Lane. Didn't know an opportunity when it bit her on the nose. Women," the baronet muttered scornfully.

This conversation threatened to restore Lord Browdie to the foul temper in which he'd begun a day that had started with a hangover and climaxed with the humiliation of parading his tawdry mistress in front of the two people he hated most in this world.

If he broadcast the tale, he would only gild Lord Rand's reputation as a virile, dashing fellow. Lord Browdie's bitterness increased. He believed himself betrayed and ill-used on all sides.

Here he was, forced to skulk on the sidelines while the arrogant, yellow-haired viscount squired Catherine Pelliston about town. Only a few weeks before, Browdie had been the chit's affianced husband, her property and money virtually in his grasp. Now the nasty, sharp-faced female had the effrontery to declare herself not at home when he called—and he her papa's oldest friend!

Miss Prim and Proper had no time for him, not when she could be flaunting herself all over London with her pretty viscount. What would Miss High and Mighty think if she heard how her golden darling spent his leisure hours—and with whom? Did Madam Propriety think she could reform Viscount Vagabond?

Lord Browdie smiled, displaying a crooked set of brown teeth to his companion. Once again the black storm clouds drifted away and he saw the happy sunshine. He could not tell the world his tale, but he must tell her. That was his duty as her papa's oldest, dearest friend.

=== 13 ===

CONSIDERING THE OUTRAGES to which he was inevitably goaded by Miss Pelliston's mere presence, it did not bode well for the viscount to be found dancing with her that evening at Miss Gravistock's birthday ball. Still, Lord Rand had action in mind, and that action required her assistance.

"Lead him on?" Catherine echoed in bewilderment when he began to describe her role. "Are you drunk yet?"

Her partner bit back a hasty retort. "You can't get information from Browdie unless you speak with him, which means you have to be more welcoming than you've been. Looking at a man as though he was something the horse left behind isn't the way to elicit confidences. You have to be more encouraging. You may even have to dance with him."

Whatever indignant response Catherine might have made to this is lost to posterity, the dance at that moment inconsiderately requiring that they separate.

As he watched her move away, Max decided that the rose silk gown became her nearly as well as the militant light flashing in her eyes and the faint flush of anger that tinted her cheeks. Something stirred within him and he grew edgy.

Miss Pelliston must have become edgy as well, because when she rejoined her partner she told him icily that she had no interest in Lord Browdie's confidences.

"Very well," said Lord Rand. "Trust him if you like. Maybe he doesn't know about Granny's. Maybe he won't say anything if he does know. Maybe it wouldn't help to find out where you stand so that you can make an intelligent decision about what to do."

Miss Pelliston did not deign to reply, though her deepening colour told him he'd struck home.

"Well?" he said after a moment.

"I concede your point," she said stiffly.

As he gazed down upon her rigidly composed features, the viscount wondered how quickly her expression would soften if he covered her face with kisses. Simultaneously he felt a surging desire to run—very, very far away.

Lord Browdie, it turned out, was eager to unburden himself. In fact, in his haste to claim a dance with Miss Pelliston, he elbowed aside one duke, two baronets, one colonel, and one affronted Jack Langdon, who would have called him out on the spot if Max had not been there to hear his complaints.

"Call him out?" Max exclaimed, as he drew his friend aside. "You don't know one end of a pistol from the other. I'll have to take you to Manton's shooting gallery for regular practice if you plan to take up this sort of hobby. Or did you mean to stand at twenty paces and throw books at him?"

Mr. Langdon thrust one aesthetically long hand into his already rumpled brown hair and reduced mere disorder to complete chaos. That his disheveled locks and distrait aspect made him seem more romantically poetical than ever to several ladies in the vicinity was a circumstance of which he was as sublimely unaware as he was of those ladies' existence. He could not know that his rumpled hair and absent expression made women want to take him in hand and smooth him out.

Jack knew only that he'd elbowed his way through Miss Pelliston's crowd of admirers—who seemed to be growing more numerous by the minute—and had been about to request the favour of a dance when some ugly old brute had rudely thrust him out of the way.

Jack Langdon was not by nature a violent man. Like Max,

he'd spent his childhood being bullied. Unlike Max, he had not rebelled by running away physically. Jack had quietly escaped into the pages of his books. He liked Miss Pelliston excessively because talking to her was like hiding in a book—an attractive book, to be sure, but a safe, quiet, pleasant one, where no emotional or physical demands were made of him.

At the moment, however, he was feeling homicidally unquiet. As he watched Lord Browdie lead the young lady out, Mr. Langdon knew an unfamiliar yearning to commit mayhem. Fortunately for the peace of the company, Lord Rand was able to appease his friend by offering him the supper dance with Miss Pelliston.

The viscount did not make this sacrifice out of pure compassion. He had suddenly produced an idea that involved action, instead of hovering about boring himself to tears at a hot stuffy party filled with the same dull people he met at every other hot stuffy party. This was a more reasonable explanation than that he was desperate to put as much distance as possible between himself and a rose silk gown.

"You see, Jack, I've just recalled an appointment," he explained. "The trouble is, I've already asked her, and Louisa will have my head if I abandon her. Won't you be a good fellow and take my place? I daresay Miss Pelliston will be delighted."

Lord Rand was not being deceitful. He was certain the young lady had rather Jack's company than his own—just as the viscount had rather Lady Diana's company. As a matter of fact, he couldn't understand why he hadn't asked Lady Diana for the confounded supper dance. Mayhap he'd known instinctively that he wouldn't stay long and therefore had better ask one who wouldn't miss him.

Perhaps Lord Rand's thinking was not as clear as it should be. That was his problem, however. Mr. Langdon, upon being granted supper with a book in the form of a most agreeable young lady, was instantly restored to his customary state of abstracted serenity.

* * *

While Mr. Langdon recovered from his flirtation with violence, Miss Pelliston was enduring a jovial, avuncular lecture from her former fiance. The lecture would have been altogether unendurable—Lord Browdie avuncular was not a pretty sight—if it had not brought her so much relief. The baron obviously believed the young woman purchased from the bawd was someone else.

Catherine could not appear relieved, of course. She had to feign shock at learning of Lord Rand's sordid entertainments. Since his vices were a sorrow to her—as they must be to any right-thinking lady—this would not have been so very trying, except that the activities Lord Browdie referred to with such sanctimonious relish were precisely those with which he entertained himself.

Hypocrisy can never be agreeable to an elevated mind. Hypocrisy mouthed by a swaggering drunkard who cares nothing for Mr. Brummell's dicta concerning clean linen, soap, and hot water is not only disagreeable but unaesthetic. Catherine was disgusted. She would have hastened to Lord Rand's defense—all in a perfectly commendable battle against hypocrisy, of course—if she had not recalled Miss Fletcher's remarks about tempering justice with a dash of common sense.

Catherine had to content herself with a show of shocked dismay. She even managed to thank Lord Browdie for his kindly meant warnings. When the ordeal was over, she searched among the crowd of faces for Lord Rand, but he was nowhere to be seen. The supper dance began, bringing Mr. Langdon to her side, full of apologies for his friend's sudden departure and hopes that Miss Pelliston would not be disappointed in his substitute.

Catherine told herself she was not in the least disappointed as she offered him a welcoming smile. Mr. Langdon's company was always soothing, and now especially so, after the emotional turmoil of dealing with first a domineering, wild viscount and then an avuncular, unwashed libertine of a baron.

The only problem was that she wanted to unburden herself, to express her contempt for Lord Browdie's pious humbug and her relief that it was only pious humbug instead of scorn and insult. Unfortunately, she could confide only in her partner in crime.

"There, Diana, did I not tell you?" said Lady Glencove bitterly. "He takes no more note of you than if you had been a stick of furniture. Which you might as well be, standing in one place the livelong night and never opening your mouth."

"Yes, Mama."

"'Yes, Mama,' she says—then does precisely as she wishes. Oh, was there ever such an undutiful daughter?" Lady Glencove dabbed her omnipresent handkerchief at her eyes.

"Mama, he is gone. I can scarcely run out of the house after him."

"He would not be gone, you unnatural child, if you would make but the smallest effort. He admires your looks, for which you ought to be thankful. How many others do you think would want such an Amazon?" the countess complained, as though her daughter had deliberately grown to this abnormal height to spite her.

"My size is hardly my fault, Mama," Lady Diana answered with a touch of impatience.

"It is your manner that concerns me. If he admires your looks, you should use the advantage. Instead you stand like a dumb statue and leave me to manage the conversation. You are not a stupid girl, Diana. Why must you let him think so?"

"I had not thought the gentlemen overly concerned with female intelligence—"

"*He* is," the mama interrupted. "Instead of talking to you, he stays forever with that blue-stocking—and her papa a mere baron, while you are the daughter of Glencove. If he likes bookish women, you must contrive to appear so."

"Oh, Mama!"

"Why not? She cannot be better educated than yourself."

Lady Glencove studied the woman in question, who was conversing with Jack Langdon. "She cannot be so bookish as all that," her ladyship went on, "or Argoyne would never go near her. Really, I do wonder what the men see in her. She is hardly an Incomparable."

"She listens, Mama. I'd scarcely said three sentences to her before she asked whether I was as devoted to hunting as my namesake."

Lady Glencove looked blank.

"She meant Diana, the goddess of the hunt. I said I enjoyed it immensely, and immediately she had a dozen questions for me. She is most knowledgeable, though she says the sport is not to her tastes. Her papa is famous for his hounds, you know."

Lady Glencove discovered in these remarks something more promising than Lord Pelliston's success in breeding hunting dogs. "Well, then, you and the girl have something in common. That is good." Her voice became commanding again. "Unless you wish to break your mama's heart, you will pursue the friendship."

"I wish you would make up your mind, Mama. I thought it was Lord Rand you wanted me to pursue."

The mother uttered an exasperated sigh. "How better than to be always in company with those he spends his time with? Really, Diana, I begin to believe you are stupid."

"I am always stupid in Town, Mama. I cannot breathe here and I cannot think and—"

She was cut off.

"You are not going back to Kirkby-Glenham, young lady, so just put that out of your mind. When I think of that person, my blood turns cold. But I will not think of him—and you know better than to do so, I trust. What you will do is form a closer acquaintance with Miss Pelliston."

"Yes, Mama."

Mr. Langdon was not accustomed to supping with debutantes. He liked women—worshipped them, in fact, but in the abstract and from afar. Up close they were problematic. His mother and sisters, for instance, were always pressuring him to marry, and marriageable women made him uneasy. He would always sense in them, after a few minutes, impatience, boredom, some vague irritation. He did not know how he provoked these reactions, but he had little doubt he did.

Catherine Pelliston was different. If he rambled off to ancient Greece or Renaissance Italy, she ambled along with him. No topic was too abstruse for her, and she never seemed to require that their conversation be interlaced with flirtation.

She was a kindred spirit, he thought. In his eagerness to pay tribute to the quiet pleasure she gave him, he piled her plate with enough tantalising sustenance to satiate a soldier after three days' forced march.

"Oh, Mr. Langdon," said Catherine with a small gasp, "are you trying to fatten me up too? If I eat but a fraction of this, you shall have to push me about the dance floor in a wheelbarrow."

Mr. Langdon's fingers promptly wrought their usual havoc with his hair. How could he be so boorish, so thoughtless? One did not offer young ladies buckets of food as though they were sows. His handsome face reddened as he watched his companion. She was studying her plate as though it were a mathematical problem

She looked up with a consoling smile. "At least you don't pretend young women live on air and nectar, like hummingbirds. All the same, I'm afraid you must come to my rescue." So saying, she took his plate from him and began apportioning the contents of hers.

A few weeks earlier, Catherine had won the affection of an eight-year-old boy with one small gesture connected to food. Mr. Langdon might have two decades' advantage of Jemmy, but his heart was equally susceptible. In a few words she had put him at ease again, and those words, like the gesture, were so fraught with overtones of domestic intimacy and tranquillity that he felt they'd been friends forever. She might have been his sister—except that any of those ladies, in like circumstances, would have either burst into tears at the imagined insult or cruelly ridiculed him.

He had no way of knowing that Catherine was accustomed to smoothing over difficulties—or at least constantly trying to do so. He knew nothing of the scenes she endured at her papa's dinner table, and the quick thinking required to spare an oversensitive aunt's feelings or distract a drunken parent from some disagreeable topic or behaviour. He did not know that she'd sensed his nervous embarrassment and had acted reflexively to remove it.

Jack knew only that he'd committed a *faux pas*. Since he'd exaggerated its importance, he likewise exaggerated the significance of her tactful response. Gazing at her with relief, he wondered if he was in love with her.

"How kind you are," he murmured as he took his place beside her. "I should know better, of course—my sisters will never take more than a mouthful in public—but everything looked so tempting."

"Yes, and all the burden of choosing is yours because you are the gentleman. Women are so difficult to please, are we not?" she asked with a faint twinkle. "If you'd left out something I fancied, I would sulk. You leave nothing out and I complain. But that is for appearances, you know," she explained, dropping her voice confidentially. "The truth is, dancing makes me so hungry I probably could eat it all— and disgrace myself in Society's eyes."

The confiding tones made Mr. Langdon feel warm and cosy. He wished they could be engaged this minute, so that he might have the privilege of squeezing one of the gentle white hands that had touched his plate.

He made do with a smile as he replied, "That is because today's modes are for sylphs. These Grecian costumes are meant for slender faeries—as you are, Miss Pelliston. If, on the other hand, this were the time of Rubens, you'd have to gorge yourself."

He took up his silverware and took a turn into the early seventeenth century, where Miss Pelliston easily followed. He was soon lost there, oblivious to the rest of the com-

140

pany, and not even altogether conscious of his companion. He never noticed the occasional frown that furrowed her delicate brow.

Miss Pelliston's partner in crime, meanwhile, was in the process of attempting burglary.

Some hours earlier, Max had made discreet inquiries regarding the baron. That is how he found out where Lord Browdie's love nest was. The viscount was now standing in a dark alleyway, staring up at the windows of that house.

Clarence Arthur Maximilian Demowery, Viscount Rand, had in the course of his chequered career scaled any number of edifices. To climb the walls of this house was child's play. He did not hesitate. He grasped a drainpipe, found a toehold between the bricks, and commenced to climb. In a few minutes he'd leapt over the wall of a narrow balcony and stood pressed against the side of the house near the French doors, listening.

He heard, as he'd expected, nothing. The house was dark. Obviously Lord Browdie's mistress had taken advantage of his absence. Either she was out or she'd gone to bed early. Max would have preferred knowing precisely where she was, and if she slept, how soundly she did so, but a man cannot have everything he wants in this world.

He moved silently towards the doors and tried them. They were unfastened—why not? The citizens of London's West End had a low opinion of burglars' intelligence. Perhaps the ground floor was secured, which meant the front door and servants' entrance were locked at night. Thieves obviously entered a house as everyone else did.

He quietly pushed the doors open and crept into the room. The interior being no darker than the alleyway, his eyes had already adjusted. In what dim light there was he could make out the outlines of furniture. His eyes sought a wardrobe and found it. His feet took him to it.

Only when he'd opened the wardrobe door did he note the flaw in his plans, such as they were. The small space contained several items of clothing, all of them female attire. So far, so good. However, while one might distinguish by touch silk or satin from muslin, one's touch was not so refined as to distinguish a peach-coloured frock from one of any other hue. He cursed softly to himself.

At that moment a candle flickered into light and a soft voice murmured, "If it *is* a dream, I do hope I don't wake up."

Lord Rand turned towards the bed and found himself staring down the barrel of a pistol.

=== 14 ===

AT THE OTHER end of the weapon was a comely brunette. The candlelight was gentler upon her countenance than the grey daylight of Hyde Park, and she was not so heavily painted now. Max judged that she was pretty, though in a rather blatant way.

He smiled, the pistol notwithstanding.

"I suppose," he said calmly, "you wonder why I'm here." He had not attended Eton and Oxford for nothing. Max knew how to preserve a mask of indifference even when in the throes of the greatest inner misery. At the moment he was not miserable, only a tad concerned that the weapon might have been constructed with a hair trigger, and thus might accidentally go off . . . in his face.

"Only if I am awake," Lynnette answered, quite as calmly as if she too had known the privileges of public school education. "If I am, I expect I'd better shoot you and have it over with, because whatever the reason, it must be a wicked one. Either you're here to murder me, or . . ." Her voice trailed off invitingly.

"Then shoot me," said his lordship. "It makes no matter. When a man has lost his heart and has no hope, it makes no matter whether he lives or dies. My heart," he went on, gazing soulfully into her eyes, "is yours. Has been since I saw you yesterday. And I have no hope because"—he hesitated meaningfully, but upon perceiving the pistol shaking, quickly continued—"because you belong to another."

143

Lynnette was no more proof against those devastating blue eyes than any other young woman. Besides, a handsome, virile lord had entered her bedroom, like manna from the heavens. She was not so ungrateful as to question the motives of Providence.

She relented, whereupon a tender scene ensued which is better left to the memoirs she will feel compelled to write when middle age begins to fasten its clammy hands upon her person and bank account.

The scene might have proceeded with dispatch to its inevitable conclusion—thereby providing Lord Rand another black spot on his conscience—had not the young woman's protector returned earlier than expected.

Since that gentleman returned drunk—as was his wont on all occasions—and therefore noisily, young love was not taken unawares. A mere twenty minutes after Max had arrived, he was once again clambering over the balcony, and Lynnette, her own conscience considerably clearer than she would have liked, appeared to be sleeping the sleep of innocent angels when Lord Browdie stumbled into her bedroom.

Lord Rand was not accustomed to failing in his enterprises. This time he had failed miserably, and now he thought on it, the enterprise itself had been hasty and ill-considered. Hasty he could understand. What baffled him was how he'd expected to steal a peach-coloured muslin frock from an ink-black wardrobe in an equally dark bedchamber. Still, he told himself, had he not been interrupted, he could have taken everything that felt like muslin—though he'd have had the devil's own time climbing down from an upper storey carrying a stack of gowns.

The whole business now struck him as patently ridiculous. Had this been an isolated incident, he might have put it down as one of his occasional aberrations. The trouble was, aberration seemed to be growing a habit with him lately—and it had all started, he now realised, the moment he'd met Catherine Pelliston.

An assortment of unrelated rash behaviours was normal. A string of freakish activities all connected to one female was not. The girl was dangerous.

Lord Rand began to wish, precisely as her papa often wished, that Catherine Pelliston would go away. Thence the viscount proceeded—again, like the parent—to wishing she'd never been born. To wish the latter was futile. He concentrated instead upon how to make her go away. How difficult could that be? Even her father had done it, though it had taken the old fool twenty-one years.

Lord Rand doubted that Lady Diana would wait patiently twenty-one years for him to disentangle himself. Strong measures were called for. He must frighten Miss Pestilence away, terrify her back to Wilberstone. That would be hard on Jack, but really, if Jack was so taken with her there was no reason he couldn't go to Wilberstone after her.

In pursuance of dark plans, Lord Rand betook himself to his sister's establishment the very next morning. Twinges of conscience he had none. In fact, as he met Molly upon the steps of Andover House the next morning, Max bestowed upon her such a dazzling smile that the abigail had to clutch at the railing to keep from stumbling headfirst onto the pavement.

He marched into the breakfast room in his usual unceremonious way and announced to his sister and brother-in-law that he'd come to take Miss Pelliston driving.

"Max, I don't care what Catherine says. You are a sad wreck. You took her driving yesterday, don't you remember?"

"Yes, and I've come to take her again. Where is she?" the viscount demanded.

"Max, it's scarcely nine o'clock in the morning."

"Confound it, I can tell time as well as the next chap."

"Catherine is still abed, you great blockhead," said his loving sister. "Now, you may either sit quietly and breakfast with us or you may go away."

Miss Pelliston chose that moment to enter the breakfast

145

room.

"There you are," said Max. "Wide awake too, I see, to give the lie to my rag-mannered sister. But she's always out of sorts these days. Will you take a turn in the park with me this morning?"

"Good heavens, but you do take hold of something and worry it to death," Lady Andover complained before Catherine could recover sufficiently to make a reply. "Will you sit down and be quiet? Catherine has not breakfasted yet."

Though Max was impatient to get his nefarious enterprise over with, he did realise that he was behaving like an idiot. He subdued himself, sat down, and dined relatively quietly, waiting until Miss Pelliston's plate was empty before he renewed his invitation.

Catherine realised quickly enough that her caller would not be so insistent about her driving with him and would not have come at such an early hour if he hadn't important news for her. She was mightily curious why he'd left the party and what he'd done. Besides, she was eager to relay her own interesting news. Now that they could be sure she was in no danger, perhaps he'd leave her alone. Certainly he would not subject her to any more disquieting physical displays and mad proposals.

Catherine, in short, grew as impatient to be gone as the viscount was. She scurried to get her bonnet, and the two were out of the house before the earl and countess had time to realise they were going.

Considering the unhappy memories of aberrant behaviour the place held for him, it was curious that Lord Rand took Miss Pelliston to Green Park. Perhaps he thought in this wise to exorcise the demon that had possessed him there. Whatever his motives, he directed the horses along a path of shifting shade and dappled sunlight. No colourful flowerbeds distracted the eye from the park's green serenity, for this was the place in which Charles II's Queen had commanded no flowers ever be planted. Here at least the straying husband could not pluck bouquets for his army of mistresses.

Max brought the carriage to a halt beside a large plane tree and turned a troubled gaze upon his companion. At least he meant the gaze to be troubled, because he meant to make her anxious. Unfortunately, he found a pair of hazel eyes gazing back. Those eyes were so unfairly large and their depths disclosed such a tumultuously thrilling universe that his own features relaxed, and the only trouble he knew was a mad desire to kiss her.

He forced the kissing part from his mind and focused on the desperation: he had to get rid of her.

He began by apologising for his abrupt departure the night before. When Miss Pelliston answered graciously that Mr. Langdon had been an altogether satisfactory replacement, Lord Rand experienced a novel, and thoroughly disagreeable, sensation—one that could not be, though it was suspiciously like, jealousy.

He forgot the slightly exaggerated warnings he'd meant to frighten her with and proceeded to relate his adventures instead, describing in unnecessary detail his meeting with Lord Browdie's mistress.

"Good heavens!" Catherine cried. "Steal back my dress? Whatever were you thinking of?"

"Destroying the evidence. You must see that the dress is the only concrete proof you were ever at Granny Grendle's. Without it, everything else is just hearsay—only the word of a tart against yours."

"Well, I do wish you'd waited a bit before rushing into such a dangerous act. Wasn't it you told me to find out how much Lord Browdie knew? And then you didn't wait to hear what I learned. Which you ought to have done, you know—and perhaps would have, if you had been sober," she added, half to herself.

Lord Rand had, all his life, considered it beneath his dignity to justify his behaviour to anyone. He knew the world called him Viscount Vagabond and he was rather proud of the title than otherwise. All the same, he was heartily sick of hearing this sanctimonious female constantly ascribe his every word, practically, to the effects of spirits.

"I wasn't drunk, dash it. Why are you always accusing me of being so?"

Being a just woman, Catherine considered the question impartially. After a moment she answered, "I suppose it is because I can think of no other explanation for your behaviour. You are very inconsistent. Sometimes you appear perfectly normal."

Max knew a dangerous wish to be enlightened. At which times, he wondered, did she consider him normal? Was it at all possible that at such times she found him pleasant company? But he didn't want to be pleasant company to her!

A light breeze rose then and a faint scent wafted to his nostrils. Violets . . . and there were no flowers in this park. There was that strange stirring, a dull ache, somewhere in his chest. Resolutely he turned to gaze straight ahead. The horses' tails restored him to objectivity.

"Consistent or not, I'm not a drunkard," he snapped. "Not yet, anyhow. But I think you'll drive me to it, Miss Pelliston. I can't open my mouth without being accused of being half-seas over. Is that some sort of hobbyhorse of yours, ma'am?"

He stole another glance in spite of himself, and his heart smote him. He had forgotten about her father. Now the wet brightness of her eyes told him he'd struck a painful spot. He felt like a brute—a great, clumsy lummox.

"Oh, drat." His instincts told him to take her in his arms and comfort her. What remained of his rational mind told him to keep his hands to himself, no matter how they itched to touch her. The two inner voices had a violent argument, and the rational mind won out. He apologised.

He told her he was out of sorts because he'd failed regarding the dress, had made such a mess of the business, in fact, that Lord Browdie's mistress was now confidently expecting to become his.

This is not the sort of talk to which a gentleman normally treats an innocent young miss. Miss Pelliston should have been insulted. She ought, at least, have pointed out the impropriety of the subject.

Like other ladies, she knew that gentlemen kept mistresses and that in the Beau Monde this was considered in light of a duty. Other women would feign ignorance of such matters. In Catherine's case, pretence was not only impossible, but absurd—after all, the man had found her in a brothel.

This was how she justified her reaction. She did not include in that justification the conspiratorial thrill she'd experienced as the viscount told his adventures. She did not even consider the relief she'd felt upon learning that the unfortunate female was not Lord Rand's mistress *yet*.

Catherine did admit—not only to herself, but aloud—that she was touched by his efforts, ill-considered though they'd been, on her behalf.

"All the same," she added, "it wasn't necessary. Lord Browdie thinks it was some other woman you paid fifty pounds for. He was so tickled that you'd paid so much only to be cheated of the girl's belongings that I wonder he hasn't told all the world about it. What was most provoking was that, in between chortling with glee about your being made of fool of, he was lecturing me on the dangers of your company."

Perhaps Lord Rand was beginning to understand how very dangerous certain company could be. Perhaps he'd begun to wish someone had warned him away weeks ago. He said nothing, however, only smiled rather bleakly.

"So there is no need to worry about the dress," Catherine went on, thinking the man was not yet convinced. "I should have realised that. Lord Browdie is not the kind of man who'd notice what a woman wore. I'm sure he never noticed any of my frocks—any more than Papa ever did."

Lord Rand's smile grew a tad more bleak. Perhaps it had occurred to him that he could, if asked, provide an accurate list of every garment he'd ever seen Miss Pelliston in, from the moment he'd seen her wrapped in a blanket.

He said, "Then we've been making mountains out of

molehills—is that it? Thinking everyone sees Banquo's ghost, so to speak."

Catherine looked puzzled.

"*Macbeth*, Miss Pelliston. Shakespeare and his confounded ghosts."

"I know—only—"

"—only you thought I didn't. I suppose, besides considering me a drunkard, you also believe I'm illiterate."

"No. I'm only surprised at your not pretending to be illiterate."

A grim foreboding began to overtake him. "Let's keep that a secret, shall we? I never meant to let on. Your happy news took me by surprise and I'm afraid I let my guard down."

"Why have it up in the first place, My Lord? Why pretend to be less than you are?"

"Don't want to raise expectations, don't you know," he answered with a fine display of insouciance. "People would start expecting me to be erudite all the time, and it's confounded tiring. It's hard enough just behaving myself without adding intellectual responsibility to the lot."

"You're a very strange man, My Lord."

" 'Mad, bad, and dangerous to know.' That's what Caro Lamb said about Byron—or so Louisa tells me. Still, the foolish creature got to know him anyhow, and look where that led."

Miss Pelliston's colour deepened about six shades, which must have brought her companion some enjoyment, because he grinned as he gave the horses leave to start.

Catherine was no more pleased with the smug grin than she was with the thinly veiled threat. He was warning her off, was he? Did the conceited brute think she was pursuing him?

"You forget," she began as soon as she'd crushed down an incipient urge to do him violence, "that Lady Caroline is also accounted mad. She became entangled with Lord Byron because she was not thinking rationally. A sensible woman would certainly keep away from dangerous men."

"Would she? But you don't keep away from *me*, though

my character failings, according to you, are legion."

"I do try to keep away," she snapped, "but you are always there."

"May I remind you that if I hadn't always been there, you'd be languishing in a whorehouse now, or getting run down by carriages, or working your fingers to the bone in a dressmaker's shop."

"Then you may derive comfort from the fact, My Lord, that I am no longer in any sort of danger, and you need waste no more of your valuable time with heroic rescues. You are at liberty to do exactly as you like. If you have accidentally got into the habit of rescuing helpless women, perhaps you should set about rescuing the one who now has my dress. I daresay that sort of activity is more in keeping with your tastes."

"Miss Pelliston, that last smacks of jealousy."

"Oh!" she cried, stamping her foot and thus alarming the horses. "What a coxcomb you are!"

"And what a devil of a temper you have. I suppose you'd like to strike me," he said with the most infuriating grin. "No, on second thought, I recall that strangling is more to your tastes. Maybe you'd like to fasten those ladylike white fingers about my throat and choke me? Be warned that there's a deal of linen in the way. Punching me on the nose would be more efficient, though more untidy. In either case, my cravat would suffer and Blackwood would never forgive you."

"You are insufferable," she muttered, clenching and unclenching her fists. "How I wish I were a man."

"I'm so glad you're not. Manly rage couldn't be nearly as entertaining as the present spectacle. You look like an outraged kitten. I shall have to call you 'Cat' from now on."

"I never gave you leave—"

"I never wait for leave, Miss Pelliston . . . Pettigrew . . . Pennyman . . . Catherine . . . Cat. What a lot of names you have, just like a common criminal."

With a mighty effort, Catherine controlled herself. She would have liked nothing better than to choke the breath

151

out of him and hated him for knowing it and teasing her with it. She folded her hands in her lap.

"I see," she said with a reasonable appearance of calm, "that you are bent on provoking me. I suppose that is the most productive activity you can think of."

"No. Kissing you would be much more productive in that way. Unfortunately, being a mere male and driven by baser instincts, I'm afraid I'd provoke myself even more. Therefore I shall not kiss you, Cat, however much you beg me."

Catherine stifled a gasp and turned her gaze towards the trees shading the Queen's Walk. Their leaves stirred in the light breeze, and above them the sky was changing from blue to grey. Her heart was stirring too, more agitated than the gently swaying branches—but that was only because she was so incensed. Of course he didn't mean to kiss her. He wanted to outrage her, and she was playing into his hands. Catherine decided she'd given Lord Rand enough entertainment for one morning.

"Very well," she said. "Since you are obviously proof against all my feminine wiles, I am obliged to turn the subject. What is this I hear about Jemmy wanting to become your footman?"

Lord Rand had lost the upper hand so quickly that he felt giddy. That must account for his witty rejoinder.

"What?" he gasped.

"As you probably know, I've continued Jemmy's lessons since that day you so thoughtfully brought him by. Lady Andover has consented to my tutoring him twice a week at the shop because it seems we cannot have him coming to the house. Mr. Jeffers claims that not only does the child distract the servants, but he is sticky. Cook evidently gives him too much jam. At any rate we have hardly begun, and Jemmy tells me he knows enough because he means to be a footman. Your Mr. Gidgeon has apparently encouraged him."

Lord Rand groaned. "I should have expected it. Well, if that's what Gidgeon means, there's nothing I can do about it. My servants do exactly as they please."

"All the same, I do not see why any servant need be illiterate. I wish you would talk to Jemmy."

"I don't see where I come into it. The boy dotes on you. I'd think he'd do whatever you tell him."

"I'm afraid he puts up with the lessons only for the sake of my company. That's flattering, of course, and I would not complain except that all he wants to do is talk about the livery he'll wear one day and tell me what fine fellows Mr. Gidgeon and Mr. Blackwood are. Mere grammar cannot compete with those paragons. However, he seems to have some respect for you as well, so I ask you to use your influence."

Lord Rand had begun to think that in spite of his earlier confusion, he'd managed to make a decent start in driving Miss Pelliston off by showing her what an ill-behaved lout he was. Now she was entangling him again in what was plainly her affair. What was it to him if Jemmy was illiterate? In fact, if she had to give up this tutoring business, that would be one less commitment keeping her in London.

The trouble with her—or one of the troubles—was her obsession with being useful. She'd returned to Louisa mainly because she believed Louisa needed her. She continued teaching the boy because she believed he needed her.

What the girl truly needed was a permanent occupation—like a husband. The sooner she got one, the faster the viscount could wash his hands of her and her plaguey problems. She needed Jack Langdon, and though Jack wanted no tutoring, he did need someone to take him in hand. They were perfectly suited. They would speak of books the livelong day and night and bore everyone else but themselves to distraction.

Lord Rand smiled benignly upon his companion. "Very well," he said. "I'll talk to the br—boy."

== 15 ==

FOLLOWING THE DRIVE in Green Park, Lord Rand took himself to Gentleman Jackson's boxing establishment. The viscount had an excess of nervous energy and physical exertion was the obvious cure. Today the Gentleman himself deigned to accommodate his lordship. At the end of the exercise Max was pleasantly fatigued, his nervous energy dissipated in perspiration.

He even lingered for a while after, watching the other gentlemen at their labors and offering the occasional piece of unwelcome advice to his less agile fellows. Thus he had the surprise of his life. He was just preparing to leave when Jack Langdon entered.

The probability of finding Jack Langdon in a boxing saloon was approximately equivalent to that of encountering the Archbishop of Canterbury at Granny Grendle's—though the odds were rather in favour of the Archbishop.

"What the devil brings you here?" the viscount enquired of his friend.

Mr. Langdon stood for a moment looking absently about him as though in search of something he'd forgotten. "Not the most pleasantly fragrant place, is it, Max?" he noted in some wonder. "Odd. Very odd. I count three viscounts, one earl, a handful of military chaps and—good God—is that Argoyne?"

"Yes. One duke."

"All come, it seems, for the express purpose of letting some huge, muscular fellow hit them repeatedly."

"So what's *your* purpose?"

"I suppose," Mr. Langdon answered rather forlornly, "I've come to be hit."

This was insufficient explanation, as Max promptly pointed out.

"I've come to be more dashing, as you advised. I've been thinking over what you said the other day, and I concluded 'Mens sana in corpore sano,' in the words of Juvenal . . . or as Mr. Locke so aptly put it, 'A sound mind in a sound body is a short but full description of a happy state in this world.' Physical prowess accords self-confidence. Boxing is reputed not only to increase physical strength and skill but to improve one's powers of concentration. Just the thing for me, I decided."

"So you mean to leave off meditating and hesitating and prepare yourself for action instead," said Max. "Well, they do say love works miracles."

Mr. Langdon flushed. "I was referring to what you said about throwing books at twenty paces. No reason I should be letting a gangly, decrepit drunkard twice my age push me about."

Jack plainly did not care to be teased about Miss Pelliston. If he wanted to believe that manly pride had brought him to the boxing saloon, that was perfectly acceptable. At least the chap was making an effort, and that ought to be encouraged. A hesitating, insecure Jack Langdon did not bode well for Lord Rand's plans regarding a certain young lady's future occupation.

"Right you are. No reason on earth, my lad. Wait here a minute and I'll find Mr. Jackson for you."

Lord Rand might have taken his friend to the famous boxer instead of the other way around, but he needed to talk to Mr. Jackson privately first. The viscount did not want Mr. Langdon discouraged in his first efforts, and decided to drop a gentle hint in advance regarding the care and handling of dreamy-eyed intellectuals.

Mr. Jackson proving a sympathetic soul, Jack Langdon's introduction to the manly art was considerably less debilitating than that, for instance, of an insolent young sprig of the nobility whom the professionals in the place all agreed wanted taking down a peg or two.

Mr. Langdon, in contrast, was handled with the proverbial kid gloves, and vigorously encouraged by both Max and the Gentleman. Both repeatedly pointed out that the neophyte, despite his sedentary habits, showed great promise with his fives.

At the end of his exercise, Mr. Langdon was glowing, literally and figuratively. In this malleable state he was open to every one of Lord Rand's suggestions regarding another manly art—courtship.

"Almack's tomorrow," Max reminded as they left the saloon. "It's her first time, and you have to get a waltz. More romantic, you know."

"I know. The trouble is, I have to face one of the Gorgons first and they all hate me because they heard I called them Gorgons."

"What in blazes are you talking about?"

"The waltz. The Gorgons—the patronesses—have to give her permission to waltz, and that means they pick a suitable partner and I'm not suitable. If I go up and ask them, they'll laugh in my face. The only reason they let me in the door is so they can humiliate me at their leisure."

"That's ridiculous."

"You've been away too long, Max. You don't know what cats they can be. If I ask to waltz with Miss Pelliston, they won't just refuse me. They might even not let her waltz at all with anyone, just for spite."

"They won't alienate Louisa."

"They don't care who they antagonise. Don't you know they wouldn't let Wellington in one night because he was a few minutes late? And another time because he wore trousers instead of knee breeches?"

"No, I don't know it, but I ain't surprised. Of all the dull, stuffy stupidity that passes for entertainment, Almack's is the dullest, stuffiest, and stupidest. So naturally that's where everyone wants most to be. If Society had half a grain of sense it'd shun Almack's like the plague."

"But it doesn't," said Jack. "So I can't waltz with her."

"All this means is you can't have the first one," Max answered bracingly. "I'll take care of that. Then you have to make sure you manage the rest."

What he meant by taking care of the matter was that he'd find someone who had less to fear from Almack's patronesses. Not himself, of course. Though Lord Rand was afraid of nobody, there was that nagging problem with Catherine Pelliston's proximity. He had enough trouble sitting beside her in a carriage. Whirling about a dance floor with his arm about her waist was an invitation to disaster.

He reported none of this to Jack Langdon because Jack would feel obliged to analyse the problem. Max didn't want anything analysed. He just wanted Catherine Pelliston to go away.

Having nudged Mr. Langdon gently but firmly down the path to matrimony, Lord Rand went home with equally charitable resolve to release Miss Pelliston from her onerous educational responsibilities.

Jemmy, Mr. Gidgeon reported, was belowstairs assisting Cook.

"Annoying him, you mean. Girard doesn't know any English and I'll eat my hat if the brat knows a word of French."

Mr. Gidgeon politely responded that the scrubbing of pots did not require bilingual skills. "Cleans 'em very well, My Lord, 'e does. As 'e does heverything. A most henterprising lad. Wotever we sets 'im to, 'e does it—with a vengeance, hif I may say so."

"Well, set him to come up to see me in my den—library—whatever you call it. I want a word with him. While you're at it, you might as well send a bottle along with him. My throat's dry as the Pharaoh's mummy."

Mr. Gidgeon withdrew. A few minutes later he returned with Jemmy, who bore a tray upon which reposed a decanter of Madeira and a sparkling crystal wineglass.

The boy carried the tray and set it down with a deft grace that astonished Lord Rand and brought a satisfied smile to the butler's face. Mr. Gidgeon had preceded the tray into the room in order to lend the ritual the appropriate dignity and ceremony. Now he withdrew.

Jemmy remained by the sturdy, marble-topped table upon which he'd placed the tray, and looked about him with an air as complacent and proprietary as that of the butler.

"You're a lad of many talents, Jemmy," said Lord Rand as he poured himself a drink.

"I hope I give satisfashun, sir."

His lordship blinked and put the glass down to stare at the boy, half expecting him to have miraculously sprouted whiskers and shot up two or three feet.

No, this was still an eight-year-old boy, but one doing an uncannily accurate imitation of Mr. Gidgeon, minus the misplaced aitches.

"So you mean to enter my employ, young man?" the viscount asked with like gravity.

"Yes, sir—My Lord. 'N' wear one of 'em blue coats wif shiny buttons, like Roger got."

"Exactly. Shiny buttons. I commend you on your choice of profession, Jemmy. The question is, what about your lessons?"

"Wot about 'em?" Jemmy asked, a guilty expression overtaking his grave dignity.

"Miss Pelliston tells me you don't attend as you used to. She's worried."

Jemmy sighed. "First it wuz the letters and then the words and still there's no end to it. Sentences, she says. And punk—punk—"

"Punctuation," Max supplied.

"Wot you said. 'N' grammar. Don't it *never* end?"

"I'm afraid not. After that, there's books. No end to them at all, as you see." The viscount gestured towards the bookshelves Louisa had crammed with several hundred tomes his lordship had no intention of opening.

Jemmy groaned.

158

"Not as interesting as the buttons, eh? Why should they be, to a lad of your talents? You have greater things awaiting you. In a few years, with diligence, you might become a footman. Or if you find your tastes don't run to fetching and carrying, perhaps you'll consider horses."

"Horses?" the boy echoed wonderingly.

"Yes. If you're as conscientious as Mr. Gidgeon says, perhaps I ought to think of training you as my tiger."

"You don't mean 'at!" The child's face glowed with excitement. Evidently he'd not dared aspire to the honour of tending his lordship's prime cattle and dashing vehicles.

"I do. But it will require a deal of work. I don't know where you'll find time for your lessons."

Gloom overtook the glow.

"What's the trouble, Jemmy? You don't care for them anyhow. You might as well give them up now and spare Miss Pelliston and yourself some pains."

"I can't," Jemmy answered in anguished tones. " 'At's the only time I get to see her. 'Cept when she comes for gowns and such—and all that time she's talkin' wif HER—Missus, I mean. Or Sally or Joan."

"So the only reason you put up with these lessons is to have Miss Pelliston's undivided attention?"

Jemmy nodded dolefully, rather in the style of Mr. Hill.

Max sipped his Madeira and thought. Buttons, even shiny ones, could not compete with Miss Pelliston's undivided attention. One had better reveal the ugly truth. The child would have to face it sooner or later anyhow.

"Jemmy, I must speak with you man to man. Do you know why Miss Pelliston is in London?"

"Parties. She dresses up fancy and goes to parties, day and night."

"She is in London, going to these parties, in order to find a husband. The parties are given mainly so that unmarried young men and women can find someone to marry. Because Miss Pelliston is a very wealthy young lady of fine family, she will marry some great lord. That lord will not want his ladywife teaching anybody—not even his own children. He will hire governesses and tutors for that purpose. Do you understand?"

"No."

Lord Rand decided to take a simpler if more brutal approach. "Miss Pelliston will marry soon—possibly within the next month. When she does, I promise you will not see her again, except when she visits the shop to buy more gowns.. There will be no more lessons."

To his credit, Jemmy did not reel from this blow. Instead he gazed upon the viscount with something very like suspicion. "Why din't she tell me, then?"

"I don't know. Today is your lesson day, isn't it? Ask her. I am not trying to deceive you. I am not so desperate for a tiger."

Immediately after this discussion, Jemmy sought out Mr. Blackwood. If anyone knew what was what, this gentleman did. To his distress, Jemmy learned that Lord Rand had spoken the truth. In fact, rumour had it that both Mr. Langdon and the Duke of Argoyne were vying—albeit slowly and cautiously—for Miss Pelliston's hand.

As Jemmy was aware, servants knew a deal more about what went on in the Great World than its members did. If you could not get the facts belowstairs, you couldn't get them anywhere in the kingdom.

"Wot about HIM?" Jemmy asked after he'd digested this catastrophic news.

"His lordship, you mean? What about him?"

"Is HE here to get married too?"

"It is his lordship's duty to marry at some point and get heirs to carry on the title. Whether he has set his mind to that matter yet is a question I cannot answer. I have heard some talk about Lady Diana Glencove, but no more than talk. To my knowledge, his lordship has called on her once and danced with her on occasion."

"Don't HE see Miz Kaffy too? Don't HE never dance with her?"

Mr. Blackwood studied the round face lifted enquiringly

towards his. He believed he could see the inner wheels beginning to turn. Mr. Blackwood approved of turning inner wheels.

By and large the aristocracy was intelligent enough. The problem was that its members had no need to live by their wits. Thus their wits atrophied. If they could not rely upon the sharper instincts and abundant common sense of their servants, the British upper classes would destroy themselves through sheer ineptness.

That was precisely what had happened in France, and look at the result. Until very recently, most of the civilized world had been under the boot of one short, ill-tempered Corsican. Compared to Napoleon, even a mad King George III was a desirable monarch, and the fat, dissolute Regent an Alexander the Great. Mr. Blackwood was no radical.

For the survival of Britannia the turning of inner wheels must be encouraged.

"Yes, Jemmy," the valet answered, "he does see her and he does dance with her and he has, to my knowledge, taken her driving twice."

"Wot for?"

"I hope, my boy, you have abandoned the notion that his lordship has designs on the young lady's virtue." Receiving a blank look, the valet explained, "He doesn't mean anything wicked, you know."

"Then wot does he mean?"

In his pursuit of wisdom, Jemmy had followed Mr. Blackwood along the hall and up the stairs. They now stood at the door of Lord Rand's chambers.

Mr. Blackwood glanced about him. Then he bent towards the boy and said in a low voice, "I think my lad, I had better explain something to you about the upper-class mind."

Lord Browdie sat in the bedchamber of his love nest glaring at the peach-coloured gown that lay in a heap on the floor. There Lynnette had dropped it after opening a large box containing the two monstrous overpriced gowns she'd insisted on having.

What a greedy creature she was. Worse, here he was, throwing away perfectly good money on a whore—captivating though she was—when he still hadn't found himself a wife. The only respectable willing females he'd met had turned out to have pockets to let. His affection for Catherine's property and dowry was increasing daily in consequence.

"Now isn't that better?" Lynnette asked coyly as she reentered the room. She made a slow, langorous turn so that her protector might fully appreciate every entrancing detail of the crimson gown and the shapely form upon which it was draped.

"Yes, better," the baron answered shortly, wondering what the bill would look like.

"There was a moment there I thought it wouldn't be ready after all, such a fuss there was at the mantua-maker's. That little girl," she went on while admiring herself in the glass. "You know—the one was with him that day—that tall one you said was a viscount." Lynnette knew very well the man was a viscount and she knew precisely how tall he was, but she didn't tell her protector everything she knew.

Lord Browdie was nudged out of his painful meditations. "Catherine Pelliston, you mean?"

"If you say so. With the great eyes and everything else so little," she added disparagingly. "I was going into the dressing room and she comes out with a horrid little boy holding her hand. Miss Hoity-Toity went all white," she sniffed. "The way she stared at my gown—she even had *me* thinking there was something nasty crawling on it. That one." She nodded towards the frock Lord Browdie had absently picked up while she was talking. "Which of course when I thought of it I had to give her some credit, as it didn't really suit me at all."

Lord Browdie stared at the gown as his brain slowly, ponderously creaked into motion.

"Such a stir she made. The boy starts howling and Madame comes running in and no one has a thought for me,

162

because they must give the delicate lady the cup of tea—so she could recover from the terrible shock of seeing a fallen woman." Lynnette smiled. "Actually, I did feel sorry for her. She looked so ill and white that for a minute she put me in mind of that poor country servant I told you about—the one that cost that viscount so much money. Remember?"

"Yes." Lord Browdie's head began to throb.

"I expect Miss Prim and Proper would faint dead away if she knew she reminded me of her fine gentleman's low sweetheart."

"No," said Lord Browdie. "She's too obstinate to faint. Did she really look like the girl? Maybe that's why Rand took up with her."

"Oh, you naughty boy!" Lynnette reached out to playfully ruffle the garish red hair, then changed her mind and settled for a coquettish smile instead. "Maybe that *is* why. I told you I never saw much of her myself. You know how Granny is—never liked the girls to get together because she thought we'd plot behind her back. I couldn't say really if she's like her or not. It was just one of those odd ideas that come into your head sometimes."

Lord Browdie had a very odd idea in his head at the moment. Lynnette had connected the dress with Catherine during her monologue. Now he made his own connection.

This was the frock Catherine had donned when she'd emerged from those unspeakable mourning costumes she'd worn for her great-aunt. The warm colour had been such a relief from the ghastly blacks and half-mourning that he'd noticed. He even recalled thinking at the time that for once she didn't look like a corpse herself. No wonder he'd remembered the gown.

Catherine's gown. Now Lynnette's gown. In between it had been, briefly, Granny Grendle's—and she had stolen it from the female Lord Rand had paid fifty quid for. In a brothel.

The idea of Catherine Pelliston—the most sanctimonious of prigs—in a brothel was so outlandish that the baron would need two bottles of wine to assimilate it. He ordered

Lynnette off to the milliner's. He was too taken up with his wonder to think of the bills that would result, and knew only that he needed to be alone, to think.

Lynnette promptly obliged him. She was gone before he'd opened the first bottle, in fact. Many glasses later, Lord Browdie's bewilderment had given way to the happiest of daydreams.

Another man might shrink at the prospect of a soiled wife, but Lord Browdie was not just any man and this was not just any wife. A soiled Catherine Pelliston was vulnerable, and a vulnerable Catherine Pelliston was the only female of that name who would agree to marry him—once, that is, he pointed out the alternative.

The precise name for what Lord Browdie contemplated was blackmail, but he was not overly concerned with semantics, any more than he was concerned with physical technicalities, such as virginity. That only meant he wouldn't have to endure any tiresome whining on his wedding night.

As long as she wasn't breeding already—and he'd make sure of that first—her maidenhead was of no concern to him. If she was breeding . . . he frowned briefly, but only briefly. In that case, the price of keeping her secret would be to let him enjoy the favours others had tasted—like that insolent Rand, for instance.

Lord Browdie refilled his glass and swallowed its contents with as much joy as if it had been the ambrosia of Olympus. After all, what greater happiness is there than contemplating the humiliation of one's enemies?

= 16 =

LORD RAND'S PLANS and Mr. Langdon's hopes were doomed to disappointment. Miss Pelliston did not appear at Almack's that evening because Lady Andover had been suddenly taken ill.

The countess was better the following day, though somewhat stunned by the experience. She had never been sick a day in her life—she scorned illness, refused to have anything to do with it.

Given her attitude, it was hardly surprising that she insisted on attending the celebration of Miss Clarissa Ventcoeur's betrothal to Lord Fevis. Louisa most certainly could not lie abed all day, and if she were forced by her brute of a husband to remain at home, she would drive herself mad. The brute, who had merely suggested—in the gentlest way—that his wife indulge in a day's rest, shook off his alarm and withdrew the hateful suggestion.

Lord Rand also attended the exuberant celebration, mainly to be at hand in case Mr. Langdon required any guidance or moral support in the pursuit of Miss Pelliston.

The party was held out of doors on the Ventcoeurs' large estate several miles from London. This meant that the guests were at liberty to join in the planned entertainments or amuse themselves by wandering about the beautiful grounds. Being at liberty to wander, Jack did so. He got into a lively debate with a literary gentleman on the merits of the Lake Poets and strolled off with him into the maze. There the two intellectuals met up with Miss Gravistock and her cousin, who promptly joined the battle.

Lord Rand decided that the mountain had better be brought to Mahomet. He found Miss Pelliston conversing with his mama and proposed that the ladies walk with him. That was perfectly acceptable—until his mother got herself lost *en route*. Lady St. Denys spied one of her friends and, in her usual fuddled manner, went where her gaze led her and forgot all about her son and the young lady.

That was when disaster struck. The maze and Mr. Langdon were due east. Due west Miss Pelliston caught sight of a Greek temple. She had never seen such an elaborate folly before, having never explored an elegantly landscaped estate. Unlike other young ladies, she was unaccustomed to discovering temples and statues, pagodas and grottoes in every nook and cranny. Instead of being overcome by ennui, she was charmed—and admitted it.

"Oh, it is like a story, isn't it?" she cried in delight. "Can one go inside, do you think?"

One could. One—or two, rather—did.

In the rotunda, she skipped from one carved deity to the next, quoting from the *Iliad* or the *Odyssey*—Lord Rand was not sure which. As she turned, smiling, to answer some wry comment he made, his heart began to thud. Her open joy warmed him.

He moved nearer and unthinkingly took her hands in his. Hers were so small and slender in their ladylike white gloves. The touch made him feel amazingly strong, but needful of something. He drew her to him.

Her smile wavered. Meaning to reassure her, he bent his head and whispered, "You're like a happy nymph."

Her eyes grew troubled, but he was already lost, searching in her gaze for he knew not what. Even as she started to answer, his head bent closer still, and his mouth covered hers.

The lips that always scolded him—that in a moment must berate him cruelly—were soft and sweet. He meant only to taste them, but the taste was a delicious surprise, and he needed to savour it. Then he knew what the shock had been

166

last time. Yearning that made no sense hammered in his heart as he waited for her to push him away. *Don't*, he thought. *Not yet*.

His arms slipped around her to keep her near just another moment and a thrill shot through him when he felt her hands move up to his neck. He sensed her answering shudder, and that was the last he knew of thought. What remained was the fragrance of violets, the clean scent of her skin, the tickle of frothy curls, and the dizzying warmth of her slim body melting into his arms. She was light and delicate, but to kiss her was to plunge into a summer storm, and that intoxicated him, as storms always did. He forgot she was small and fragile, and crushed her to him.

Catherine was lost. Whatever inner warnings she tried to heed at the start stilled when his lips sought hers—perhaps because that seeking was so gentle, coaxing, surprisingly tender. The taste of him, the scent of him, drew her as easily as his encircling arms.

She had not expected the gentleness or the sweetness or the sense of homecoming, still less the longing he so easily kindled. As his mouth grew more insistent, she answered helplessly. The frantic pumping of her heart warned her she was being drawn to danger, but the alarm was muffled in the sweet chaos of physical sensation. He surrounded her and she, trusting him, abandoned herself to him. The strong arms about her and the press of his hard chest secured her, even as she felt herself sinking into warm, enticing, turbulent darkness.

Falling, she thought vaguely, as her lips opened in answer to some felt command from his. Falling. Fallen. Her eyes flew open and she jerked her head back.

"Good heavens! What are you doing to me?" she asked, horrified, as reality crashed down upon her.

The viscount's blue eyes were dark as midnight. "Kissing you, Cat," he answered huskily. "Surely you remember what a kiss is. I gave you one just a few weeks ago."

"This was not at all the same thing."

"No, it wasn't," was the grave reply. "This was a deal bet-

167

ter. This time you cooperated."

She pulled away and was alarmed to find herself still weak-kneed. Embarrassed, she glared at him. "You tricked me!"

"On the contrary, you tricked *me*. You are very deceitful. Never once have you hinted that you were passionate. You were most unsporting to take me unawares. I might have fainted."

Two bright spots of colour appeared in Miss Pelliston's cheeks.

"Passionate? How dare you!" she cried, furious with herself for the humiliating proof she'd given him. "Oh, you are the most provoking man!" She stamped her foot. Then, realising she was having a childish tantrum, she raised her chin, collected her dignity, and marched out of the ersatz temple.

Lord Rand might have been more tactful, but misery loves company. Being agitated himself, he felt obliged to vex his companion. Now, as he watched her storm off, he was torn between wanting to follow her to apologise, as he should, and remaining to dash his head against the temple's stone pillars. Though the latter course of action promised more relief, he decided he had better go after her.

Another moment's delay and he would have lost track of her. She was moving very quickly. As he hastened down the path they'd come, he saw a flash of white muslin before she turned down another pathway.

That way led to Lord Ventcoeur's man-made grotto, Max knew. He also knew that if she continued at that pace, she'd stumble and probably fall into the (also man-made) lake. The path was narrow and inclined steeply. It was meant for leisurely exploration, not foot races. Damning her temper and himself for goading it, he hurried along in pursuit.

Because of the turns and angles of the walkway, the heavy plantings and occasional rock outcroppings, she disappeared from view for a few minutes. Then he caught another glimpse of white at the grotto's entrance. At that moment, his foot slipped on a patch of moss, he lost his balance, and landed on his backside.

Cursing softly, he got up, brushed himself off, and hurried on. He had just turned towards the cave entrance when he heard a disagreeably familiar voice—Lord Browdie's—crying, "Hold a minute, Cathy. I want a word with you."

There was a muttering of male voices, then Max saw Sir Reginald Aspinwal give a shrug and turn back onto the lower path by the lake's edge.

Apologies of the sort Lord Rand contemplated cannot be made in the presence of other gentlemen. On the other hand, a gentleman cannot leave an innocent young lady—especially one in an emotional state—alone with a lecherous old sot. And, the viscount was curious what Lord Browdie wanted to talk about. Very likely he had more slander about Max, which would be entertaining. And if there was the least sign of danger to Catherine, Max would be on hand. Perhaps afterwards he would reward the brute with a broken jaw.

By now Sir Reginald was out of sight. Lord Rand took up a position under an enormous rhododendron at the grotto's entrance. He leaned back against the smooth stone, folded his arms across his chest, and eavesdropped.

In a few minutes he'd unfolded his arms and was clenching his fists.

"Me?" he heard Catherine cry in affronted disbelief. "In a—in such a place? You are mad—or drunk—I do not care which—"

"No, I ain't—and there's a peach-colour frock your Aunt Deborah'll recognise fast enough if I show it to her. Which I can, you know, if you won't be sensible."

"I will not stay and listen to this, this—I hardly know what to call it."

"I wouldn't run off if I was you, Cathy. Not unless you want the world to know what you been up to."

Lord Rand made up his mind to hear no more, but to commence immediately upon the breaking of jaws. He was about to turn into the entrance when he caught Miss Pelliston's surprising response.

"You have my leave, sirrah, to tell anyone you like. Tell them this instant, do."

Max hesitated. What was she thinking of?

"I should," Browdie growled. "After the sorry trick you've served me. If it wasn't for your papa—"

"Oh, pray don't trouble about Papa. Do tell your filthy slander to the world," Catherine urged. "I should like nothing better than to see you made the laughingstock of London."

"Ain't me they'll be laughing at, Miss Hoity-Toity, and laughing'll be the kindest of it. You won't be marrying any of your fine beaux, I promise you. Too good for me, are you? Well, you won't be good enough for anyone else, not even your randy viscount. Not that he'd marry you anyhow when he can get what he wants without."

"Now I see what this is about, My Lord. You have lost a dowry and a rich piece of property, have you not? And this is how you think to get them back."

"Your papa promised—"

"Let me make you a promise, sirrah." Catherine's voice deepened, became ominous. "Do you so much as breathe a hint of this scurrilous tale and I shall take it up and trumpet it abroad."

Max heard Browdie's outraged gasp and smiled. She had called his bluff, the clever Cat. Browdie could not publicly condemn her, then turn around and marry her after.

"Yes, I think you understand me," Catherine went on. "Even you would not wed a woman the world believes is damaged goods. Tell your slander, then. I have always lived a retired life, and if one must remain a spinster, it is best to be a rich one. Perhaps I shall bequeath my great-aunt's property to a charity. Coram's Foundling Hospital, I think. The children would do better for country air."

Lord Rand decided that it was high time to make his presence known. Catherine may have vanquished her foe, but that foe was likely infuriated enough at present to drown her. The viscount picked up a stone and skimmed it over the water. Then he sauntered into sight. Without looking towards the entrance, he picked up another flat stone and skimmed it. He was bending to find another when he heard footsteps echoing. Lord Browdie, his face an interesting display of swelling veins and maroon coloration, stomped into the sunlight.

Max feigned surprise and offered an amiable greeting to which the baron muttered some surly response before tramping away. Max turned and strolled into the grotto.

Inside were a few statues of mythological figures connected, aptly enough, with water. These were set in niches carved for that purpose. In one corner a stone nymph was reclining, her hand trailing in a shallow pool. Near her, on a seat carved into the wall, sat Miss Pelliston, her head in her hands.

"Cat," he said.

Her head went up, but she did not appear surprised to see him. "We were wrong," she said simply. "He knows everything."

"Yes. I heard."

"Oh Lord." She resumed her posture of despair.

Max moved closer. "What are you so unhappy about? You were brilliant—but I knew you had it in you, Cat. Though I did feel rather a fool, about to dash to your rescue and then finding you quite capable of rescuing yourself."

"Yes, with a great pack of lies."

" 'Truly, to tell lies is not honourable, but when the truth entails tremendous ruin, to speak dishonourably is pardonable.' "

"You need not quote me Sophocles, My Lord. Even the devil can quote scripture to his purpose."

"Oh, I hadn't any purpose. Only wanted to show off my formidable knowledge, ma'am."

"I think you have shown me quite enough of your knowledge for one day," she answered tartly, apparently beginning to recover her natural waspish spirits.

"Yes, I know. I came after you to apologise. At the moment that seems anticlimactic. Besides," he went on, feeling at a loss, "I'm not sure if I am sorry."

"Why should you be?" she answered angrily. "You had your amusement and didn't even get slapped for it. I raised no objections. Why should you be sorry?"

He moved nearer still, and knelt so she would not have to crane her neck to look at him.

"Oh, Cat, you're having an attack of conscience. You let me kiss you, then you told fibs to Browdie, and now you think you're completely corrupt. Shall I make an honest woman of you? Will you marry me?"

Catherine gazed into his lean, handsome face and wished that the eyes, for this one time at least, truly were windows to the soul. If she could have but one glimpse inside, and if that glimpse could give her some reason to hope . . .

"Why?" she asked.

He glanced away at the nymph. "Because I do keep kissing you, it seems. If I keep it up, people will begin to talk."

"I have no intention of allowing you to keep it up," was the indignant answer.

"What about Browdie? You may have called his bluff this time, but surely you don't trust him to keep his tongue in his head."

"I see. You want to marry me to protect my honour. I think you are having an attack of *noblesse oblige*."

He rose abruptly. "I wasn't brought up by wolves, if that's what you mean," he snapped. "I have got some honour, some sense of what's right. If you weren't so stubborn, you'd admit it's right. If it weren't you, but another woman in your predicament, wouldn't you advise her to marry me?"

Catherine stood up as well. Shivering, she drew her shawl more tightly about her. "That would depend upon the woman. There is some risk that Lord Browdie will repeat the tale and ruin me, but that's his gamble, as I told him. Shall you and I gamble on marriage, My Lord? Considering how ill we suit, are the stakes not excessive? Should we hazard a lifetime of wretchedness simply because there's a small chance Lord Browdie will be foolish enough to reveal my secret? If this were a card game would you risk your entire future upon it?"

"I've risked that most of my life," Max answered, his face darkening. "But we're not talking about me, are we? It's you. You're afraid of me, aren't you?"

Catherine had given her troubling feelings about him many names, but fear was not one of them. Now she realised he was right. She had met him only a month ago, yet he'd changed her. Every moment spent with him released demons. Lord, how many had escaped today? Her horrid temper. Those blustering denials and threats—she who abhorred falsehood had uttered lie upon lie.

Worst of all was the passion. He had touched her and she succumbed instantly. Even when she was away from him, he tormented her. Wicked dreams, harking back to that night at Granny Grendle's, recollections of a strong, beautiful physique, shirtless—and she in a whore's *negligee*.

It was the lust—there was no pleasanter name for it— she feared most of all. He had sensed it, as he sensed every other flaw, and would use the power it gave him over her, just as he used her other weaknesses. If not for that, she might have risked marriage, been happy to abandon her fears for her reputation, and devote her energies instead to helping him overcome his own frailties. She could never reform him altogether, and perhaps she didn't quite want that. But these were naive fantasies. She could never change him, because he could master her with the merest glance, the lightest touch.

She saw all this in an instant and answered quickly, "If you mean I am afraid of spending the rest of my life as I have the beginning, you're right."

"I ain't your father, damn it!"

"At the moment the resemblance is quite strong. He too bullies when he is contradicted."

"I'm not bullying you!" he shouted.

"How unfortunate you have not a bottle or a mug handy," said Miss Pelliston as she moved towards the entrance. "Then you might throw it at me, and the resemblance would be complete." With that, she left him.

* * *

To Catherine's relief, no one remarked her overlong absence. Lady Andover had been preoccupied with casting up her accounts and the members of her family had devoted all their anxiety to her.

When Catherine returned, therefore, she heard no awkward questions, only the brief announcement that they would be leaving as soon as the carriage was brought round. She might remain if she wished—Lady Glencove had offered to chaperone her—but Catherine had no desire to stay. At home she might look after Lady Andover, and that would help keep her miserable thoughts at bay.

If Lord Rand had any troubles of his own, he must have vanquished them after a very brief battle, because he left the grotto shortly after Miss Pelliston did, though taking a different path, and went in search of Lady Diana. When he found that goddess he was all affable gallantry and devoted so much time to her that Lady Glencove spent the next twenty-four hours in a state of paradisiacal bliss.

Gentlemen cope with rejection in different ways.

Lord Rand had all the resiliency of young manhood. After being spurned for the second time by Miss Pelliston, he decided he could take a hint and would go where he was more welcome.

Lord Browdie was not so resilient. When confronted with failure, he produced no creative alternatives. He fell into a sullen fit and his mind scraped back and forth upon the same narrow path until he wore the way so deep he could not see beyond it.

He also left the party early, in a bitter rage, vowing inwardly to publish his tale far and wide. He could not commence that publication at the Ventcoeur party because Lord Rand was too much in evidence. The fellow had aready turned up once at an inconvenient moment and might get into the habit. Lord Browdie's was not an enquiring mind. He was not eager to relive Cholly's experience of having his

174

nose broken.

The return trip took an hour and a half, and he sulked the whole way. In the course of this exercise he experienced some doubts, one of which loomed increasingly larger the closer he got to Town. By the time he reached his love nest, the doubt had swelled to huge proportions. The little shrew had insisted she'd never been in that brothel. One would expect denials from the average lady. The trouble was, this was Catherine Pelliston, and one of her least agreeable traits was her appalling honesty.

London Society may have changed her—it changed everyone—and certainly she looked different. If she hadn't changed, though, and he started an ugly rumour that proved to be unfounded, he'd have Pelliston, Andover, Rand—and Lord only knew who else—all fighting for the privilege of putting a sword or a bullet through his heart.

There was only one way to get the truth. Accordingly, Lord Browdie had his horse stabled, then made his way by hackney to a less prosperous neighbourhood.

Fortune must have been smiling on him that day because as he was approaching the brothel he met up with Cholly, and thus avoided a far more costly confrontation with Granny herself.

A pint of gin and a single gold coin made the taciturn Cholly talkative. That is to say, he described the "country servant" in question as having great "rum ogles" of a sort of yellowish-greenish-brownish color and a rat's nest of curly hair. The girl, who had disembarked from the Bath coach, was rather small and very skinny—which Cholly had pointed out to Granny. She'd answered that the girl looked like a child, which was what plenty of the gentlemen wanted, because they believed that children wouldn't give them the pox.

"Then why, I ax you," Cholly went on in aggrieved tones, "does the old witch give her to *him* first, when she knows he likes the jolly big ones and not no babies? I knowed there was goin' to be trouble as soon as she done it, but she don't listen to me—and whose nose gets broke? Not *hers*."

He glared at his glass. "Not as it ain't been broke afore, but that was in a good row of my own. This were all on account of that old witch thinks she's so sharp. I seed it comin'—but it's wot she pays me for. That cove," he added in mingled resentment and admiration, "got a fist like a millstone."

Lord Browdie was not a man of many ideas, but hunger for revenge, like love, works miracles. He had something like an idea, and if he worked on it—and had some help— he might end up with a real one.

"How'd you like to get even, Cholly, without so much as going near the fellow? How'd you like that, and getting yourself a nice pile of those shiners besides?" He nodded at the coin that lay between them on the rough table.

Cholly expressed the opinion that he might contrive a liking for such matters, if properly persuaded.

$=17=$

LORD RAND HAD survived neither his numerous youthful escapades nor his adult ones through sheer luck. His instincts were finely tuned. He knew the exact odds of his surviving any given danger because he knew how much trouble he could handle.

He could, for instance, hold his own against two great, hulking brutes determined to tear him limb from limb, as he had at Granny Grendle's. He knew the odds in his favour when a harlot pointed a gun at his head. He knew, therefore, that with Catherine Pelliston he hadn't a prayer.

He'd been upleasantly surprised by the depth of his dismay when she'd rejected his proposal again. He'd thought he was offering for exactly the reasons she'd cited. Now he realised there was more, that in spite of her being everything he thought he didn't want in a woman, he was very fond of her, and fascinated, and possibly—contrary or demented or whatever it was—well, very possibly he was rather *in love* with her, drat it.

Still, that didn't mean it wasn't a mistake or that marrying her wouldn't be a grievous error. She was right, of course: they didn't suit and one or both of them would be wretched. Besides, she didn't want him. To her he was a younger version of her papa, and she was afraid of him and despised him and that settled matters, didn't it?

Lord Rand was not one to mope. Life was filled with disappointments. He picked up his battered—but not really broken, he told himself—heart, dusted it off, and decided he might as well drop it upon the goddess's altar.

For nearly a week after the Ventcoeur party, the viscount kept clear of Miss Pelliston. If they happened to attend the same events—and that was unavoidable—he reduced their interactions to the minimum courtesy required. He stopped dancing with her and danced attendance upon Lady Diana instead.

He would have preferred to keep away from Almack's as well, but he couldn't, because he'd promised to help Jack. Besides, the goddess would be present. Accordingly, the viscount made his way to the sanctum sanctorum of snobs, that stuffiest and stupidest of places.

He arrived at Almack's earlier than he would have normally because he had to find Catherine a suitable waltz partner—as he'd promised Jack a week ago—and needed time to investigate prospective victims. Why his sister was incapable of managing so simple a matter was a question that did not occur to him.

His sister herself did not occur to him even when she was standing in front of him, offering an unsolicited opinion of his new neck-cloth arrangement, an original creation of Blackwood's. All Max saw at that point was Miss Pelliston in a white muslin gown. There was nothing remarkable in that, certainly. White muslin was the usual debutante costume. She might be a bit older than the others, but the simple innocence of her frock complemented her delicate features.

Brunettes there were aplenty at Almack's that night, as well as blondes and one unfortunate redhead, but there was no one in the cramped assembly rooms whose carefully groomed *coiffure* was such a tantalising froth, a light brown faery cloud flecked with golden light where the candles' glow caught it.

From her hair his gaze dropped to her great hazel eyes, gleaming now with the militant light that always seemed to blaze up the instant she spotted him. Thence his scrutiny proceeded to a pair of soft pink lips. He remembered how sweet they were, while his survey continued, trancelike, down the silken whiteness of her neck. It was then he realised that her neckline was cut more daringly than any she'd worn before; simultaneously he became aware of the fragrance of violets and his head began to spin. He panicked.

He mumbled some answer—he hardly knew what—to her cool greeting, then fled as quickly as he could . . . and walked straight into Sally Jersey's arms, in a manner of speaking, because he nearly knocked that lady down in his blind haste to escape.

Regardless of Jack Langdon's characterisation of Lady Jersey as one of several Almack Gorgons, she was an attractive matron, many years from her dotage, and not at all averse to having a handsome young lord fall on top of her. She offered Max an indulgent smile and waved away his apologies.

"Oh, I know what you're about," said she. "I saw you looking at Miss Pelliston and I expect you want to waltz with her. Well, come along, and I'll do the honours. It's either you or Argoyne, I suppose, though Langdon wants the same thing, but I'll see him turn to stone first, since he tells everyone I can do it, and Argoyne is such a clumsy idiot he'll trample her toes and put her off waltzing forever."

Silence Jersey had more to say on this and other subjects as she led the hapless viscount inexorably back to the peril he'd just escaped. Then the chatter ceased. Lady Jersey resumed her patroness's dignity and presented Miss Pelliston with her waltz partner.

After that there was nothing to be done because the music had started. Max led Miss Pelliston out, placed his arm about her waist, and promptly lost his mind.

The waltz, like Lord Bryon, had become all the rage the previous year and was still considered by Society's more conservative element as fast at best and lewd at worst, which is more or less what these persons thought of the poet.

For the first time in his life Max wished that older and wiser heads had prevailed, and that the curst dance had been banished to benighted Germany, which had spawned it. To hold Miss Pelliston in any way was to wish to hold her closer. That was humiliating. He gazed longingly over his partner's head at the blonde Juno, who was whirling about the dance floor with a tall military gentleman.

Lord Rand looked down at Catherine. He noticed that her head came to his breast and immediately he felt a dull ache there.

"I wish you would say something," Miss Pelliston complained. "I'm still inept at small talk, but if you would help get me started, I might manage something."

"If you get *me* started, you'll be sorry. You usually are."

"Nonetheless, I shall keep a brave smile on my face, so long as we appear to be holding a conversation. At present you are wearing what your sister calls your 'caged animal' look and everyone will think I am a thoroughly disagreeable partner."

If he did feel like a trapped beast, Eton and Oxford quickly came to his rescue. "Oh, you're not disagreeable at all. Tonight, in your maidenly white, with that pink in your cheeks, you put me in mind of apple blossoms. You're as light in my arms as so many flower petals and your voice—"

"Oh, dear," she murmured.

"The sound of your voice," he went on, determined to make her as unsettled as he was, "is a breeze ruffling the leaves."

"What on earth am I to say to that?" she asked, rather breathlessly, because she was at the same time recovering from a turn that had brought her up against his hard chest. Between that and the warm gloved hand which seemed to burn all the way up her spine, Catherine felt rather like a stack of very dry kindling. These circumstances as much as his words set her cheeks aflame and made her wish fervently that she were in St. Petersburg in the dead of winter.

"Really, Cat, must I tell you everything? Haven't you told me repeatedly that you have no further need of my assistance?"

"Yes, I have—and you are still there. Everywhere I go, there you are."

This was monstrous unfair—he'd kept away from her for ages, it seemed—but he chose to agree.

"Like a bad penny."

"Very like," she concurred.

How tiny her waist was. He could easily span it with his two hands, he was sure.

Aloud he said, "Actually, I'm here tonight as a favour to Jack. He'd much rather have the first waltz with you. Unfortunately he's antagonised all the great ladies, so he has to wait for the next one." Max briefly outlined Mr. Langdon's difficulties with the patronesses.

"I see," she said in a subdued voice.

"I hope you're not disappointed."

"Why should I be?" she answered a tad too quickly.

"I mean, that it's me instead of Jack."

"Well, My Lord, if you'll leave off about apple blossoms and talk of Aristophanes instead, I might more easily pretend you are Mr. Langdon."

She had recovered sufficiently to score a hit, but Lord Rand was not one to yield at the first blow.

"I wish you'd call me Max," he said, deciding distraction was the best tactic. " 'My lord' always makes me feel I should be in armour, clanking about and trodding on helpless peasants. Most disconcerting when a chap's trying to be graceful."

"I most certainly cannot. That is disrespectful and far too intimate."

"If you call me Clarence Arthur Maximilian, I'll shoot you."

He heard a faint tinkling sound: Miss Pestilence was giggling!

Though she quickly squelched the giggle, she could not suppress the smile as she gazed up at him. "Clarence Arthur? No wonder you prefer Max."

"Just so." He answered the smile, despite the sudden, inexplicable thundering in his ears. "Now you've said it, I feel warm and friendly and very light on my feet."

"I wish you did not feel quite so friendly. I believe we are supposed to be twelve inches apart. Not"—she glanced down briefly—"five."

Lord St. Denys stood listening to his daughter talk, but his eyes were upon the dance floor, and, in particular, upon his son. When Louisa chided him for not attending, he smiled. "Remember the half-drowned kitten Max brought home that day? He dropped it at your feet and told you to nurse it back to life."

"I remember. The kitten. A robin. A bat. I spent my childhood nursing a menagerie."

"I was thinking how that tiny creature terrified my great mastiff out of its wits. I could not understand it then and I cannot now."

Lady Andover followed her father's gaze. "If it's any comfort, Papa, I'm sure he doesn't understand, either."

"Of course he doesn't," the earl snapped. "The boy's a fool."

By the time the waltz was over and Max had relinquished his partner to Lord Argoyne, the viscount was beside himself. How dare she be so cool and proper when she made him so heated? How dare she giggle and act human for once and set off all those warm, cosy sensations and weaken his already beleaguered resistance even further?

He had weakened, he knew. For one chilling moment he would have promised anything—complete reform, a transformation into a stodgy pillar of Society, not a drop of liquor again as long as he lived, not another tavern wench—anything, if she would give him her hand and allow him to make love to her all the rest of his life.

He had stood on the brink of the precipice, looked down, and thought, in that terrifying instant, "Very well, I'll jump." Now he drew back in horror. That awful girl could do whatever she liked with him! It was not to be borne, not by Clarence Arthur Maximilian Demowery. He would not be managed and reformed by an obstinate little prig.

Could the objective observer have looked into his mind,

he or she would have concluded that Lord Rand was hysterical. Unfortunately, the viscount had no disinterested parties to point this out. Therefore, not half an hour later, when his dance with Lady Diana had concluded, he had asked for and received permission to call upon her papa the following day.

"My dear, you do deserve a severe scold, but in the circumstances, I forgive you."

Lady Diana gazed wearily out the carriage window. "Yes," she murmured, "at last you have your wish."

"All the same, you are not to dance with that man again, even after you're betrothed. The effrontery of the creature—to dare show his face at Almack's. I cannot imagine what the patronesses were thinking of, to allow that fellow entrance. It is the coat, of course. Women are altogether too susceptible to a dashing uniform."

Lady Diana said nothing.

"Still, we will say no more on that head. I'm very pleased with you, Diana," said her ladyship. "I was sure Lord Rand must come to the point soon, once you made an effort, but tomorrow is better than I expected. Lady St. Denys—just as your papa and I have always hoped." Lady Glencove sighed happily. "I can hardly think how your sister Julia can do better."

"Oh, you'll think of something, Mama, depend upon it."

Word of Lord Rand's proposal was all over London by teatime the following afternoon, Lady Glencove's servants proving even more assiduous than their mistress in relaying the momentous news. This was no doubt because the betrothal was to be kept secret until Lord Glencove might make a formal announcement at an appropriately grand party.

Catherine was told the secret by Molly, who announced it as one would an unnatural death.

"I ought to've told her ladyship first," said Molly, shaking her head in sorrow, "only she's sick again and his lordship there with her and them having a row about sending for the leech. That's the trouble with folks as are never sick. When they are, they won't believe it and act like it'd go away on that account."

What Catherine did not believe at the moment had nothing to do with Lady Andover, but with the cold sensation in the pit of her stomach. "Offered for Lady Diana? Are you certain, Molly? That is to say," she added hastily, "I would have thought he'd have mentioned his intentions to his family."

"I don't see how he could, Miss, as he never comes no more and even her ladyship says he hardly says two words when she sees him anywhere else, either." She cast a reproachful look at Miss Pelliston, who did not see it, the maid being at her back unfastening buttons.

"That will do, Molly. I can manage the rest myself."

Molly departed with the air of one following a funeral procession, and Miss Pelliston stumbled to her dressing table. Perhaps she had tripped over the truth, because she sat for a long while staring at her reflection in the glass, then spent another long while after, weeping.

That night Catherine attended a rout with her host and hostess. Lady Andover seemed to be in excellent health and spirits, despite the "shocking squeeze" that signifies a successful entertainment. She was well, that is, until they were heading home again. She climbed into the carriage wearing a very odd expression, sat down, and fainted dead away.

Sir Henry Vane, the family physician, was sent for the following morning. Half an hour after he departed, Catherine was summoned to her cousin's study.

When she entered, the earl was standing by his desk, an odd, faint smile on his noble face as he gazed at the papers neatly arranged there.

"My Lord, is she all right?" Catherine asked immediately, forgetting her manners in her anxiety about the countess.

The earl came out of his daydream though the smile remained.

"Catherine, you are very obstinate. You have been living under my roof at least a month now. You are my cousin. Ours is a distant kinship and I know you like to be respectful, but surely you might omit my style. Louisa threatens to wash your mouth out with soap if you 'my lady' her again."

"Cousin Edgar," Catherine said obediently, "do tell me. What did Sir Henry say?"

"That is better. I had meant to save the physician for last and tell you my news in order of social consequence, but I see you have contracted the Demowery impatience. Please sit down, my dear." He indicated the chair by his desk.

Catherine sat, wishing she could shake the news out of him. Her cousin had such a fondness for roundabout preambles.

"As you must know by now," he began, "once Louisa gets a notion, there is no preventing her putting it into action. According to Sir Henry, my lady wife has taken it into her head to commence a family. Reasoning with her is of no avail."

"I beg your pardon?"

"Louisa plans to present me with a son or daughter before Christmas. There is no stopping her, according to Sir Henry." Lord Andover did not appear in the least desirous of halting his wife's impetuous progress. His dark eyes glowed with pride and happiness.

Catherine jumped up from her chair to hug him. "Oh, that is wonderful news!" she cried. "I know how you have wished for children. How excited you must be, and how happy I am for you both. Louisa is going to have a baby." Her eyes grew moist. "That is marvelous news."

Abruptly she realised that in her enthusiasm she'd crushed her elegant cousin's neck-cloth. She let go of him with a stammering apology.

"Don't be silly, Catherine. On such an occasion even my dour valet must forgive you. Besides, Louisa has already made rather a shambles of my *ensemble*, and in all the excitement I forgot to change before sending for you. Really, this has been a very busy day. Do sit down, Cousin. I have something more to tell you."

Though Catherine had much rather dash up to her ladyship's chamber, she quelled herself and sat down once more.

"As you know, Catherine, your papa has entrusted you to my care and engaged me to act in his behalf, which was wise of him. Once cannot forever be consulting him on every question. The distance is most inconvenient and his self-imposed isolation from his peers equips him ill to judge objectively."

Isolation—intoxication was more like it, Catherine thought, though she said nothing.

"While I act in his stead, there are some matters in which your opinion is paramount."

Papa would hardly thank you for that, was the silent reply—but I do.

"Lord Argoyne has asked permission to pay his addresses."

Catherine immediately abandoned all thoughts of her papa to turn a startled gaze upon her cousin.

"His timing was unfortunate," the earl continued. "I was expecting Sir Henry at any moment. I explained that my wife was ill, and in the circumstances I could not possibly give proper attention to any other subject. He seemed to find that startling. It is just as well. That is a man who wants startling at frequent intervals. He may be a duke, but he is a very dull duke. He has no business being so. It sets a bad example. I hope you have not conceived a *tendresse* for him, Cousin. I should, of course, accede to your wishes, since it is you who would have to marry him. Still I must warn you that if you do, Louisa and I cannot possibly visit you above once a decade."

"Good heavens—a duke—offered for me—why, I hardly know him."

"That is just as well. He does not improve upon acquaintance. I take it, then, I might tell him to go to blazes?"

Catherine thought rapidly. "It is a very good match. He might have looked much higher. Perhaps I'd better have him. I can scarcely expect a more advantageous offer—or even another," she added, frowning.

She had rather have Mr. Langdon, she thought, ruthlessly banishing another image from her mind. He was most attentive, but he was so shy and so preoccupied with matters literary that likely he'd never come to the point this century. She began to wish she'd acquired a few of those feminine arts she'd always scorned. Sometimes men required firm guidance. Now, with Louisa *enceinte*, there was no time to waste. Catherine could not expect to reside with her cousin forever, and Louisa would soon be unable to chaperone her.

"Maybe it would be best to accept him," she said with a dreary sigh.

"Catherine, it is most unlike you to be so silly. Argoyne only wanted to be ahead of the other fellows. I must say I find his haste indecent. You have only been out a few weeks. Perhaps he takes his example from my impetuous brother-in-law."

He must have noticed Catherine's wince, because he added, "Still, as you appear so terrified of finding yourself on the shelf, I shall ask him to call again in another month or so if he is still of the same mind."

With that, and reassurances about Louisa's health, and further assurances that the Dowager Countess of Andover would be delighted to take over as chaperone whenever Louisa was prevented by her condition, the earl dismissed his cousin.

=== 18 ===

"WHERE THE DEVIL'S Jemmy? I haven't seen him in days."

Lord Rand tore off his coat, neck-cloth, and waistcoat, and flung himself onto the bed. He had not drunk an unusual quantity of wine, but lately he did not require very much alcohol to become dizzy and tired. Perhaps that was because he'd spent the past eight nights thrashing among the bedclothes instead of sleeping like a good Christian.

"I couldn't say, My Lord. Evidently, Madame Germaine is extremely busy these days. He has not been by since—" The valet hesitated.

"Since when?"

"I beg your pardon, My Lord. As there has been no formal announcement in the papers, the matter at present is mere household gossip."

"What matter? What in blazes are you talking about?"

Blackwood bent to retrieve the abandoned articles from the floor. "There is word that your lordship has contracted an alliance with one of England's great families."

"Oh, that." Lord Rand scowled at the bedpost.

"When Jemmy received that word, he left the house. He has not been seen since." Blackwood straightened and draped the garments over his arm.

"Just like that—not a word?"

"Actually, My Lord, he had a great deal to say on that occasion. If you'll excuse me, I'd rather not repeat it."

The viscount transferred his scowl from bedpost to servant. "No, I won't excuse you. What did the brat say?"

"He found fault with your thinking processes, My Lord."

"None of your euphemistic translations, Blackwood. What did he say?"

"His words, as I recall, were, 'He's got no more brains 'an 'at shoe.' He pointed to his footwear. He followed that with a long, not entirely coherent speech about his education, in which Miss Pelliston's name recurred repeatedly. He expressed doubts regarding a profession as a tiger. Mr. Gidgeon pointed out alternatives, to which Jemmy responded he'd rather live in the Hulks."

"Spoiled," said the master. "That's what comes of indulging the whims of—of maternal butlers. You're excused, Blackwood. Wait—where are you going with my clothes? I'm going out again."

"Yes, My Lord. I was taking them away to clean them. There is a spot of wine on your coat and what seems to be a gravy stain on your waistcoat."

"Well, what do you expect? I'm a barbarian, ain't I? Barely civilized, you know. Brought up by wolves. And illiterate. Not to mention a drunkard."

A light flickered very briefly in the valet's eyes, but his face was otherwise expressionless as he responded, "I beg leave to disagree, My Lord."

The figure sprawled on the bed heaved a great sigh.

"You're loyal, Blackwood, besides being a paragon. Because you're loyal, I'll share my secret with you. There's been no announcement in the papers because the girl's parents want to bore everyone to death with another overcrowded party where they'll make the announcement and expect the world to be astounded. Ask Hill when that is— I don't remember. End of the week, I think. In short, I am engaged to be married to Lady Diana Glencove."

"Then may I take leave to wish you happy, My Lord?"

"You may wish," the viscount answered gloomily, "all you like."

To find Lady Diana Glencove in the drawing-room was hardly surprising. She was, after all, engaged—though un-

189

officially at present—to Lady Andover's brother. What did surprise Catherine when she joined the sisters-to-be was that Lord Rand's fiancee had stopped by primarily to ask Miss Pelliston to accompany her to Hatchard's.

"Lord Rand tells me you are a prodigious reader," Lady Diana explained. "It would be a great pleasure to have the company of one who shares my fondness for books."

To refuse would be rude, to make excuses cowardly. Catherine had no reason, she told herself, to avoid Lady Diana's company. Lady Andover having an errand or two to be performed in Piccadilly, the matter was speedily settled. Catherine would shop for a while with Lady Diana before going on to Madame's for her regular Wednesday appointment with Jemmy. The Andover carriage would retrieve her at the usual time.

When they reached Hatchard's, Lady Diana suggested that her abigail perform Lady Andover's errands.

As soon as the reluctant maid departed, Lady Diana turned to Catherine and said in a low voice, "I'm afraid I asked you here under false pretences, Miss Pelliston. The plain fact is that I am in need of a friend at the moment. Lord Rand has spoken so highly of you. Your efforts on behalf of that poor orphaned boy I found particularly touching."

Catherine abruptly realised that her mouth was hanging open. She shut it, but continued to stare in bewilderment at her statuesque companion.

"That is why," the goddess continued, "I dared hope that perhaps you would act the part of a friend for me."

Catherine stammered something that must have sounded like agreement, because Lady Diana quickly explained her difficulty. There was a gentleman, a member of her brother's regiment, who had formed an attachment for her some months ago. Unaware that her parents had ordered her to see him no more, he had followed her to London.

"It is very difficult to explain, Miss Pelliston, but I must speak with him. My engagement came as a shock to him, and I feel I owe him a proper good-bye."

Catherine might have made a speech about filial duty,

but her heart was not in it. She only nodded sympathetically and pointed out to her companion that they could not remain whispering in the street.

The fair Juno glanced over her shoulder, then led the way into the bookshop and stopped in an unoccupied corner.

"He is waiting for me near the theological books. I will be no more than five minutes. I would not involve you, Miss Pelliston, but Mama has set my maid spying on me. If Jane comes back too soon, I had rather she didn't see me with him. Will you help me?"

Catherine examined her conscience. She did not understand what needed explaining to the fellow. Wasn't Lady Diana's betrothal to another gentleman sufficient? Still, the lady wanted only five minutes and her disappointed suitor might be entitled to a kindly farewell. Miss Pelliston agreed to help. She would wait by the door. If the abigail made an unwelcome appearance, Catherine would distract her, loudly enough to alert Lady Diana. Would that do?

"Oh, yes. Bless you, Miss Pelliston." Lady Diana squeezed her companion's hand, then hurried off to the religious works.

The kind farewell took nearly half an hour, and Catherine grew mad with frustration. After reading the titles displayed by the door at least a hundred times, she lost all patience with Lady Diana and her thickheaded suitor. Miss Pelliston was also most displeased with Lord Rand. If he had not praised her to his fiancee, Catherine would not be in this awkward position now.

Lady Diana should not be meeting clandestinely with other men, regardless the reason. It was improper and equivocal. She should not engage in any behaviour that might trigger nasty gossip, that would make vicious-minded people laugh at or kinder hearts pity her affianced husband.

Not that Catherine pitied him, she thought, glaring at an innocent volume of the recently published *Pride and Prejudice*. His fiancee was beautiful. She did as her parents commanded and all the world knew they'd ordered her to have the future Earl of St. Denys. He would marry her and do as he pleased, and so would she, after presenting him with the requisite male offspring. They would live as others in the Great World did—serene and comfortable. There would be no battles of will and none of that passion that gnawed at one and frightened one and made one so very unhappy.

Lady Diana finally approached, carrying two of Hannah More's pious works. The tall fair one had time only to assure Miss Pelliston that "everything was settled" before Jane appeared, her face a mask of suspicion. Not another world could be uttered on the subject after that, because the abigail was at their elbows all the rest of the time they shopped.

As previously arranged, Lord Glencove's carriage deposited Catherine at the dressmaker's. The coachman was about to start the horses again when his mistress cried out to him to wait. She turned to her maid.

"Go see if my bonnet is ready, Jane," the lady ordered, indicating the milliner's shop opposite.

"If it please your ladyship, Mrs. Flora did say it wouldn't be ready until Monday."

"Well, I have a mind to wear it tomorrow. See if you can hurry her."

The sullen maid took herself across the street and disappeared into the milliner's shop.

"Oh dear," Lady Diana exclaimed. "I forgot to tell her about the ribbon." She disembarked. "We may be rather a while, John," she told the coachman. "Perhaps you would like to walk the horses."

John would like, actually, to stop at a friendly place around the corner and refresh his palate with a pint of something. Visits to milliners, he knew, consumed at least half an hour. He smiled and drove down the street.

Lady Diana Glencove gave one quick glance towards the milliner's, another at the window of Madame Germaine's, then hastened off down the street in the direction opposite the one her papa's carriage took.

Miss Pelliston had entered the dressmaker's shop in no pleasant temper. In the last hour she had come to a most distressing—and maddening—realisation. The maddening part was that her distress was all her own doing.

The sight of Madame Germaine in a fit of hysterics being comforted by the odious Lord Browdie was not calculated to lift her spirits. Madame sat in a chair talking agitatedly as tears streamed down her cheeks. Lord Browdie was alternately patting her elbow and clumsily waving sal volatile under her chin.

"What are you doing to that poor woman?" Catherine shrieked, hastening to Madame's side.

"Oh, Miss Pelliston, how glad I am you've come," the *modiste* gasped. Impatiently she brushed the man away. "It's Jemmy. One of those dreadful street boys came running in—not ten minutes ago, was it, My Lord? When you had come to pick up that cerise gown for—" She stopped abruptly, having recollected, evidently, that as far as young ladies were concerned, gentlemen's mistresses did not exist.

"One of those boys came running in," she repeated, turning back to Catherine, "and said Jemmy was taken up as a thief—a thief, Miss Pelliston!" Madame's voice rose. "Which of course he is no such thing, and it is a terrible mistake, but what am I to do with Lady Ashfolly coming any minute and Miss Ventcoeur's *trousseau* scarcely begun and that dreadful contessa quarrelling about the silk—"

"There, there," Lord Browdie interrupted. "No need to trouble yourself. I'll just pop down to the magistrate and see everything sorted out. Have the boy back before you can wipe your nose."

Catherine stared at her ex-fiance in disbelief. Lord Browdie had never in his life rushed to the rescue of anything, except perhaps a bottle in danger of toppling.

"You?" she asked incredulously, having already abandoned all pretence of politeness.

"Certainly. Can't have an innocent lad tossed in with a

lot of thieves and cutthroats, and his poor mistress breaking her kind heart. Just tell me what he looks like and I'll be off."

Madame's description was rather skimpy on physiology and elaborate in details of attire.

"Brown hair, brown eyes, and about so high?" Lord Browdie gestured at a level with his belly. He shook his head. "To tell the truth, that sounds like anybody. There's bound to be dozens of boys—always is—and he could be any of 'em."

Catherine sighed in exasperation. The man was obviously incompetent. Why could it not have been Lord Rand in the shop? That was just like him, wasn't it? Always there when he had no business to be and not there when you truly needed him. Which of course was monstrous unfair, but Miss Pelliston was not in an impartial frame of mind.

"I had better go with you," she said. "Every minute we stand here giving you particulars is another minute wasted, and I will not have that child thrust among the lowest sort of criminals."

Lord Browdie objected that the criminal court was no place for a young lady.

That was all Catherine needed to hear. If he would not take her, she snapped, she'd go alone. It was a fine Christian world, wasn't it, when a poor helpless boy, little more than a baby, must be left to languish among London's foulest vermin while one stood idly by on pretext of being a lady.

Madame protested that Miss Pelliston truly must not go. Madame would go herself. She would close up the shop. She hoped she was as much a Christian as anyone else.

Catherine, however, had already worked herself up into the fury of an avenging angel. She was prepared to tear apart the temples of justice with her own bare hands if need be. She swept out of the shop. Lord Browdie hurried after her.

"Afraid we'll have to take a hackney," he said apologetically. "My carriage is in for repairs."

Miss Pelliston did not care if they rode donkeys, so long as they went *now*.

"Well," said Max, peering owlishly over his glass at the gentleman who'd just entered his study. "Well. There you are."

Mr. Langdon took in the owlish expression and the empty champagne bottle standing on the desk. "You're foxed," he said.

"I'm celebrating," the viscount announced, waving his glass airily. "Now we can celebrate together. I'm going to be married. Ring for Gidgeon, Jack. We want another bottle. 'Fraid I couldn't wait for you. Too impetuous, you know."

"No, I think I'd better not. You're going to have a devilish head by nightfall as it is, and I thought we were going to the theatre."

Lord Rand hauled himself out of his seat and yanked on the rope. A minute later Mr. Gidgeon appeared, bearing a fresh bottle of champagne. In response to orders, he uncorked it with all due solemnity, though he cast a worried glance at his master. He shot another worried look at Mr. Langdon before exiting.

Mr. Langdon had no choice but the accept the glass thrust in his face. "All right, then," he said. "Congratulations."

"Don't you want to know who the lucky bride is?"

"All London knows. Alvanley has lost a pony to Worcester on account of your haste. He gave you another week."

"No matter. Somebody will propose to somebody in another week. You, maybe, Jack. Why don't you offer for Cat?"

Mr. Langdon's posture stiffened. "I presume you mean Miss Pelliston."

"As you say—Miss Pestilence. I expect she's well? Preachy as ever?" The viscount stared dolourously at his glass. "I ain't seen her in seven days. Couldn't, you know. Had to sit in what's-her-name's pocket. Minerva. Athena. One of 'em. Diana," he said gloomily.

"Lady Diana Glencove," the friend reminded. "What on earth is the matter, Max?"

"Nothing. Couldn't be happier. She's just in my style. Tall, you know. I like to look a girl right in the eye. Small women give me a crick in the neck. And a headache," he added, tapping his chest, having apparently misplaced his skull.

Mr. Langdon liked accuracy. He pointed out that his friend's head was located several inches above his breastbone.

"Who cares?" Max scowled at the bottle for a moment before refilling his glass. "Is she?" he asked. "Is she preachy as ever?"

"Miss Pelliston is never preachy," was the reproachful reply.

"Not with you, I'll warrant. You never do everything wrong. You talk to her about books and never put her in a temper or tease her just to see her eyes flash and her chin go up and her face turn pink. And her hands." He stared at his own. "Small white hands all balled up into fists. It's completely ridiculous. Why, if she hit you, you'd think maybe a fly had landed on your face."

Jack's countenance grew very grave. "Max," he began. Then he stepped back, startled, as the door flew open and a hideous little goblin burst into the room.

=== 19 ===

UPON CLOSER EXAMINATION, the goblin turned out to be Jemmy, sporting a bloody nose, a cut lip, and what promised to become an organ of such magnificent colour that "black eye" could scarcely do it justice. At present that eye was swollen shut.

"What the devil happened to you?" Lord Rand asked the apparition. "Trampled by a horse, were you?"

Jemmy burst into rapid speech, or what would have been speech to Mr. Blackwood. As far as Mr. Langdon was concerned, the boy might as well be speaking Chinese.

Lord Rand's perceptions were at present not very quick. Even he needed several minutes to decipher any part of this oration.

"I see," he said finally, as he refilled his glass. "A thief taker grabbed you. You bit him. He hit you. You kicked him where it matters and escaped. You have had an interesting adventure. Now go and wash yourself."

Jemmy turned to Mr. Langdon. "Is he deaf? Din't I jest say as she went off to the beak's wif him in a hackney and him been hangin' 'round like that every Monday and Wednesday. I was goin' to tell her about it too today, only what happened—"

Here Lord Rand interrupted, mainly because the mention of "Monday and Wednesday" shot a beam of light into his clouded mind. Catherine went to the shop on those days to give Jemmy lessons. Therefore this hysterical speech had something to do with Catherine. Now that he'd identified "she," he demanded to know who "he" was.

Given that Lord Rand was a trifle foxed and Jemmy incoherent, it was some time before the viscount began to grasp the problem.

"Are you telling me Miss Pelliston has gone off in a hackney with Lord Browdie and they're headed for the magistrate's? Why?"

"Because she thought 'at trap took me there. Which he tried, like I said, only—"

"Only you got away. Well, when they get to the magistrate's, they'll discover their mistake, won't they?"

"If 'at's where he was goin'," Jemmy hinted darkly.

"Why do you suppose otherwise?" Mr. Langdon asked.

Jemmy gazed at him in exasperation. "Din't I jest tell you? He's been spyin' on her and askin' fings all week. Besides, 'at big one 'at grabbed me ain't no trap, neither. Almost as big as you are," he told Lord Rand, "only fatter and his nose all mashed in. I knows all on 'em and he ain't one."

"Are you sure? He might be a new officer who mistook you for another boy."

"Not him. He wouldn't be nowhere's near 'em traps and horneys."

This Lord Rand translated for Mr. Langdon as referring to thief takers and constables respectively.

"I seen him once at a gin shop when I went arter me mum. She wanted him to get her a job in 'at house he worked at, but he wouldn't on account he said she was too old and ugly an' 'd fright the customers."

Lord Rand abruptly became sober and asked if Jemmy was referring to a brothel.

"A bawdy house she wanted. 'At's wot she allus said in the winter, as how she wanted a nice warm house and not out in the streets."

"Good God!" Mr. Langdon exclaimed. "He speaks of a whorehouse as though it were the vicarage. How do these children survive?"

"The question at the moment may be Miss Pelliston's survival, Jack. Save your aristocratic dismay for later."

The viscount turned back to Jemmy. "Do you know the fellow's name? Was it Jos, perhaps? Or Cholly?"

"Cholly," was the prompt answer. "Jolly Cholly she called him. But I tole you about him. It's 'at other one got Miz Kaffy. 'At tall one wif orange hair."

Lord Rand stood up. "If that other one did not take her to the magistrate's, our friend Cholly may be the only one who knows where they did go."

He summoned Mr. Gidgeon and told the butler to send up a bucket of cold water to his chamber and have someone get them a couple of hackneys. Then the viscount strode from the room. Mr. Langdon and Jemmy followed.

Some minutes later, the two watched in amazement as Lord Rand, naked to the waist, bent over his washbasin and poured the cold water over his head. After towelling his head quickly and vigorously, he tore off the rest of his clothes. With Blackwood's assistance, he changed into the attire of his pre-heir days. This business was speedily accomplished, the viscount having no patience with idiotic questions from his audience. When he was ready, he turned to Jack.

"Now," he announced, "you're going to rescue her."

"I?" Jack asked, taken aback. "Well, of course I'll help."

"No, I'm helping. You're going to rescue the damsel in distress—which she'd better be, or we're going to look like a pair of bloody fools."

Mr. Blackwood was dispatched to investigate the two likeliest magistrate's offices—at Great Marlborough Street and at Bow Street. If Browdie and Miss Pelliston were at either of these places, the valet had only to inform them that Jemmy was safe, and to make sure the lady was brought home safely herself. Lord Rand and Mr. Langdon, meanwhile, would seek out Cholly.

Accordingly, Mr. Blackwood set off in one shabby hired coach and the two gentlemen, accompanied by Jemmy—who vociferously objected to being left behind—went off in the other.

The coach windows were so encrusted with soot and

grime that Catherine could scarcely make out the passing scene. Her sense of direction being as deplorable now as when she first arrived in London, looking did her precious little good anyhow. Still, she did know that the nearest magistrate was at Great Marlborough Street. She pointed out to Lord Browdie that the carriage seemed to be heading the wrong way.

"Oh, he won't be there. From what I heard, the crime happened in Bow Street territory, and you know how jealous those fellows are. Sounds like Townsend himself picked up the boy," Lord Browdie added, carelessly dropping the name of a famous Bow Street officer.

Catherine was duly impressed, having heard the name before. She did not know that Mr. John Townsend—whose clients included the Bank of England and the Prince Regent—would never trouble himself with such small potatoes as an eight-year-old boy accused of pilfering a pocket watch.

"Not to mention," the baron went on airily, "Conant's a friend of mine, and since he's the chief magistrate, we'll have all this set straight quick enough."

"Is that not the place?" Catherine asked a while later, as the coach turned onto Bow Street. "I'm sure Lord Andover pointed it out when he took me around town."

"Oh, that's the office all right. But they hold the prisoners a bit further on, at the Brown Bear."

"Good heavens—isn't that a public house?"

"It is. Didn't I tell you it wasn't a place for ladies?" Lord Browdie smiled contemptuously. "I expect you've changed your mind about your Christian duty?"

"You might have mentioned we were going to a public house. Obviously, I cannot enter such a place."

"No, of course not. Only brothels, eh, Cathy?"

Miss Pelliston drew herself up. "You will have the courtesy, I hope," she replied with cold dignity, "to refrain from raising that objectionable topic again. It does not become you as a gentleman to mention such matters in a lady's presence."

"Oh, don't get on your high ropes, gal. I was only teasing. And you ain't so missish as all that. Your papa talks plain enough in front of you."

Lord Browdie was highly pleased with himself. He thought he was the cleverest fellow in creation. How easily she'd come! He needn't have wasted so much time planning how to coax her. Not a word about needing her maid by, or demanding the dressmaker come along, or sending for her cousin. He was in such high spirits that he took no offence at her shrewish remarks. She could say what she liked now. She'd learn humility soon enough.

" 'Course I don't believe it, m' dear," he went on unctuously. "Fact is, I was a trifle foxed that day. Wanted to apologise, but you're devilish hard to get at lately. All them chaperones and maids, not to mention them beaux of yours. Heard Argoyne offered for you and Andover put him off. Holding out for Rand, were you? Well, it's an ill wind blows nobody good. Might as well be a duchess if you can."

Though this topic was even less agreeable than bawdy houses, Catherine contented herself with a disdainful sniff. She was immediately sorry. The interior of the coach smelled like something had died there days ago. She was not certain whether this fragrance emanated from the vehicle itself or from the gentleman sitting opposite, and was not eager to find out. All she wanted was to get out of this foul, jolting cage.

The hackney finally rattled to a stop. Lord Browdie alighted first and offered his hand to help her. She pretended not to notice and climbed down the steps unassisted. She began to draw a deep breath, then realised the air outside the coach was scarce fresher than that inside. She also noted that they were no longer in Bow Street, and with a vague stirring of alarm asked where they were.

"Just around the corner from the Brown Bear. Since I can't take you into the place with me, I figured you could wait here."

He gestured towards the entrance of a building whose soot-encrusted windows were crammed with a haphazard display of articles that included gentlemen's coats of the previous century, broken swords, rusty toiletries, crumpled bonnets, and other objects too moldering to be easily identified. Three balls hung over the door.

"This is a pawnshop," said Catherine unhappily.

"Well, it ain't a public house and it's the best there is in the neighbourhood," he lied. "Friend of a friend runs it. You'll be safe as houses. Soon as I can get the boy moved to the office, I'll come back and get you."

Miss Pelliston struggled for a moment between Scylla and Charybdis. The hackney had already departed. She could not accompany Lord Browdie to a public house, and certainly not the Brown Bear. She dimly recalled Lord Andover's remarks about the place being no better than a thieves' den, filled with law officers as corrupt as their prisoners.

She could not wait on the street, either. The unsavoury block brought back memories of Granny Grendle's and the foul alleys Lord Rand had carried her through on the way to his lodgings.

She gazed at the pawnshop door and swallowed. "I see there is no choice. I will have to make the best of it. But you do promise to hurry?"

"Of course I'll hurry. Now, now, you'll be fine," he went on in those falsely avuncular tones that made her skin crawl. "Mrs. Hodder has a quiet back room where you can sit and have a cup of tea while you wait. I know it don't look like much, but she's a good old gal. Wouldn't hurt a fly. You'd be surprised how many of the gentry come here— ladies too—like when they had a bad night at the faro tables and don't like to tell their husbands."

So saying, Lord Browdie yanked open a sticky door. Catherine reluctantly entered.

An enormously fat woman sat by a counter, knitting. She gave a curt nod as they entered. Lord Browdie spoke briefly with her in a low voice. She shrugged and made a vague gesture towards the rear of the shop.

The baron led Catherine in this direction and pushed

open another sticky door.

Miss Pelliston had had a trying day. She'd been coaxed into the role of bosom-bow by Lord Rand's fiancee, whose height, classical proportions, and serene, fair beauty had made Catherine feel like an ugly little dwarf. That fiancee had taken advantage of Catherine's good nature, engaging her as co-conspirator in a most improper situation. The goddess had compounded the error by dragging out the business for a full half hour, and Catherine had not even had the opportunity to deliver the lecture that lady so richly deserved.

Add to that the incompetence and corruption of a legal system that must persecute innocent boys, Madame's helpless hysteria in the face of this injustice, Lord Browdie's swaggering imbecility, and the provoking unavailability of the one man who could have quickly set matters right, and one had a young lady in a most unladylike state of temper.

From the time she'd entered the dressmaker's shop, Catherine's thinking—what there was of it—had been dictated by blind rage against a world that today utterly refused to behave itself. Being in such a state, it had not occurred to her to do anything but dash recklessly to Jemmy's rescue since no one else was capable of handling the matter intelligently.

As she entered the back room of the shop, Catherine's anger began to recede, and second thoughts crowded into its place. The room was a dark ugly one whose sole window was boarded up. The space contained two rickety chairs, one filthy mattress on an equally filthy floor, and nothing remotely resembling accoutrements for the tea Lord Browdie had promised.

It abruptly occurred to her to wonder how Lord Browdie proposed to have Jemmy removed from the Brown Bear when the baron was unable to identify the boy.

The door slammed shut and Catherine heard a key turn in a lock. A cold chill ran down the back of her neck as she turned to Lord Browdie. His avuncular smile had vanished, replaced by a sneer.

"Now, Miss Hoity-Toity," said he, "we're going to settle this business once and for all."

Mr. Langdon had not much to say for himself during the bumpy ride that seemed to taking them into the very heart of London's underworld. He knew a good deal about it, having read many works on the subject—among others, the anonymously published *Letters from England*, Mr. Patrick Colquhoun's *Treatise on the Police of the Metropolis*, and the recently published report of the Parliamentary Select Committee that had enquired into the state of London's Watch. He knew, therefore, that London's criminal classes and their habitations flourished much as they had in Sir Henry Fielding's time.

Mr. Langdon had never explored this world firsthand, however, and he was appalled. Around him he saw filth and wretchedness of every description, the population resembling rodents as they darted nervously into alleys and doorways or else stared with undisguised hostility at the vehicle that dared venture into their noisome haven. No wonder Max had not wanted to take his own carriage.

Mr. Langdon was equally shocked by the confident familiarity with which his friend directed the increasingly reluctant coachman. Occasionally Max halted the vehicle, alit, and disappeared into a noxious hole of a gin shop or a black alley that looked like the entrance to hell. Rarely did he stop more than a few minutes—though to Jack every second dragged by like centuries—before emerging with new directions for the driver.

Jack had a pistol, courtesy of the viscount, and was determined to use it if necessary. He would have preferred that he knew how to use it, and cursed himself for wasting his life away in books and never acquiring a productive skill. What earthly good was a bookworm to a young lady in danger?

Now, as the coach halted before a decrepit tavern, Mr. Langdon decided that if he was to be of any use at all, he must be confident. He'd been visiting the boxing saloon religiously for a fortnight and, according to his instructor, was making rapid progress. He told himself he was not completely helpless.

Reassured, he contemplated the damsel in distress. Miss Pelliston was so agreeable. She always had intelligent comments or questions for him, never seemed bored or impatient. In fact, she was the only woman he'd ever met who understood him at all. He was not sure if he understood her—he sensed there was more to her than one saw on social occasions. That "more" occasionally made him uneasy. It was rather like the faint rumblings of a storm many miles away.

All the same, to be understood by a woman was a rarity. He doubted he'd ever find another with whom he felt so comfortable. Their acquaintance was developing into genuine friendship, and what better match than one between friends? A marriage begun in friendship could ripen into deep affection . . . even love.

Naturally he was willing to do or risk whatever he must to rescue her. He was not sure the very proper Miss Pelliston would, as Max had claimed, throw herself into his arms with admiration and gratitude and be swept completely off her feet. If that did happen, though, Jack must offer for her immediately. He who hesitates is lost, as his friend had repeatedly reminded him.

The trouble was, he rather suspected . . . but that was absurd. Max was engaged to Lady Diana Glencove. Those comments about Miss Pelliston and the bitterness Jack had heard must be blamed on the champagne. Max was having typical second thoughts about being leg-shackled and the champagne had made him maudlin. Whatever was troubling Max was Max's problem. One had better concentrate on acting heroic.

Mr. Langdon stopped raking his hair and squared his shoulders instead. He met Jemmy's puzzled gaze and flushed.

The coach door opened and Max climbed inside. "He just went into that coffee shop a couple of doors along."

"Are we going in after him?" Jack asked, fumbling for the pistol.

"Of course not. The place is jammed to the rafters. We can't take on the whole murdering crowd at once. We've got to get him out. There's an alley next to the building. I should like to speak with him there, I think." Max smiled thinly at Jemmy.

"Want me to get him out?" the boy asked eagerly. "I ken do it."

"Good God, no!" Jack cried.

Max ignored his friend. "You'd better do it," he told Jemmy, "or we'll have to wait until he comes out on his own and that could be hours. He went in with a female companion—Bellowser Bess, I think the name is."

"I knows her," said Jemmy. "Her old man got lagged."

"Transported," Max translated for his friend. "Thus the nickname—'bellowser' is cant for transportation for life. Add that to your etymologies." He turned back to Jemmy. "Can you do it, then, and not get your head broken? Because as it is Miss Pestilence is going to ring a peal over me about that black eye."

Jemmy threw the viscount an indignant glare. "A baby could do it," he retorted, "in a minute."

In a fraction of that time he was out of the coach. The two men followed. The boy waited until they had turned into the alley before he disappeared into the coffee shop.

True to his word, Jemmy was out again in less than a minute, with Cholly in hot pursuit. Jemmy dashed into the alley. Cholly followed, but as he rounded the corner, he stumbled over a boot. A hand grabbed his shoulder, righting him roughly, and an instant later a fist that closely resembled a millstone drove itself into his face. Reeling from the blow, Granny's employee fell back against the side of the building.

Lord Rand grabbed him by the throat and banged his head against the wall a few times, perhaps to clear Cholly's mind.

"Good Lord, Max," Mr. Langdon gasped. "He won't be

206

any good to us dead."

"He ain't any good to anybody alive that I can see," Max answered. "Are you, Cholly? No good to anyone."

Cholly's response was unintelligible.

"Get over here, Jack," came the curt order. "Just rest the muzzle of your pistol against his ear."

Mr. Langdon obeyed. He was amazed to discover that his hand did not shake.

"Now, my lad," Max said to Cholly, releasing his grip just enough to allow the man to speak, "maybe you'll tell us exactly what possessed you to kidnap this lad of tender years. Maybe you'll tell us who paid you to do it and why and what else you've been doing lately that you shouldn't. And you'd better say it fast and not think of calling for help because I'd as soon dash your brains out and my friend would like to shoot 'em out and maybe we'll both get our wish if you make us impatient."

=== 20 ===

CATHERINE STARED COLDLY at her captor. She hoped her heart was not pounding as loudly as she thought it was.

"It is obvious what has happened," she told him. "This is what comes of incessant gluttony and drunkenness. Your dissolute habits have led to mental decay. Don't expect any pity from me. You have brought it all upon yourself."

Lord Browdie was beginning to believe he *would* go mad if he spent another minute with this termagant. He had thought that the bare room and impossibility of escape would awaken her to a sense of her peril, that within five minutes at most the witch would be terrified into submission—but no.

For more than half an hour Catherine Pelliston had stoutly denied ever having been in the brothel. She had plenty else to say besides, enough to make his head throb. If it had not been for those rich acres and the dowry and a gnawing hunger for revenge on Lord Rand, the baron might have been more sensible and beaten a tactical retreat.

He was not sensible. A fortnight of watching, waiting, and plotting had in fact made Lord Browdie a trifle mad.

He was moody by nature, vengeful when thwarted in any whim. Catherine had thwarted him repeatedly since the day she'd run away and he blamed every unpleasantness that followed, from the humiliating rebuffs of other marriageable females to the tradesmen's bills Lynnette mounted up, on her. Besides, Catherine had played him for a fool—was even now doing so, the lying slut.

"Going to keep it up, are you?" he growled. "Going to keep pretending it wasn't you? Don't think I've got witnesses? Well, I do, and you ain't changed all that much they won't know you close up. Lynnette seen you and Granny and Cholly and Jos."

Catherine stared coldly past him at the wall, which enraged him further.

"You remember Cholly, don't you? Big, handsome fellow. He told me you was pretty entertaining between the covers, for a beginner and one mostly asleep."

The colour drained from Catherine's face and her knees buckled. She had been standing behind one of the chairs. Rather inelegantly she sat down in it.

"Oh, that jogged your memory, I guess. Surprised? Don't see why you should be. That's what they always do with the new ones—give 'em to Cholly or Jos first—so when the gal wakes up, it's too late to be crying about her honour."

The possibility that she'd been deflowered while unconscious had never occurred to Catherine, and the thought was devastating. Still, that could be lies. Lord Browdie did look half-demented. No wonder, she thought sourly. He hadn't had a drink in over an hour at least.

Whatever happened, she must not give him the upper hand. She had betrayed herself for a moment, which was dangerous. Summoning up twenty-one years of rigid training, she stiffened her spine and retorted icily, "You are not only mad, but a swine. I have nothing further to say to you."

He would like to beat her until she screamed for mercy, but he knew from painful experience that women didn't fight fair. They kicked and clawed and yanked your hair and bit, behaving generally in the most unsporting way. Also, Catherine may have inherited her father's temper, and that was an ugly thing unleashed. He'd rather save beating as a last resort. Besides, his throat was parched with all this palavering.

"The trouble with you, my girl, is you ain't thinking straight. I'm going to get us something to drink, so we can sit and be cosy until you get sensible. Just remember that

209

if you're gone too long—like 'til tomorrow morning, maybe—you'll have a lot of explaining to do."

He moved to the door. "Oh, by the way—your hostess is deaf as a post when she's paid to be and screams ain't nothing special around here. I won't be but a minute, but no one'll pay you any mind, m' dear, so make all the noise you like."

True to his promise, he returned in a very few minutes with two bottles of wine and two greasy mugs. When Catherine disdainfully declined the cup offered her, he flung himself into the other chair and attended to quenching his own thirst. A bottle and a half later, he grew imperiously confident. She was only a slip of a girl, after all, easily overpowered if it came to that. Not a bit like the buxom milkmaid he'd tried to rape a few years back.

He pointed to the mattress and jovially informed her that while she was thinking things over she might as well show him what Cholly and Rand found so entertaining. Catherine suppressed a shudder and resolutely refused to understand him.

Lord Browdie rose unsteadily from his chair and staggered towards her. He was breathing hard and she felt a surge of nausea as the wine-laden fumes rose to her nostrils. Then she saw a hairy hand reaching for her bodice. Shuddering, she knocked it away, and hastily made herself stand to face him.

Her limbs weak with fear, she clutched the chair back for support, but the chair overbalanced and she stumbled with it. As she was righting herself, he grabbed her hair, making her cry out with pain. Fear blazed into rage. How dare he touch her!

Furious, she dug her nails into his hand. He jerked away with an angry yelp.

"You little hellcat!" he screeched. Then he lunged at her.

There was no time to think and nowhere to run. Catherine grabbed the chair and swung it at him. He tried to dodge her, but wasn't fast enough. The chair caught him on the hip before it finally broke against the wall. Lord

Browdie stumbled backwards, cursing. More cautious now, he stood a moment, eyeing her with hatred as he gasped for breath.

"That ain't smart, Cathy," he warned, his voice hoarse. "No use fighting me. It'll end the same whether you do or don't, only you'll make me mad and that'll be the worse for you."

Yes, the end would be the same, she knew. There was no way out of this filthy room, and he meant to rape her. She could not dwell on that, because the thought sickened and weakened her. She focused on him. How long could she fight him? He was bigger, stronger, but she was younger. Who would tire first? The longer she held out, the greater chance that her family—someone—would realise something was amiss and try to find her. But how? When? How long?

Then she saw his body tense. Catherine darted towards the pile of broken wood. Just as he threw himself at her, she snatched up a chair leg and swung it at him. He dodged, then lunged again. She quickly sidestepped him and swung her weapon once more, lower this time, aiming for his knees. Had she aimed higher or lower she'd have only struck padding and done little damage, but she aimed true.

She heard a crack as wood struck bone. Pain shot through her wrists from the force of the blow, making her eyes fill with tears, but she didn't dare let go of the chair leg. In a wet blur she watched Lord Browdie topple to the floor while his howled curses pierced the air.

There was another, more resounding crack. The heavy door shook and shuddered an instant before swinging into the room and crashing against the wall. Lord Rand came crashing in after it, Jack and Jemmy at his heels.

Catherine still held the chair leg. She swung it again reflexively, too blinded with pain and rage to know what she was aiming at. Lord Rand caught her wrists midswing.

"That's enough, Cat," he said. "You can't kill everybody, just because you're a trifle out of sorts."

She stared blankly at him for a moment. Then the chair

leg dropped from her suddenly nerveless hands and she threw herself against his hard chest.

"Oh, Max," she cried. "I thought you'd never come."

Lord Rand must have forgotten who was supposed to be the hero in this scene, because he never looked at Mr. Langdon. He never looked at anybody. His arms closed around Miss Pelliston in a crushing embrace, and he buried his face in her hair.

"Oh, Cat," he murmured. "My poor, dear, brave girl." His hands stroked her back, then the back of her neck, while she sobbed against his chest. "It's all right now, sweetheart," he comforted softly. "It's all right, my gallant darling."

He uttered more tender praise and endearments, and even some gentle teasing, as he told her she might have left him something to do besides clean up the mess she'd made. Fortunately, most of this was unintelligible to all but the young lady. That she understood was evident, because the sobbing gradually eased, though her face remained buried in the viscount's coat.

Mr. Langdon politely looked away . . . and caught Lord Browdie attempting to crawl out the door. Jack drew out his pistol and pointed it at the baron's head. Lord Browdie froze.

Jemmy, for once in his life, was mute. Less courteous than Mr. Langdon, he watched the embracing couple with every evidence of satisfaction. He had not been able to contribute much to the rescue beyond tripping up Mr. Langdon when the viscount kicked in the door. Even though Lord Rand had not looked like he meant to wait for his friend, the boy must have recalled Mr. Blackwood's advice regarding the gentry's need for firm guidance.

Catherine, trembling in Max's arms, had evidently forgotten that the man holding her so possessively belonged to someone else because she remained there quite contentedly even after her tears had ceased. When she did finally remember, there was a brief struggle—the viscount's memory proving more sluggish—before she managed to break free.

Lord Rand gazed blankly at her for a moment while his handsome face coloured. Then he cleared his throat and turned to Lord Browdie, who was cowering by the door, alternately moaning and muttering imprecations.

"We seem to have a problem of protocol here," said the viscount, "and of course I want to do the proper thing. What would that be, I wonder? Do I beat you to a bloody pulp? Shall I give Jack leave to pull the trigger? Or, since you've lost your way to Bow Street, shall we simply take you there and let the magistrate sort out etiquette? Let me see—kidnapping, violent assault, and attempted rape of a gentlewoman. I wonder if they'll hang you, send you to the Hulks, or simply transport you for life."

"Assault?" Browdie screamed indignantly. "I never touched her. I'll have her up on assault, the murdering jade! And tell some things about her. I've got witnesses too."

"The man is unhinged," said Mr. Langdon. "We'd better bring him to a lunatic asylum instead. He wants treatment."

"Do I? Then fetch a doctor. We'll see how crazy I am. Maybe that doctor'll want to have a look at you as well, eh Missy?" He shot Catherine a murderous look.

Catherine glared right back. "You are a filthy, lying swine," she snapped. "I wish I had dashed out your brains."

Mr. Langdon's jaw dropped, though he did not take his eyes off his captive. Perhaps it occurred to him that the storm had finally moved in to burst about his ears.

"Harlot!" shouted Browdie. "Slut!"

Mr. Langdon hustled Catherine and Jemmy out into the shop. "This is no spectacle for a lady," he said. Then, his own face reddening, he returned to the back room.

Lord Browdie's compliments had abruptly ceased meanwhile, because in one graceful movement Lord Rand had yanked him up by his coat lapels and knocked his head against the wall.

"You'll keep a civil tongue in your head, Browdie, if you know what's good for you."

When he saw that his interlocutor was more disposed to listen, the viscount added, "There's nothing I'd like better than to kill you. But that just might get me hanged, and you aren't worth swinging for, are you?"

Another crack of skull against plaster was deemed a necessary aid to decision-making. This must have helped, because Lord Browdie shook his head.

"I'm so happy we agree," said Lord Rand amiably. "Since you're disposed to be reasonable, let me offer you two courses. The first is that you get on the very next ship leaving England. I can recommend North America from personal experience, but you can go where you like, so long as you never come back—except perhaps in a casket."

"I ain't going nowhere," the baron growled.

"The alternative," the viscount continued, unheeding, "is that I take you to Bow Street and bring the charges I mentioned. You may say what you wish in your behalf—but do rest assured, dear fellow, that if you're indiscreet and a softhearted magistrate releases you, I'll find you, wherever you hide, and break every bone in your filthy body. Oh, I should mention there's a fellow named Cholly who'll be looking for you as well. He's disappointed about something—I think it's a broken jaw. Coarse fellow, that Cholly. Doesn't care a bit for gentlemanly codes of honour. Has a way with a broken bottle, I understand."

Being bested in physical combat by a mere slip of a girl cannot be agreeable to a man's *amour propre*. Instigated by a combination of too much wine drunk too fast and humiliated rage, the baron had been incautiously belligerent. Lord Rand's suggestions, along with the occasional physical reminder, had restored Lord Browdie's reasoning powers. Being a coward, he would have run very far away on his own, if Mr. Langdon had not prevented him.

The baron elected exile, though he did so most ungraciously.

"That's settled, then," said the viscount. He abruptly released his hold on the man, who crumpled to the floor.

"Jack, you'd better take Cat—Miss Pelliston—home to Louisa. I want to take our friend to an acquaintance of mine who'll make sure he keeps his promise."

"Why don't you let me go with him?" Jack offered. "It seems there's something . . . well, maybe you and Miss Pelliston need to talk—"

Lord Rand's face hardened. "No. Take her and the boy back and tell Louisa I'll explain everything later. On no account is she to trouble Catherine. Is that clear? Just tell her to put the girl to bed."

En route to Andover House, Jemmy was deposited at the dressmaker's with adjurations not to reveal unpleasant details to Madame. The lad having a discretion beyond his years, all the *modiste* ever learned was that he had been mistaken for another, but had managed to escape. She believed that Lord Browdie and Catherine had simply been delayed at the magistrate's office by the usual bureaucratic incompetence.

Lord and Lady Andover were told only to wait for Max, who would explain everything. Fortunately, these two had not had time to become unduly alarmed. Catherine customarily lingered two hours or more at the dressmaker's, and their carriage had returned without her scarcely half an hour ago. If they were alarmed now, they were too tactful to show it. They assured Mr. Langdon they would do as he asked. They would wait up for Max, however late he returned.

Spared an interrogation, Catherine escaped to her room. She found a hot bath waiting for her, but there was no ease in it, except perhaps for her aching muscles. Even though she was safe, she could not stop trembling. She would never feel safe or right again, would never feel clean again.

Why had she gone with that horrible man? How could she have been so foolhardy? Though Jack had promised that Lord Browdie would never trouble her again, Catherine knew he would. All the rest of her days Lord Browdie would haunt her because he'd told her about Cholly, told her she was soiled, polluted, foul.

She could never marry. She would never know the quiet

215

joy of being cared for, of having children to care for. Still, since it would never be Lord Rand caring for her or his children she might love, it was just as well there would be no one.

She'd convinced herself that she could be happy with Jack, or at least content. Now she realised how selfish that was and how unfair to Jack. She'd seen that when she'd drawn away from Max and caught a glimpse of his friend's face, so shocked and—oh, she hoped he wasn't hurt. Jack was so kind and gentle. It wasn't fair that he should be hurt because she was a fool.

Catherine crawled under the bedclothes and buried her face in the pillow, but the tears she expected wouldn't come. Her throat raw, she lay curled up in a tight ball, unable to weep.

"My brave girl," Max had called her—that and so many other tender words—as his strong arms sheltered her. He had been her shelter from the start, hadn't he? She had trusted him instinctively, from the moment she'd first asked his help. She'd continued to trust him, though she hadn't realised it because she'd been too busy finding fault with him.

How could she have believed he was her bad angel, when all he ever drew from her was honesty—the truth of her feelings. In response, she'd insulted him repeatedly. Instead of appreciating Lord Rand's kind, noble heart, she'd fixed instead on trivial misbehaviours, exaggerating them into major character flaws.

How on earth could she have believed he was just like Papa? When had Papa ever been kind or gentle? When had Papa ever tried to comfort or help her or even tease her out of her overnice notions of propriety? When had anyone in her whole life ever made her feel so interesting and feminine and special?

With his teasing and prodding, Viscount Vagabond had uncovered the real Catherine: the short-tempered, passionate, willful, occasionally improper young woman under the stiff schoolmistress's pose. Along the way, he'd revealed himself as well, only she had been too stubbornly blind to see who the real Max was and how much she loved him. Oh, she did love him dearly, passionately, and would always love him . . . hopelessly.

Utterly hopeless. She gasped as despair flooded her heart. The dam gave at last, and she broke into wracking sobs that shook her frame until she wept herself empty. Finally, exhausted, she fell asleep.

Max did not arrive until after midnight. Lord Andover had had an urgent summons from Lord Liverpool meanwhile, and was not yet returned. Thus Max had only his sister to tell his tale to, and because she was his sister, he found himself telling her everything.

She bore the news about the brothel with not a hint of swooning. Rather, she spoke with admiration of Catherine's courage. "That is one of the things I like so much about her, Max. She is a perfect lady, yet amazingly capable and fearless. Not nearly as fragile as she looks. From the first moment I saw you with her, I rather hoped—"

"I know you're breeding, Louisa, but even in that condition, sentiment doesn't become you," he interrupted hastily. "Anyhow, whatever you hoped, the fact is, I offered twice for her and was rejected in no uncertain terms."

Louisa sighed. "I can think of a dozen reasons for her to refuse when she would rather accept, but you are determined to be thickheaded."

"I'm engaged to be married, Louisa," was the quiet answer. "To Lady Diana Glencove, remember? Maybe you also remember that a gentleman can't jilt a lady. I might as well be thickheaded, don't you think?"

=== 21 ===

FOR A MAN whose head is not only thick, but hard, two glasses of brandy cannot be sufficient to induce unconsciousnes if he is otherwise inclined. Lord Rand was not so inclined. He did not fall asleep until well after daybreak. Thus he slept soundly until midafternoon, when he was awakened by a pair of rabbits hopping on his chest.

He opened one eye to discover not rabbits, but two small grubby fists. He opened the other eye and discerned that the fists were attached to a pair of short arms, in turn attached to the personage known as Jemmy.

"Get away from me," his lordship grumbled. "What the devil are you about? Curse me if the boy has any manners at all, and respect for his betters is out of the question."

"Get up, will you? Wot are you waiting for?"

"Judgement Day. What in blazes do you want?"

Blackwood appeared at the bedside, having entered the room in his usual noiseless fashion. He pulled Jemmy away and apologised for the lad's outlandish behaviour. Unfortunately, the boy had dashed up the stairs so quickly that Mr. Blackwood had been unable to catch him in time.

"There is rather odd news, My Lord," he explained.

"She's bolted," Jemmy cried, thrusting himself in front of the valet. "Run off wif a sojer."

Lord Rand jerked himself upright. "What? Cat? When? What soldier? Drat her, why don't that woman stay put?"

He threw back the bedclothes, thereby presenting Jemmy with the interesting spectacle of a naked aristocrat. Duly impressed, Jemmy backed away as the viscount scrambled out of bed and ripped the dressing gown out of his servant's hands.

"I beg your pardon, My Lord. The young lady in question is Lady Diana Glencove."

Lord Rand, who had hastily wrapped the dressing gown around himself, was about to tear it off again, having evidently decided on dressing immediately and eliminating the middleman. He now sat back down upon the bed.

"Lady Diana?" he echoed blankly.

"Your fiancee, My Lord," Blackwood clarified. "I'm afraid the news is all over Town because Lord Glencove's servants have been everywhere looking for her since yesterday afternoon. I heard from his lordship's footman that the family received a message from the young lady this morning. She was married by special license last night, as I understand. Her message said nothing regarding her subsequent itinerary. One imagines that was in order to elude pursuit."

"Well," said Lord Rand.

"Indeed, My Lord, most shocking. Lord Glencove sent the footman round with a message asking you to call upon him at your earliest convenience. I believed it proper that his lordship should break the news to you, but unfortunately, Jemmy has anticipated that."

"Yes," said Lord Rand with a dazed look at Jemmy.

"I heard it at the shop first," the boy said defensively. "They come by asking for her yesterday and today again and today when they come they tole HER and SHE tole Joan and she tole me so I come to tell you."

"I see," said the viscount, still looking blank. "I had better get dressed."

Lord Rand's interview with Lord and Lady Glencove was not the most agreeable of his life. Lady Glencove was beside herself with grief. She raved about annulments and having the fiend horsewhipped, hung, drawn and quartered. Occasionally she remembered to feel sorry for the betrayed fiance and that was even worse.

Lord Glencove, fortunately, was of a more philosophical temperament. He had, not an hour since, received encouraging news about his daughter's new husband. Though the man's immediate family was relatively obscure, the late father had been a man of property, which compensated somewhat for the maternal connection with commerce. The son—Colonel Stockmore—had a respectable income. He also had prospects: that is, he had a very ill, very old eccentric bachelor cousin who happened to be a viscount. From this cousin Colonel Stockmore would inherit a title. A prospective viscount was not a prospective Earl of St. Denys, but a man cannot have everything. Or a woman, either, as Lord Glencove was forced to remind his wife at tediously frequent intervals.

Lord Rand was also philosophical. He bore his disappointment with a most becoming manliness, which provoked Lady Glencove to another plaintive outburst after he was gone.

From the home of the Earl of Glencove, the viscount proceeded to Lord Browdie's love nest. There he purchased a peach muslin gown for five hundred pounds. Being philosophical enough for any two aristocrats, Lynnette bore her own assorted disappointments like the Stoic she was.

Molly related the news of Lady Diana's elopement before Catherine had even opened her eyes, and accompanied the dressing process with recitals about the mysterious ways of Providence, and human beings refusing to understand what was good for them, and the course of true love being a rocky one. The maid concluded with fervent thanks that she herself was content to love from afar, because getting close made folks act so foolish.

Fortunately, Lady Andover had very little to add at breakfast or thereafter.

"I suppose Molly has told you," she said, "with more detail, I am sure, than I could. It is astonishing. I had always thought Diana completely under her mother's thumb. I am relieved she is not. Their temperaments were badly unsuited. She would have bored Max to distraction and he would have taken up a life of crime in consequence."

Catherine mumbled something about being amazed. That was the end of the subject.

Chastened by the revelations of the previous night, Miss Pelliston elected to spend the afternoon in the library reading Foxe's *Actes and Monuments of These Latter Perilous Days*. Her mind, however, refused to concentrate on the Protestant martyrs of the sixteenth century.

One did not require above-average intelligence to ascertain that Lady Diana's rendezvous with her forbidden love had been devoted primarily to plans for immediate elopement. As participant, however unwitting, Catherine should at least be displeased with herself for not sensing what was afoot and striving to set Lady Diana back upon the course of duty.

Miss Pelliston could not be displeased or even surprised, considering the startling insights she'd had regarding her powers of perception. She could hardly expect to read another lady's mind when her own was such a miserable muddle.

Besides, she defiantly admitted to herself that she was pleased with the news. Even though it changed nothing for her—Lord Rand was still forever beyond her reach—he at least would have a second chance. Perhaps this time he would find a woman who truly loved him. That could not be difficult. Only fools like herself were blind to his perfections.

All she could pray for was an opportunity to apologise for more than a month of ungrateful, childish behaviour. For more than that she could not hope. She was beyond the pale.

This morning, after a long struggle with her conscience, Catherine had decided no useful purpose would be served by confessing her shame. To tell her cousin or Louisa about Cholly would only distress them needlessly. She would plead exhaustion and tell them she wished to go home.

After that, the years seemed to stretch out interminably.

Perhaps she would sell Aunt Eustacia's property, invest the money, and live quietly, humbly, alone. She would devote herself to good works among those even more wretched than herself. She would work among the poor. Perhaps she would contract some loathsome disease that would put a period to her vile existence.

Thus she reduced herself to a deeply penitential, utterly tragic state with no assistance from *The Book of Martyrs*. The volume proving useless, she very sensibly closed it and commenced to dolefully studying the carpet.

There was a tap at the door. She looked up to meet Jeffers's dignified gaze.

"Lady Andover's compliments, Miss, and would you please be so kind as to join her in—"

"Oh, do be quiet," Lord Rand snapped, pushing past the butler. "I ain't sitting in some damned parlor waiting for tea and making small talk with my own sister. Go away, Jeffers."

Jeffers sighed and went.

Lord Rand strode towards her. Under his arm he had a package which he now dropped at Catherine's feet.

"There's your dress," he said. "It cost me five hundred pounds. Then there's the fifty from a month ago. Altogether I've paid five hundred fifty quid for you."

Catherine's heart immediately commenced a steady *chamade*. She stared blindly at the package. Then she slowly dragged her gaze up to the viscount's face. His eyes were the blue of a frosty moonlit night, chilling her. He hated her. She deserved to be hated, she told herself. Even so, temper began to rise within her. He needn't be so callous . . . and mean.

"I can do sums," she said rather unsteadily. "I shall write to Papa for five hundred fifty pounds. Or do you require interest as well?"

"You will write to your papa, young lady, to tell him we're going to be married."

Inelegantly, she gulped. "I beg your pardon?" she said stupidly. She would like to say—and do—a thousand

222

things, and could not think where to begin.

"You're not deaf, Cat, so don't pretend to be. We're going to be married, as we should have done at the start."

The viscount looked hastily away from her face and began pacing the room.

"I don't know who had the training of you," he continued determinedly, "but your morals are shocking. You spent a night in my bed, remember, after a night in a bawdy house. You go about collecting street urchins and letting inebriated vagabonds kiss you, and then you get into brawls in pawnshops. You are probably past all redemption, but I'm going to reform you anyhow. If you behave yourself, perhaps I'll let you reform me on occasion, but I make no promises."

"Oh, Max."

He did not seem to hear the pitiful sound, because he went on heatedly, "There's no point telling me everything that's wrong with me, because I know all that by heart. I'm a bully and a ruffian and a drunkard and a gambler and I act before I think, always. I'm also short-tempered—and yes, mad, bad, and dangerous. Just as you are—which is why we suit so admirably."

"Oh, Max," she said once more, as a tear trickled down her nose.

He stopped pacing to glance at her. "There's no use crying," he said, his voice less assured now. "You can't manipulate me with tears. I've made up my mind. . . . " His voice trailed off. "Drat," he muttered.

He stood uncertain for a moment, clenching his fists. Then he sighed, moved closer, and knelt before her. "Come, sweetheart, is it so bad? Don't you like me even a little?"

"Oh, Max," she cried. "I love you madly."

In the moment it took him to digest this stupendous news, Lord Rand's face lighted up. It turned, in fact, slightly red about the cheekbones.

"Do you, darling?" he asked tenderly, taking her hand. "Do you really? But of course you do—you must—as I love you."

She stopped him with a small, sad gesture. "Still, I can't marry you." Before he could argue, she plunged on, desperate to put this agonising scene to a speedy end. "I can't marry you—I can't marry anyone—because I'm—oh, Max, I'm ruined, truly ruined."

Lord Rand patiently told her that she was hysterical. Citing her shocking travail of the previous day, he generously excused her, in between telling her not to be silly.

Catherine knew she was not being silly—not, at least, about this. She found her handkerchief, wiped her eyes and nose, and confided as calmly as she could what Lord Browdie had told her about Cholly.

When she'd come to a shuddering end, Lord Rand drew her up from her chair and into his arms. "I'm sorry, sweetheart," he said softly against her curls. "That was a terrible thing for him to tell you, but it's past and done. We're going to be married. Forget Cholly and think about us—about our happiness."

She pulled away slightly to examine his face. "Didn't you hear me, Max? I just told you I'm not—not pure."

"I'm not exactly Sir Galahad myself, sweet."

"That's different. Men are expected—oh, Max, you can't marry me. A gentleman expects his bride to come to him untouched," she patiently reminded, while her heart fluttered madly between hope and despair.

"I'm not like other gentlemen, as you well know." He brought her near again and let his fingers play among the light brown curls. "Nor are you like other ladies. You're Cat, the lady I found in a brothel, the lady who scolds me endlessly, the lady I love madly. Put Cholly out of your mind." He lightly kissed her nose.

"Come, sweetheart," he added when she did not respond. "It can't be so hard. Browdie could have been lying—and if he wasn't, you weren't even conscious at the time. Besides, didn't I break Cholly's nose that night? And yesterday I broke his jaw, I think. If you like, I'll break everything else, but I do think the poor fellow's paid dearly already."

This was reasonable enough, though it was his peculiar sort of reason. Catherine let her anxieties evaporate in the warmth of his love.

"I suppose," she murmured to his lapel, "if I don't believe you, you'll dash my head against the wall until I do."

"I might," he answered. "I'm very stubborn and ill-behaved."

"Yes. No wonder I love you so."

There was only one possible conclusion to this sort of intellectual exchange. Lord Rand tightened his clasp and kissed his darling thoroughly and repeatedly until they were both in a highly agitated state, not at all conducive to abstract reasoning.

Fortunately, Lady Andover put her head in the door at this perilous moment.

"That will be sufficient for the nonce, Max," she said composedly. "You are wrinkling Catherine's dress and Molly will be in fits. Now come out and talk to Edgar like a gentleman."

Not all the viscount's ranting, raving, and threats of violence could hasten the wedding day. Six unbearably slow weeks crept by because Lady Andover insisted that any earlier date would be unseemly as well as inconvenient. This would be the wedding of the year.

If Society was duly impressed with the result, Catherine and Max were not. They were oblivious to all that went on about them. Except for the moment when they were pronounced husband and wife, all that stood out for Max among the blur of chaotic activity was meeting Catherine's formidable papa.

From all he'd heard and all he'd guessed, Lord Rand was expecting Attila the Hun. During the wedding breakfast, the viscount found his eyes drawn repeatedly to a pear-shaped man of middling height who hovered about his baroness like a sycophantic courtier.

Since Lord and Lady Rand would not commence their

bridal trip until the following day, they spent their first night as a married couple in his townhouse amid a staff of deliriously happy servants. What the house needed, they'd all agreed long since, was a mistress. The master was universally adored, but he needed a deal of looking after. According to young Jemmy and the all-knowing Blackwood, Miss Pelliston was the only woman capable of managing this fearsome task. His lordship, Mr. Blackwood pointed out, was a handful, but his new wife was more than a match for him, despite her modest physical stature. Even Mr. Hill agreed dolefully that his master might have done worse.

That evening, therefore, Lord Rand and his bride supped quietly at home, surrounded by a beaming staff and a smug Jemmy, who insisted upon waiting at table with the other footmen.

After dessert was served and the room emptied of fawning menials, Lord Rand remembered the papa and teased his bride with charges of calculated overstatement.

"He was meek as a vicar, Cat. I'm sure he never had more than two glasses of champagne the whole time, and he sipped them like a deb at her first party."

"I know," she answered distractedly, her mind on other matters. "I scarcely recognised him myself. My stepmama appears to be an extraordinary woman."

"Must be. Between her and my own Old Man, they've convinced your papa to take his seat in Parliament."

"I can only hope the country will not suffer for it. Still, she has a way about her. She has only to raise an eyebrow at him and he's subdued. I saw how she looked at him when he came up to greet us. He took my hand in the most courtly way and said I was a good girl and made him proud, and kissed me." She touched her cheek. "He has never done that before. I nearly fainted from shock."

Lord Rand casually mentioned that if such a trivial matter shocked her, he must be sure to bring burnt feathers and sal volatile to their bedchamber tonight. He glanced at her untouched dessert and wondered aloud if she was quite finished.

She had no time to answer. Jemmy instantly darted in and snatched up her dish. Likewise he removed the viscount's plate, and with a knowing wink, took himself away.

Mr. Langdon had been awarded the signal honour of standing up for the friend of his college days. Rather like a consolation prize, he thought, as he settled himself into an armchair and opened his book. If the experience had not been altogether consoling, neither had it been a bitter punishment. One could not, should not feel bitter. Not when one saw the clear, bright face of love shining so happily upon its object. He had seen this when his two friends gazed at each other, and somehow that had heartened him.

Besides, as the Bard had said, "Men have died from time to time and worms have eaten them, but not for love." Jack would not die, would not even sicken. Though the blow had staggered him it had not crushed him. He had actually gained a great deal from the experience. The trouble was, among the bits of wisdom he'd acquired was one new sensation: for the first time in his quiet, dreamy life he was lonely.

He closed his book and departed from his club unremarked by the increasingly boisterous crowd gathering as the evening wore on. He stopped briefly at his home, where he collected a few belongings and ordered his horse. As the watchman announced to interested listeners that the sky was clear and the time was eleven o'clock, Mr. Langdon rode off into the night.

Lord Rand drew his bride close to him. "Are you all right, Cat?"

She didn't answer for a moment, being preoccupied, perhaps, with locating a comfortable spot near his shoulder where she could nestle her head.

"Cat?"

"Oh, yes. I'm . . . well, that was rather . . . "

"Shocking?"

227

She sighed. "I'm afraid not. I ought to have been shocked, but . . . how gentle you are, Max. I shall have to leave off calling you a bully, and your reputation will go all to pieces."

"We'll keep that private, shall we, m'lady?"

She giggled and snuggled nearer.

"I'm glad you're all right, because you are, you know—or were—pure as the driven snow. Browdie lied, sweetheart. There's no question about it. Will you put Cholly out of your mind now?"

"I will endeavour to do so," she whispered, "though I may want help."

"Very well. Just let me know when he pops into your mind. I'll try to think of something to distract you."

"Max?" came a shy voice, a while later.

"Yes, sweet?"

"I wonder if you might think of something . . . *now*."

The Devil's
Delilah

1

Rain drummed furiously against the sturdy timbers of the Black Cat Inn. Within, its public dining parlour, tap-room, and coffee rooms overflowed with orphans of the storm. From time to time a flash of lightning set the rooms ablaze with glaring light, and the more timid of the company shrank in terror at the deafening cannonade of thunder which instantly followed.

"Filthy night, sir," said Mrs. Tabithy, approaching one of her guests. "There'll be a sight more of them"—she nodded toward the group crowding the main passageway—"unless I miss my guess. If you'd come but a quarter hour later I couldn't have given you a private parlour, not if my life depended on it."

"Very kind of you, I'm sure," said the guest, gazing absently about the room.

His hostess eyed the thick volume in his hands and smiled. His mien was that of a gentleman. The quality and cut of his attire, despite its untidiness, bespoke wealth. He was a good-looking young man—not yet thirty, she would guess—and, judging by both the book and the rather dazed expression

1

of his grey eyes, one of those harmless scholar types. This fellow would offer no trouble at all.

"Just down that passage," she said aloud. "Third door on the left. I'll send Sairey along to you as soon as ever I can—but she has her hands full, as you can see."

The young man only gave a vague nod and wandered off in the direction she indicated.

His hostess had guessed aright. Mr. Jack Langdon was a quiet, bookish sort, too preoccupied with his own musings to take any note of the service accorded him. At present he was more preoccupied—or muddled, rather—than usual. This was because Mr. Langdon was recently disappointed in love.

Retiring by nature, he was now sorely tempted to betake himself to a monastery. Unfortunately, he had responsibilities. Therefore he was taking himself to the next best refuge, his Uncle Albert's peaceful estate in Yorkshire. His uncle, Viscount Rossing, was a recluse, even more book-minded than the nephew. Jack could spend the entire summer at Rossing Hall without once having to attempt a conversation. Better still, except for servants, he need never see a single female.

Sadly contemplating the particular female who had cast a blighting frost upon his budding hopes, Mr. Langdon lost count of doors and opened the fifth.

The room was exceedingly dim, which was annoying. He could not read comfortably by lightning bolts, frequent as they were. He'd scarcely formulated the thought when the lightning crackled again to reveal, lit like a scene upon the stage, a young woman pressing a pistol against the Earl of Streetham's breast.

Without pausing to reflect further, Mr. Langdon hurled himself at the young woman, knocking her to the floor and the earl against the wall. Lord

Streetham's head cracked against the window frame and his lordship slid, unconscious, to the floor.

The young woman remained fully conscious though, and in full possession of the pistol. As Jack grabbed for it, she jammed an elbow into his chest and tried to shove him away. He thrust the elbow away, and went again for the weapon. Her free hand tore into his scalp. He tried to pull away, but she caught hold of his ear and yanked so hard that the pain made his eyes water. While he struggled to pry her fingers loose, she brought up the hand wielding the weapon behind his neck. Just as the pistol's butt was about to slam down on his skull, Jack seized her wrist. He squeezed hard and the weapon dropped to the floor a few inches from her head. He lunged for the pistol, but her nails ripped into his scalp once more, jerking him back.

Mr. Langdon was growing distraught. To have assaulted a woman in the first place was contrary to his nature. Now he seemed to have no choice but to render her unconscious. He knew he could, having been well-trained at Gentleman Jack's, yet the idea of driving his fist into a feminine jaw was appalling.

While he struggled with his sense of propriety, she struggled to better purpose, punctuating her blows with a stream of choked oaths that would have shocked Mr. Langdon to the core had he been able to pay full attention. He, however, had all he could do to keep her down. He prayed she'd tire soon and spare him the shame of having to beat her senseless. But she only writhed, elbowed, scratched, and pummelled with unabated ferocity.

Mr. Langdon's prodigious patience began to fail him. In desperation, he grabbed both her wrists and pinned them to the floor. She cursed vehemently now, but her heaving bosom showed she was finally weakening, though she continued twisting frantically beneath him. That is when his concentration began to fail.

The form beneath his was strong and lithe, and he became acutely aware of supple muscles and lush curves. As her writhings abated, a warmth more beckoning than the heat of combat began to steal over him. In a moment it had stolen into his brain, along with a host of other inappropriate sensations, all of which loudly demanded attention.

Mr. Langdon attended and—alarmed at what he found—hastily lifted his weight off her. His adversary promptly thrust her knee against a portion of his anatomy.

Jack gasped and rolled onto the floor, and the young woman scrambled to her feet, grabbed her pistol, and dashed out of the room.

Moments later, as Jack was struggling to rise, he heard a low groan and saw the earl painfully raising his head from the floor. Jack crawled towards him. Blood trickled past Lord Streetham's ear along his jaw line.

"My Lord, you're hurt," said Jack. He fumbled in his coat for his handkerchief.

Lord Streetham pulled himself up to a sitting position, clutching his head. "Damned madwoman," he muttered. "How was I to know she wasn't—what are you doing?" he cried.

"Your head, My Lord—"

"Never mind that. Go find the she-devil. I'll teach her to—well, what are you waiting for?"

From his earliest childhood Jack Langdon had run tame in the earl's house, dealt with on the same terms as his lordship's son, Tony. Jack had played with Tony, studied with Tony and—periodically—been flogged with Tony. When, therefore, Tony's father told Jack to do a thing, Jack did it.

He stumbled to his feet and out of the room.

* * *

4

"Well, Delilah, and now what have you been up to?" said Mr. Desmond as he coolly studied his daughter's disheveled appearance.

Delilah glanced at the pudgy little man who stood, perspiring profusely, beside her papa. "Oh, nothing," she said, airily indifferent to the scene of carnage she'd recently left. "A misunderstanding with one of our fellow guests. Two, actually," she added, half to herself.

"Good heavens, Miss Desmond, it appears to have been a great deal more than that. I hope one of the gentlemen has not behaved uncivilly. A terrible thing, these public inns," said the damp fellow. "You really should not have come unattended. Your maid—"

"My maid has a sick headache, Mr. Atkins, though I have told her repeatedly that only women of the upper classes are permitted the luxury of me-grims. I fear she has aspirations above her station." Miss Desmond impatiently thrust her tangled black curls back from her face.

"Mr. Atkins is right, my love. You should not have come."

"Of course I should, Papa. The matter nearly concerns me—as I hope you've explained to Mr. Atkins." She turned to the small man. "I believe Papa has already informed you of his change of plans. Therefore I cannot think why you have travelled all this way on a fruitless errand."

"Oh, Miss Desmond, not fruitless, surely. As I was just explaining to your father—" Mr. Atkins stopped short because at that moment the door flew open.

The woman Jack sought stood with her back to the door, but as he drew on his remaining strength for a second assault, he heard a low, lazy voice say, "Ah, the guest in question, I believe."

Mr. Langdon stopped mid-lunge as his gaze

5

swung towards the voice. There were others in the room. Two others.

One was a small, rather plump, exceedingly agitated creature with a moist, round face. At the moment he was nervously mopping his forehead with his handkerchief.

The other—the voice's owner—was a tall, powerfully built man with a darkly handsome face and riveting green eyes. He stood coolly, almost negligently, surveying the intruder, yet his very negligence was threatening.

It occurred to Mr. Langdon that when and if the Old Harry took human form, this was the form he must take. The man exuded force, danger, and something else Jack couldn't define.

"I beg your pardon for interrupting," said Jack, bracing himself for he knew not what, "but I've been sent to apprehend this woman."

"You apprehended me once already," said she. "This smacks of obstinacy."

"Ah, it *is* the guest," said the satanic-looking fellow. He took a step towards Jack and smiled. The gleam of his white teeth was not comforting. "My dear young man, you must give up your pursuit of my daughter. She objects to being pursued by gentlemen to whom she has not been introduced. Objects most strongly. She is likely to shoot you."

"I don't doubt it," said Jack. "She just tried to murder the Earl of Streetham."

"Dear heaven!" cried the small man. "Lord Streetham? Oh, Miss Desmond, this will never do!"

"No, it will not," the man who claimed to be her father agreed. "How many times have I told you, Delilah, not to murder earls? Really, my dear, it is a very bad habit. Steel yourself. Overcome it. Mr. Atkins is quite right. Won't do at all." He turned to Jack. "My dear chap, I'm terribly sorry, but this is a fiend we never have done wrestling with. Rest assured that I will speak very firmly to my daughter later. Pray don't trouble yourself further about it. Good-bye."

Though this response was hardly satisfactory, there was something so assured in the man's tones that for one eerie instant, Jack, half convinced he was acting in a comic play, very nearly took his cue. He had even begun to back out of the room when he felt the young woman's gaze upon him. He turned towards her and froze.

In the heat of battle he had become conscious of her lush person. Now he saw that her heavy black hair framed a perfect oval face startlingly white in contrast, smooth and clear as his mother's precious porcelain. Her eyes, the grey-green of a stormy sea, had a slight upward slant. As she watched his baffled face, her generous mouth curved slightly in an enigmatic, maddening smile that made his heart lurch within him. Jack suddenly needed air.

All the same, he could not retreat. This young Circe had attempted the worst of crimes.

"I'm very sorry, sir, but I'm obliged to be troubled," said Jack, attempting similar nonchalance. "I'm afraid this is a matter for the constable."

"Dear God!" Mr. Atkins sank into a chair.

"As you like," said Miss Desmond. "I wish to speak to a constable myself. Perhaps he can explain why your Lord Streetham is permitted to wander about public inns assaulting defenceless young women. He cannot be very successful at it, since he requires accomplices. I shall recommend he find a hobby better suited to his limited skills."

"Assaulted *you*! You were holding a pistol to his heart."

"Ah, now I understand. His lordship is a tall man?" Mr. Desmond enquired.

"Yes, but that—"

"There you have it. She could not hold the pistol to his head. Much too awkward. As you can see, Delilah is scarcely above middle height."

"This is hardly a time for humour," said Jack, much provoked. "Lord Streetham lies bleeding just a few doors away."

"There you are mistaken," said Delilah's father. "He is bleeding slightly, but he is standing right behind you."

Jack whipped around. Sure enough, there was his lordship, leaning weakly against the door frame and pressing a handkerchief to the side of his head.

Mr. Atkins scurried towards the earl. "My Lord, you are hurt. Here, take my handkerchief. Shall I send for a physician? Shall I send for water? Shall I send for brandy?" The man continued babbling as he alternately thrust his handkerchief in the earl's face and mopped his own moist brow.

"Who *is* this person?" the earl demanded. "Why does he wave that filthy rag in my face?" He nodded to Jack. "Remove him, Jack. This is a private matter."

Mr. Atkins did not wait for removal. He shot past the earl out of the room.

Lord Streetham's icy glare now fell upon the dark gentleman, who produced another gleaming grin. The earl's hauteur faltered slightly. "So it *is* you, Desmond," he said. "When I heard that voice I was certain I'd passed over. Where else but in Hades would one expect to see *you* again?"

"But not, surely, where you'd expect to find yourself, eh, Marcus?" Mr. Desmond returned. "You are, I promise, still in this sad world, and this poor hostelry is hardly the Other Place, though the Devil himself takes refuge here from the storm."

Lord Streetham manufactured a taut smile. "Then I may take it this young woman belongs to you?"

The green eyes glittered. "Young *lady*, if you please. This is my daughter, Delilah."

"Daughter?" the earl repeated weakly.

8

The tension in the air was palpable. Once more Jack braced himself.

To his amazement, the earl's hauteur vanished completely, replaced by a rather white expression of solicitude. "My dear young lady, a thousand apologies," he said. "The poor light—and my eyes are not what they used to be. I took you for that saucy maid. A terrible misunderstanding."

Miss Desmond stared coldly at him.

"Nearly fatal, actually," said her father. "Now I suppose I must call you out. How tiresome."

"Too tiresome, Papa," said Miss Desmond. "His lordship has apologised. I am unharmed." Obviously, his lordship was not, but the young lady tactfully forbore to mention this. "Now if his accomplice will apologise as well," she added with an amused glance at Jack, "we might all continue peaceably about our business."

Jack was certain that some sort of signal passed then from daughter to father, but he could not perceive what it was. A flicker of an eyelid . . . an infinitesimal movement . . . or even—impossible—no one could read another's mind.

He looked to the earl for guidance.

"A misunderstanding, Jack," said Lord Streetham. "That's all."

All. He, Jack Langdon, had violently assaulted an innocent young woman who had only been attempting to defend her honour. He wished the floor would open up and swallow him, but as floors are rarely accommodating in this way, he reddened with mortification instead.

"I—I do beg your pardon, Miss Desmond," he stammered. "I'm dreadfully sorry—and—and—" Abruptly he recalled the appalling urges she'd aroused. "I hope I caused you no injury."

"Oh, no," she answered soberly, though her eyes were lit with amusement. "And I trust I caused *you* none."

Mr. Langdon's colour deepened. "N—no. Of course not."

"Very well, Mr.—?"

"Langdon," the earl impatiently supplied. "Jack Langdon. Known him since he was a babe. Wouldn't hurt a fly."

"Very well, Mr. Langdon. Apology accepted."

Mr. Langdon begged pardon of the room at large, then fled.

He found the correct parlour this time and sat staring at the table for half an hour before he remembered that he'd dropped his book during his scuffle with Miss Desmond. Reluctant to risk bumping into any of the witnesses to his humiliation, he sent a servant to retrieve the volume.

Once it was safely in his hands, Jack relaxed somewhat, and even managed to order his dinner without stammering. This was about all he could manage. He ate his meal without tasting it, and read his book without comprehending a syllable. The storm continued with savage fury, and he noticed nothing. Hours later, when all was quiet within and without, he crept to his room and stared at the ceiling until daybreak.

While Mr. Langdon was trying in vain to find oblivion in his book, and Miss Desmond was recounting her adventure to her papa, Lord Streetham was relieving his own frustrations at the expense of the hapless Mr. Atkins. After berating the poor fellow unmercifully for nearly revealing their connexion, his lordship proceeded to an unkind analysis of said connexion.

The world knew Lord Streetham as an enthusiastic book collector. Mr. Atkins knew him as a secret partner in his publishing business. That this was a closely guarded secret was perhaps because of the firm's tendency to offer the British public some of the naughtiest volumes ever to be hidden under mattresses or tucked away in locked drawers. Despite readers' regrettable affinity for anatomy manuals, directories of prostitutes, reviews of *crim con* cases, and guides to seduction, the business had not done well of late—as the earl was at present pointing out.

Atkins was obviously a failure, his lordship observed, perhaps a fraud as well. Be that as it may, he now had leave to plunge into bankruptcy solo. In short, Lord Streetham proposed to cease tossing good money after bad.

"But, My Lord, to give up now—when a brilliant success is practically in my grasp—virtually in the printer's hands." Mr. Atkins squeezed his eyes shut and bit his lip. "Oh, my. I had not meant—oh, dear me."

Lord Streetham paused in the act of bringing his glass to his lips and studied his companion's face over the rim. Then he put the glass down and fixed his pale blue eyes on the publisher.

"What hadn't you meant?" he asked.

The man only stood speechless and terrified, gazing back.

"You'd better speak up, Atkins. My patience is quite at an end."

"My—My Lord, I c—cannot. I'm sworn to s—secrecy."

"You have no business secrets from me. Speak up at once."

The publisher swallowed. "The memoirs, My Lord."

"I am not in the mood to catechize you, Atkins, and you are provoking me."

"*His* memoirs," the publisher said miserably. "Mr. Desmond has written his memoirs and I have paid him—partially, I mean, as an incentive to complete them speedily. That is why I am here. I learned he was travelling to Rossingley to visit relatives, so I came up from Town to—to spare him the trouble of bringing them to me."

"Written his memoirs, has he?" Lord Streetham asked as he absently poured more wine into his still nearly full glass.

"Yes, My Lord. I saw them—at least part of them—myself. He had written to ask whether I had any interest, and naturally, being familiar with his reputation—as who is not?—I made all haste to examine the work. I had to travel all the way to Scotland, but the journey was well worth my while, I assure you. All of Society will be clamouring to read Devil Desmond's story. We'll issue it in installments, you see, and—"

"And have you got them?" his lordship asked.

Mr. Atkins was forced to admit he had not, because Mr. Desmond had raised difficulties.

"Of course he has," said the earl. "If you know his reputation, you should know better than to give Devil Desmond money before you have the goods in your hands. You are a fool. These memoirs do not exist. He showed you a few scraps of paper he'd got up for the purpose, and you were cozened."

The publisher protested that the manuscript must exist, or Miss Desmond would not have been so eager to interrupt the meeting with her father. "He's ready to publish," Atkins explained, "but she won't let him. She's afraid of the scandal. The girl's looking for a husband, you know. That's why Mr. Desmond has returned to England."

The earl sneered. "Devil Desmond's daughter? A husband? The wench must be addled in her wits. I suppose she means to find herself a lord—a duke, perhaps?" Lord Streetham chuckled. "Silly chit. What's one more scandal to her? As it is—but no, ancient history bores me. Still, the public dotes on such sorry tales, and you are correct. These memoirs, if they truly exist, are certain to be popular. Unfortunately . . . " He paused and lightly drummed his fingers on the table.

"My Lord?"

"People change, Atkins," said the earl, without looking up. "Some of those with whom Desmond consorted in his wicked youth have died of their excesses. Those who survived are today men of prominence, highly respected. They will not take kindly to such an exposure of their youthful follies. If you are not careful, you will be sued for libel."

"My Lord, I assure you—"

Lord Streetham continued, unheeding, "Furthermore, libellous or not, there may be information that would destroy the peace of innocent families. We can't have that." His lordship sipped his wine with an air of piety.

Mr. Atkins panicked. "Oh, My Lord. For fear of a few domestic squabbles you are prepared to deprive the world of these recollections? I promise you, they'll be pounding at the doors every time a new installment is announced. I beg of you, My Lord, reconsider." Tears formed in the publisher's eyes.

Lord Streetham reflected for several agonising minutes while Mr. Atkins mopped his brow and waited.

"Very well," said the earl at last. "It would be wrong to deprive the public. He has lived an extraordinary life. You may publish, if you can—but on one condition."

"Anything, My Lord."

"I must approve the material first. A bit of editing here and there will do no harm, and may spare some of my colleagues considerable pain."

Having agreed to accept any condition, Mr. Atkins could hardly quarrel with this modest request. Some time later, however, as he took himself to bed, he bewailed the cruel fate that had brought Lord Streetham to this accursed inn. By the time his lordship had done "approving" Devil Desmond's memoirs, they'd look like a book of sermons, and Mr. Atkins would consider himself very fortunate if even the Methodists would buy them.

* * *

Lord Streetham took to his own bed in bad humour. He might have known this would be a night of ill omen from the start, when his mistress had failed to appear. Then, when Desmond's chit had entered his private parlour, he'd mistaken her for the tart, and nearly had his claret spilled. After that, he'd narrowly escaped certain death at Devil Desmond's hands, had had to truckle to the monster—with Jack Langdon, the soul of rectitude, a witness to the whole tawdry scene. Worst of all were these curst memoirs, whose pages must surely reveal secrets of his own to the unsympathetic London mob.

His lordship was not altogether easy in his mind about the publisher, either. The choice between certain success and certain ruin is not a difficult one, and a desperate man is not a patient one. Suppose Atkins betrayed him, and made off with the manuscript? Suppose, even if he didn't, the book was so scurrilous that editing would not be enough? Perhaps it were safest to destroy the work altogether. With these and hosts of other, equally unsettling questions did Lord Streetham while away the long, dreary night.

2

Hoping once again to avoid his fellow travellers, Jack stole out of his room shortly after dawn. As he was about to turn the corner towards the stairs, there came a noise from a room nearby. Jack glanced back at the precise instant that another gentleman came hurrying around the corner. The two collided, and Mr. Langdon was sent staggering against the wall.

"Drat—so sorr—Jack!" exclaimed the gentleman. "Is that you, truly?"

He reached out a hand to help, but Jack had swiftly recovered his balance, though he was still rather dazed. He glanced up into what most women would have described as the face of an angel. It was a face that might have been painted by Botticelli, so classically beautiful were its proportions, so finely chiseled every feature, so clear, blue, and innocent its eyes, so golden the halo of curls that crowned it.

This, however, was not only the face of a mortal man, but of a most unseraphic member of that gender. Lord Streetham's son, the Viscount Berne, was well on his way to becoming the most dangerous libertine the British peerage had ever produced. He was also Jack's oldest friend.

"Yes, it's me—at least I think so," said Jack with a grimace as he rubbed the back of his head.

"What brings you here—up and about at this ungodly hour? And as usual, never looking where you went. Why, I nearly threw you down in my haste."

"That's quite all right, Tony," said Mr. Langdon. "I'm growing accustomed to falling on my face."

Lord Berne's innocent countenance immediately became pitying. "Oh, yes, I heard about that. Too bad about Miss Pelliston."

Mr. Langdon winced. He had not been aware that his failure was common gossip.

"Still, that's the way of love," the viscount consoled. "Plants you a facer every now and then. The secret is to pick yourself up and march on to the next battle. We civilians must take our lesson from Wellington."

He threw an arm about his friend's shoulder and led him down the stairs. "First, you want sustenance. We shall breakfast together. Then, you must return with me to the ancestral pile for a long visit. I'm forced to ruralise because I am obliged to court Lady Jane Gathers. Of course she'll make a paragon of a wife. My sire's judgement is infallible, as he incessantly reminds me."

Since Lord Berne had a tendency to run on wherever his fancy took him, his monologues could continue for hours if not ruthlessly interrupted and hauled back to the point.

Accordingly, Jack cut in. "You don't usually ruralise at inns—at least not so close to home. What brings you here?"

"A wench of course. What else? Perhaps you have not yet met the fair and saucy Sarah? No matter. I scarcely saw her either, for I'd no sooner stepped into the coffee room than I spied a high flyer sitting lonely and neglected amid the storm-tossed rabble.

16

What choice had I but to come to the dark-haired damsel's aid?"

"Lady Jane will hardly appreciate that sort of knight errantry," said Jack as they stepped into the main passage.

"Lady Jane is determined to know nothing about such matters, which is most becoming in her. I only wish her face were more becoming. But no matter. We'll woo her together, you and I," Tony offered.

He deftly steered his preoccupied friend into the public dining room. "Perhaps you'll steal her away. Actually, Jack, I wish you would. She's all very well, but I'm not ready—Good God! Where did *she* come from? With my noble sire, no less. Where in blazes did *he* come from?"

Mr. Langdon followed his companion's gaze past the enormous communal table to a quiet corner near the fireplace. There Mr. Desmond and his daughter sat breakfasting with the Earl of Streetham.

Though the last thing in this world Jack wanted was interaction with any of the three, he could hardly expect Tony to ignore his own father, particularly when that parent was in the company of a beautiful young woman. There was no escape, because Tony had a firm grip on his friend's arm and was propelling him towards the table.

Jack employed the next few minutes examining with apparent fascination a small landscape containing several evil-looking sheep which hung upon the wall some inches above Miss Desmond's head. Dimly he heard introductions and a number of what he was certain were falsehoods as the earl and his son respectively accounted for their appearance at the Black Cat.

Mr. Langdon nudged himself to proper attention when he heard the earl renew his pleas that the Desmonds be his guests at Streetham Close. Since his lordship addressed his requests primarily to the

17

daughter, Jack gathered that she was the more reluctant of the pair. In the next moment, however, Tony added his persuasions, and, as might be expected, Miss Desmond capitulated.

Having completed their meal, the trio soon left, one of them followed by a look of such languishing adoration from Lord Berne that the waiter knocked over two chairs in his haste to reach the table, so certain was he the young gentleman was about to perish of hunger.

Mr. Langdon, being inured to his companion's fits of romantic stupefaction, took no notice. Their breakfast was speedily served, and while they ate, Jack calmly explained why he could not visit Streetham Close. His uncle was expecting him, he said. He was not in a humour to be sociable. He had not read a book through in months. These and other lame excuses received short shrift from the Viscount Berne.

"You only want to go off to hide and feel sorry for yourself, Jack, and that's unhealthy. To wish to be elsewhere when this exotic flower will be under my roof is evidence of mental decay. We must make you well again. If those grey eyes of hers don't restore you to manhood, I don't know what will."

"They're green," said Jack.

"Grey."

"Green. And I don't need to be restored by anyone's *eyes*. I want peace and quiet, Tony, and I must tell you there's nothing peaceful about the pair of them." Jack was on the brink of revealing the previous night's adventure when his friend blithely cut in.

"I don't expect them to be peaceful," said Lord Berne. "Don't you know who that is? Devil Desmond, the most infamous rogue in Christendom. Adventurer, charlatan, and—at least until he wed—corrupter of feminine virtue the like of which has

18

not been seen since Casanova. His conquests would populate—"

"Thank you, Tony. The broad outlines will do."

"He's a legend in his own time, I tell you. Never thought he'd return to England after that duel with Billings—but that's aeons ago, isn't it?"

Mr. Langdon scowled at his coffee. "Then I wonder at your father's taking him under the ancestral roof."

"His lordship grows pious in his dotage. Maybe he means to reform the Devil. Still, what do I care about the reasons? Delilah." Lord Berne sighed. "Even her name throbs with sinful promise. She has not touched a hair of my head, yet I feel the strength ebbing from my very sinews."

His friend sighed inwardly. Tony fell in love on a daily—sometime hourly—basis, and the results, in the view of some, amounted to a national tragedy. The pitiful remains of the feminine hearts Lord Berne had shattered lay strewn in a broad path from London to Carlisle. One more scrap of wreckage would not change the course of history—though, unless Jack much missed his guess, Miss Desmond's heart was made of sturdier material.

For the philosopher, their interchange would provide an interesting study, but Mr. Langdon was not in a philosophic mood. He stubbornly insisted on going to his uncle's.

Lord Berne played his trump card. "You must come, Jack, to save me from myself."

"Rescue is not in my style," was the irritated reply.

"But who else can keep me from straying beyond light dalliance into dangerous depths? Very dangerous, I promise you. You will not want to see the Devil put a bullet through my too-tender heart, will you?"

"Then keep your hands to yourself."

"But Jack." Lord Berne fixed his friend with a wide-eyed gaze. "You know I can't."

Mr. Desmond and his daughter travelled in their own carriage, the earl preceding them on horseback. After they had driven some time in silence, Mr. Desmond remarked, "That young man interests me."

"Which young man, Papa?"

'My dear, you can hardly think I find that fair-haired coxcomb interesting. I have met his type across the world, through several generations. I refer to the Guest in Question. The unhappy young man with the rumpled brown hair and poetic grey eyes."

"I did not find him poetic."

"You most certainly did. Also, you felt sorry for him. I nearly swooned with astonishment."

Miss Desmond gazed stonily ahead. "I did neither. Your eyesight is failing you, Papa, just like poor Lord Streetham's."

"You are very cross today, Delilah. Is it because the poetic young man turns out to be heir presumptive to Viscount Rossing and you regret your decision?"

Miss Desmond's head snapped towards her father so abruptly that her gypsy bonnet tipped over her ear. As she straightened it she said angrily, "I am not going to force a man to marry me on some trumped up pretext of being compromised. It's absurd."

"He would have done it, though."

"Because he's an innocent babe. Oh, Papa, that's not how I wish to begin—yet there's no fresh beginning, is there? My feet scarcely touch English soil before I become embroiled in a dreadful scene. I *wish* I could act like a lady. I can act everything else, it seems," she added ruefully.

"Had you acted a helpless female—which I take

is your definition of a lady—you would have been dishonoured by that sanctimonious old hypocrite."

"If I'd waited for my maid or kept to my room I should not have invited incivility."

Mr. Desmond smiled, a far gentler smile than the one Mr. Langdon had observed the previous evening. "You were concerned that Mr. Atkins's pleas would soften my susceptible heart. A natural anxiety, my dear, though quite unnecessary. In fact, I've given the matter a great deal of thought. Perhaps I should destroy those paltry literary efforts of mine, so we might proceed in this enterprise with easy minds. I made a great mistake in contacting Atkins, I know. But I wanted to ascertain the value of the work. Suppose I died suddenly?"

Delilah shuddered. "Don't say such things, Papa."

"It might have easily happened but a year ago. You and your mama would be left destitute, with no prospects of aid from either of our callous families. Insurance, I thought. A nest egg in case of calamity. Naturally I had to make sure the egg was a golden one."

"Of course you did. And not another word about destroying your wonderful story, after all your months of work. As you say, calamities happen. I may never find a husband."

"Or you may fall in love with a penniless young man."

Miss Desmond sniffed disdainfully. "I have no intention of falling in love with anybody. One cannot preserve a clear head and be in love at the same time. My marriage wants a clear head."

"You mean a cold, calculating one, I suppose." The parent sighed. "I fear your mama and I went sadly astray in your upbringing. We have failed you."

"Oh, Papa." Miss Desmond hugged her father, setting her bonnet askew again. "You have never failed me. I only hope I might be clear-headed enough to find a man half as splendid as you."

"That, my love, wants a muddled head. What a silly girl you are. But at least you have recovered your temper. I shall endure the silliness."

Whatever objections Lady Streetham had about entertaining the notorious Devil Desmond were ruthlessly crushed by her lord and master.

"I have reasons," said he, "of a highly confidential and political nature. You may treat him with civility or you may blight my Cabinet prospects. The choice is yours."

After subduing his wife, Lord Streetham called upon his most trusted servants and, again citing national security, ordered them to search the Desmonds' belongings.

While Lord Streetham and his minions laboured on behalf of the imperiled kingdom, Lord Berne took his guests on a riding circuit of the park. Mr. Langdon went as well, though he knew every stick, stone, and rabbit hole of every acre. He had his book with him, however, and whenever the group had occasion to pause, would take it out to stare blindly at the pages.

Miss Desmond found this behaviour most curious. As they were returning to the house, she asked Lord Berne, "Does he *always* have a book with him?"

"Always," said her companion, glancing back at his friend, "even in Town, at the most magnificent balls, routs, musicales. There you'll unfailingly find Jack Langdon with a book, which he unfailingly loses at some point, and must of course go poking about for. Drives the ladies wild. Not that I blame them. It must be most exasperating when you're just commencing a bit of flirtation to see his eyes glaze over and then watch him wander off, talking to himself." His own appreciative gaze dropped from her eyes to her lips. "Though I cannot understand his behaviour in the present case."

"I find it perfectly understandable," Miss Desmond answered lightly. "What lady can compete with Plutarch?"

The viscount opened his mouth to answer, but she added quickly, "Pray, My Lord, do not say it is myself, when the facts contradict you. Besides, that is too easy a compliment. You cannot think I was angling for it."

"You need never *angle* for praise, Miss Desmond," was the prompt reply.

The exotic countenance grew blank with boredom, and Lord Berne was wise enough to revise his tactics.

"Actually," he said, dropping his voice, "Jack is more than usually abstracted because"—he paused dramatically—"he has had a disappointment."

Miss Desmond was intrigued. "Really? What sort? It cannot have been love, since you say he eludes feminine wiles. What can it be?"

"To disclose that would be dishonourable."

"Then you were dishonourable to mention it at all," she retorted, tossing her head. This tipped her beaver riding hat over her forehead, causing several black tendrils to escape from behind. She impatiently thrust these back under the hat while Lord Berne watched with every evidence of enchantment.

"As long as I am sunk beneath reproach, I suppose one more indiscretion can scarcely matter," he said, when hat and hair had been jammed into order. "Yes, there was a lady in the case. Amazing, isn't it?"

"She must have been extraordinary to distract him from his books."

"Not at all. From what I've heard, she was a mousy little model of propriety—and a blue-

23

stocking. I think he's had a narrow escape, though it wouldn't do to tell him so, of course. A friend is obliged to sympathise and console."

"Then I keep you from your obligations, My Lord. You must attend to Mr. Langdon, and leave Papa and me to make shift without you." So saying, she rode ahead to catch up with her father.

"Bored so soon?" asked Mr. Desmond. "I told you he was like everyone else."

"On the contrary, he's a wonderful gossip. In less than an hour I have learned the entire past Season's *on-dits*."

"Then doubtless the conversation grew too warm for your maidenly ears."

Delilah shot him a disbelieving glance. "His lordship was courteously amusing, no more. Still, if the prey is not elusive, the hunter soon loses his relish for the pursuit, as you have told me a thousand times."

The father grinned. "I am always right, of course. You've set your mind on Streetham's heir, then?"

Delilah shook her head. "His parents would never condone it. I was most surprised by his lordship's invitation. I don't think he likes you, Papa."

"Loathes me," the Devil replied easily. "Still, he wouldn't want his *faux pas* to be noised about—and even I am not so low a cur as to tattle on my gracious host, am I?"

"What an old hypocrite he is! Naturally his son is out of the question." She smiled into the sunlit distance. "As a husband, I mean. But as a pursuer, he could prove useful. It would be pleasant to have at least one suitor on hand when the Little Season begins. Let us hope he pursues me as far as London."

It was fortunate that Lord Streetham was not a superstitious man, else he had concluded a curse had fallen upon him from the moment he'd strayed past the Black Cat's portals. A diligent search of all of the Desmonds' belongings, including their carriage, had yielded nothing.

Lord Streetham now had two choices. He could offer Desmond an enormous sum for the memoirs. Though the earl was tight-fisted, he was prepared to pay in so urgent a case. The trouble was, he must pay Desmond, and to admit himself at that creature's mercy was unthinkable. The second choice—to seek his irresponsible son's help—was nearly as unthinkable. Yet this was one of the few enterprises in which Tony's narrow talents could be useful. Thus, as soon as the group had returned to the house, Lord Streetham sent for his son.

"I suppose you are on your way to making a conquest of Miss Desmond," said the earl, once the door was closed.

Tony shifted uneasily. "I was only trying to entertain them, sir. That is one's duty to one's guests."

"I'll tell you your duty," the earl snapped. "I didn't ask them here for their amusement or yours, and I mean to be rid of them as soon as possible. Your mother is still in fits, and she doesn't know the half of it." Lord Streetham proceeded to tell his son the whole of it—or most of it, for he did not reveal precisely what revelations he feared. He dwelt instead upon the ignorance of the public and the jealousy of political rivals. The latter, he insisted, would snatch at any straw that might discredit him.

"They will twist minor peccadillos out of all recognition and make me appear unfit to lead," he stiffly explained. "What you or I, as men of the world, would shrug off as youthful folly they will exaggerate into weakness of character. Mere boyish pranks will be transformed into heinous crimes."

He turned from the window in time to catch his son grinning. The grin was hastily suppressed.

"I'm delighted you find this so amusing," said Lord Streetham coldly. "Doubtless your mother will find it equally so, particularly when she grows reluctant to go about in public, for fear of hearing her former friends snickering behind their fans, or—and I'm sure this will be most humorous—enduring their expressions of pity."

Lord Berne became properly solemn. "I beg your pardon, My Lord. I did not mean—"

"I'll tell you what you mean, you rattle! You mean to relieve Desmond of that confounded manuscript."

"I?"

"The girl, you idiot. If you must dally with her, then do so with a purpose. I am unable to locate the memoirs. That does not surprise me. Desmond is cunning. She may be equally so—certainly her mother is—but she *is* a female, and all females can be managed."

Since Lord Berne had never met a young woman he couldn't manage, he could hardly find fault with this reasoning. Nor, being sufficiently intelligent, was he slow to grasp what his father wished him to do.

"You believe I might persuade her to turn this manuscript over to me, sir?" he asked.

Lord Streetham uttered a sigh of vexation. "Why else would I impose so on that depraved brain of yours? Of course that is what I wish. Now go away and *do* it," he ordered.

Lord Berne went away not altogether pleased with his assignment—which was rather odd, considering this was the first time his father had ever trusted him with any matter of importance. Furthermore, what was at stake was power, and the viscount had selfish reasons for preferring that his father's not be diminished in any way. Lord Streetham's influence had more than once saved his son from an undesirable marriage, not to mention tiresome interviews with constables.

The trouble was, the son was accustomed to pursue pleasure for its own sake. Though he would have been delighted to dally with the ravishing Miss Desmond, doing so as a means to an end was very like *work*, and his aristocratic soul shuddered at the prospect.

Still, he thought, his noble sire could not possibly expect him to begin this minute. Consequently, Lord Berne took himself to the water tower for a cold bath, and remained there, coolly meditating, for two hours.

3

Though she had bathed and dressed leisurely, Miss Desmond discovered she had still the remainder of the afternoon to get through and no idea what to do with herself.

Lady Streetham, Delilah knew, was not eager for her company, and the feeling was mutual. Papa was having a nap. Her host was closeted with his steward. Lord Berne, according to her maid, had not yet returned to the house.

Clearly, Miss Desmond would have to provide her own amusement until tea. The prospect was not appealing. She could not play billiards, because that was unladylike. She doubted very much her hosts would approve her gambling with the servants. For the same reason, she could not spend the time in target practice. This enforced inactivity left her to her reflections, which were not agreeable.

Though she'd made light of it to her father, last night's contretemps preyed on her mind. It was no good telling herself, as her father had assured her, she hadn't had any choice. She might have attempted at least to reason with the earl before drawing out her pistol. Certainly she needn't have *wrestled*, for heaven's sake, with Mr. Langdon. She might have pretended to faint or burst into tears, but not one of these alternatives had occurred to her, though they would have been instinctive to any truly genteel young lady.

Delilah Desmond had a great deal to learn about ladylike behaviour, that was for certain. She hoped Lady Potterby would be up to the task of re-educating her grand-niece. Otherwise that grand-niece would never attract the sort of gentleman she needed to marry.

Right now, for instance, she ought to make an effort to impress her stony hostess by conversing with her on some suitably dull subject, preferably while doing needlework. The trouble was, Delilah was heartily sick of Lady Streetham's condescension and would be more likely to plunge her needle into that lady's starched bosom.

Miss Desmond decided her wisest course was to take a stroll in the gardens. At least they were extensive enough to make the walk something like real exercise.

She crossed the terrace and followed one of the neat gravel paths bordered by low, scrupulously manicured hedges until she came to an enormous fountain where water spewed from the mouths of four enraged stone dolphins. Staring raptly at the carved monstrosity was Mr. Langdon, book clamped to his side. He seemed oblivious to her approach.

"I wonder if they bite," said Delilah.

He spun round to face her, his countenance colouring slightly.

Miss Desmond was surprised to feel her own cheeks grow warm. She wished she hadn't struck him quite so violently last night—or at least not in that unseemly way. She shook her head to drive off the recollection, and two pins flew out of her hair to drop with a faint tinkle upon the paving stones.

As his glance went from her hair to the pins, his eyes seemed to darken, but Delilah could not be certain because he immediately bent to retrieve the pins. In her experience, gentlemen invariably used the return of her hairpins as an excuse for squeezing her hand. Mr. Langdon, however, gingerly dropped them into her outstretched palm as though he were afraid of being contaminated.

"Thank you," she said with an inward twitch of irritation, "but you needn't have bothered. I'm forever losing them. Papa says he can always tell where I've been because I leave a trail of hairpins behind me."

"Then why pin your hair up at all?" he asked.

She glanced at him suspiciously, but his expression was innocently enquiring. Thrusting the pins back any which way, she said, "Little girls may leave their hair down, Mr. Langdon. A young lady who does so may be mistaken for a demi-rep. At least, so my abigail repeatedly tells me. I have enough problems being mistaken for what I am not," she found herself adding under his sober grey gaze.

He winced as though she had struck him. "Miss Desmond, no words can express my shame and sorrow regarding my behaviour last night," he said hurriedly. "I should have realised—I should have tried to think first at least—it might have been obvious to an imbecile—"

"That I was only demonstrating the use of a pistol to his lordship?" Delilah smiled in spite of her discomfort. "Even I must admit the circumstances were most incriminating."

"That hardly changes the fact that my behaviour was ungentlemanly, to say the least."

How unhappy he was! That rather took the sting out of her own embarrassment. "Mine was unladylike," she said. "That makes us quits, Mr. Langdon. Shall we forgive each other—and ourselves?" She held out her hand.

He hesitated a moment before accepting the

handshake. His clasp lingered just an instant longer than pure sportsmanship required, but after the business with the hairpins this might be accounted a minor triumph, and Miss Desmond had never been one to quibble over instants.

"As long as you've given me your hand, may I have your arm as well?" she asked lightly. "Will you walk with me and talk amiable inanities, as though we'd only now met in these sedate circumstances?"

"With pleasure," said her companion. He did not look pleased, however. He looked as though he'd much prefer to run away.

Though common sense told her he had good reason to avoid her, Miss Desmond had sufficient vanity to be piqued by this show of reluctance.

"If you think it a pleasure, oughtn't you smile at least?" she chided as she took his arm and they began to walk. "You look so grim, as though I had asked you to commit treason—" She caught herself up, struck with a disconcerting possibility. "Or have I stepped wrong again? Was it forward of me to ask for your company?"

"Forward?" he asked, plainly bewildered.

"Fast. Bold. Vulgar. I don't know. Was it wrong?"

He considered for a moment. "Not wrong certainly. I mean, it can't be a hanging offence," he said with a faint smile, "though there were over two hundred of them at last count. As to bold or forward or fast, I am the last man on earth who'd know. There are some subtleties of social behavior that utterly elude me. My friend Max always says any behaviour that's pleasant can't be correct. If I employ his measure, I must conclude," he said, his smile broadening and lighting up the clean, straight lines of his profile, "that it is incorrect."

He turned the smile full upon her then, and Miss Desmond felt a tad breathless, but she answered sturdily enough. "Of course it must be. I fear the subtleties elude me also, Mr. Langdon, but I assure you I mean to learn them. In future I will not make such unseemly requests. Lud, I hope I commit no *faux pas* at tea. As it is, her ladyship seems in constant expectation of some outrage. I daresay she's certain that Papa and I will swing from the draperies or slide down banisters or, heaven help us, treat the servants like human beings."

"You had better not say 'lud' then, Miss Desmond. I distinctly recall my mother ringing a peal over my sister Gwendolyn on that account."

"Fast?"

"Vulgar."

"How tiresome."

"Then we shan't speak of it," said Mr. Langdon, and immediately turned the subject. "I understand you plan to visit your aunt?"

"My great-aunt. Lady Potterby."

Her companion started. "Lady *Millicent* Potterby?"

"Yes. Do you know her?" Delilah asked, wondering why he'd changed instantly from amiability to discomfiture. Was there some dreadful scandal about Mama's Aunt Mimsy as well?

"I know her very well. She is a near neighbour of my uncle. The properties adjoin, actually. What a small world it is," he added uneasily. "I was on my way to visit him."

They had reached the shrubbery, but instead of taking the narrow pathway between the tall hedges, he steered her along the outer border.

Miss Desmond did not at first notice the abrupt change in direction. She was too taken up with the unsettling news that Mr. Langdon would be her next door neighbour—if, that is, he persisted in his intention to visit with his uncle. Perhaps now he would change his mind—and why on earth were they circling the hedges instead of entering them?

"Oh, Mr. Langdon, is it not a maze? I should like ever so much—"

"Another time, perhaps," he said stiffly.

She felt the warmth rising in her cheeks. "Lud—I mean, good heavens—I had not thought—but these tall hedges would screen one from view of the house, and we are obliged to keep in plain sight, are we not?"

"Miss Desmond—" He hesitated. Then he drew a long breath and said, "It is not a true maze, and we are indeed so obliged, particularly as your maid is not with you."

"To protect me, you mean. But from what, sir?" she could not help asking. "Do wild animals lurk there? Or is the danger in your company?"

"No—at least—*no.*"

She felt the muscles of his arm tighten under her hand and wondered if he would bolt now. Instead, he bent a searching look upon her and after a moment's hesitation asked, "Miss Desmond, are you . . . *flirting* with me?"

"Yes," she answered in some surprise. "I believe I am."

"Then I am obliged to tell you that is a prodigious waste of time."

"You are impervious to my charms, of course," she said, as he steered her back to the rose garden.

His face instantly became shuttered. "You must be well aware no man can be that, so long as he is breathing."

"Then perhaps you do not approve of flirtation," she persisted, intrigued. "You consider it indecorous."

"I am only a book-worm, Miss Desmond, not, I hope, a prig. I make an excellent book-worm, I'm told, but a most disappointing flirt."

"Now who told you that, I wonder?"

"No one had to tell me. It's perfectly obvious."

Her pique gave way to curiosity. He meant what he said. What an odd man he was.

"Not to me, Mr. Langdon," she answered, "and I assure you I am an excellent judge. Ah, now I *have* shocked you at last."

She found that steady, studying look upon her again and once more felt rather short of breath.

"Miss Desmond, only your beauty shocks me," he said as though the words were wrung from him. "A man could look upon your face for the next one hundred years and never grow tired of it. But you would soon grow tired of that, I think," he added more briskly, "when he could not simultaneously amuse you with witty gallantries. Nor, surely, could you amuse yourself by fencing with an unarmed man."

"Unarmed?" she repeated, bemused.

A voice called out then, and Delilah turned to see Lord Berne, his golden hair in damp ringlets about his head, sauntering up the pathway toward them. She simultaneously felt her companion gently disengage her hand from his arm. When the viscount drew near, Mr. Langdon, with some vague remark about "letters to write," excused himself and quickly strode away.

Mr. Langdon must have had a great many letters to write—or perhaps only one very long and difficult one—because he did not emerge from the library again until it was time to dress for dinner.

He was there the next day as well, with even less prospect of completing his task, for he spent most of his time wandering aimlessly about the room or staring out the windows. At the moment, he was engaged in the latter occupation, and it was not an especially agreeable one.

Really, the situation was absurd, he thought. He could hardly dash out and haul Tony away from the shrubbery. If that's where the reckless fool wanted to take Miss Desmond, that was the fool's problem.

All the same, Mr. Langdon continued to watch. Just as the pair approached the perilous pathway, he saw Lady Streetham shoot out of the house like a rocket and draw Miss Desmond back to the terrace. Jack smiled. Now the countess would send Tony off on one of her errands, as she had been doing practically from the moment the Desmonds arrived.

That was not at all surprising. Lady Streetham had been snatching her son out of the jaws of romantic disaster for years, and entanglement with the penniless daughter of the notorious Devil Desmond was obviously in that category.

Mr. Langdon left the window and reseated himself at the writing desk. Miss Desmond ought to have known better, he told himself, especially after he dropped his hint about the perils of the hedgerows to her yesterday. If she was so set on learning decorum, she really oughtn't encourage Tony. Surely by now she must have recognised what a rakehell he was. Or at least her father might have warned her. But no. In a mere twenty-four hours she had developed all the usual symptoms. True, Tony had needed to add a few coals to the blaze of his charm, but Miss Desmond appeared ready enough now to be consumed.

Jack threw down his pen and went in search of a book sufficiently taxing to occupy his brain more profitably. His fingers flicked over volumes of Euripides, Aristophanes, Aristotle, and Herodotus, but each was rejected as too familiar, even in Greek. Then he found a large, moroccan-bound, heavily gilded volume whose title and author were unknown to him. He drew it out, selected a capacious leather chair, and settled himself to read.

What he found within the covers was not exactly what he'd expected, but after an initial gasp of surprise and a few moments of confusion, he became entirely deaf, dumb, and blind to all else but what he found in those pages.

Utterly absorbed, Mr. Langdon continued reading as late morning warmed into early afternoon and luncheon passed unnoticed. The household being familiar with his ways, a modest array of sustenance was brought to him on a tray. It remained untouched and was later carried away by the same servant, who smiled indulgently as he closed the library doors behind him.

The servant speedily erased his smile a moment later when he met up in the hall with his mistress and Miss Desmond.

Lady Streetham frowned at the tray and then, more deeply, at the servant. "This will not do," she said. "You will bring him another, Nicholas, and this time be sure he is eating *before* you leave the room."

"I am sure I have told them a hundred times not to leave it to him," said Lady Streetham after the servant had bowed himself away. "One would think after all these years they would learn, but they do not. Of course that tiresome boy will neglect his tea as well, and what good dinner will do him I cannot think, when he only daydreams at the epergne."

Miss Desmond suppressed her own smile. "I hope Mr. Langdon is not ill," she said.

"It is a miracle if he is not. He is always engrossed in one book or another, to the exclusion of all else—friends, family, even his own health. I do what I can, because he is very like a son to me, but one cannot watch him every minute."

Especially not, Delilah added inwardly, when one is maintaining unwinking guard over one's actual offspring. She had no opportunity to make the obligatory sympathetic response because the butler now approached to inform the countess that Lady Gathers and her daughter had arrived.

"So soon?" said Lady Streetham. "But Tony is

not yet retur—Well, no matter." She turned to her guest with an expression of cold resignation. "Miss Desmond, if you are not too fatigued, perhaps you would enjoy meeting my neighbours."

"I should like nothing better," Delilah answered. Her hostess's features grew more rigid.

"Unfortunately," Miss Desmond went on, "I find myself unusually susceptible to the heat and am sure to make but poor company as a result. Would you think it unconscionably rude, My Lady, if I excused myself?"

"Not at all," said the countess with a shade of eagerness in her customary chilly tones. "Quite oppressive, the heat. Perhaps you will want a long nap before tea?"

"Actually, I had thought I would sit quietly in your cool library with a book. If Mr. Langdon is still there, I will certainly urge him to cease insulting your excellent chef."

Lady Streetham's frigid countenance thawed ever so slightly. "Very well," she said, and took herself away.

"Yes, it is very well, you stuck-up old battle-axe," said Delilah under her breath. "Far better than having to introduce Devil Desmond's daughter to your exalted friends." Not, Delilah told herself as she moved down the long hall towards the library, that she *wanted* to meet them. Lady Gathers was doubtless another battle-axe and her daughter a demurely proper nincompoop. The entire conversation would be devoted to tearing their friends' reputations to shreds.

All the same, it was rather hard to be treated like a leper, for heaven's sake, when one's blood was every bit as blue as theirs. Bluer. In Charles II's time, the Melgraves had been mere jumped-up squires, while her papa's family had been Norman barons long before the Conqueror was an illicit gleam in his father's eye.

Caught up in her angry reflections, Delilah neglected to knock. As soon as she entered she perceived that knocking would have been futile anyhow. Mr. Langdon did not even look up when she flounced into the room.

He ought to look up. He ought to have looked up at least once in the past twenty-four hours. She had not needed Lord Berne's lyrical compliments last night to be assured that her new amber gown became her. Even this simple sprigged muslin fit her to perfection, and it had cost Papa a substantial sum. Mr. Langdon might at least show some aesthetic interest.

What on earth was so fascinating about that stupid book? She crept noiselessly to his chair and glanced down over his shoulder at the volume that lay open on his lap. Then she gasped.

Mr. Langdon came abruptly to attention. "Miss Desmond," he began, but the look on her face stopped him.

"You!" she cried. "You—you *beast!*"

"Miss Desmond—"

"Don't you speak to me, you wretched man. How dare you?"

"I—I beg your pardon?" said Mr. Langdon, much taken aback. Bent over him was a flushed, furious, and blindingly beautiful countenance whose wrath seemed to set the very air throbbing. Certainly it had his senses reeling.

"A sneak. A horrid, sneaking thief. And I felt sorry for you. Oh, I wish Papa had killed you. No, I wish I had done it myself." Her hand went to the neckline of her frock, then halted.

It dawned on Mr. Langdon that he was for some unaccountable reason in very real danger. The gesture had puzzled him only for an instant, until he'd guessed that she'd gone for her pistol, which, luckily for him, was not at present upon her person.

Quickly he stood up, the volume clutched under his arm.

"Miss Desmond, you are distressed. Shall I—"

"Distressed?" she echoed wrathfully. "You have stolen my father's manuscript and sit here coolly reading it, when anyone might come in and—and—" She paused. "Good Lord, are you mad?"

"I am not mad, Miss Desmond," he said in the soothing tones usually reserved for sufferers of delirium. "I fear, however, that you are hysterical. This volume belongs to your father?"

"No," she snapped. "It is the property of the Archbishop of York. Of course it's my papa's. Surely you noticed that the pages are handwritten—that it is a manuscript, in fact—that it is my father's?"

"Yes, I noticed all that."

"Well?"

"I also could hardly fail to notice that it was here on the shelves with the rest of our host's collection. I assumed your father had given it to Lord Streetham. My own collection contains some unpublished efforts by friends—though I must say this is far more worthy of publication."

The angry flush on her cheeks faded to a more becoming pink as her fury subsided, to be replaced by discomfiture. She did not answer, however, only gazed unhappily at the book he held.

"You are telling me, Miss Desmond, that this book does not belong to Lord Streetham?"

"No, it does not," she answered in a choked voice.

"Then why was it here, and enclosed in this odd binding?" He moved closer to show her the richly tooled cover. "This is supposed to be a work on horticulture."

"Yes, I know. I can read Greek," she said stiffly.

"You can?"

"Don't patronise me, sir."

"I beg your pardon. I meant no offence. It's just that young ladies—"

"Oh, *don't*, please."

To his surprise, Miss Desmond threw herself into the chair he'd vacated and clutched her head in her hands. Several pins flew out, and the gleaming black tresses they'd contained slipped out after them to dangle against her shoulders.

Jack politely looked away.

"Young ladies," she muttered. "Yes, a fine lady I am, don't you think? Make a fool of myself first, then think after. That's the way of it. Good grief." She looked up, her grey-green eyes clouded with remorse. "I'm sorry I called you those horrid names. In case you had any doubts, I have a beastly temper. And no one knows where I get it from because Mama and Papa both are so—oh, never mind."

Though he was unaccustomed to coping with overwrought young women—that was more in Tony's line—Jack had lived with three short-tempered sisters. "I don't mind," he said, trying for the airy tone he often took with Gwendolyn. "It was all very exciting, actually—though I was grateful you hadn't a weapon handy. As the child's rhyme goes, names will never hurt me."

"Oh," she moaned, twisting herself into the corner of the chair and burying her face in her arms. "Now you're going to be gallant. I can't bear it."

"Shall I call *you* names, then, and make us even?"

"Yes," was the muffled response. "And you'd better not be gentle."

"Very well." Holding the volume against his breast, Jack recited calmly. "Virago. Hellcat. Beldam."

She winced.

"Is that enough?" he asked.

She shook her head.

Jack thought. "Termagant," he said.

"Yes."

"Shrew, fury, tigress, she-wolf. Ah, here's an excellent one: cross-patch."

Miss Desmond giggled weakly and raised her pale face towards him.

"Shall I commence in Latin or Greek, or is that sufficient?"

"That will do, Mr. Langdon. I feel much better." She rose. "Now if you will please to give me the book."

Jack's face fell and he backed away. He was, of course, a gentleman to the very core and would do anything to assist a damsel in distress. Anything, that is, except relinquish a book before he'd finished reading it. Especially this book, which was a revelation to him.

"But Miss Desmond, I'm scarcely halfway through it," he said uneasily. "Your father's hand is not always decipherable."

Her slanted eyes narrowed. "Sir, that work is not intended for public consumption," she responded with the exaggerated patience of one addressing a half-wit. "I am not certain why Papa placed it here, though I would guess it was his idea of a perfect hiding place. He has used that false binding before," she explained. "Greek is unenticing to the average person. The topic is even less inviting. The combination is guaranteed to drive off all potential readers. Except," she added with a small sigh, "*you.*"

"I see." He gazed disconsolately at the volume. "I had better put it back." He turned towards the shelves.

"No!" she cried. "You must give it to me. It's obviously not safe here."

"Of course it is," he said, growing stubborn. "Lord Streetham only collects books for show. He never reads anything but political tracts. Tony is interested only in sporting journals. The countess is addicted to gothics. As you said, no one but I

41

would ever muster any interest in so forbidding a volume. Your father obviously knew what he was about. Besides, I might still finish it."

"No! I don't want you to read any more," she blurted out.

Though he was convinced Miss Desmond was a tad unbalanced at present, Mr. Langdon felt guilty. Unbalanced or not, she should not be tormented. He saw her eyes glisten then, and he was undone. He had never in his life made a woman cry, and he was certain this woman was not one to weep easily. He felt like a monster.

He took a step towards her, then paused. She wanted the book, not comforting, and it was not his place to comfort her anyhow—not at least in the way he'd instinctively wished to.

"I do beg your pardon," he said quietly. "I've been most inconsiderate. I'm afraid I thought only of finishing this wonderful story and not—"

"And not about entertaining the ladies, eh, Mr. Langdon?" came a low voice from the doorway.

42

4

Miss Desmond whirled round. "Papa," she breathed.

Her father was glancing over his shoulder into the hall. "In here, Marcus," he said in more carrying tones. "As her ladyship promised, Delilah has come to rescue Mr. Langdon from eyestrain."

Mr. Desmond stepped into the library. An instant later, Lord Streetham appeared.

"Ah, still here," said the earl to Jack. "My lady wife tells me you've been holed up all day, neglecting your meals. Won't do, you know. You must relinquish your books and tend to the ladies at least, if you will not attend to your victuals." He glanced at the volume Jack clasped to his breast. "What have you got there? Greek? You are a sorry rogue, indeed. What do you want with such dusty stuff?"

"Mr. Langdon does not find the work at all dull," said Delilah smoothly when Jack proved mute. "He's spent the last quarter hour explaining it to me. How remarkable, is it not, that he understands Greek so well, to be able to translate such complicated horticultural theories?"

The earl's eyes glazed over. "Yes, yes, I daresay. All the same, Jack, you must come off your hobby-

43

horse and be sociable. No more reading. Take the book home with you when you go, if you like it so much. It's yours. I'm sure I'll never miss it, and Greek is not Tony's forte, as you know."

"You are too generous, My Lord," said Jack, nervously eying Mr. Desmond. "I can't possibly accept."

"Take it, take it," said the earl irritably as he moved to the door. "But mind you appear for tea or her ladyship will be most vexed with you."

"But My Lord—" Jack called after the earl's retreating back.

"Don't be ungrateful, Mr. Langdon," said Mr. Desmond. "Mustn't hurt his lordship's feelings, you know." He winked and followed the earl out of the room.

Delilah was just opening her mouth to speak when her papa put his head back in the door. "My dear, hadn't you better go upstairs and let Joan do something about your hair? I'm afraid you're all atumble again. You will not wish to outrage your hostess's sensibilities, I'm sure."

Miss Desmond shot Mr. Langdon a resentful glance and hastened from the room.

Mr. Langdon had scarcely a minute to recover his composure before Nicholas appeared, bearing a heavily laden tray. "If you please, sir," he said, "her ladyship has asked me to convey her wishes that you take a bite to sustain you until tea time."

"Yes, yes, of course," Jack muttered.

The servant deposited the tray upon a side table, drew out a chair, and stood waiting.

"Was there anything else, Nicholas?"

"I beg your pardon, sir, but she told me I was not to stir from the room until I actually saw you begin to eat," the servant said apologetically.

Jack sighed, placed the troublesome volume upon the writing desk, and sat down before the repast.

He lifted a napkin, glared at it, and dropped it onto his lap. With the air of a man condemned to hard labour, he took up his silverware and began to eat.

Nicholas waited a few minutes, then bowed and exited.

"I shall not need to enter a monastery," Jack grumbled to himself when the door had closed. "By nightfall they'll have packed me off to Bedlam."

When he'd made a reasonable show of attending to his victuals, Mr. Langdon took up the so-called work on horticulture and went in search of Mr. Desmond. He finally ran that gentleman to ground in the billiard room, where a thick grey haze showed that Mr. Desmond had retired to enjoy a cheroot in solitude.

"I must speak with you, sir," said Jack without preamble.

"Yes, I thought so. Well, have a seat. Will you join me?" the older man asked as he offered his cigar case.

Jack, whose meal had not settled very well, shook his head. "I won't be but a moment," he said. "I only wanted to return your manuscript to you."

"Ah, but I'd much rather you didn't," said the Devil, sending up a lovely grey billowing cloud that curled about his head much as darker, more ominous smoke must hover about his namesake. "You see, it's no longer safe in my custody," he explained. "That is why I'm obliged to relinquish it to yours."

Mr. Langdon had already had one disagreeable experience in connexion with this volume. Now he began to scent danger, an aroma as palpable as that of Mr. Desmond's cigar. Jack also sensed that he'd have a very difficult time dissuading this gentleman from involving him.

Mr. Desmond's easy courtesy and low, drawling tones could not disguise a most formidable will. He was, Jack thought, the Irresistible Force personified. Obviously, more than the man's escapades had earned Desmond his nickname.

"I'm flattered you repose such trust in me," Jack said cautiously, "but I really don't deserve it. I'm not reliable. Ask anybody."

"I have," said the Devil, "and what I hear only confirms my belief that you are exactly the man for the job."

Jack sat down, taking the volume upon his lap. It had grown much heavier in the past few minutes.

"Perhaps I had better explain," said Mr. Desmond.

"Yes, thank you. I would appreciate that."

Mr. Desmond began by describing the near-fatal illness which had inspired him to write his recollections. He had intended that, in the event of calamity, their publication would obtain his wife and daughter a respectable sum. Invested wisely, the sum would earn them a modest but reliable annual income.

There being no calamity at the moment, Mr. Desmond was not inclined to stir up old animosities against himself and his family, particularly in the present circumstances. His daughter was unwed. As it was, she would have sufficient difficulty being accepted by a Great World which had decades ago shut its doors to her parents. To publish now was to eliminate any possibility of a respectable marriage to one of her own class.

"Delilah must marry into that class, of course, Mr. Langdon. Though her mama trod the boards for a brief time, she is still an Ornesby and Lord Stivling's niece. Nor am I precisely a parvenu. The barony my brother inherited is an ancient one. Besides, we cannot shackle Delilah to the blacksmith or the tavern-keeper. Their tastes run along more oxen-like lines, I think. Poor child. She's neither fish nor fowl. You have seen for yourself how unrefined her manners are. Not to mention that beastly temper of hers. She will not count to ten."

Without appearing to notice his listener's faint flush, Mr. Desmond went on, "Lady Potterby, my wife's aunt, has courageously agreed to transform Delilah into a Society miss and attempt to launch her in the Little Season."

Lady Potterby must be addled in her wits to take on this Augean task, Jack thought. Still, who was he to judge? What else could a young lady do but wed, especially if she is not a well-heeled young lady? The only gainful employment open to her was as governess, companion, or prostitute. For the former two Miss Desmond's personality appeared profoundly ill-suited. The third alternative was not to be contemplated.

"I understand your reasons for suppressing your story," said Jack, when he belatedly became aware that a response was awaited. "I simply don't understand the difficulty in doing so. Why did you say the manuscript was no longer safe in your custody?"

"Atkins wants it, apparently more desperately than I'd believed. He has hired confederates to invade this household and search our belongings. I made the discovery this morning. Fortunately, I'd already thought to store the manuscript in that false binding. Whoever examined my room did not trouble with a book left out in plain sight. After breakfast I took the book to the library, just as though I'd borrowed it. I had no fear of discovery. I knew that whatever Marcus pretended to be these days, he was no bibliophile. Further, his Greek and Latin were always abominable."

"This sounds so—so conspiratorial," said Jack uncomfortably. "Are you certain, sir, these intruders were not simply common burglars?"

"Then why has there been no general alarm? Why trouble with the belongings of obviously down-

at-heel guests when there are richer pickings elsewhere? No, sir, I'm convinced Atkins is at the bot-
tom of this. Admittedly, I did wonder at first
whether our host had set his servants to search for
deadly weapons. After all, we Desmonds might run
amok and embark upon a murder spree." Mr. Desmond chuckled.

Mr. Langdon's sense of humour had deserted him.
Nor were his spirits raised when Mr. Desmond went
on to describe Mr. Atkins's grief in learning the
book would not be his after all. This had upset the
publisher far more than hearing he must be patient
for his money.

"I had not expected such intrepidity from him, I
must confess," Mr. Desmond continued. "But with
your help we will keep this desperate fellow at bay
until I come up with the blunt to repay him."

The reminder that he was to be the memoirs'
guardian made the hairs at the back of Jack's neck
rise. Unfortunately, he could contrive no reason for
declining the honour that did not sound discourte-
ous or cowardly, especially after Mr. Desmond
pointed out Jack's advantages as custodian.

Jack was fully aware that everyone in the world
knew he was bookish. He always carried volumes
about with him. He might carry this tome wherever he went and not arouse the least speculation.
He was, in short, doomed.

"It was Destiny brought you to the Black Cat the
other night, sir," said the Devil, as though he had
read Jack's mind. "The gods knew we wanted help
and wisely sent the perfect man for the job."

Having bent Mr. Langdon to his will, Mr. Desmond was next confronted with the more onerous
task of pacifying his daughter, who appeared moments after Mr. Langdon had dazedly departed. In
fact, judging from her high colour, she had probably collided with that young man in the hall.

"Oh, he is impossible!" she snapped, slamming the billiard room door behind her.

"Not at all. Mr. Langdon is most accommodating. He has agreed to assist us, Delilah, so I recommend you mind your manners with him. From his expression earlier, I guessed you had treated him to a tantrum, then apologised with the usual fit of self-flagellation. Never before has a young man seemed so relieved at my untimely entrance. I thought he would collapse, weeping, in my arms."

"He is stupid and obstinate. What on earth were you thinking of, to leave him with your book? He had it with him just now. How could you, Papa?"

Mr. Desmond unperturbedly explained precisely how he could, and turned an amiable deaf ear to all her ensuing protestations. He pointed out that Lord Streetham's was an enormous old house which would crumble to pieces if not constantly kept in repair. Of the hired labourers who frequently came on this mission, any one might be Atkins's accomplice. Until the Desmonds were securely housed at Lady Potterby's and could safeguard against further intrusions, Mr. Langdon must keep the manuscript.

His daughter replied that they had better leave immediately for Elmhurst, because she would not sleep a wink until the manuscript was back in her father's possession. Mr. Langdon would be sure to bring the book to dinner, where he would inevitably drop it into his soup. Miss Desmond had never met such a muddled, stupidly oblivious person in her whole life. With these closing remarks, she stormed out of the billiard room.

Mr. Atkins had been told he would not be welcome at Streetham Close while the earl's guests remained. The publisher had therefore taken rooms in a small, uncomfortable inn nearby. The inn's main asset was its tap-room, a gathering place for all the local idlers and gossips. Virtually all that occurred at Streetham Close was a matter of public information within hours.

Mr. Atkins was swallowing a mug of ale he was certain had been made with his hostess's laundry water when he learned the Desmonds had departed for Rossingley. An hour later, the publisher was in Lord Streetham's study, ostensibly to seek his lordship's advice regarding the memoirs.

His lordship was decidedly ungracious. This did not disturb Mr. Atkins, who was accustomed to being treated like the lowest species of insect. He knew less noble investors might be more amiable, but they were not likely to prove useful when a libel suit was imminent. In these litigious times, when a royal whim might land a man in prison for sedition, a wise businessman sought as backers not merely men of wealth, but men of influence. Lord Streetham being such a man, his lack of amiability might be overlooked.

What did disturb the publisher, however, was the earl's curt announcement that Mr. Atkins need not concern himself about the manuscript, since Lord Berne had been charged with "persuading" the Desmonds to relinquish the work.

"With all due respect, My Lord," said Mr. Atkins, "why should they do that? Lord Berne has not paid for it."

"One fool throwing away money is sufficient, I should think," said the earl. "We are dealing with an exceedingly devious man. In self-defence we must be devious as well. You've paid him for goods which he now refuses to deliver. In that case, someone must deliver them for him. Your ignorance of such simple economic logic is the reason you are on the brink of bankruptcy."

What Lord Streetham called "economic logic" sounded remarkably like theft to Mr. Atkins, but he held his tongue, endured a few more insults, and humbly took his leave.

He then took himself back to the inn, where he argued with his landlady for an hour over the reckoning. Finally, having paid his exorbitant shot, Mr. Atkins set out for Rossingley.

Rossingley, as Lord Berne pointed out to his father, was twenty-five miles away. The viscount could hardly visit Miss Desmond every day, claiming he was merely passing through the neighborhood. He could not stay with Jack at Rossing Hall because Lord Rossing hated company, and Lord Berne's company especially.

"There won't be any need to stop every day if you would but apply yourself," the earl retorted. "You might have had the manuscript by now if you had not been gadding about the countryside."

This was grossly unfair. Lord Berne had tried to apply himself to Miss Desmond, but his officious mama had constantly interrupted, sending him on one cork-brained mission after another. That same mama, he now told the earl, would go off in an apoplexy if he commenced regular visits to Lady Potterby's house. "As it is she's prodigious displeased with my neglect of Lady Jane," said Tony.

"Lady Jane will not elope with one of the grooms while you are gone—and so I shall assure your mother. Nor need you blame her for your ineptitude. You were not on errands last evening, yet you allowed Miss Desmond to spend the whole time flirting with Langdon."

Lord Berne frowned. That had been most disconcerting. Jack had been totally oblivious to all Miss Desmond's efforts to draw him out, yet she'd persisted. She'd even resorted to Latin epigrams, for heaven's sake!

Since no woman in his vast experience had ever favoured dull Jack Langdon over himself, Lord

Berne had assumed Miss Desmond was simply attempting to spur a rivalry. Still, it was rather lowering to find he could not understand a word of the Latin which has roused Jack from his reveries. What business had the chit knowing the language in the first place?

"You know, Father, she is a very strange girl," said the viscount thoughtfully.

"Of course she's strange. Look who her father is. And her mother was an actress. What do you expect?"

The frown deepened. Desmond behaved very oddly, too. Most fathers of young women instinctively viewed Lord Berne with a wary eye, if not outright hostility. But Devil Desmond was not remotely hostile. He appeared to regard the viscount as an endlessly amusing joke. Whenever and whatever the Devil was about, Tony always felt as though the man were laughing at him, even when there wasn't the faintest flicker of a smile on his satanic face. Desmond would not, Tony reflected, be quite so amused when his memoirs disappeared.

"Well?" said Lord Streetham. "Do you mean to stand there sulking all day?"

"I can hardly run after them this very moment, sir. They've scarcely left. And it would look too particular if I did so tomorrow—unless they've left something behind?"

"No," was the curt reply. "I had their rooms sear—inspected shortly after they left."

"Doubtless Jack's forgotten something. He always does when his valet isn't by to look after him. I'll go to Rossingley in a day or two to return whatever it is, then call on Lady Potterby. I hope that's satisfactory?"

Lord Streetham was about to voice his opinion that it was *not*, but a moment's reflection stopped him, for he did not want to awaken any suspicions at Lady Potterby's. Oddly enough, there was some

sense in Tony's arguments. Thus the earl answered
sarcastically that he must, by all means, patiently
await his son's convenience.

5

Her restless hands folded tightly before her, Miss Desmond stood listening with increasing dismay to her great-aunt. It was late afternoon and the still air which hung like a thick blanket over the countryside hung heavier still in her luxuriously appointed guest chamber. Lady Potterby flitted about the room like a fussy little white-capped bird, taking up one after another the garments draped upon the bed, shaking her head and twitting unhappily. At the moment, she was frowning at the beloved amber silk.

"Good heavens, child, were you so distant from civilisation that you could not obtain a copy of *La Belle Assemblée*? When girls straight from the schoolroom bare their bosoms in public it is absurd for a woman of twenty to be swathed up to the neck. I realise your endowments are excessive," she added, flicking a reproving glance at her grandniece's bosom, "but if you hide them, the world will think you hide some deformity. That is, if they do not conclude you are a strumpet trying to pass as a chaste maiden."

"Then the world," said Miss Desmond irritably, "is an ass."

"Even if that is so, it is most impolite to mention it, particularly in those terms. Where did you learn such language? But why do I ask? Your papa never troubles to curb his tongue, regardless who is present. Don't slouch, Delilah. Poor posture is both unbecoming and vulgar, and it will only draw added attention to your figure."

Certainly there was no hint of vulgarity about Lady Potterby. Her lace cap was immaculately white. Her grey afternoon gown was the epitome of tidy elegance. She might flutter, but she did so with all the dignity appropriate to her station. Everything about her was exactly *comme il faut*. As a consequence, she made Delilah feel too large, too clumsy, too noisy, and altogether too much of everything.

"I'm sorry, Aunt, that my figure is so unfashionable, but I'm afraid there is no way to amend it."

"Sadly true," said her ladyship with a sigh. "Yet we must not be cast down. In that matter at least, the gentlemen are not such slaves to fashion as ourselves." She brightened and patted the amber silk with something like satisfaction. "Mrs. Archer can drop the neckline an inch or so, and when we get to London, we will leave everything to Madame Germaine. She is frightfully dear, but her taste is impeccable. As to workmanship, there is scarce another dressmaker in Town who can touch her."

"Aunt, I do hope you are not saying I need a new wardrobe," said Delilah with alarm. "Papa really cannot afford—"

"Well, who asked him?" Lady Potterby now took up a light green muslin frock. "This will do for church, I think—at least in Rossingley," she muttered to herself. Then more distinctly she said, "Your papa has nothing to do with it. I told your mama I would move heaven and earth to see you wed. I should hardly stop at a trifle such as a wardrobe. Besides, there is my late elder sister's be-quest. She urged me to use it on your behalf. The poor dear had so many regrets towards the end. We always doted upon your mama, you know, but neither of us wished to stir up more ill-will in the family. Really, sometimes it is very difficult to know what is right."

This Delilah understood too well, in spite of her irritation. Her great-aunt's fault-finding, which had commenced the instant Delilah had alit from the carriage, had continued almost unceasingly since. Still, one was forced to admit the elder lady had the right of it most of the time, and certainly she meant well. One ought to strive for patience, considering the risks her ladyship was prepared to run. The entire Beau Monde was certain to believe Lady Potterby had lost her mind, and the Ornesbys had already ceased communicating with her.

The best return Delilah could make was in striving to be a credit to her great-aunt. Only thus could she hope to overcome the world's prejudices.

"I understand, Aunt," Delilah said, "and I'm deeply grateful for your kindness. I only wish this business were not so expensive."

"Frankly, child, expense is the least of our problems," her aunt answered as she put the green frock aside. "With a mama once an actress and a papa a notorious adventurer—and of course with such a face and figure—you will be prey to every evil-minded man in the kingdom. They will be endlessly casting out lures. I hope you are prepared."

"Yes, Aunt, I know my position is precarious, to say the least. I only wonder," Delilah added dolefully, "if it can ever be made secure. If the men are so busy casting out lures, they may not have time to consider offering marriage."

"It is up to you to behave in such a way to force them to consider it," was the brisk reply. "That wicked Letty Lade got herself a title. Lord Berwick married Harriette Wilson's sister, Sophia, only last

56

year. If noblemen wed demi-reps, why should they not marry a good-looking, blue-blooded maiden?"

"Yes, there must be some senile lord or ambitious Cit who'll be sufficiently blinded by my looks to tumble onto his knees."

"You will not even contemplate marrying into trade, miss," said Lady Potterby sternly as she took up a dark green riding habit. "This is better," she murmured. "Quite dashing."

Then she recollected her grand-niece. "Good heavens, why that long face?" she asked, putting her head to one side like a puzzled sparrow to study the girl. "I hope my frank speech has not lowered your spirits. I only wanted us to face the obstacles squarely, not be overcome by them. Ornesbys are never overcome by obstacles, and certainly not the Desmonds, either." She glanced at the watch dangling from her waist. "Gracious, how late it grows. No wonder you are cross. It is past time for tea."

Tea, it turned out, was an opportunity for a lesson in deportment. Delilah was called upon to pour, so that her great-aunt could size up her command of common etiquette and ability to take instruction. In Lady Potterby's opinion, few exercises so clearly demonstrated a lady's character as her manner in presiding at the tea table.

"Doubtless you observed how Lady Streetham conducted herself," said the great-aunt, watching narrowly as her niece lifted the delicate teapot. "I suppose you were shocked, so stiff she is and lacking in grace."

"My daughter was too busy talking at Mr. Langdon to remark Lady Streetham's skills," said Mr. Desmond as he accepted his cup with a gracious nod. "I am sure Delilah never even glanced at the tea tray—if she did, I cannot think why such an innocent object should cause her to blush so prettily."

"I am vastly relieved to hear she can blush at all," her ladyship returned tartly, "considering your notions of parental guidance. I distinctly heard her utter two oaths when Joan was pinning up her hair."

She turned to Delilah, who was fuming at the teapot. "In future, my dear, you will confine your exclamations to 'good grief' or 'dear me.' But what is this of Mr. Langdon? What on earth could that diffident boy have said to put you to the blush?"

"Perhaps I blushed at my own forwardness in attempting to draw him into conversation, Aunt," said Delilah, darting a quelling glance at her parent. He knew perfectly well why she'd been talking frantically at Mr. Langdon. She'd been terrified the muddled creature would blurt out some quote from her papa's memoirs. She would not have been placed in so awkward and frustrating a position if her papa had not been so obstinate.

Delilah's scowl turned into an expression of dismay as she recollected that Mr. Langdon still had the book. Where *was* the stupid man? He should have returned it immediately. He'd left Streetham Close hours before they had—and without so much as a farewell.

"What on earth is the matter, miss? Have you spilled tea on your skirt? Did I not just tell you to keep an easy, amiable countenance, as though the activity required no effort or concentration whatsoever?"

"I fear we must look deeper than the teapot, Millicent. Obviously, Delilah is pining for Mr. Langdon." Mr. Desmond turned to his daughter. "I beg your pardon, my dear. I should not have brought his name into the conversation."

"Certainly not in so absurd a way," said Delilah indignantly. "Pining for him, indeed. What nonsense. I hope you will pay Papa no mind, Aunt. He

58

is an incorrigible tease." She picked up a plate of pastries. "Will you try the seed-cake, My Lady?"

Lady Potterby smiled approvingly. "Very well done, my dear. Just the right air. Is it not, Darryl? Could Queen Charlotte do any better, I ask you?"

"Not when His Majesty is by. I understand he has long, bawdy conversations with the cucumber sandwiches," was the irreverent reply.

"That is cruel, Darryl, and possibly seditious. You cannot know how the poor man suffers."

"Of course I know. Am I not acquainted with his sons? It's a wonder to me he went on producing offspring. Surely the first half dozen must have shown him his seed was cursed."

"You will not speak of such topics before the girl, sir. If she has had a steady diet of such conversation, it is a miracle she can blush as you claim. A young lady must be capable of blushing," Lady Potterby pointed out to her grand-niece, "or she will appear hardened in iniquity."

"No fear of that," said Mr. Desmond. "She colours very nicely when a certain gentleman who must remain nameless is by, I assure you."

"Papa, you are most tiresome today," said Delilah, putting down her cup and saucer with a clatter that made her great-aunt frown.

"Indeed you are, Darryl. Why do you tease so about poor Mr. Langdon? I cannot believe he has been making sheep's eyes at Delilah—or any young lady, for that matter. Lord Berne is another case altogether," the lady went on, instantly reverting to an earlier bone of contention with her male relative. "You should never have stopped there when that wicked young man was at home. I could not rest easy a moment after I got your message. Do you know the dreadful boy took Annabelle Carstairs into the hedgerows—on his own father's property—and now she calls herself Mrs. Johnson and

59

lives in Dublin, and there never was a Mr. Johnson, not that ever stood before the parson with her."

"Oh, not that rattle," said Desmond. "Delilah took his measure quickly enough. Didn't you, my precious?"

Miss Desmond's cheeks were tingling. The hedgerows. No wonder Mr. Langdon had steered her away so firmly. If Lady Streetham had not rushed out of the house . . . but that was absurd. Delilah Desmond was no naïve Annabelle Carstairs. She was not about to be seduced in *bushes*, for heaven's sake.

"He is obviously a rake," she said primly.

"He most certainly is—and that is the kindest name one can give him," Lady Potterby agreed. "You did well to devote your attention to Mr. Langdon instead."

"I did not—"

"I admit he's excessively shy," the great-aunt went on unheedingly. "But he at least is a perfect gentleman. I am sure he subjected you to no over-warm compliments."

"Well, he must have said something to raise her temperature. I am sure she turned pink every time she was in his company," said the pitiless father.

"Papa!"

Lady Potterby was at last goaded into giving the matter serious attention. "Good heavens, Darryl, are you certain? Do we speak of the same Jack Langdon? That absentminded creature who always has his head in a book? He exerted himself to have a conversation with my grand-niece? He did not hurry off to hide in a corner with his tiresome Greeks?"

"He tried," said the Devil gravely, "but Delilah wouldn't let him."

Miss Desmond took up her teacup again with an air of resignation. For some unaccountable reason, her father was set on provoking her. Well, she would not give him the satisfaction of appearing at all vexed.

"Yes, Aunt," Delilah concurred. "I am afraid I am very forward. Just one more character flaw I shall strive to overcome, with your assistance."

"But you obtained his attention?" asked the lady eagerly.

"Fortunately, Papa has overseen my education. I took refuge in Latin epigrams, and Mr. Langdon was sufficiently dazzled to respond in kind."

"Indeed," said her ladyship thoughtfully. "Latin epigrams. My, my. That was very well done of you, I must say." She meditated.

"Shall I add water to the tea leaves, Aunt? Or is it too cold, do you think?"

"Bother the water," Lady Potterby muttered. "I am thinking." She meditated a few minutes longer, then nodded to herself. "Yes, it will do. We will have them to tea, of course. Tomorrow."

Delilah shot a suspicious glance at her father, who only smiled inscrutably. "Whom do you mean, Aunt?"

"Why Rossing, of course, and his nephew. Good heavens, why did I not think of it myself? He is perfect. The soul of rectitude—and staying right next door. Mr. Langdon is one of the few gentlemen in Society who will not automatically make assumptions about your character based on your parents' behaviour. Absent-minded he may be, but he is also fair-minded. If you can win his admiration, you will have won a staunch ally. I will look no farther than that, of course, for the time being. We must not put all our eggs in one basket, my dear."

Lady Potterby, looking altogether pleased with the eggs she had found, got up and ambled out of the drawing room mumbling to herself about orders she must give Cook for the morrow.

"So that's what you were about," Delilah accused her father when the elder woman was gone. "Why did you not simply come out and ask her to invite them?"

"Because it was more amusing to entice her into proposing the matter herself. People are always more enthusiastic about their own brilliant ideas."

"I still do not see why it was necessary to utter such fabrications about my blushes. 'Pining away,' " she said scornfully. "I thought I would be ill."

"Oh, you were not pining?" the father asked, all innocence. "How stupid of me. I thought that was why you were languishing by the window this morning as Mr. Langdon rode away."

Miss Desmond feigned a yawn. "How very amusing, Papa. But do divert yourself as you like. I shall occupy my time in praying my muddled swain remembers to bring your manuscript with him when he comes."

Mr. Langdon hastily put down his coffee cup. The hot liquid splashed over the rim and onto his fingers, but he didn't notice. He blinked at his uncle.

"Tea? With Lady Potterby?"

"Yes. She sent a message late yesterday, but I'm afraid it slipped my mind. You're making a mess, Jack," said Lord Rossing, peering over his newspaper. "You had better not do that at Millicent's. As it is she thinks us incapable of taking care of ourselves. Always sending her jellies and bouillons and I don't know what else. The poor creature's been like that ever since Potterby passed on—what was it—five years ago? Then she was nursing her old fright of a sister. Might have expected this. She always wants someone to look after. Pity she hasn't any children. Well, we must go and meet her relatives, I suppose." He put down his paper and took up his silverware.

"Actually, Uncle, I've already met them. I thought I'd mentioned it."

"So you did, so you did." Lord Rossing stabbed

62

his fork into a piece of ham. "So have I. Desmond, I mean. Intriguing fellow. Quite a rogue in his day. Pursued your mama for a while. Did you know that?"

"No, I did not."

"Didn't catch her, lucky fellow. But then, he did catch more than his share, I'll warrant. Rather like your swell-headed friend, Melgrave, in that way. Only Desmond had more address. Or maybe it was simply intelligence. I don't know. At any rate, he was the only one of those loose fish I ever could have a conversation with." He gazed at the forgotten fork in his hand for a moment as though wondering what it was doing waving about in the air. Then he put it into his mouth and reverted to his customary silence.

Mr. Langdon contemplated his plate. He had completely forgotten about returning Mr. Desmond's property. Not that Jack had forgotten the property itself, though. The manuscript had rarely left his hands. He'd felt guilty, at first, about continuing to read, given Miss Desmond's violent opposition to his doing so. However, she was not by to harass him, and the book was irresistible. Now his neglected conscience sprang to agitated life. What had he been thinking of, to keep the manuscript overnight? He should have returned it immediately.

The trouble was, he was extremely reluctant to confront Miss Desmond. He had managed, with the memoirs' help, to put her out of his mind during his waking hours. When he slept, though, she crept into feverish dreams—of tumbled black tresses and hot, angry eyes and silken white skin . . . of heated struggles that subsided into long and languorous joinings of another kind. He would awake perspiring, to find the bed-clothes tangled into knots and his breath coming in gasps.

Jack Langdon was accounted an eccentric and

63

known to be shy of women. All the same, he had the normal urges of any healthy young man. He knew what desire was and how to assuage it, but he had never felt anything like desire—rather the opposite—for women of his own class. Only Catherine Pelliston had awakened in him something like passion. Certainly it had thrilled him to discover a kindred spirit in female form. Whenever he'd dared imagine an ideal mate, such was the character he'd conjured up.

Miss Desmond was no kindred spirit. She was wild, brazen, hot-tempered, and completely unpredictable. Every time she spoke to him she set his nerves jangling so he couldn't think straight. With Miss Desmond, Jack's normal discomfort in feminine company increased a hundredfold, because added to his usual consciousness of his dull inadequacy was the disconcerting awareness that he'd wanted her from the moment he'd knocked her down.

Jack forced a bit of his omelette into his mouth and with a mighty effort, swallowed it. He must go, like it or not. He dared not entrust the ersatz book to his uncle, because the viscount was certain to open it and read it on the way, as he walked.

Jack would have to return it himself. He would have to converse with the Desmonds and hope the ugly thing consuming him was not evident in his countenance. Then he would be done with them. As to the thing itself—this unspeakable desire was nothing more than an appetite. Like others, it might be channelled into more appropriate directions, if he would but apply himself.

6

Mr. Langdon was so eager to be rid of the manuscript and thereby end all reasons for communicating with the Desmonds that he hurried his uncle out of the house well in advance of the time appointed for tea.

Lord Rossing and his nephew entered the vestibule just as Mr. Atkins was being handed his hat by a haughty Bantwell. Mr. Atkins did not appear happy. Miss Desmond, who stood beside her father, appeared even less so. Lady Potterby, who'd evidently conceived a keen dislike for Mr. Atkins, threw him a baleful glance before taking up the introductions.

"Ah, yes," said Mr. Atkins, when Lady Potterby had condescended to acknowledge his existence. "Mr. Langdon and I have briefly met, though not formally."

Jack pronounced himself pleased at the acquaintance, though he felt anything but. The sham book was under his arm, and Mr. Atkins was eying it with curiosity.

"What a handsome volume you have there, Mr. Langdon. I fancy myself rather a connoisseur, and it seems a rare specimen. Greek, is it?" he asked, oblivious to the company's blatant impatience with him to be gone.

"Yes," said Jack, looking to Mr. Desmond for guidance. That gentleman, however, had turned his attention to Lord Rossing to commence a review of their mutual acquaintance.

"It was a gift from Lord Streetham," Jack added uneasily, "and—and I brought it to show Miss Desmond."

"How thoughtful," said Lady Potterby with an indulgent smile. "A book of poetry, is it?"

"No, Aunt," Delilah said quickly. "Horticulture. Mr. Langdon has a perfect passion for horticulture, do you not sir?" She turned to Jack with a dazzling smile.

Jack nodded.

"Since we have some time before tea will be served, you may wish to examine her ladyship's garden." Delilah moved closer to take Jack firmly by the arm. "Perhaps you'll be kind enough to explain the differences between the Greek techniques and modern methods of cultivation."

Mr. Langdon stiffly avowed himself delighted.

If Lady Potterby thought her grand-niece rather forward, she must have also recollected that Mr. Langdon, being an exceedingly shy gentleman, might require firm guidance. After giving the young pair permission to retire to the garden, she tried with all the frigid courtesy at her disposal to rid her hallway of the unwelcome visitor.

"What is that fellow doing here?" Jack asked, when they had turned into the path leading to the decorative herb garden. "I thought your father sent him about his business."

"Papa told you about him?" said Delilah, dismayed.

"Your father was kind enough to enlighten me concerning your difficulties—and I do wish you had,

Miss Desmond. Had I understood the enormity of the problem, I would never have behaved so—so childishly. To me it was simply a wonderful story," he explained. "I never thought of the difficulties it presented you."

"Well, now you know. So you can guess that Mr. Atkins has come to plague my father again. Has Papa told you he was paid five hundred pounds?"

"No. I take it the money has been spent?"

She shook her head and appeared embarrassed. "We dare not spend it. It's been put aside as—as my dowry. Papa's income comes from cards," she explained quickly. "And no one in England will play him for high stakes. He must send money to my mother in Scotland as well as keep himself here, which means we have nothing to spare." Miss Desmond's smooth brow became furrowed. "Meanwhile, I must have a marriage portion. If I don't marry reasonably well, then we'll probably have to publish—some day. My parents are not getting any younger. It's most vexing, yet we seem to have no choice but to put Mr. Atkins off indefinitely."

"I see," Jack said thoughtfully.

"I know it sounds horribly mercenary—" she began.

"Miss Desmond, I have three sisters," he interrupted gently. "The youngest, Gwendolyn, has been paraded on the Marriage Mart for three Seasons now. I understand the business fully—and it is a business, a most expensive one. In the circumstances, I fully understand your father's caution."

"Still, there's no denying we've played Mr. Atkins false."

Jack smiled. "That's absurd. Murray had to wait months while Byron agonised about publishing *Childe Harold*."

They had reached the herb garden, an extensive formal planting that radiated out from a central sun-dial. Miss Desmond gazed about her unhappily.

"At any rate, even if we could repay Atkins, Papa's sure he won't take the money back—not while there's any chance of publishing and making a great fortune," she added cynically. "I fear he's right. Who'd have thought such a nervous little man could be so obstinate—or so devious? Papa says Mr. Atkins sent someone to Streetham Close to steal the manuscript. Now I'm sure he'll send someone here. We can't carry that tome about with us everywhere and we can't watch it every minute. The house is too large," she said, glancing back at the immense stone building. "She has nearly as many servants as Lord Streetham does, and I don't know a quarter of them."

Jack followed her gaze. The late Lord Potterby's ancestors, like everyone else in the shire, had competed fiercely when it came to home building. Though none could compare with Blenheim, all the great houses for miles around were enormous structures, built to awe the beholder. Rossing Hall was the sole exception, because there had been more than one reclusive Langdon in the family tree.

The second Lord Rossing had built his house in Elizabeth's time, but had not included lodgings for her majesty's household in the modest plans. The queen and her entourage were a deal too noisy for his simple tastes.

Jack knew every servant, down to the lowest pot boy. The labourers who maintained the building and grounds had been doing so for decades. Every face was familiar and trusted.

Stifling a sigh, he said, "I suppose, then, the book will be safest at Rossing Hall." Reluctantly he went on to outline the advantages of his uncle's house, the viscount's reclusive habits, and the virtual impossibility of strangers invading the premises, but Miss Desmond broke in abruptly, her grey-green eyes alight with inspiration.

"No," she said. "I have a better idea. We'll bury it."

"We'll what?" cried Jack, aghast.

"Here. In the garden." Miss Desmond abruptly released his arm and began walking quickly down the path which led to the perennial beds.

Mr. Langdon hastened after her. "Miss Desmond, you cannot dig up your aunt's flower beds. Don't you think the gardener will remark it?"

"She's made him move something. I heard her complaining about the bees. There!" she cried triumphantly as they reached a bed entirely stripped of the bergamot it had once contained. "He hasn't replanted yet."

"Of course not, in this heat. If you knew anything about gardening, Miss Desmond—"

"I don't need to know anything." She turned shining eyes upon him. "Because she knows nothing of ancient Greek horticulture. We'll tell her it's an experiment."

She dragged Jack off to the potting shed, where, after a brief discussion with the distracted gardener, they possessed themselves of a few tools and several healthy seedlings.

After a brief argument, Jack dug the hole. Miss Desmond placed the book in its grave, waited until he had thrown some dirt upon it, then began stuffing plants into the loose soil. Jack knelt beside her.

"They'll die," he said, eying the seedlings. Some were packed into dirt so deeply that only the very tops showed. "It's too hot and I'm sure you've done it wrong."

"Then we'll blame it on the Greeks." Miss Desmond thrust a stray lock of hair back from her face.

It was very hot, indeed. The air was as thick as new-churned butter. Mr. Langdon had removed his coat, but his waistcoat was plastered to his shirt, which was stuck to his skin. He noted that Miss Desmond had rubbed a dirty smudge onto her right cheekbone. He was about to offer his handkerchief when he saw a bead of perspiration trickle down from her temples past the smudge, along her slender white neck, past her collarbone and on down until it disappeared at the edge of her bodice. The air must have grown heavier still, because Mr. Langdon suddenly found it quite impossible to breathe.

Miss Desmond looked towards him then. Her eyes widened slightly and her cheeks began to glow faintly pink. She scrambled up very quickly. Too quickly, apparently, in the heat, because he saw her hand go to her head as she began to sway.

Jack rose hastily. "Miss Desmond, are you ill?" he asked, putting out his hand to assist her.

"No," she said, backing away. "Just dizzy for a moment. I—"

She did not complete the thought because she tripped on the trowel and lost her balance.

Fortunately, she stumbled forwards instead of backwards, and Jack was able to catch her before she fell. Unfortunately, once he'd caught her, he was presented with an interesting example of the mind-body dichotomy. His mind told him to let go of her. His hands clasped her upper arms more firmly. Then his gaze locked with hers and, drawn like the tides to the moon, his head bent slowly until his lips met soft ones, tasting slightly of salt, and while his brain watched, horrified and helpless, he kissed her.

Mr. Atkins had no business in the garden. Though Desmond had put him off in his usual urbanely evasive way, Lady Potterby had made plain her disapproval of the publisher's unexpected visit. Naturally she would not approve. He carried with him that distasteful aroma of the City which only aristocrats could discern. No doubt she thought him a mushroom, presuming upon a chance acquaintance with the Desmonds in order to encroach his way into noble households.

Mr. Atkins could not afford to be thin-skinned, however. He had delayed his departure well beyond the limits of her ladyship's patience because he must leave empty-handed, which meant he would be ruined, and he was as reluctant to face ruin as any more sensitive fellow.

He had stolen into the garden because he was grasping at straws. Why had Mr. Langdon clutched that curious volume to his breast as though it were his firstborn? Why had Miss Desmond been so eager to hustle the young man out of the house?

Hoping desperately that the answers to these questions would somehow lead him to the manuscripts, Mr. Atkins trespassed quietly past the herb garden and on towards the perennial beds. There he found the puzzle solved and his hopes dashed. In short, he caught sight of the pair at the precise moment in which Mr. Langdon was confronting the mind-body dichotomy.

Mr. Atkins's head began to throb as he turned and headed back to his gig—and, he was certain, bankruptcy.

Miss Desmond was not altogether shocked at first. She had seen the same hot light before in other men's eyes. Though she was surprised to see it in Mr. Langdon's, she'd sensed what was coming and instinctively backed away. The trouble was, this sober young man had an uncanny knack for leading her to step wrong—today quite literally.

Once she found herself in his arms, she'd decided she might as well let him steal his kiss—only because she was curious—and thereafter reward him with severe bodily injury. These admirable intentions had been delayed of execution because the first tentative touch had softened her stony heart. He was too shy to *really* kiss her, poor man. In a moment he would jump back, embarrassed, stammering every sort of apology.

What followed in that moment could not have been more opposed to her expectations. His hands slid to her back, and in an instant, it seemed, the kiss became sure, thorough, and ... debilitating.

Miss Desmond had rarely before suffered a kiss for more than a few seconds. She knew too well the consequences, especially for one of her dubious heritage. Now those seconds had passed, she found herself slipping into uncharted and surprisingly stormy waters.

As his mouth, tender but sure, moved over hers, she was strangely unable to do anything but respond in kind. In the next moment, without warning, the bright afternoon sun was submerged in the dark wave that engulfed her as his lips grew more demanding and his hands pressed her closer. Her mind grew dark as well.

There was far too much warmth, suddenly, and something like electricity darting through her as his arms tightened about her to crush her against his chest. Her own muscles grew weak, as though his drew their strength from them. It was, finally, the trembling of her weakening limbs that alerted her, that made her recollect to what—and whom—she was succumbing.

She jerked herself free and slapped him as hard as she could. Then she only stood where she was, because though she was furious—and perhaps a tad alarmed—she was too weak-kneed to storm off as she wished to.

Had she been herself, the blow would have staggered him. As it was, he scarcely winced, only stared at her in horror. "Oh, my God," he said, as his face reddened to match the mark she'd left there.

"You—you cur!" she spat out. "How dare you?

But of course you dare, you—you wolf in bookworm's clothing. You're just like all the rest."

"Miss Desmond, please. I beg your pardon. I cannot think what I—"

"I can think what you are. You can count yourself lucky I hadn't my pistol with me or you'd never think again."

"Oh, my God." He stared blindly about him, his expression that of a man who has just trodden upon a nest of angry cobras. "Am I losing my mind?" He turned to her then, and in his grey eyes she saw, outraged as she was, genuine anguish.

"As an excuse, that is hardly original—or complimentary," she said tartly.

"Miss Desmond, I cannot make any excuse. I can scarcely imagine any apology that would be remotely adequate. It is simply—" He hesitated.

"Yes, it is simply a matter of taking me for a lightskirts—which is, naturally, what everyone does, and I suppose I should be used to it by now."

"It's nothing of the sort." He ran his fingers through his hair, which she noted was already untidy.

Good grief, Delilah thought, had she made it so? She could not remember where her own hands had been a few moments before. She wanted to dash into the house and up to her room where she could hide under the bed, but she had too much pride to retreat. She stood waiting, watching, as he seemed to struggle with something. Finally, he spoke.

"Miss Desmond, I find there is—I mean, I have an intensity of . . . feeling for you that . . . that I cannot understand—or control, apparently," he ended feebly.

"It is usually called lust, Mr. Langdon," she snapped as the recollection of his recent power over her stirred up her fury again. "Though I'm relieved to hear you don't understand it, because I certainly could not. After all, I am not paper and ink and

73

bound in morocco. Or will you claim you were touched by the sun and took me for a volume of Ptolemy? That would be far more original than this equivalent of 'I don't know what came over me.'"

His grey eyes darkened, and his face became rigid. Even before he spoke, Delilah knew she'd gone too far.

"Whatever my tastes, madam—and I do admit I am more than average fond of reading—I am not made of paper and ink, either," he said coldly. "I am still a man. I suppose I may have moments of weakness like other men? We all of us, despite our best intentions, occasionally forget we are gentlemen. I had such a moment, and I do humbly beg your pardon. Or is there some further penance you wish to exact?"

Delilah knew what penance he referred to. She knew she had, technically, a right to claim he'd compromised her. For an instant she was even tempted to do so, because she could think of no more fitting punishment than to make him marry her, disgrace his name, outrage his family, and be miserable all the rest of his days. Pride—and perhaps a twinge of guilt—overcame anger, however. She was not so desperate for a husband. Furthermore, it was most unwise to arouse his enmity, considering all he knew about the manuscript.

"Now you are being unfair," she said. "It's the lady's prerogative to be insulted and the gentleman's to be penitent. You did far better when you were all abject apologies. You were so beautifully insincere."

"I was entirely sincere," he returned angrily.

"If you were, then why do you pick on me now? If you must be wicked enough to try to seduce me in my great-aunt's garden, you might at least allow me to be insulted and faint and scream and become hysterical. That's *supposed* to be how it's done."

He opened his mouth to retort, then shut it and

74

looked around instead for his coat. He snatched it up from a bush and shrugged himself into it. It was a very well-made coat, Delilah noted, even as she was wondering how to mollify him. It fit him quite nicely.

"You hate me," she said.

He gazed at her in exasperation. "I was not trying to seduce you, Miss Desmond."

"Well, I most certainly was not trying to seduce *you*. Why are you so angry with me?"

"I wish," he said quietly, "you had your pistol. I wish you would just shoot me and be done with it."

Delilah sighed. "Oh, very well, have it your way," she said. "I apologise for whatever it is I've done, though I do think you are monstrous unjust and ungallant in this. Still, I can't let you go in to tea looking like an outraged Zeus or Aunt will be scolding me for hours. She'll probably send me back to Scotland," she added.

"She ought to," said Jack. "You are perfectly impossible."

"I know," she said, her face penitent.

Delilah Desmond penitent was a sight calculated to unman the most obdurate of tyrants, which Mr. Langdon certainly was not. He was, in fact, painfully aware that his behaviour had been criminal in the first place and rude and insolent in the second. Even though she had slighted his masculinity, he had no business being enraged. He'd slighted it himself often enough. All the same, he was very upset. Her sarcastic remarks still smarted, and he wanted to throttle her. He wondered fleetingly if he were possessed, because by rights he should throttle himself.

"Miss Desmond, I am not angry," he said wearily. "I am deeply ashamed of my behaviour. I promise never to repeat it. We've disposed of the book. Can we please dispose of this distressing conversation?"

75

"Yes," she said in an oddly subdued voice. "Do I look a fright?"

No, he thought, only more maddeningly beautiful than ever.

"Yes," he said. "You have dirt on your face and the state of your hair makes you look like Medusa. You had best go tidy up or we'll be subjected to a most intensive interrogation. No one will mind me," he added with a wry glance at his stained trousers. "It's exactly what they expect."

As an unusually docile Miss Desmond took herself away to be tidied, it may have occurred to her that, in Mr. Langdon's case, people really had better not place too much reliance upon their expectations.

Mr. Atkins returned to his latest inn, which was only slightly less uncomfortable than the first, with every intention of proceeding to Streetham Close as soon as he had revived his sagging spirits with food. His hostess was slow, however, and by the time he had finished his meal, the sky was darkening ominously.

He had just climbed into his vehicle when lightning crackled. From a distance followed the low boom of thunder. In the next moment, the heavens burst about his ears, and by the time he'd regained the shelter of the inn, he was drenched.

Nonetheless, he set out for Streetham Close the following morning, sniffling and sneezing the whole way. The earl, never eager for his company in the best of circumstances, did not trouble to disguise his disgust with the repellent spectacle before him.

Mr. Atkins refused to be cowed. Doggedly, between blowing his nose and sneezing, he reported what he'd seen. He declared that even a simple man like himself could see Lord Berne would have a very difficult time obtaining the young lady's trust when she was so busy trying to ensnare Mr. Langdon.

"I think, My Lord, we'd best increase our offer," the publisher went on. "The alternative I shudder at—though I suppose it can be done. That is to say, the manuscript must be somewhere in the house, and I understand there are persons who may be hired to—to deliver it up to us."

Lord Streetham drew himself up. In no uncertain terms he informed the publisher that bribery and theft were not in his line. Persuasion was another matter. "As I have already pointed out to you," he said, "my son is perfectly capable of persuading the young lady."

"He hasn't done it yet," Mr. Atkins muttered, rubbing his red nose.

Of this his lordship was frustratedly aware. Aloud, however, he only cited the heir's many responsibilities, and advised Mr. Atkins to return speedily to London where Mrs. Atkins might give him proper care.

After Mr. Atkins had taken his nasal leave, Lord Streetham summoned his son.

"I see I must deal with this myself," his lordship said frigidly. "Obviously you cannot be counted upon to assume any of the responsibilities of your position. While you amuse yourself at common hostelries, Jack Langdon is seducing Miss Desmond—in her great-aunt's garden, no less."

Lord Berne was, sad to say, a very fickle young man. His interest in Miss Desmond had dwindled with every passing hour of her absence, which time he had pleasantly whiled away in a rendezvous with his father's former mistress and a lively flirtation with the fair and saucy Sarah. Along with decreasing interest in Miss Desmond had grown an increasing reluctance to antagonise her formidable parent.

Men far more reckless than himself became circumspect when dealing with Devil Desmond or anything connected to him. To deceive his daughter, especially for a useless lot of ink and paper, seemed wantonly self-destructive.

Now, however, as he left his irate father, Lord Berne was outraged. That poky Jack Langdon should succeed with the girl so easily—in a mere day or two—when that same young woman had proved so incomprehensibly indifferent to the viscount's own irresistible charm . . . it was not to be endured.

7

DELILAH GAZED IN disgust at the Gordian knot of stitches that was supposed to pass for embroidery. "Isn't that typical?" she muttered. "I make a mess of everything."

Her father looked up from his sporting journal. The two were spending a few quiet hours together while Lady Potterby visited an ailing neighbour, and they were abnormally quiet. Normally, Delilah and her father could converse endlessly. Today she was unable to find any entertaining topic because yesterday's garden episode preyed on her mind.

She still could not believe that she, Delilah Desmond, had very nearly succumbed to the clumsy embrace of the provoking, stodgy Mr. Langdon. She had travelled over half the globe with her parents and encountered every sort of scoundrel. She had met with every seductive trick and heard honeyed speeches in half a dozen languages. Always she had been immune, observing her pursuers' efforts with the same cool detachment with which she studied her cards and bluffed her way to victory over the most cunning Captain Sharps.

She could not understand why her instincts had failed her yesterday—and with him, of all people, a muddled, naïve book-worm. It was too humiliating for words.

Now, as Delilah met her father's calm scrutiny, her conscience pricked her. She was not used to keeping secrets from him.

"Papa, if I tell you something," she began, "will you promise not to do anything violent?"

"If I didn't yesterday, why should I today?" was the disconcerting reply. "As you say, Mr. Langdon left with all his limbs intact—though I cannot speak for his mind."

The daughter's eyes widened. "You saw?"

"The entire household might have seen, for all I know. The corner window of the drawing room looks out over that section of the perennial beds. Luckily, Lord Rossing and your great-aunt were dithering at each other on the opposite side of the room, so I had no need to act the role of outraged parent, thank heavens. Beastly weather, worse than the West Indies. At least last night's storm has cleared the air somewhat."

Miss Desmond's embroidery had fallen unnoticed to the carpet. "It was an accident, Papa, I assure you."

"Indeed? Which part?" he asked as he laid his journal aside. "Did you entomb my memoirs accidentally on account of sunstroke or are you referring to the subsequent performance?"

Embarrassed, Delilah took the offensive. "You were spying on me!"

"Not at all. I was looking out for Mr. Langdon. When you hauled him so hastily out of doors, I began to fear for his life. I grew increasingly alarmed when I saw that trowel in your hand. Awkward things, trowels."

Delilah glared at an insipid porcelain shepherdess standing on the small table at her elbow. "I suppose you found the entire scene immensely entertaining," she grumbled.

"More entertaining, I think, than Mr. Langdon

did. When he came in to tea he looked as though he'd been fighting the Thirty Years' War single-handedly. I wish you would not plague him so, Delilah. He is supposed to be our ally."

"I—plague him! When he took advantage—"

Her father raised an eyebrow.

"I certainly did not encourage him," she said hotly.

The door opened and Bantwell entered to inform Mr. Desmond that Lord Wemberton had arrived.

"We'll pursue this discussion later, Delilah," said her papa as he rose from his chair. "Wemberton has very kindly offered to have a look at the grey. He has a taste for ill-behaved beasts. Takes it as a challenge, I suppose."

While her papa was occupied with Lord Wemberton, Delilah decided to work off her irritation with a walk into Rossingley. No wonder her brain was fuddled. She was not used to being so inactive. Gad, but ladies had a dull life of it.

She knew she ought to take Joan along, but the abigail always whined if she had to stir more than a few yards. Instead, Miss Desmond strapped her knife sheath to her calf and tucked her small pistol into her reticule. If she were in danger, these two would do her a deal more good than Joan would.

Delilah had walked scarcely half a mile before she met up with Lord Berne travelling in the opposite direction. As soon as he caught sight of her he brought his curricle to a halt and offered to take her up.

"I will take you out of your way," she said as she took in the dashing picture of snug blue coat, nankeen breeches, and gleaming top boots. His beaver hat, slightly tilted, gave him a rakish air which his angelic blue eyes stoutly contradicted. He was a devastating combination of dangerous masculinity and boyish innocence—and he knew it.

"That is impossible, since it was you I came to see," he answered with a winning smile.

Miss Desmond was not in a humour to be won so easily. She pointed out that she'd already outraged propriety by going out without her maid. She would not compound the error by driving with him when he was without a tiger.

"I had not thought we needed bodyguards, Miss Desmond," he said. "It is broad day, and no highwayman has been seen in these parts in over a decade."

"My reputation can bear a highwayman, My Lord. A libertine is another matter." She offered a brilliant smile and proceeded on her way.

The viscount promptly turned his carriage and came up beside her again.

"If you mean to follow me to Rossingley, I shall be cross with you," she said. "You raise a deal of dust and my frock will be spoiled."

"I can't help it. I'm curious."

She paused. "About what?"

He glanced at the cushioned seat of his equipage, then at the floor, then turned round to study the small rear seat where his tiger would normally be perched.

"About how I can possibly seduce you in the curricle without relinquishing the reins," he answered ingenuously. "With, in fact, any degree of safety and comfort."

His baffled glance met an amused one.

"Clearly, I am not as imaginative as you are, Miss Desmond. Would you be kind enough to explain how the thing is to be accomplished?" he asked.

"Certainly not." She went on walking, and the curricle went on beside her. After five minutes of silence, she swore to herself, stopped, and looked up at him.

"You are very obstinate," she said. "Do you really intend to follow me all the way into town and make a spectacle of me?"

He nodded.

She sighed. "Very well, I'll ride. But only back to Elmhurst. I don't mean to set the whole village buzzing."

As he moved to help her, she waved him back, telling him to mind the horses. "You can't be chivalrous when you've no tiger to take the reins," she said, climbing up easily.

"That's better," he said as, to the great annoyance of his cattle, he turned the curricle once more. "Now you might satisfy my curiosity more comfortably. On another topic, I mean," he added quickly as her eyes narrowed. "What is all this about your reputation? What harm is there in a short drive in broad day, even with a libertine?"

"That should be obvious."

He only looked baffled.

"My parents," she said impatiently.

"What has that to do with you? You haven't joined a theatre troupe or carried on a series of dazzling escapades and love affairs. Quite the opposite. You've been exceedingly decorous, and I can't tell you how depressing I find that." He shook his head sorrowfully. "You wouldn't even drive with me, simply because I came without my groom. I hope you won't think me vain, Miss Desmond, if I tell you no one has ever done that before."

"Well, I'm here now," she said. "Pray be as vain as you like."

"I can't. I'm consumed by guilt. I never considered the damage my coming to call might do. I've been inexcusably thoughtless."

"I would not refine upon it too much, My Lord. Lady Potterby will not allow you past the doorstep anyhow. If we manage to reach Elmhurst without being seen, then I may escape this unscathed."

She felt his gaze upon her. As she turned to meet it, she saw a flicker of something in his eyes, but it was gone in an instant, and she could not tell what it was.

"Miss Desmond, I think this is monstrous unfair," he said, sounding indignant. "People have no right to judge you by your parents, even if they were right in judging your parents so harshly—which I do not accept, either."

"In the abstract, perhaps they have no right, but this is the real world. In the real world, Lady Potterby's neighbours want nothing to do with her while Papa and I are about. I had not expected to be welcomed with open arms, but I had thought at least one or two people might give me a chance before snubbing me." She smiled cynically. "I was mistaken."

"Jealousy," he said. "Envy. That's what it is—and a deal of hypocrisy besides."

She shrugged.

They drove on in silence for a while, the viscount appearing lost in thought. Then, as they were turning into the drive leading to Elmhurst, Lord Berne spoke.

"I wonder what the world would think," he said, "if the Devil's daughter reformed the libertine."

She stared at him.

"Reflect, Miss Desmond. How would the world regard a woman who could make me mend my wicked ways?"

She considered."I daresay she would be proposed for sainthood. The job is worth half a dozen lesser miracles, I'm sure."

"Then I recommend you be measured for a halo as soon as may be. I'm not joking, you know. The miracle can be accomplished," he promised, "because I mean to help you. Miss Desmond, I wish to be reformed."

"And I should like to be Queen of Egypt."

"I am quite serious," he insisted, with another melting smile. "You have no idea how much you've alarmed me. If you're never invited anywhere, when am I to see you again? You tell me your aunt

84

will send me packing if I come to the house, and I cannot possibly expect to happen on you in the road every time I come to Rossingley. I must be reformed because there appears to be no alternative."

She could not help smiling in return. He was not to be trusted, but she appreciated charm, and that he had in abundance. All the same, she pointed out rather sternly that his motives did not seem remotely saintlike.

"My motives are selfish, Miss Desmond," he said softly, "and selfishness is always to be relied upon."

It must be acknowledged with regret that Mr. Langdon was not a devoted churchgoer. Since he was given to quiet pursuits, he found Sunday no longer or drearier than any other day. Normally, he was content to spend the Sabbath with an improving book.

This Sunday, however, he rose from a breakfast he must have been trying to read—for he certainly didn't eat any of it—and told his uncle he thought he might find out whether Mr. Blenkly's sermons had improved at all in the last decade. The uncle only nodded absently and returned to his dog-eared copy of Mr. Jeremy Bentham's *Introduction to Principles of Morals and Legislation*.

Oblivious to the stares and whispers about him, Mr. Langdon took his place in the family pew. He studied the stained glass which had for centuries illuminated in picture form what the uneducated faithful could not read in the Bible. He gazed up at the ceiling and admired the skill of twelfth-century craftsmen, while absently noting several stains bespeaking an urgent need for roof repairs. Then, almost but not quite as absently, his gaze drifted to the pew where the late Lord Potterby's ancestors had attended divers lessons in Christianity.

Miss Desmond wore a pale green bonnet with

dark green ribbons, under which her wayward hair must have been throttled into submission, for not one disobedient strand escaped. Her high-waisted frock was the same cool colour, embroidered with sprigs which matched the ribbons on her bonnet. She was a cool bouquet of mint, and he wanted to crush her and inhale the fragrance of her . . . which was *not*, he angrily reproached himself, the sort of thought to be having at all, let alone on the Sabbath, in church.

Mr. Langdon was so busy rebuking himself and trying to tear his gaze away that he never noticed how the whispering had swelled into a communal gasp. He saw only that Miss Desmond had turned to look over her shoulder, and that for three full seconds her gaze locked with his before jerking unsteadily to the rear of the church.

He turned as well, and instantly joined in the general astonishment. Lord Berne had entered.

The viscount serenely returned the parishioners' bold survey, then catching Jack's eye, made for him.

"Couldn't keep away either, I see," Tony whispered as he slid in next to his friend.

"I only came to find out whether old Blenkly is as rambling as ever," Jack said stiffly.

"And to assure yourself she isn't a figment of your overheated imagination. I see your case is nearly as bad as my own. Gad, how cool she looks—and how I should like to warm her."

Mr. Blenkly's entrance spared Lord Berne the throttling his friend was instantly most eager to administer. Mr. Langdon was forced to make do with a murderous glance and the fervent wish that lightning would, as the congregation seemed to expect, strike the spot where the provoking viscount stood.

The service was thoroughly incomprehensible from beginning to end. Mr. Blenkly had wanted only one glimpse of the two gentlemen in a pew which had stood empty for most of the past decade before what little poise he possessed flew up to the heavens. He had planned to enlighten his parishioners regarding the Parable of the Sower. Unfortunately, the sight in the Langdon family pew—especially the taller, golden-haired spectacle—was too much for him. He became hopelessly entangled between the Parable of the Prodigal Son and vaguely related proverbs dealing with loving parents, sparing the rod, wise and foolish offspring, and some deranged reference to loaves and fishes.

Even if he had managed a more logical discourse, it would have been utterly wasted on its object. Lord Berne had long since mastered the art of appearing devotedly attentive while his mind fixed on other topics altogether. Since the minister did not expound upon the Song of Solomon, the viscount's present meditations could scarcely be deemed appropriate.

Mr. Blenkly knew nothing of this. He saw a notorious libertine gravely attending his speech and wondered if the end of the world had come. He was dumbfounded when, after the service, that same young libertine engaged him in a brief conversation, at the end of which Mr. Blenkly possessed a pledge for repairs of the church roof.

In ten minutes, all the parishioners who'd lingered to stare at Lord Berne and exchanged speculative whispers were also possessed of the information. Thus the news reached Lady Potterby's ears.

She had fully intended to keep Lord Berne at a safe distance from her grand-niece, but his appearance at the service elicited certain interesting speculations of her own. His astounding act of philanthropy gave her further reason to ponder. Thus, when he approached, Lady Potterby was too curious to be as unwelcoming as she'd intended. She even went so far as to applaud his generosity.

"I wish, My Lady, I could say I fully deserved your kind words, but the credit does not belong to me. I only acted upon inspiration—and it was your young relative who inspired me."

The young relative looked blank.

"Delilah told you the roof leaked?" Lady Potterby asked, her dignified countenance belying certain agreeable surmises within. "But she has not been in the church before today."

Mr. Langdon, who had lingered in the cool, dark church after everyone else had exited, joined the small group as Lord Berne was answering.

"Miss Desmond awakened in me yesterday a lively concern for the state of my immortal soul," said the viscount, bestowing an adoring glance upon that fair evangelist. "Accordingly, I came to church, and as I gazed heavenward, hoping my prayers for forgiveness would be heard, I noticed the stains on the ceiling. As I looked downward to confirm my suspicions, my eyes lit upon Miss Desmond's bonnet. If it rained—as it has almost incessantly—and the roof leaked, her bonnet would be ruined. The thought was insupportable."

Miss Desmond glanced away to hide the smile she could not suppress . . . and met Mr. Langdon's sober grey scrutiny. Her smile vanished, though her colour increased.

"You would have done better, My Lord," said Lady Potterby as severely as she could, considering the hopes blossoming within her breast, "to have reflected upon your soul—not young ladies' bonnets."

"One should never underestimate the power of a bonnet," his lordship returned. "It is the ladies who teach us to be good—but first they must obtain our attention."

"It is certainly not good of you to insult their intelligence," Mr. Langdon put in. "You speak as though Miss Desmond would stand there witlessly, allowing the roof to leak upon her."

The image conjured up was evidently more than Miss Desmond's composure could withstand, because she giggled.

Lord Berne was good-natured enough to chuckle and Lady Potterby permitted herself to smile. "Indeed, I hope my grand-niece has better sense," said she.

"My Lady, your grand-niece is the most level-headed young lady I have ever met," said Lord Berne. "A great many others would do well to emulate her—though that would be difficult," he added solemnly. "They have the advantages neither of your kinship nor your wise guidance."

"Yet you believed I had so little sense I would stand under a dripping roof," said Delilah. "You contradict yourself, My Lord."

"His lordship is confused," said Jack. "Clearly, the experience of hearing a sermon was too great a shock to his senses. It has addled his wits."

"Mr. Blenkly was addled enough himself," Lady Potterby calmly intervened before Lord Berne could retort upon his friend. "I could not make heads or tales of his homily. Yet I still retain sufficient perception to note that the sky darkens. Dear me, and the day had begun so bright. We had better go home, Delilah."

"I do not know whether this is very good or very bad," said Lady Potterby when they were safely within the carriage. "To attend services here instead of at home . . . to travel at least twenty-five miles in each direction . . . and after the same journey yesterday . . . and to behave so respectfully towards you. That is most puzzling."

"I may take it then, that unlike his friend, Mr. Langdon regularly attends services?" Delilah asked.

"Dear me, no. Only a marriage or a baptism might lure him here. Still, there is no predicting what that young man will do. He may have come to admire the architecture—or a young lady," she added slyly.

The grand-niece frowned.

"You needn't look so grim," said Lady Potterby. "I admit he's not dashing, but he's perfectly eligible. He has twenty thousand a year of his own. When he comes into the title the figure will increase considerably. You could do worse."

"I will, of course, do as you tell me, Aunt, but I hope you will not let Papa's ill-considered remarks influence you. I'm sure the only reason Mr. Langdon tolerates me is out of respect for your longstanding friendship with his uncle. Whenever Mr. Langdon looks at me he makes me feel there's dirt on my nose—or that I've got my bonnet on backwards."

"That is merely his way," Lady Potterby said dismissively. "At least you have nothing to fear from him. On the other hand, Lord Berne is a sorry rascal. Still, a new roof does give one pause. The expense is not inconsiderable."

So Lord Streetham pointed out to his son some hours later when that young man described his recent activities. Nor was the earl in any way appeased when Lord Berne embarked upon an impassioned soliloquy regarding the young lady's numerous perfections, among which her intriguing hard-headedness figured most prominently.

He had no business being intrigued, his father retorted. Mindless infatuation had no place in business matters. All Tony had accomplished was to degenerate himself into a moonstruck schoolboy, while both the young lady and the memoirs remained as unapproachable as ever.

Lord Streetham coldly observed that he'd erred

gravely in entrusting so sensitive an enterprise to his fribble of an heir. Accordingly, he ordered his son off to Brighton, where the fresh salt air might clear his fevered brain.

Lord Berne hastened to defend himself. He'd made an excellent start, he insisted. Even the formidable aunt had behaved almost amiably. "In another two days they'll be convinced I mean to offer for the girl. What better way than that to obtain Miss Desmond's confidence and trust?"

"What better way for them to trap you is more like it," Lord Streetham returned.

"So you'll keep me in leading strings to protect me from an inexperienced miss? And while I'm safely in Brighton, Langdon will seduce her."

"Inexperienced—hah! That embrace Atkins reported was the chit's doing, rely upon it. Jack has never seduced anyone in his whole life. She was trying to ensnare him—as she will you. You are too much taken with her. You are sure to forget yourself, and her family will be quick to cry Dishonour if you so much as kiss her hand. Remember, Desmond is not like the other fathers you've outraged. He will not be quieted with a bribe—not when he can make that black-haired wench of his a countess."

"But surely your influence—"

"One has no influence over knaves who leap out of alleys in the dead of night. You forget of whom we speak. Besides, if he has made a laughingstock of me in his curst story, I will have as much influence in the world as the coal scuttle. As usual, the Devil holds all the winning cards. You will go to Brighton or I shall cut off your allowance."

8

WHILE LORD BERNE was quarrelling with his father, Delilah was confiding in hers. Until the viscount had appeared at church, she had not permitted herself to consider his scheme seriously. Now she was forced to consider it, but she wished to have her father's perspective as well.

When she was done, Mr. Desmond leaned back comfortably in his chair and acknowledged that Lord Berne's was an interesting approach to the problem.

"It is brilliant, Papa," she answered. "I only wish you could have seen the parishioners today. They were positively agog. Even Aunt Millicent was impressed. Lord Berne's reputation must be far worse than I thought, if one appearance at church could cause such a stir. Still, I cannot help but question his motives. Though it seems a deal of trouble to go to, I do wonder if he only wants to win my trust so he can seduce me."

"That's simple enough," said her father. "Don't get seduced."

She did not appear to hear him. Her brow furrowed.

"I find your expression ominous, Delilah," said

Mr. Desmond. "You are hatching something, and I am certain it is mischief."

She was staring at the carpet, and when she spoke, it was as though she were simply thinking aloud.

"Not being seduced is simple," she said. "What is difficult is maintaining his interest. He is reputed very fickle." Absently she rose from her chair and began pacing the room. "If it could be done, he might be brought round—eventually. But is there time—and is he worth the effort, I wonder? Still, he will be Earl of Streetham one day and—" She glanced at her father, who was watching her with every evidence of amusement.

"He is very beautiful, Papa. That we must admit."

"I am sure there is not a prettier fellow in the kingdom."

"He is exceedingly conceited," she went on, "yet he is amusing. He is rather wild—"

"Very wild."

She bit her lip. "Well, I'd rather not marry some dull, conventional fellow if I can help it. I should be bored to death and driven to some atrocity sooner or later, I know it. At any rate, Lord Berne is at hand and wishes to pursue me. I think I may let him do so . . . until I catch him," she finished with a faint smile.

"And if you do not?" her papa enquired.

She shrugged. "Then I'm no worse off than before. I'll go to London with my aunt as planned and try to catch someone else."

Mr. Desmond gave a theatrical shudder. "Such a cold-blooded creature you are, my dear. Whenever you begin making wedding plans I feel I have entered a damp, chilly dungeon. No more, I beg you."

He rose from his chair and crossed the room to her. "Your aunt is napping," he said. "If I swear the servants to secrecy, will you indulge your aged parent in a game of billiards?"

Her smile broadened into a mischievous grin. "I promise to trounce you soundly."

"I shall see that you don't. You know, while we are on the tiresome subject, I ought to remind you of *his* parents. Your behaviour must be most circumspect if you wish to enslave them as well. I'm afraid that will tax your patience."

"I will do my part not to make a scandal, Papa," she said with some indignation. "I only wish you would do yours. Something must be done about that odious Mr. Atkins."

"Leave him to me. If worse comes to worse, and he proves recalcitrant, we shall simply burn the manuscript."

"Actually, I begin to think we should do so immediately."

"So confident of your viscount, eh?" Mr. Desmond offered his daughter his arm.

As she took it she said, "It would be one less worry."

"My dear, a single young lady has only one true worry, which is not getting seduced. All you need do is not believe anything an idle young man says until he says it before the parson and witnesses, pursuant to placing a ring upon your finger."

She squeezed his arm affectionately. "I will remember, Papa," she promised. "Now—to battle."

Lord Berne spent his first day in Brighton dutifully inhaling the salt air during a restless walk upon the Steyne. In the usual way of things, he would have promptly banished Miss Desmond's image by fixing on one closer to hand. The circumstances were not usual. He had not wandered away on his own caprice, but had been sent away against his will, like a naughty child ordered to bed without his supper. Now, precisely like a spoiled child,

94

Lord Berne wanted no other treat but the one denied him.

Consequently, he persuaded himself there was no other female upon the earth as desirable as Delilah Desmond; that, furthermore, he had never loved before, all the rest being puerile infatuations.

That her image haunted him (at least twice a day) proved beyond doubt he'd come upon the grand passion of a lifetime. Yet what had he done? He'd scurried off to Brighton because his father threatened to stop his allowance. An idle threat. Lord Streetham had too much pride to allow his son to wander about the kingdom on foot, in rags, like a beggar.

Meanwhile Lord Berne's beloved would have concluded he'd abandoned her—that he was a worthless, unreliable knave. She must not.

Lord Berne hastened back to his lodgings and penned a very long letter full of bad grammar and execrable verse, in the course of which he claimed to be called away to sit by the sickbed of a friend. Then he ordered his curricle and posted off to Rye.

In the country, one day can be so tediously like all the rest that the smallest piece of news becomes a nine-days' wonder. All the same, few of Lady Potterby's neighbours could work up much excitement about Squire Pegham's sow's difficulties in labour and the consequent suffocation of three of her numerous offspring. This local sensation was cast entirely in the shade by the bizarre behaviour of Lord Berne.

Streetham Close might be twenty-five miles away, but Lord Berne's periodic sorties into the Rossingley environs and the feminine devastation he left in his wake had made him a common foe. The local gentry were therefore mightily curious about the young lady who had (if reports were to be believed) so far subjugated this enemy as to lure him to church, where—and this was utterly confounding—he had not nodded off at once. He had capped this miracle by pledging a large sum of money for repairs to a church not even in his own parish, thus sparing the Rossingley parishioners the disagreeable necessity of reaching into their own pockets.

All this he had done, it was said, in an effort to overcome Miss Desmond's prejudices against him. Miss Twiggenham herself had heard him say as much, having on Sunday been placed by an accidental though fortunate conjunction of circumstances close enough to overhear his lordship's remarks. Miss Twiggenham's evidence was strengthened by Mrs. Blenkly's avowal that Lord Berne had said practically the same thing to the minister.

In short, as Lord Berne had predicted, and more speedily than even he could have guessed, Rossingley developed a lively interest in Miss Delilah Desmond. Lady Potterby was besieged daily by callers, all of whom had hitherto been studiously unaware of the Desmonds' entry into the neighbourhood.

They came primarily out of curiosity and went away still curious. Admittedly Miss Desmond was handsome. All the same, Lord Berne had his pick of not only rustic beauties, but Society's most dazzling Incomparables. There must be something more than her looks.

Unfortunately, no one could ascertain what the "more" was, exactly. Miss Desmond's manners were unexceptionable, and her conversation was very properly limited to deference to the opinions of her elders. She seemed very much like any other gently-bred young miss. Only when people recollected she was Devil Desmond's daughter did this conclusion appear at all remarkable. Thus she became a mystery all Rossingley was in a fever to solve.

Miss Desmond might have enjoyed her triumph

whole-heartedly had she not been so acutely aware that Rossingley's interest in her would fade as abruptly as it had blossomed if the reason for its interest vanished. The reason—Lord Berne—showed every evidence of doing so.

When he had not called by Friday, Miss Desmond's spirits—already sorely tried by the necessity of behaving circumspectly before an endless stream of company—sank into the Slough of Despond.

Lord Berne was obviously as fickle, selfish, and thoughtless as everyone said. She must have been totty-headed to have taken him seriously even for an instant, especially on such light evidence as one whimsical promise. She had not been her usual hard-headed self, that was certain. Delilah reflected as she wandered unhappily out to the garden.

The sun shone, but today its beams were gentle, and a cool breeze drove away all traces of the unusual humidity which had oppressed the countryside. The milder weather had not, she soon discovered, been of much use to her horticultural experiment. Two more seedlings had succumbed. As she gazed sorrowfully upon their withered remains, she made a mental note to speak to Jenkins, the gardener. Until she thought of a better hiding place, there must be no more planting here. Mr. Langdon had not dug a very deep hole. He'd been too busy demonstrating his prowess in other ways. Well, he'd discovered his mistake soon enough and had slunk off to hide among his dusty volumes.

By now he must have persuaded himself the embrace had been all her doing, because she was a wanton adventuress, bent on entrapping him. *Was there some further penance she wished to exact*, he'd said, in those cold, patronising tones. The nerve of the man! He was despicable.

She stomped down the path until she came to a

wrought iron bench placed conveniently in a shady corner. Muttering imprecations upon Mr. Langdon and occasionally—when she remembered—Lord Berne, Delilah flung herself onto the seat and fell into a sulk.

She had been thus amusing herself for about ten minutes when her maid appeared bearing a letter, as well as a lengthy recitation of her trials and tribulations, the letter being the most recent affront to Joan's dignity. She did not see why a lady's maid must act as messenger when there were plenty of footmen lazing about the house, gaping and gawking the livelong day for want of anything to do. Her ill-tempered mistress only added to these injuries by curtly dismissing her.

While Joan marched back to the house in high dudgeon, Miss Desmond was eagerly tearing open the letter. She quickly scanned the bold, black lines, then, with her first genuine smile in at least three days, sat back to read again more slowly.

When she had finished savouring Lord Berne's lyric prose for the tenth time, Delilah made for the house, to acquaint her father with this latest, most promising development on the rut-ridden road to matrimony.

She found him in the late Lord Potterby's study, perusing an epistle of his own and grinning. "Ah, there you are," said he. "I was intending to come out to share this with you but you've spared my aged body that labour. What do you think, Delilah? We have yet another publisher who wishes to become my bosom-bow—and at twice the price."

He handed the letter to his daughter, whose joyous countenance reverted to its previous gloom while she read.

"This is dreadful, Papa," she said when she was done. "I thought Mr. Atkins assured us of secrecy. How on earth did this man learn of your memoirs?"

"Easy enough," said the parent with a shrug. "I

daresay one of Atkins's clerks has a passion for listening at keyholes and a loose tongue. An unfortunate combination, but one prevalent, I fear, in every class of society."

"Indeed. I expect all of London knows by now."

"If that were the case, I should receive a great many more offers than this. Rest easy, my dear. Businessmen are always spying upon one another and they are not above paying their rivals' employees for useful tidbits."

Delilah could not rest easy. She began pacing frantically, her skirts whirling about her in a manner which would have sent her great-aunt into paroxysms. Fortunately, the only observer at the moment was her papa.

"Yes, my love," he said. "I am certain you have inherited your legs from your mama, but I hope you will be cautious about revealing that circumstance beyond our small family circle."

Miss Desmond dutifully threw herself into a chair. "Thank you for the reminder, Papa. Aunt Millicent has told me a hundred times to move with more decorum. But it will scarcely matter whether I lift my skirts and run howling through the village if we do not silence this horrid man."

"Silence him? But my dear, he offers double what Atkins did. If I accept, I might repay our nervous friend and commence a less tiresome relationship with his colleague. Although I must say," he added, "Atkins has astonished me by keeping away this whole week. I wonder if he's returned to London?"

Delilah had no time for wonderings. The crisis at the moment was this letter. It must be dealt with. If her papa accepted the offer, she might as well go back to Scotland to her mama. She could not endure any more anxiety.

"What on earth is there to be anxious about?" her father asked mildly. "My memoirs are safely entombed. Another few weeks of rain and they will have rotted away. Or is it your elusive golden prince who troubles you? You should not be cast down, my dear. Reformation is a most wearisome enterprise, particularly for fickle young libertines. You cannot be surprised that after an eternity of five whole days he has altogether forgotten your existence."

"Oh, has he?" was the arch response. "Then I wonder why he writes so desolately of missing me." Delilah bounced up from her chair to wave Lord Berne's letter triumphantly in her father's face.

Mr. Desmond smiled. "Has he, indeed?" He took the letter and skimmed it. "Defy his parents . . . his life heretofore a shallow mockery . . . nothing but this pernicious accident could have kept him away. Good heavens," he said, looking up. "His courage and resolution take my breath away."

Whether he was breathless or not, Delilah told her parent, he must wrench his mind from Lord Berne for the moment and fix it on this new publisher, who must, she averred, be answered immediately.

"You must tell him he is mistaken, Papa. Tell him the memoirs do not exist. If you do not, the rumours will be all over London in another week and I will not dare show my face there until I am as old as Aunt Millicent."

Her papa sighed and declared his only wish, of course, was to cater to her every whim, regardless how silly. He obediently took up his pen and wrote as his adamant child dictated. When the letter was sealed up, the two departed for Rossingley. Nothing would do, certainly, but to post it themselves, forthwith.

Lord Streetham had reached an unhappy conclusion. Desmond's daughter was far more wily than the earl had imagined. Whatever favours Tony might eventually obtain from her, the manuscript was not one of them. Having admitted his error—a painful enough exercise—the earl must now face an even more disagreeable fact. There were only two ways left to get the manuscript away from Desmond. One was to steal it, which was now not only impossibly difficult but exceedingly risky. The other was to buy it, which was demeaning and expensive. On the whole, Lord Streetham thought he'd rather swallow his pride than risk swallowing a much harder object—like the end of Desmond's sword.

No man had ever run afoul of the Devil and emerged from the experience intact. Lord Gartwaite's jaw had been so severely dislocated that he'd been subsisting for the past twenty years on gruel. Billings was mouldering in the family crypt because he'd made an ill-chosen remark about the former Angelica Ornesby. Even the Devil's own brother had walked with a limp ever since attempting to cheat the Devil of the few trinkets left in their father's will to the younger son.

These represented the smallest fraction of gentlemen who had at one time or another taxed Devil Desmond's patience too far. The curst fellow always found out somehow what was said or attempted behind his back.

Lord Streetham gave a superstitious shudder as he turned his carriage through the gates of Elmhurst, then shrugged off the sensation. Desmond could not have known his belongings had been searched at Streetham Close, or he'd have given his host a most unpleasant time of it. The man did not have eyes in the back of his head, regardless what others believed.

Having steeled himself for a humiliating interview, Lord Streetham was both relieved and frustrated to learn, shortly after he met his hostess, that Mr. Desmond and his daughter had driven into Rossingley. The earl was relieved enough to wish to return home immediately, his purse and dignity still intact, but that would only mean he must repeat the same unpleasant journey Lady Potterby was at the moment commiserating with him about.

"Such unusual heat we have had, My Lord," she said as she led him into the drawing room. "So oppressive. We are sadly behind in our baking because the dough will not rise properly. Even when it does, who is to do anything with it, with the kitchen hot enough to bake bricks and the staff collapsing into the soup kettle?"

Lord Streetham agreed that the weather had been most un-English of late. Even the rain was far more like that of India in the monsoon season.

"Whatever it is, it cannot be like Greece," said Lady Potterby. "Those seedlings my grand-niece and Mr. Langdon planted are half of them dead already. Indeed, I do wonder they made such an experiment. Surely Mr. Langdon knows ours is not a Mediterranean climate. Jenkins is most distressed," she added, shaking her head. "But what could he do? They were so eager to test one of the theories in that lovely volume you so generously gave Mr. Langdon."

Lord Streetham had prepared himself to endure Lady Potterby's endless prosing for hours, if necessary, and had assumed the same state of half-attention he usually accorded his wife. He could not help wondering, however, why two young persons of the upper class (Miss Desmond was at least technically a member) should be labouring over seedlings. Why hadn't they left it to the gardening staff, who were paid to make themselves hot and dirty? Or was Miss Desmond's planting merely some needlessly laborious pretext for taking advantage of a naïve young man?

"I'm afraid I am not familiar with the book's contents—which does not surprise me," said the earl. "My collection is so extensive and the demands on my time so great. Yet I supposed Mr. Langdon's interest was purely academic. After all, did not the ancients place great reliance upon conjunctions of certain planets and sacrifices to their pagan deities? Hardly the sort of theories to put to scientific experiment, I should think."

Though he spoke casually, Lord Streetham's mind was working at full speed. The massive tome Jack had clutched . . . the panicked look he'd darted at Desmond. The pages themselves . . . something odd . . . not thick and rough-edged—because, perhaps, they had never required to be cut?

Lady Potterby sighed. "I do not know what Mr. Langdon was thinking—who ever does? But he was a perfect sight when he came in to tea. Lord Rossing said he put him in mind of the grave-diggers in *Hamlet,* and asked whether they'd unearthed poor Yorick's skull." She did not notice the earl's slight start. "Delilah's maid declares she will never be able to remove the stains from that frock. How odd," Lady Potterby added, glancing toward the corner windows, her brow knit. "Now I think of it, I do not recall seeing the book again. Dear me, I hope Mr. Langdon did not leave it in the garden. He is dreadfully absent-minded, you know."

Lord Streetham too looked towards the window, though what he perceived was in his mind's eye— the stunning reality of what had occurred.

It had been Desmond's book contained in that elaborate binding, and the earl himself had given it to Jack. Then Jack, so easily manipulated, had done the Devil's bidding and buried it—there, just a few steps away, in the garden.

Not the slightest flicker of excitement was visible in his lordship's countenance, however, as he turned back to his hostess to agree in a good-natured, avuncular way that Jack was indeed absent-minded.

"We are still collecting articles that he left behind, poor fellow," he said with a small smile. "When his valet is not with him, one can only pray he will not present himself at dinner in his nightshirt. Very likely he did forget the book, and one day he will appear upon your doorstep, flustered and embarrassed, looking for it."

"One day!" cried Lady Potterby. "In the middle of February, no doubt. Good heavens, that fine volume might be lying in the dirt yet—and we have had two storms since Friday. I had better send one of the servants to look."

Lord Streetham rose. "No need for that. You've made me most curious about his experiment. If you don't mind, I'd like to have a look myself."

They went out to the garden, where they found the plants, as Lady Potterby had predicted, in various stages of decline. The book, however, was nowhere to be seen.

Lord Streetham stared hard at the woebegone flower bed. "You know," he said thoughtfully, "I wouldn't put it past the lad to have inadvertently buried the book in the process of turning the soil."

"Buried it! Good heavens, he could not be so muddled as that—and with Delilah by. Surely she would have noticed."

"If Jack was declaiming on Greek wisdom, she very likely had given all her concentration to follow his discourse," said the earl smoothly. "I think I had better find a spade."

Less than an hour later, Lord Streetham was once more upon the road. A thick tome, its cover damp and dirty, lay at his feet. One quick glance at the contents had been sufficient to assure him of what he'd found.

Obtaining possession of the volume had been simple enough. He'd insisted upon doing the digging himself, because it would never do for the gardening staff to know of Mr. Langdon's folly. Then the earl had only to express the charitable wish to have the book repaired secretly, to spare Jack embarrassment. Lord Streetham had solemnly assured Lady Potterby the restored volume would be discreetly returned to the young man. All they had to do was keep the matter to themselves. After all, Jack was a very good fellow, and absent-mindedness was a trivial flaw in the great scheme of things, was it not?

Lady Potterby, properly impressed by this show of magnanimity, had yielded up the book without argument.

While his father was returning home with his ill-gotten goods, Lord Berne was gazing discontentedly in the general direction of France. To soothe his troubled soul, he compared his beloved's hair to a waterfall of black pearls, her ears to shells, her lips to pink oysters, and her eyes to the rolling ocean. He made a mental note to jot down these revelations for future use as soon as he returned to his lodgings.

He gazed with lackluster eyes upon a fancy bit of muslin who smiled encouragingly as she passed. He looked away towards the ocean once more and sighed heavily. These activities being not quite so productive as when performed for an audience, he resolved to leave for home first thing tomorrow.

Lord Streetham closed the cover of the book and smiled at the soiled binding.

The references to himself were so easily amended that it was foolish to destroy the manuscript, as he had in certain panicked moments thought of doing. The book would take England by storm, just as Atkins had insisted. The lively adventures, the impudent, witty style, together with the occasional scandalous revelation, guaranteed tremendous popular success. There might be lawsuits, but the profits could easily absorb the legal costs—and since Desmond had taken care to show Prinny and his siblings in a favourable, indulgently humourous light, there was small likelihood of sedition charges from that quarter.

At any rate, being the largest shareholder of the firm, Lord Streetham had a right to make the occasional correction. Even Desmond must admit as much—if, that is, he ever got wind of the matter.

Lord Streetham opened the book, carefully removed the pages from the false binding, and carried them to his writing desk.

Half an hour later he sat, pen poised in mid-air, exactly as though some evil spirit whispering in his ear had distracted him.

Here was a remarkably tactful though highly entertaining account of Lord Gaines's drunken interview with a notorious bawd of the day.

Lord Streetham recalled the episode, having formed one of the small party of revellers, and wondered now why Desmond had been so discreet. He'd left out altogether the best part: the bawd's loud expressions of pity for poor Lord Gaines. His lordship had tried every one of her girls with so little success that she'd recommended he avail himself of Dr. James Graham's Celestial Bed as the only certain cure for impotence.

Lord Gaines had recently subjected one of Lord Streetham's proposals to a scathing satire in the House of Lords, resulting in a most humiliating defeat. It would serve the foul-mouthed rascal right, said the fiend at the earl's ear, to have his personal inadequacies exposed to John Bull's mockery.

And what of Corbell and Marchingham? These thorns in Lord Streetham's side had once been numbered among Desmond's cronies. What amusing tales could be told of those two! With a judicious phrase inserted here, a short passage there, an occasional substitution of one word for another, these recollections would do a great deal more than make a fortune.

Lord Streetham smiled and set to work.

9

"To dinner?" Jack echoed hollowly. "Here?"

Lord Rossing removed his spectacles and placed them on his writing desk. "That's what I said. There's no need to make a Greek tragic chorus, Jack. I've asked the Wembertons, which means, as it turns out, we must expect Lord and Lady Gathers and their daughter as well, because they're visiting. Also, Streetham and his countess—though I never dreamed they'd accept, considering the distance."

"Good God," Jack muttered.

"I believed I ought at least offer to repay their hospitality to you—though one dinner can hardly repay a lifetime of it. They propose to stay with the Wembertons as well, and I daresay they'll all be quite cozy." Lord Rossing sniffed in disdain, then went on. "Also, Blenkly and his wife, and Lady Potterby and her guests. I've already sent out the other invitations, but Lady Potterby's ought to be delivered personally. Just run across, will you, Jack?" said the viscount as he handed his dismayed nephew the invitation. "I'd go myself, but last night's storm has stirred up my rheumaticks again."

Jack looked down at the folded sheet in his hand and sighed. "I wish you had war—mentioned this to me sooner. I was planning to return to London."

"Your valet has just come up from Town. Why did you make him take the journey if you only meant to go back again? Really, Jack, I begin to wonder at you. I would assume you had a touch of the sun, but you haven't been out of the house in nearly a week—and all you do in it is take out books and leave them strewn about while you gape out the windows. You're not ailing, are you, boy?"

"No, Uncle."

"Well, you'd better not. Let Fellows attend to you before you go. If you appear at Millicent's with that woebegone expression and your hair all up on end— stop that!" Lord Rossing commanded, as Jack's fingers began raking his hair. "One look at you and she'll start dosing you with brimstone and treacle and heaven knows what other foul concoctions."

Jack's hand dropped to his side and he walked slowly from the room.

Only when the door had closed behind him did his uncle give vent to a low snort of laughter.

"Mr. Langdon," said the valet reproachfully.

"Yes, yes, I know. My uncle just told me. I suppose I'd better comb my hair," said Jack, moving to the dresser. "He wants me to deliver an invitation to Lady Potterby. To dinner. Can you believe it?" He stared at his reflection in the glass. "I've been coming here since I was in skirts and not once do I recall my uncle entertaining. Not once."

"If you mean to go out, sir, you had better change. With the Hessians it must be the green coat and buff pantaloons," said the valet. He collected these objects and laid them out.

"I'm only running next door, Fellows."

"Indeed, sir, but you are not departing in that

costume, unless you plan to muck out Lady Potter-by's stables. As it is you will astonish the horses."

Plainly, Mr. Langdon's valet was not of the stoically all-enduring, self-effacing variety. Mr. Fellows had tried that technique early in his employment and found it unproductive. He had learned that if his master was not to disgrace him in public, the servant must speak his mind and maintain a tight rein.

Mr. Fellows was well aware that his employer, having recently suffered a setback in an affair of the heart, required a suitable period of mourning. That is why Mr. Langdon had been indulged a solo trip to his uncle's. However, in Mr. Fellows's considered opinion, a week or so was quite sufficient a period of lamentation for a healthy young man. It was now time for Mr. Langdon to be marched back—properly attired—to the world of the living. Besides, there was a young lady next door whose abigail's acquaintance Mr. Fellows had made this morning and wished to pursue. If the lady thought Mr. Langdon's appearance shabby, her maid would entertain similar conclusions about the gentleman's gentleman.

Immaculately groomed but heavy-hearted, Mr. Langdon walked slowly along the path which intersected the graceful line of tall elms forming the boundary between the two estates. Ahead the way cut through a rolling expanse of lawn dotted with oaks and more elms. In the shade of one venerable oak a herd of sheep languidly graced.

All about him was the familiar tranquillity Jack had left London for. He'd come here hoping the serenity and isolation of Rossing Hall would soothe away all memories of his failure with the one young lady who might have made him happy. True enough, the disappointment and shame had subsided—but only because they'd been so violently uprooted and hurled aside by a tempest in the form of Delilah Desmond.

Jack knew he was infatuated with her. He had sense enough remaining to recognise that. But for the life of him he could not understand why. Always before his senses had responded in accord with his character and tastes. Even the impures he'd occasionally taken up with had been the quieter, more genteel of their breed. He loathed noise, confrontation, violence, and argument, yet he was obsessed with a Fury in human form. Well, not exactly a Fury, he amended, but she was at least as capricious and temperamental as any of the ancient female deities.

She screamed at him and struck him and humiliated him and scorned him, and through the turbulence that seemed to whirl constantly about her—even on those rare occasions when she was relatively subdued—he wanted her. That was all, and that was everything.

This morning, after another tormented, sleepless night, he'd reviewed his situation and concluded he must either return to London and trust time and absence to cure him, or offer for her and let *her* cure him—or kill him. The last, he thought, was a deal more likely.

Though she despised him, she might consent. Given Society's prejudices, she may not have another suitable offer. He felt, as he always did when he considered her situation, a surge of compassion for her and anger at his fellows.

That was almost the worst of it. If the world had not persisted in visiting the sins of the parents upon the offspring, Miss Desmond might never have crossed his path. She might have been shackled as soon as she emerged from the schoolroom, and he would not be in so pathetic a case as to contemplate wedding a woman so admirably designed to make him wretched.

Besides, he chided himself as he took a shortcut through Lady Potterby's garden, marrying Miss Desmond was too extreme a remedy, even if she were desperate enough to consent. It was like cutting off one's head to cure a toothache. He would return to London directly after this curst dinner party.

As he approached the terrace, he came upon Miss Desmond, who, head bent and skirts whirling, was agitatedly pacing. Mr. Langdon had but a fleeting glimpse—though one sufficient to make him groan inwardly—of a pair of exceptionally fine ankles before she became aware of his presence and abruptly halted.

Then she did the strangest thing. She smiled, and the upward curve of her sensuous mouth sent every thought of London flying from Mr. Langdon's head.

As she stepped forward to greet him, he apologised for interrupting her meditations.

"You're a very welcome interruption, Mr. Langdon," said she, to his inutterable amazement. "We've been plagued with company all day. I only came out to talk to myself, since that was the only party with whom I could have a natural conversation. Decorum is heavy work," she explained.

"Then I fear you'll recall the welcome when you learn my errand, because I'm sent to bring you more of the same." He held up the invitation. "My uncle desires the pleasure of your company—and that of your father and Lady Potterby as well—at dinner Wednesday evening. I hope this is not excessively short notice. You might have wished more time to plan an escape to Mongolia perhaps."

Another smile. Mr. Langdon grew dizzy.

"You know there's no escape for me, Mr. Langdon. Anyhow, I did have notice. Lord Rossing was by earlier in the week to ask my aunt whether the date was convenient. Your errand only formalises the plans."

Mr. Langdon was too stunned by his remarkable fortune in finding Miss Desmond in gentle humour to think of questioning why his uncle had withheld this information.

"As long as my errand is not urgent, perhaps we might delay the formalities," he said, moved to unheard-of boldness by her amiability. "May I pace the terrace with you awhile and eavesdrop upon your 'natural conversation' with yourself?"

A faint colour tinged her cheeks as she shook her head. Several pins dropped to paving stones, loosening the long black curls they'd held. Jack looked at the pins and at the hair, and he was done for.

"Pacing is forbidden before company," she answered. "In fact, I'm supposed to restrain myself even in private so as not to feed a bad habit." She sighed. "The trouble is, I'm so full of bad habits that when I leave them off there's hardly anything left of me."

"Only a beautiful shell? Well, I shall have to make do," said Mr. Langdon. "Since you're so dangerously inclined to pace, perhaps we'd better avail ourselves of that genteel-looking bench behind you."

When they were seated, Miss Desmond told him of her trials and tribulations with all the callers who came expecting a "common little baggage," as she put it, and must be conquered by her unspeakable propriety. "It is perfectly excruciating," she complained. "After an hour I want to scream. After two hours I want to commit murder."

"You remind me of my friend Max," said Jack, smiling. "He's always complaining that propriety wrings all the spirit out of a chap and Convention is just another word for Strangulation."

"A man after my own heart," said Delilah. "You've mentioned him before, I think? Is this not the same fellow who claims that if something is pleasant, it cannot be correct?"

Mr. Langdon must have appeared very surprised

because she laughed and said, "You needn't look so stunned. Sometimes I do listen, you know—and when I do, I usually remember. I have an excellent memory—comes of all those card games, I suppose."

"Then I'll be sure not to play you for high stakes, Miss Desmond. And I'll certainly be careful what remarks of Lord Rand's I share with you. Some of his pearls of wisdom are not fit for feminine ears."

"Yet you seem to admire him—or like him at least."

"He's one of the finest fellows I know," said Jack, neglecting to add that this noble fellow had stolen away the love of his life. "An old and trusted friend."

"Lord Berne is another such, I take it? He told me you've been friends since you were babies. I find that intriguing. You're a most puzzling man," she said. "From what you repeat of Lord Rand's wisdom and what I've seen of Lord Berne, they seem not at all the sort of friends I'd expect you to have."

"Because I'm so dull and conventional, you mean?" he asked. "Because I always have my nose in a book?"

"You mustn't imagine insults where none are intended. Besides, you know perfectly well that if I meant to insult you I'd do so without roundaboutation," she rebuked.

"Then what is so puzzling about my choice of friends?"

"I only meant that you're contemplative and serious," she answered, looking down at her hands. "Lord Berne has probably never had a serious thought in his entire life. I cannot understand what would make his company rewarding for you."

Jack smiled ruefully. "I can't expect all my friends to be Aristotles. I'd probably be bored to death if they were. Maybe I cling to these fellows because they make a change from the monotony of my own company. Is that so odd? Would you wish all your bosom-bows to be exactly like yourself?"

"Egad, no," she answered with a show of horrour. "I should throttle them all in five minutes. Only I haven't any bosom-bows. Nor will I get any," she added, glancing towards the house, "if anyone learns I've been entertaining you all this time unchaperoned."

She rose and Jack was obliged to follow, though it was not at all what he would have preferred. For nearly an hour they'd talked and she hadn't berated him or hit him once. He hadn't felt so serene in weeks.

Perhaps it was simply the vehemence of her behaviour—the flurry and collision and high emotion—which triggered so much emotion in himself. Maybe now that she had settled somewhat into her new life, she would not agitate him quite so much.

The end of this tranquil interlude, could Jack but have known it, appeared early Wednesday afternoon in the form of a cloud of dust. This gradually resolved itself into a pair of sweating horses pulling a dashing black curricle upon whose seat Lord Berne was perched. He'd decided that while rivals were all very well in the case of puerile infatuations, they would not do at all when it came to a Grand Passion. The enemy must be routed. There would be no more clandestine embraces in gardens or anywhere else, save where Lord Berne played the male lead.

The viscount did not customarily abuse his cattle, and would have arrived with a deal less lather if he hadn't needed a potent excuse for stopping at Rossing Hall. Jack's uncle might have easily enough walked over or around Lord Berne had that young man been lying mortally wounded in his path, but for dumb animals Lord Rossing had compassion.

For the weary horses' sake, then, he grumblingly allowed Lord Berne entrance. This did not mean the reluctant host wished to talk to his guest, however. He promptly abandoned Lord Berne at the library door and headed in the opposite direction.

Wasting no time, Tony launched his offensive as soon as he entered the library. Citing Atkins's report of what had transpired in the garden, the viscount demanded to know Jack's intentions toward Miss Desmond.

Being not only greatly taken aback by this unlooked-for assault but altogether unable to satisfy himself upon this very subject, Mr. Langdon was utterly incapable of responding.

Since Lord Berne had no intention of heeding any reply in the first place, Jack's stammering bewilderment spared his having to feign attention. The viscount mounted his attack.

"You cannot toy with her affections, Jack. I know what her father is and what he's done, and I know what people say of her mother, but that is no reason to take advantage of an innocent girl."

"Take advantage?" Jack repeated, dazed. "What are you saying?"

"You know very well what I mean. You think—" Lord Berne stopped short to stare at his friend in consternation. "Oh, Lord, what *am* I saying? Forgive me, Jack. I must be mad." He began pacing, speaking rapidly as he did so. "I don't know what's happened to me. I tried to stay away, truly I did. But she draws me. No woman has ever—no, you will not believe it. You'll laugh—no, your heart is too generous for that. Oh, Jack, your friend is brought low, indeed." Lord Berne threw himself into a chair.

"Good God, Tony, what on earth is the matter?"

"The matter," the viscount repeated bitterly. "Everything is the matter. I can't eat, can't sleep, can't think. Oh, Jack, I love her. Can you believe it?"

"Well, yes, actually, I can. You're always in love with somebody," said Jack rather unsympathetically.

"Never like this. When before could I find no comfort elsewhere? But how can I think of my comfort, knowing the undeserved burdens that innocent angel must bear? An ill-fame, not of her making, blights her youth even before it blossoms. How can I find happiness anywhere, knowing the world is determined to destroy any chance of hers?"

His stunned foe sank into a chair.

Lord Berne got up from his to recommence his agitated march upon the carpet. "She wishes nothing to do with me, and I cannot blame her. Yet how can I keep away when there remains any hope I might be able to help her? Perhaps that would make her think a little more kindly of me. Only a little, Jack. I know I can't expect her to care—and I'm sure she deserves a worthier fellow. Yet if she'd but smile kindly upon me once, I think I could live on that, and die, if not happy, then a better man for it."

Any expression of selflessness was so utterly foreign to Lord Berne's character that Mr. Langdon might be excused for blinking once or twice to assure himself he was not dreaming. This could not be Tony Melgrave who strode back and forth before him declaiming upon his unworthiness of the seraphic being known as Miss Delilah Desmond. Tony deserving of her—of any woman's—scorn? Impossible, Jack told himself.

Aloud he said, "I see what the matter is, Tony. She's the first woman in your experience who did not collapse helpless into your arms the instant you smiled upon her. The novelty of the experience has obviously been too much for you. You're merely frustrated, and having never been so before you confuse the emotion with love."

"Why should you believe me?" Lord Berne ceased his pacing to take up a tragic pose at the mantel. "You know what a paltry, insensible beast I am. No one would believe me, and there's no one to blame but myself. Perhaps my family has indulged me overmuch, but I cannot blame them. A man makes his own character. Only I bear the guilt, and only I can make amends." He turned upon his friend a gaze so desolate that Jack experienced a profound twinge of guilt.

"No more," said Jack hastily. "You're making yourself overwrought, which always makes you behave recklessly. I'll ring for wine and you must try to collect yourself."

"I'm perfectly collected. You needn't fear I'll do myself—or your neighbours—an injury. I've thought the matter over long and hard, and I cannot bring myself to believe the situation is hopeless."

Lord Berne moved from the fireplace to perch on a chair opposite his friend. "You've seen her recently?"

Jack admitted he had.

"Did she speak of me? Did she mention what I said to her when we last spoke?"

"You were mentioned only in passing."

The viscount nodded sadly. "She suspected I wasn't in earnest, and my going away only confirmed her suspicions. But enough self-pity. I'd better tell you what I proposed." He proceeded to repeat the scheme he had suggested to Miss Desmond.

"So that explains the business at church," said Jack. "No wonder she was complaining of the visitors and calling herself a curiosity piece."

"Then they've begun to relent?" the viscount asked eagerly. "They've welcomed her?"

Jack admitted that such appeared to be the case.

"Then there's hope!" Lord Berne exclaimed. "That's all I wanted. My way is clear now. I will not rest until she's securely established, until no one will dare breathe a word against her."

The wine was duly provided, but it refreshed neither party. Lord Berne was too busy talking to remember to drink his, and Jack was too busy with his troubled thoughts to taste what he drank.

Mr. Langdon examined his own feelings and found them base. He was tormented only by lust, which had certainly not inspired him with any true compassion for its object or any heroic plans for her future happiness. He'd thought only of his own needs and railed inwardly against her for arousing them. There was nothing of finer sentiments in this, nothing remotely worthy of the name Love. Being a just man, he felt he must ease his friend's mind regarding the "intentions" referred to earlier.

"I hope, Tony, you won't give the business in the garden another thought," he said, feeling very awkward. "You see, she tripped and stumbled into my arms and . . . and I lost my head. I got soundly slapped for my impertinence. I was also told in no uncertain terms that my attentions were profoundly unwelcome. That was and is the end of it, I promise you."

After a moment's reflection, Lord Berne responded magnanimously that he had been over-hasty in seeing evil where it was not, and pronounced himself satisfied.

Not to be outdone in generosity, Mr. Langdon revealed that the subject of their discussion would be dining at Rossing Hall this very evening. He said he'd be most pleased if Tony would make one of the party, and later avail himself of a guest chamber.

"I'll make it all right with my uncle," Jack added with a weak smile. "Now you're here, he'll think the damage done. Besides, if he can tolerate

Blenkly, he can endure your company as well, I expect."

Having transformed himself into a model of unselfishness, Lord Berne offered to absent himself from the house for a while—after, that is, he had washed and changed—to spare Lord Rossing unnecessary irritation. There was no need to explain that his chosen place of exile would be the house next door. Jack was intelligent enough to recognise the impossibility of his friend's doing anything else.

Lord Berne was just turning into the front walkway of Elmhurst when he came upon Mr. Atkins, who'd recently been turned out.

Mr. Atkins's lot was not a happy one. Following his last interview with Lord Streetham, the publisher had returned to London to nurse his cold and contemplate ruin. No sooner had he arrived than he'd had the idea of appealing to Desmond's greed by forging a letter offering more money for the manuscript. The reply had been most disheartening. Today he'd come hinting at legal action, only to meet a stone wall of injured innocence.

Desmond had claimed to be the victim of scoundrels. His manuscript had disappeared, he'd insisted. After observing that one couldn't get blood from a stone, and assuring the publisher something would turn up, and vowing an unspeakable vengeance upon those who had stripped him of the fruits of his labours, the Devil had politely eased Mr. Atkins out the door.

Now the publisher was faced with the unenviable task of discovering whether it was his business partner or his author who was playing him false, and the hopeless task of wrenching the manuscript from either of these fellows' grips.

Mr. Atkins cast an unfriendly eye upon Lord Berne. Had the earl not placed so much confidence in this young coxcomb, the matter might have been handled in a properly businesslike way from the start.

Lord Berne immediately took umbrage at being glowered at by this low, sweating tradesman.

"Still nosing about, Atkins?" said he. "Looking for more scurrilous tales to carry to my father? You'd better take care. Neither Mr. Desmond nor Lady Potterby will be best pleased to hear how you lurk about the property spying upon the family."

Mr. Atkins answered that he had not been spying on anyone. A man was entitled to professional interest in the products of his trade, he hoped. "I only wanted—"

"My good man, what you want can be of no possible interest to me, I am sure," said Lord Berne in perfect imitation of his father at his supercilious best. "I hope you will not tax my credulity too far by attempting to persuade me Lady Potterby now cultivates literature in her garden. She's growing a library there, perhaps, and you were curious about her choice of fertilizer? Or did you suspect your publications were the manure used to enrich her soil? Indeed, that would explain your obsessive interest. Good day, sir," his lordship concluded, rudely bushing past him.

Mr. Atkins stood a moment staring after the viscount in mute indignation. "Insolent, sarcastic puppy," he muttered to himself. "You feign to misunderstand me, do you, and insult my trade—as though it did not pay for your coats from Mr. Weston and your starched cravats and all the rest. Manure, indeed. *My* work enriching the soil and—"

And then Mr. Atkins had a vision—of a spade handle standing a foot or so from an embracing couple. He saw as well Mr. Langdon coatless and spattered with dirt. Mr. Atkins asked himself, much as Lord Streetham had a few days earlier, why two members of the idle upper class should take to agriculture on such a punishingly hot day.

* * *

Lord Berne discovered to his regret that he'd been overtaken by Time's winged chariot, for he was shown into the house just as the two ladies were about to go upstairs to prepare for the dinner party. He therefore had the honour of a mere ten minutes' visit, during which he found no opportunity to speak privately with Miss Desmond.

Still, he made the most of the precious minutes. He appeared as subdued, chastened, and decorous a visitor as any fastidious duenna could wish. His speech had just the right air of mournfulness to persuade any onlooker he was the hapless victim of a merciless conqueror. The sad, furtive way in which his gaze helplessly sought Miss Desmond's left no doubt as to whom this tyrant could be.

"Plague take the fellow," the Devil muttered under his breath, when the viscount had taken his dejected leave. "Kemble is a clownish amateur compared to him."

The fair despot might have been touched by the moving sight of a young lord in the last stages of romantic decline had she been able to spare him her attention. This was impossible, because Delilah's mind was taken up entirely by Mr. Atkins. His reappearance had been most disquieting, and she had not been at all appeased by her father's entertaining reenactment of his performance.

If they had not been engaged for the evening, Delilah would very likely have dashed out to the garden, dug up the manuscript—had it been there to be disinterred—and either burned it or thrown it into the duckpond. Unfortunately, they were engaged, and she must bathe and dress and then sit still for an eternity while Joan battled with her mistress's unruly hair.

10

THE DINNER PARTY turned out to be a foreshadowing
of the reception Delilah might expect in London.
Even the tentative acceptance she'd recently
achieved in Rossingley was not reflected in the
manner of Lord Rossing's more prominent guests.

Lord and Lady Streetham were more patronising
than ever, while their Gathers counterparts simply
pretended Miss Desmond was an uninteresting
piece of furniture. Since the former were now, like
the latter, houseguests of the Wembertons, even
that heretofore kindly group appeared stiffly ill at
ease.

Delilah's situation was not at all improved by
Lord Berne, who hovered about her constantly, despite his mama's apparently inexhaustible supply
of stratagems to call him back to Lady Jane's side.
Though Delilah wished he would consider her predicament and not make such a cake of himself, she
was not entirely displeased with his behaviour.

Lady Jane was all sharp angles. Her chin was
small and pointed. Her nose was narrow and
pointed. Her eyes were very black and very sharp,
and her voice, in perfect keeping with all this staccato, was high and clipped. She had curtly acknowl-

edged their introduction with a snap of her chin, as though she were a pair of scissors and would like to snip Miss Desmond out of the scene altogether. Lord Berne's devotion was some recompense to Delilah for this rudeness.

Still, it was a relief to be seated by Mr. Langdon at dinner, with Lady Jane and Lord Berne the length of the table away. As usual, Mr. Langdon was the soul of courtesy. He did not gaze upon Delilah with moonstruck eyes, nor heap fulsome compliments upon her aching head.

After dinner, though, he had to remain with the gentlemen, while the ladies retired to await them in the drawing room.

There Lady Potterby was drawn into conversation with Mrs. Blenkly, while Delilah, pointedly ignored by Lady Jane's allies, struggled to keep up something like a conversation with an excessively nervous Miss Wemberton. The latter was too tender-hearted to snub Miss Desmond, yet too aware of the ill-feeling towards her to converse enthusiastically. She kept glancing uneasily across the room at her mother, who was deeply engrossed with her houseguests.

"Is it wise, do you think, Eliza," Lady Gathers was saying, "to allow Mary to sit with her?"

Though Lady Wemberton was torn between loyalties, Lady Gathers's hint that Mary might be easily led astray was not at all acceptable.

"A few minutes' conversation will hardly corrupt my daughter," said Lady Wemberton, drawing herself up. "Besides, Millicent is a dear friend. One cannot choose one's relations, you know."

"One can decide whether or not to acknowledge them," Lady Gathers retorted. "But I daresay she grows senile and you tolerate her frailties for old times' sake."

"I can hardly cut the grand-niece without cutting the great-aunt," said Lady Wemberton.

"Yes, I suppose that is also Lord Berne's problem," snapped Lady Jane.

"The young men must sow their wild oats, my dear," said Lady Streetham, hastening to her darling's defence. "If he had any respect for that creature he would not subject her to such unseemly ogling."

"Indeed, you know you would blush, Jane, to be regarded so," Lady Gathers concurred.

All the same, the ladies must have agreed it was more unseemly that Lady Jane not be regarded at all, for they soon united to place that paragon center stage.

The men had scarcely appeared when the ladies began hinting for music. Naturally, Lady Jane must perform first, since she had precedence over the other maidens.

"I knew it," Lord Rossing muttered to his nephew. "Sooner or later we must be treated to a lot of amateurish caterwauling and applaud it as musical accomplishment." More audibly he pronounced himself enchanted with the prospect, and begged Lady Jane to offer the company her Euterpean tribute.

When all the ladies except Miss Desmond looked blank at this, Jack seconded his uncle with the more lucid request that Lady Jane accommodate them with a song.

Lady Jane made a proper show of modest hesitation, then took her place at the pianoforte and trilled out a sharp staccato version of "Barbara Allen." Perhaps she ought to have sung "Greensleeves" instead, but Lady Jane had too much dignity to sing of being cast off discourteously. Nevertheless, her voice did grow a tad more shrill as Lord Berne crossed the room to stand near Miss Desmond and drop several sad, tender glances upon her.

He proved equally deaf to Miss Wemberton's melodic offering, though her tones were sweeter and softer than Lady Jane's. By the time Miss Desmond's turn came, there were several pairs of hostile eyes fixed on her.

Colouring somewhat, she demurred.

"Come now, Miss Desmond," said Lady Streetham with excessive condescension. "You needn't be shy. There are no harsh critics in this informal group."

Miss Desmond flushed more deeply then, though she dutifully moved to the pianoforte. With a brief glance about her she removed her gloves. Then she sat down and struck the first notes of an unfamiliar melody.

It was nothing like the old ballads typically heard at such small gatherings in the country. The song was Italian, and Jack noted with dismay that the lyrics were not precisely proper for polite company. He glanced about him nervously, but all he saw was wonder in most of the faces about him as Miss Desmond's mezzo-soprano easily conveyed every throbbing nuance of the passionate song. Evidently few of her listeners were well-versed in Italian. He breathed a small sigh of relief as he turned his gaze to her.

When she'd seemed so reluctant to begin, Mr. Langdon's heart had pounded in sympathy for her apparent stage fright. Now, as he listened to her rich, beckoning voice, his heart beat with pride . . . and a longing that made him ache.

He glanced at Lord Berne and saw the same feelings openly displayed upon his friend's handsome countenance. Of course Tony loved her. He couldn't help it, any more than he could help showing it. Still, he might have been a tad more discreet. Miss Desmond would surely be the one to suffer for his lapse, as the expression on Lady Jane's face clearly augured. Her eyes were narrowed to two black points like stilettoes aimed at her rival's heart.

When the applause had died away—Lord Berne contributing a solo tattoo for a few seconds after the others had stopped—Lady Gathers smiled, showing all her teeth and most of the gums as well.

"Very pretty, Miss Desmond," said she with excessive condescension—and loud enough to drown out the other compliments. "You are generous indeed to treat so small a group to a display of your considerable gifts—though one trusts you plan to share that gift with a wider audience in time. No doubt you have thought of going upon the stage, as your mama did. I never had the pleasure of seeing her perform, but I daresay you have inherited her talents."

Jack heard more than one gasp, but his eyes were on Miss Desmond's father. The Devil said nothing, only gazed about him with a cynical smile before turning back to his daughter. Though she was rather pale as she rose from the piano seat, the face which met her father's glance was inscrutable. She turned towards Lady Gathers and smiled.

"You are too kind, My Lady," she said.

"Not at all," said Lady Jane, taking up the gauntlet. "Mama is quite right. Talent such as yours ought not be hoarded for small private gatherings, when it might delight the public."

"Ah, you believe one's skill should be used to the common good."

"Indeed it must. That is virtually an obligation."

"Then I wonder, Lady Jane, why you have not offered the public the benefit of your exquisite taste and elegance by becoming a couturière," said Miss Desmond sweetly.

Before Lady Jane had time to counterattack, Jack leapt into the fray.

"Really, it is most gratifying to hear the ladies speak so knowledgeably of Benthamite philosophy," he said hurriedly. "In order to be good, according to them, the object examined must be useful. The object, of course, refers to the matter under discussion, whether it be an abstract quality or a physical fact."

Apparently oblivious to the bafflement of most of his audience, Jack soared into the empyrean realms of the most abstruse philosophy, citing Plato, Aristotle, St. Augustine and others with no regard whatsoever to relevance or coherence, and with a great deal of Greek and Latin thrown in for good measure. He continued in this vein for at least a quarter hour, at the end of which time most of the company had withdrawn from the battlefield to less mystifying conversations. At last, when even his uncle had apparently dozed off, and Tony had retreated to the window—where he stood looking bored and cross—only Miss Desmond of Jack's listeners remained.

As he paused to look about him and draw his breath, Jack found Miss Desmond's eyes upon his. She smiled, and in that smile was so much gratitude that he could not resist drawing closer to bask in its warmth. He drew near enough to join her at the pianoforte, where she still stood.

"You are a 'verray, parfit, gentile knight,' " she said softly. "Thank you for coming to my rescue. I'm afraid I nearly provoked a scene."

"It was *she* provoked it," said Jack heatedly. "The effrontery of the woman, to speak to you as though you were a damned organ grinder's monkey. And her ill-bred daughter to take it up—pure, malicious ignorance. But that is what you get, Miss Desmond, for casting your pearls before swine. You sang like an angel, and made me wish I could banish this common herd from the paradise you created."

He had not meant to say so much, and for an instant wished he could recall the words. But only for an instant, until his gaze was drawn once more to hers and he discovered a soft light shining in her grey-green eyes.

"How beautifully you smooth my ruffled feathers," she said. "As beautifully as you routed my enemies. You have depths, sir, I had not imagined."

As a man accustomed to consider himself the most uninteresting, prosy fellow who ever existed, Mr. Langdon could not help but be agreeably surprised. Her words set chords vibrating within him, and this inner music crept to his tongue. "I wish," he began—then a shadow fell upon him. He looked around to meet his erstwile friend's frown.

"Really, Jack, I do think you've edified the company sufficiently for one evening," said Lord Berne. "Have some consideration for our fair songbird. You give her not a moment to catch her breath." He bent a killing glance upon Miss Desmond.

She appeared not to notice, but another young lady must have because the latter was, as Jack noted, making her way towards them with all deliberate speed.

"I am hardier than you think, My Lord," said the songbird. "One tune is not so great an exertion as to require extended convalescence."

"But perhaps you want a change of scenery," he hinted.

"Now that is what I should like," said Lady Jane as she nipped out a position for herself between Lord Berne and Miss Desmond. "We spend every summer in the country, though I beg Papa to take us to Brighton instead. Everyone is there now, it seems. Is that not so, Tony? Aunt Lilith wrote that you were upon the Steyne every day. I wonder you did not remain longer. I daresay Brighton was as lively as London in the Season."

Lord Berne looked abashed, and to Jack's surprise, allowed his chattering companion to lead him away.

As Jack turned back to Miss Desmond, he experienced a disagreeably familiar sensation of something throbbing in the air about him, like the first ominous rumblings of a volcano.

"I wonder," she said in suppressed tones, "what invalid makes his sickbed upon the Steyne."

Mr. Langdon looked baffled.

"He wrote me, you know," she explained, her eyes very bright. "He was called away to some bosom-bow's bed of pain. In Rye. Really, what a full evening this has been. Most enlightening. I have learned precisely in what estimation I am held by the lords and ladies. She sings and remains a lady. I sing and immediately descend to the ranks of ballet dancers—only a bit higher on the social scale than the village idiot *he* appears to take me for."

Her low tones were crisp enough, but the glitter of her eyes and the slight trembling of her lower lip betrayed her. With a sinking feeling Jack perceived it was this last—Tony's falsehood—which had made the deepest cut.

"Miss Desmond, the ladies had to strike at the only place where they thought they could wound you, because you wounded their pride," Jack said quietly. "You know how matters stand with Lady Jane. Surely you're aware of her—and his—parents' plans."

"Indeed, I am sorry their plans do not proceed apace," Miss Desmond answered, lifting her chin. "Yet that is certainly not my doing. It's all his, but he lets them make a scapegoat of me—after he's made a fool of me."

Mr. Langdon underwent a short, fierce struggle with his conscience. Though he didn't want to defend Tony, the impassioned speech of this afternoon had left its mark.

"I know that can't be, Miss Desmond," he said finally, unhappily. "He should not have lied about where and why he'd gone. I suppose it was improper of him to write at all—yet I'm sure he did so because he feared you'd despise him otherwise. His father sent him away, you know," Jack added, growing uneasy under her searching scrutiny, "and his father controls the purse strings. It was only Tony's pride prevented his confiding this to you. That he's returned, in defiance of his parents' express command, speaks volumes, I think, of his regard for you."

Unable to meet her gaze with equanimity, Jack had dropped his own. It fell upon one white hand whose fingers nervously traced a corner of the pianoforte. Though her hands were graceful, they were not small and delicate. They were strong and expressive, with long, slim fingers that could play a deadly tune upon a pistol as easily as they could a passionate one upon the pianoforte. He thought sadly, that she might play any tune upon him she liked. He longed, even as he defended his friend, to feel those fingers in his hair.

He could not know that Miss Desmond, at this precise moment, had any thoughts of obliging him. She had struggled with her rage and hurt while he spoke. She had struggled, too, with embarrassment at what those feelings had caused her tongue to reveal. She should not for worlds have anyone know just how deeply she had been hurt, repeatedly, this evening. She too had her pride.

But pride, hurt, and rage had gotten all mixed up somehow with another sort of agitation she could not or would not define. She saw her companion's clear, compassionate grey eyes cloud over with some inner sorrow, and she wanted to comfort him as he'd tried to comfort her. She wanted, at least, to push back the errant lock of hair that had fallen onto his forehead, as though by smoothing out his hair she might somehow smooth away his trouble as well.

Lord, what was she thinking of? She was not the maternal type. Delilah glanced towards the window where Lord Berne stood, entirely self-assured, his arrogant self again as he talked with Lady Jane. He certainly wanted no mothering, any more than Papa did. She looked away from Lord Berne and sighed.

While Lord Rossing's guests were either enjoying or making themselves miserable according to individual inclination, Lady Potterby's servants were engaged in the usual modest dissipations attendant upon their mistress's being out for the evening. The human denizens of the stables had settled down in their quarters to cards and drink, while the household staff had retired either to the housekeeper's room or the servants' hall, according to rank, to partake of punch and gossip about their betters. In their innocent enjoyment of an evening's freedom, not one loyal retainer suspected that a serpent lurked in their beloved mistress's garden.

If there was nothing sleek and sinuous about him, if his form was more porcine than reptilian, and if he was insufficiently cold-blooded for his task and trembled with terror every step of the way, Mr. Atkins could lurk as well as the next man, and lurk he did. He crept into the garden as the sky began to darken and slunk uneasily, starting at every imagined sound, to the bed where the ill-fated seedlings had been planted.

He would have felt a bit less terrified—but only a bit—if this had been an utterly black, moonless night. In such a case, however, his task would have been more difficult than it was already. He dared not carry a light and, not being as familiar with the site as he could wish, must find the spot before the descending sun made its departure from the heavens altogether.

What with starting and hesitating and imagining footsteps where there were none and turning back half a dozen times for every dozen he went forward, he discovered the one barren square of soil just as darkness truly fell. Still, having come so far, he could not—would not, for fear and greed drove him on—go back and wait for a better opportunity. He drew out his few hand tools (he had not dared bring anything so loudly incriminating as a shovel) from the pockets of his overcoat and began to dig.

He dug a hole, not so deep as a well nor so wide as a church door but, as Mercutio had once observed, it would serve. The excavations Mr. Atkins effected might have served, in fact, to bury a host of volumes and one or two owners besides. These efforts, to his unspeakable despair, did not serve sufficiently to produce what he sought.

Hours after he'd begun, as a few bold stars twinkled defiantly through the heavy overcast of late-night sky, Mr. Atkins sank down on his knees, defeated and near tears with frustration. It must be here. There was no other explanation. Yet there must be some other, because it was not.

He sat and mourned and raged by turns and rubbed his dirty, blistered hands against his forehead and got dirt into his eyes, which made them water, and up his nose, which made him sneeze. A slug began oozing over his fingers towards his shirt cuff. Shuddering, the publisher struck at it with the trowel, but only succeeded in gashing his wrist. While the slug crawled away unharmed, Mr. Atkins, eyes smarting, nose running, muscles aching, and wrist throbbing in excruciating counterpart to his head, collected his tools, rose, and trudged out of the garden.

11

Though he'd experienced some confusion the night before, an untroubled night's sleep was sufficient to revive Lord Berne's customary aplomb. He appeared at Elmhurst the morning after the dinner party, fully prepared to recover whatever credit he had lost. When the butler informed him that Miss Desmond was not in, Lord Berne was not too shy to ask where she had gone.

Bantwell certainly had no business telling him. Unfortunately, the butler was suffering the after-effects of dissipation and, due to what seemed like a hundred nails driving themselves into his skull, was not thinking clearly.

Thus Lord Berne learned Miss Desmond had gone riding. He had only to bribe a groom to obtain a mount. Finding the young lady was not difficult, either. Forbidden any pace speedier than a trot and not allowed beyond the park boundaries, she could not go very far.

He found her decorously following the bridle path which circuited the park, her groom trotting at a discreet distance behind her. Peters, the groom, looked even more ill than the butler had. He was, in fact, rather green about the gills.

Lord Berne smiled. The gods were with him this morning. He erased the smile as soon as he was alongside his beloved, whose expression was not at all welcoming. Without further ado, Lord Berne threw himself at her mercy. He was despicable, he declared. He wished he might be flogged—no, a rack would be better—for the falsehood he had, in a moment of utter despair, committed to paper.

He was informed in flinty tones that his wishes could be of no possible interest to her.

Miss Desmond's icy hauteur immediately aroused Lord Berne as no coquetry could have done. Perhaps this was because, as Jack had supposed, such treatment was a novelty. Lord Berne had encountered feigned indifference before, but this Arctic fury was another species altogether, and held all the exotic thrill of travel in uncharted lands.

"It's as I feared, as I knew it would be, then," he said. "You will not forgive me, and it were futile to explain, to exonerate myself."

"I wish, sir, you would divest yourself of the delusion that anything you do or say could be of any possible concern to myself."

"Is it a delusion, Miss Desmond? Would you be so angry—would you hate me so if what I had done were a matter of indifference to you?"

Her eyes flashed, telling him he had scored his point.

"Spoken with all the conceited arrogance of a true coxcomb," she retorted hotly. "But what do you care how you insult me? I only wonder you take the trouble with one so utterly beneath your notice."

No woman in his whole life had ever spoken to him so, and no one could look so ravishingly enraged while she did. Lord Berne grew giddy with desire.

"Despise me, then," he said. "Loathe me. Tell me I disgust you. At least there's feeling in that. At least I inspire you with some sort of passion." He saw her raise her riding crop. "Will you strike me? Do it," he urged. "I cannot tell you the relief it would bring me."

"How dare you!" she gasped, goaded nearly to tears. "But of course you dare. You think you can say any filth to me you like. And like a fool I remain passively enduring it. Well, I've amused you long enough." She spurred her horse and dashed ahead.

Being by no means taken unawares, Lord Berne set off in pursuit, as did the less prepared groom. Unfortunately, Peter's physiology was in no state amenable to a gallop. In less than a minute he was forced to halt, so that he could dismount and vomit into the bushes. By the time he could look up again, Miss Desmond and her pursuer were out of sight.

"Atkins, I admire persistence. A man gets nowhere in this wicked world without it. But I must tell you frankly, sir, that your case now passes the bounds of British tenacity and hovers on the brink of obsession. I told you I haven't got it. You may offer a million pounds, and the Crown of England in the bargain, and I still won't have it. The manuscript is no longer in my possession."

Mr. Desmond's smile was regretful, even pitying, yet something in his eyes caused Mr. Atkins to step back a pace.

Desmond, even at his amiable best—which he was not this morning—was a formidable figure. All the same, Mr. Atkins was desperate. If he was obsessed, he was entitled to be, when his entire future was at stake, when ruin and desolation stared grinning into his face.

"Are you quite sure, Mr. Desmond," he asked poignantly, "you have no idea who *has* got it? No suspicions?"

"If I had suspicions," the Devil answered, "I would act upon them, don't you think? If I suspected, for instance, that you would not accept the word of a gentleman, don't you think I might be a little affronted?" He went on, still smiling, but with a warning in his voice that matched the warning in his glittering green eyes, "Yet as you see, I am perfectly at ease. I imagine no such slight to my honour. You are only concerned I may have experienced a momentary absence of mind—a failing, like physical enfeeblement, regrettably common among men of my advanced age."

As he spoke, Mr. Desmond advanced upon his guest, who found himself backing towards the door.

"I appreciate your concern," the Devil added, as Mr. Atkins collided with the door handle, "but I do hate to be fussed over, you know. Ungrateful creature that I am, it makes me irritable. I had much rather, Mr. Atkins, you ceased fussing."

Mr. Atkins's courage—no reliable quality in him anyhow—deserted him entirely as the towering dark figure closed in on him.

"In—indeed, sir, I understand per—perfectly," he stammered. "Most annoying, I'm sure. Very sorry to have troubled you. Good day, sir." He grasped the door handle, wrenched the door open, and stumbled into the hall and against a very large potted palm. The tree tottered and Mr. Atkins made a grab for it, dropping his hat in the process. The tree swayed back into place, its fronds quivering. Trembling likewise, Mr. Atkins turned to retrieve his hat and found Mr. Langdon standing in the way, frowning at him.

Mr. Langdon's frown was attributable to the fact that his life had become a burden to him. From the moment last night when he'd caught Miss Desmond's furtive glance at Lord Berne and heard the ensuing sigh, Mr. Langdon had seen the light. Or perhaps the darkness was more apt a metaphor, because what he saw threw gloom upon every facet of his existence.

137

It was Tony she sighed for, Tony she longed for, which ought to be perfectly agreeable, since Tony was sighing and longing for her and they were well matched in every way, from their physical beauty to their restless, passionate natures. Yet try as he might, Mr. Langdon could find no joy in contemplating this pair formed by nature for each other. He found so little joy in it that he wished he were dead.

Still, whatever he felt, he knew he had no business behaving so rudely to Mr. Atkins. Though he would like to knock the fellow down for continuing to plague the family, Jack had no right to do so. No one had appointed him guardian of the Desmonds' peace.

Accordingly, he schooled his features into a thin semblance of politeness and—perhaps to make up for this poor show, retrieved the publisher's hat and returned it to him with something like a pleasant greeting.

"Th-thank you, sir. Kind of you, I'm sure," Mr. Atkins mumbled, turning the hat round and round in his hands. "So clumsy of me. Business, you know. So pressing." He darted a frightened look at the sturdy door, then, with a stammered "Good day," scurried away.

Mr. Langdon scarcely heard the farewell, being preoccupied once more with the matter of hands. How curious that so well-fed and well-groomed a City-bred fellow should have such ill-cared-for hands. Mr. Atkins's fingernails had been ragged and grimy, the digits themselves red and blistered. This was odd in a man whose primary labour was the shifting about of pieces of paper and the consumption of vast quantities of ink.

The butler appeared, breaking in upon Mr. Langdon's reflections.

"Her ladyship has just come in from the garden," said Bantwell. "She says that if you will be so kind as to excuse her appearance, she will be pleased to meet with you in the drawing room."

Mr. Langdon was duly led in and announced in unsteady tones by the red-eyed, but otherwise pale, butler.

Lady Potterby looked rather peevish and ill as well, an appearance she explained was the result of unwelcome news from her gardener. "He insists we are overrun with moles, Mr. Langdon, which is most distressing."

"Moles?" Jack echoed blankly.

She nodded. "Jenkins tells me there are holes everywhere. He's beside himself. The lavender half uprooted and the lilies a shambles and I don't know what else. At least the worst of the damage was—" She caught herself up short as Mr. Langdon's eyes widened. "Well, it is most tiresome, and I shall spare you the details."

Mr. Langdon, upon whom an awful suspicion had just dawned, hurriedly dispatched his errand by returning Lady Potterby's fan to her. He then asked after Miss Desmond.

Upon learning the young lady was sufficiently recovered from last night's jollities to go riding, he expressed his satisfaction and made a hasty departure.

He had just broken into a run, preparatory to a mad dash back to the Rossing stables for his horse, when, turning the corner of the hedge, he narrowly missed colliding with Mr. Desmond.

"All this dashing about in the height of summer—it is a wonder you young people have not succumbed to heat prostration," said the Devil. "Well, you *are* young."

Mr. Langdon rather incoherently concurred with this observation.

"Since you are thirty years at least younger than myself, Mr. Langdon, I wish you would get my horse back for me, and save me some exertion."

"I beg your pardon?" said Jack distractedly.

"That knave—Berne, I mean—has borrowed Apollyon and gone gallivanting with Delilah. I particularly wanted to ride today and I particularly want my own horse," said Mr. Desmond in aggrieved tones. "Apollyon and I are accustomed to each other. We are quite intimate. I got him from Wemberton two days ago in trade for an ill-natured grey."

"Indeed, sir," said Jack, practically hopping with impatience.

"So will you not borrow a mount and get my horse back for me? Her ladyship's stable is nearer to hand," the Devil added, "and I am in rather a hurry."

No horse can sustain a gallop forever, regardless how inconsiderate its rider. Miss Desmond was boiling mad, but she was not inconsiderate. Out of compassion for dumb beasts she was eventually compelled to slow her mount. She glared at Lord Berne when he rode up alongside her once more.

"Go away," she said, panting. "Go to the devil."

"I come to his daughter instead. Gad, but you ride well," he said admiringly. "We must hunt together one day."

"Are you deaf? You are not wanted. Go away."

"You know I can't. You are the woman I've been searching for my entire life." His voice dropped to low, thrilling tones of urgency. "You must let me speak."

"To insult me further?"

"There was no insult in what I said. Only you made it so. Still, it served my purpose."

"Your *what*?"

"I wanted to be rid of the groom, which you did for me by becoming enraged and galloping away. Were you not aware he was too ill to follow?"

Miss Desmond glanced behind her and knew an

instant of alarm. She was alone and unprotected in the company of a libertine who had deliberately manipulated her into this predicament. Nonetheless, she reminded herself, this was her great-aunt's property. He would not dare misbehave. She willed herself to be calm as she turned to meet his gaze, and was taken aback by the piteous longing in his countenance.

"It was only because I could not speak what was in my heart while others were by," he said tenderly. "I must speak because, despite your mistrust—oh, I admit you have reason—but despite that, despite my parents' warnings, Hope persists. How can I help it, worshipping you as I do? I must hope . . . or die."

In her short life, Delilah had heard enough sweet talk to fill all seven volumes of *Clarissa*. Since she had never, however, heard Lord Berne at his heart-stirring best, she might as well have spent her twenty years in a convent. His voice easily drowned out the one in the back of her head which was shrilly recommending she return to the house immediately.

He raised every objection she could have to him just as though he had direct access to her brain, then answered each objection as brilliantly as if he had been on trial for his life. It was not so much his rhetoric that held her, however, as the boyish innocence of his handsome face and the sincerity of his tones as he gave her to understand she was the most beautiful, brilliant, altogether admirable woman who had ever existed.

Upon Delilah, who had endured virtually unceasing disapproval in recent days, his idolatry fell like rain upon an arid field. Even had she been less vulnerable, she would have been hard put to resist the kind of heartfelt declarations which had so effectively crushed a considerably more objective Mr. Langdon only the day before. When it came to the game of love, Lord Berne was a tactical genius. Had Napoleon been a woman—though every bit as brilliant a commander—the viscount might have dispatched him in a week.

It was not so surprising, then, that even Miss Desmond's skeptical heart was touched. Though she said little, her countenance must have spoken for her, because Lord Berne's tones changed subtly from pleading to coaxing. In a remarkably short time he had persuaded her to dismount and walk with him, so that he might pick a nosegay of wildflowers for her.

They walked, and he picked the flowers, and looked so much like a schoolboy experiencing his first calf love that he made her laugh, which undermined her defences even more effectively than the rest.

"You don't laugh nearly enough," he said tenderly as he presented the posies to her. "If you were mine—"

He did not complete the sentence because, evidently, his heart was too full. Or perhaps his arms were too full, since they'd already encircled her. In the next instant, the bouquet fell neglected to the ground as he kissed her.

It began with a mere touch of his lips upon hers, light and teasing—but clearly skilled, because in seconds and virtually without her realising, the kiss grew deeper and more fervent, just as the light circle of his arms strengthened into a crushing embrace. He worked so subtly and quickly, in fact, that Delilah felt like one caught in a treacherous undertow which was tugging her gently but inexorably towards the open sea of destruction.

Just as it was dawning on her to disentangle herself, Lord Berne drew away and apologised. Then he promptly embraced her again, declaring himself helpless, lost, confused, bewitched, overcome.

He did not, however, declare himself in the more

formal, accepted manner. This is to say, no hint was given concerning rings or parsons or a company of witnesses, and Delilah, though rather giddy, only teetered on the brink of being swept off her feet. Then she regained her balance and pushed him away.

His eyes glistening with tears, he begged her to take pity on him. He worshipped her. Just one more chaste kiss—that was all he wanted. He took both her hands and kissed the fingers, then the palms. Then he fell to his knees, still firmly clasping her hands, and—apparently too distracted to realise what he was doing—began pulling her down to him.

Though Delilah was not a fragile young miss, she was hardly a match for a six foot, twelve stone male in excellent physical condition. She tried to pull free, but his grip was relentless. He was deaf to her protests, being utterly absorbed in his all-consuming passion for her, and she had neither dagger nor pistol with which to restore him to full consciousness.

She would have to kick him in the usual place, she concluded—though, despite her apprehension, she rather wished she didn't have to. Still, Papa had ordered her not to be seduced, and she most certainly had no intention of being ravished in a field, like some unfortunate dairy maid. She closed her eyes, steeled herself, and was just raising her foot from the ground when she heard what sounded like thunder.

She opened her eyes again and looked towards the sound. Lord Berne, surprised, looked too, and released her hands abruptly when he saw what it was.

Though his was not a violent nature, the spectacle which met his eyes as he rode across the meadow threw Mr. Langdon into a towering rage, and an

143

impulse seized him to trample his childhood friend into a bloody pulp.

Fortunately, Jack's better nature reasserted itself. Masking his fury, he coldly informed Lord Berne that Mr. Desmond's horse was wanted.

"You'd better go at once," said Jack, "because you're wanted at Wemberton as well. A message came from your mother not an hour ago," he lied, "and I've been looking everywhere for you."

Though Lord Berne's mother was forever summoning him and he saw no greater urgency in this latest demand, he did suspect that withholding the Devil's horse while simultaneously attempting to ravish his daughter was a tad excessive. Besides, with Jack by, there was nothing more to be accomplished with Miss Desmond at present. Quelling his frustration, Lord Berne consoled himself with one languishing glance at his beloved before taking his leave.

Jack now turned his own gaze to that dazzling object. "Where's your groom?" he demanded.

"I haven't the slightest idea," Delilah answered with great nonchalance. "Probably several miles back, casting up his accounts. Not that it is any concern of yours, sir," she added haughtily, though two spots of colour blazed in her cheeks.

"If you ride with Tony unescorted the matter will be everyone's concern, Miss Desmond."

"I am still unescorted, as you put it," she returned. "If you have so much regard for petty gossip, you would be better employed finding Peters." She marched towards her horse, which was tethered to a nearby bush.

Jack quickly dismounted and followed.

"Since I am obviously not a lady, I can mount without assistance," she told him as he came up beside her.

Mr. Langdon lost his temper. "Damn it all!" he snapped. "I'm very sorry I interrupted your *tête-à-*

tête, Miss Desmond, but I wish you'd save your righteous indignation for later. I only came because we have a problem. That is, *you* have a problem. Really, I don't know why I've been galloping about Rossingley like a lunatic and telling lies to my friends when you're so splendidly capable of managing your affairs." So saying, and oblivious to her sputter of outrage, he flung her none too gently into her saddle.

A stunned Delilah gazed for a moment speechlessly down upon the unkempt brown head of this unexpectedly masterful Mr. Langdon.

"What problem?" she finally managed to gasp out.

"I saw Atkins just now," said Jack, glaring at her right boot. "His hands were all blistered and dirty. Then your great-aunt told me some nonsense about moles invading her garden. I think Atkins has got hold of the memoirs. I thought you'd wish to know. I should have told your father instead," he grumbled. "He at least doesn't use me as a whipping boy."

He stomped back to his own beast and mounted.

Delilah drew up beside him. "Are you sure?" she asked, alarm quickly superseding all other emotions. "How could he possibly have found out? And why would he be at the house again if he's already got them?"

"I don't know. I know only what I saw and heard," was the grudging response.

"Oh, please, don't be angry with me now," she begged. "I'm sorry I was nasty, but I was—" She hesitated.

"Was what?" he asked testily.

She bit her lip and dropped her eyes. "I was embarrassed."

Her frankness was disarming and Jack was, in spite of himself, disarmed. She had only to appear the slightest bit repentant or troubled and his heart

145

went out to her, in spite of his brain's warnings that she was a consummate actress. Really, it was no good his brain telling him anything, because he just wouldn't listen.

Suppressing a sigh, he told her he was not angry, only anxious. They had better hurry back to find out if they could whether his suspicions were founded in fact.

With a nod, Miss Desmond urged her horse on, and the two hastened back to the house.

"Oh, Lord," Delilah cried as they arrived, panting, at the book's grave-site. The flower bed looked as though it had been bombarded with cannon.

"If he did find it," said Jack, "it was obviously not on the first attempt. And one cannot tell from this whether he did dig in the right place."

"Well, I'm going to find out," said Delilah. She started moving down the path towards the potting shed, but Jack stopped her.

The gardener, he told her, was already beside himself. Jenkins would not remain quietly elsewhere if anyone set foot in his domain with a spade in hand. Furthermore, he'd be sure to inform Lady Potterby, and how did Miss Desmond propose to explain further outrages to the garden?

"I'll make some excuse," she answered impatiently.

"You have no more excuses. There's no sign of the seedlings. They're obviously destroyed."

"So I'm to stand idly by, not knowing whether the manuscript is already on its way to print?" she cried.

"I wish you'd keep your voice down," Jack warned. "Do strive for a little patience, Miss Desmond. I'll come tonight and search. Tomorrow morning first thing I'll report to you."

"No, you will not. I can search tonight myself—"

"You most certainly cannot. A young woman—at

146

night—all alone—digging in the garden? Are you mad? If Atkins failed last night he may try again—or he may send someone better adapted to such labour. You don't know who you may run up against."

Delilah glared at him. "What does that matter? I'll bring my pistol."

"This is no enterprise for a lady."

"Since I'm obviously not—"

"Miss Desmond, I just told you I'd see to it—and I'll see to it *my* way. If you even think of leaving the house tonight I shall—" He paused briefly, then in steely tones went on, "I shall *spank* you."

Delilah stared at him. As usual, his hair was untidy and his clothes had subsided into their customary matching state. At the moment, however, his face was that of a stranger. It was positively feudal. The eyes gazing down his long, aristocratic nose at her were as steely as his voice, and the set of his jaw was the very model of dictatorial obstinacy.

She was not in the least impressed by this display of masculine arrogance, she told herself, though her heart proceeded to raise a fuss all the same.

"How dare you?" she said, rather breathlessly. "I am perfectly capable of digging a hole." She lifted her chin and turned to leave.

He seized her wrist. "What *you* are capable of is beside the point. I'll do what needs to be done, and that doesn't include spending the night worrying about the safety of a rash female."

Worrying? Was he truly anxious about her safety? Really, that was rather ... quaint of him, she told herself, while her heart drummed against her ribs. Then she became acutely aware of the hand closed about her wrist and a most puzzling sensation of weakness in her limbs. Baffled, she stared hard at his hand. He quickly released her.

"Excuse me," he said. "I did not mean to man-handle you."

"No, I suppose not," she answered, feeling dread-fully confused. "Not unless I'm disobedient, I gather."

He gave her a faint smile. "But you won't be, will you, Miss Desmond? You won't try my patience, I hope?"

Miss Desmond sighed and promised to do as he bid.

12

As he learned a while later, Mr. Langdon had not
told falsehoods after all. There had indeed been a
summons for Lord Berne, who had already left to
accompany his parents back to Streetham Close by
the time Jack returned to Rossing Hall.

Relieved that he would not have to endure his
friend's quizzing, Jack quickly set about preparing
for his evening's skullduggery. The first order of
business was to get rid of his valet, who was given
the night off. Though Mr. Fellows lingered in the
house until after dinner—to make certain his master donned proper attire—he did leave at last, and
Jack could ransack his own wardrobe free of prying
eyes and ironic comments.

Eventually he found an old set of clothing suitable to his purposes. After donning these, he sat
down with a volume of Andrew Marvell's poetry to
wait.

Delilah had intended, as soon as she returned to
the house, to inform her father of Atkins's apparent
treachery. She could not. Mr. Desmond had gone
out and did not plan to return until very late that

evening, Lady Potterby disapprovingly informed her grand-niece.

"Some card game or cock fight, I suppose," Lady Potterby muttered. "But that is to be expected. I only wonder he has remained so quietly at home all this time."

As predicted, he did not return for dinner and when, several hours later, he had not yet put in an appearance, Delilah decided this was just as well. She really ought not say anything to him until she was certain the memoirs were gone. Otherwise he might go after Mr. Atkins and get himself taken up for assault on an innocent man.

Since no festivities were scheduled for tonight, the household made an early bedtime. By ten o'clock, having dismissed her maid, Delilah was curled up in the window seat of her bedchamber, gazing out at the darkened expanse of park towards Rossing Hall.

She would have preferred a view of the garden, but her room was on the wrong side of the house. As it was, she doubted she'd be able to see anything, even if Mr. Langdon did come that way, and she had no way of knowing whether he would.

Still, she waited and watched as the old clock in the hall downstairs tolled eleven o'clock, then midnight. The clock had scarcely left off chiming when she discerned a faint light moving between the row of elms. Immediately her heart began pounding.

Lud, wasn't that just like him—to bring a lantern. What if one of the grooms was up and about in his quarters by the stable and spied the light?

Jack darkened his lantern and placed it on the ground. Having decided that, if caught, he would simply confess all, he had brought along a spade, which he now plunged into the earth. He had just emptied his third shovelful when he heard a faint creak, then rustling. There was a light patter of footsteps, and Jack looked up to see a dark figure approaching. It was not a tall, dark figure. He uttered a sigh.

"I told you to keep away," he whispered as the figure drew near. "Must you be so pigheaded?"

The object of his rebuke hesitated but a moment before stepping closer. In the moonlight Mr. Langdon was able to ascertain that Miss Desmond had thrown on a coat obviously not her own. The coat, which dragged on the ground, would have comfortably covered two or three Miss Desmonds. Though she clutched her large wrapping tightly about her, a peep of white at the neck and another near the toes sufficiently indicated what was beneath.

Drat the woman! She'd come out in her night-rail, for heaven's sake. How in blazes would he explain *that* if they were caught?

"Go back in the house this instant," he whispered harshly.

This Miss Desmond firmly refused to do. Since arguing with her was bound to prove only an exasperating waste of time, Jack decided to ignore her and go on digging.

Because he had not dug a very deep hole originally, not many shovelfuls were required to confirm their fears: The false book and its contents were gone.

Miss Desmond stared for a long while at the empty hole. Then her head bent and her shoulders began to shake, and in another moment Jack heard the unmistakable sounds of weeping.

He thrust his spade securely into the dirt and stepped back to take her in his arms. Accepting the offer of comfort without protest, Miss Desmond pressed her face against his chest and sobbed like a child while he patted her back and muttered every sort of consolation he could think of.

Even if Atkins had the memoirs now, there was no reason her father could not get them back again,

Jack told her. Was her papa not a brilliant man? Besides, Atkins was terrified of him. One confrontation and the nervous little fellow would give up his purloined goods. He must. Since he hadn't yet paid in full for them, he didn't legally own them.

Under this calming influence, Miss Desmond's weeping gradually abated. Regrettably, Mr. Langdon did not have the same tranquilizing effect upon himself. At the moment, the young lady was a somewhat awkward bundle, but it was *she*, all the same. The feel of her face pressed against his coat was very pleasant. The proximity of her person, even with all that coarse wrapping, was agreeably warm. His comforting pats gradually became gentle stroking, and very soon, Jack was in agonies.

He wanted to bury his face in her hair. His fingers itched to caress her neck, her shoulders, to fling away the dratted coat and . . .

She raised her head just as his right hand was about to plunge into her tangled hair. The hand paused mid-air.

"Oh, Jack," she said softly. "You're always so sensible."

Jack? "Jack?" he echoed stupidly, stunned by the beckoning sound of his own dull name. His hand dropped to her shoulder. His face was beginning to lower to hers when another word intruded upon his consciousness: *sensible*?

As she saw him withdraw, Delilah immediately set about persuading her crestfallen self she was vastly relieved. She had a sensed a kiss coming, and certainly he had no business . . . but that was no good, she realized with dismay as she drew away from the comfortingly strong arms. She'd wanted him to kiss her. Good heavens—she'd even called him by his Christian name!

"Excuse me, Mr. Langdon," she said, backing away and nervously rubbing her nose on her coatsleeve. "I should not have been so familiar. I was—

distraught. Thank you so much. You have been very—very—kind. I—I had better go in now, I think. And you had better go home. The night air, you know. Most insalubrious, my aunt says," she babbled. Then she turned and fled.

She sped up the backstairs, pausing only to return Bantwell's overcoat to its peg, and on to her room.

She threw herself down at the dressing table and began savagely brushing her hair. Two minutes later she put down the brush and went again to the window. By now he was gone, and what possible consolation watching the faint light move through the park could have been to her, she could not imagine.

Delilah leaned her head against the glass. How very comfortable and safe she had felt, held securely against his hard chest. Well, that was nothing. Jack Langdon was as safe as houses, quiet and diffident and scholarly and serious.

She blinked. Not when he kissed her, though. Not when he lost his temper and *threw* her onto her horse. That had left her dumbfounded. She hadn't realized he was so strong. After all, hadn't they been well matched during their tussle at the inn? Or had that been more of his chivalry? Very likely. He'd held himself back because a gentleman could not hurt a woman, murderess or not. Damn his gallantry. Why must he be so honourable, always, and make her feel more ill-bred than ever?

Her eyes itched, threatening tears. Angrily she rubbed them away, telling herself it would serve him right if she used that honour to manipulate him into marrying her. Certainly that would solve her problems very easily. She'd never need have a moment's anxiety about her parents' future. After all, Papa was not getting any younger. He could not go on living by his wits forever.

Mr. Langdon would take care of her parents. She needn't fear they'd be tossed into debtors' prison or be left to languish in a workhouse or spend their declining years in sordid lodgings, waiting to die. At the same time, their daughter would be spared the mortification of striving to be accepted by a Great World which didn't want her.

Given the way Lord Berne's family and friends had reacted, gaining acceptance was going to be a more formidable battle than Delilah had imagined—even if her own heedless behaviour did not continue to trip her up. Now, with the memoirs gone, it seemed she was to be defeated before she'd even begun.

All the same, she chided herself, Delilah Desmond was no coward. Here was a man who, while perhaps physically attracted—which was nothing, since every male seemed to be—could barely tolerate her, and who only irritated her and made her behave badly. A choice between entrapping him and tackling Society was no choice at all. She left the window, kicked off her damp slippers, and crawled into bed.

Directly after breakfast the following morning, Delilah asked her father to ride with her. As soon as they'd left the stables, she informed him of all—or nearly all—that had transpired the previous day. She thought it wisest not to mention her struggle with the love-crazed viscount.

Though mildly amused at Mr. Atkins's intrepidity and unable to suppress a chuckle when he learned of Mr. Langdon's midnight assault upon the unfortunate flower bed, Mr. Desmond endeavoured to show a proper sympathy for his daughter's distress.

"In truth, my dear, I do curse the day I ever began the dratted thing," he said. "I never dreamed my paltry tale would arouse so much powerful emotion in so many breasts. Chicanery, collusion, deceit on every side. Conspiracy in the dead of night. Where it will all end, I shudder to guess. No doubt we can expect rioting in the streets of London. Wellington will have to be recalled to restore the peace. Prinny will be most cross with me. I will probably be imprisoned for sedition."

Delilah gasped. "You're teasing, I hope, Papa."

Her father smiled. "Exaggerating, perhaps. Yet he was not happy with the Hunts. They were sentenced to two years in prison for the unflattering portrait of him they printed in the *Examiner*."

"Surely far worse insult than what you wrote appears in the print-shop windows daily."

"Florizel is capricious, and at present we have insufficient funds for lawyers."

"Good grief," she said, dismayed. "And all I worried about was scandal."

"You worry far too much, my dear. I do not understand why you cannot be like your peers and leave worrying to the lower orders."

Mr. Desmond appeared to study his daughter with profound curiosity. Then he shrugged and said, "All the same, I suppose I had better attend to Mr. Atkins forthwith. I shall depart for London tomorrow."

"*We* shall depart," Delilah corrected.

The parent raised an eyebrow, but the stubborn set of his daughter's mouth boding a tiresome argument, he resignedly agreed she might as well see a bit of London before the Ton descended in force.

The matter settled between them, it remained only to be settled with Lady Potterby, who at first, as was expected, made every objection. She was no match, however, for two persuasive Desmonds. By mid-afternoon, her ladyship was driving herself and her servants distracted with a frenzy of packing.

So great was the uproar within Elmhurst that time for only the barest exchange of civilities could be spared the two visitors who simultaneously appeared upon the doorstep. Lord Berne and Mr. Langdon were hustled in and out of the house so speedily that their heads were spinning as dizzily as those of the servants.

Dear Mr. Langdon,

I hope you will excuse the family's rather cold reception today, and in particular my own inability to express my gratitude for your exceedingly kind assistance. Papa has asked me to convey his thanks as well as his apologies for the great inconvenience we have caused you.

We were unable to thank you properly because we have been all about the ears, trying to do a week's worth of packing in twenty-four hours. As you may expect, we leave immediately for London, in pursuit of The Odious Mr. Atkins (though, naturally, my aunt believes it is on other business).

I supposed it is improper of me to write you, but Papa could not, being occupied with supervising arrangements. I thought it the lesser impropriety to write than to leave without a word. You will pardon me, I know. You are too chivalrous to do otherwise.

Please believe me your most grateful,
                                    Delilah Desmond

Of course she'd go, Jack told himself as he stared numbly at the paper in his hand. He'd known that even before he'd entered the frenzied household next door. Her father would be off in pursuit of Atkins, and the daughter must go with him because she refused to believe men were capable of managing their own affairs.

All the same, if the Devil was so clever, why did he not pack his daughter back to Scotland at least, out of harm's way, while he handled matters himself? In London she was bound to get herself into some sort of trouble or other. Town held too many temptations, too many ways of going wrong, and being Delilah Desmond, she was sure to plunge headlong into all of them.

Slowly Jack traced the handwriting with his finger. He'd never seen her writing before, yet that too was what he would have expected. It was strong and bold, nothing delicate or ladylike about it. But it was a woman's hand nonetheless, just as hers was a woman's body, supple and curving . . . and he had just better not think about *that*.

The trouble was, as it had been from the start, he could not stop thinking about her. He had not known a minute's genuine peace since he'd met her. Now at last he would be rid of her maddening presence. Rossingley would be tranquil again, and he might read his beloved books in untroubled solitude.

He gazed about him at the rows of volumes which filled his uncle's library and grew unbearably weary.

"Don't," he murmured to himself. "Don't be stupid."

He got up and took a turn about the room, stopping once at a window to gaze disconsolately at the row of elms that blocked his view of the house nearby. Then he left the library, walked upstairs to his room, and summoned his valet.

"I'm leaving for London," said Jack. "Tonight. You may follow tomorrow or the next day—whatever is most convenient. I shall want you to bring all my things."

Mr. Fellows might have raised a protest had he not previously learned that a young person named Joan was to be hauled to London much against her will the next day. Therefore he merely nodded and immediately set about packing his master's belongings.

While the Desmonds, accompanied by a greatly baffled Lady Potterby, were completing the first stage of their journey to Town, Lord Berne was having another row with his father. This was not surprising, for the viscount was very much out of sorts.

He had been on the brink of achieving his heart's desire with Miss Desmond when Jack Langdon had rudely interrupted. Now the dazzling enslaver was on her way to London, where private audiences would be a deal harder to come by. Nonetheless, Lord Berne was not daunted by the challenge, nor by his sire's thundering and threatening when informed of the son's intentions to depart for Town.

Lord Streetham might as well rail at Fate or the weather. He could not disown his heir, whatever he threatened, and the bills would come regardless of the stoppage of allowances. The earl elected another tack.

"I appreciate your conscientiousness, Tony, but it is quite absurd to keep after the chit. I have no use for her now. The memoirs are safe in hand. I was able to deal with Desmond myself," the father mendaciously added.

Lord Berne returned that he didn't give a bloody damn about any stupid book. Some matters had a greater claim on a man than tiresome business dealings. Furthermore, he was not to be imprisoned in the country with a lot·of razor-tongued, narrow-minded, sharp-faced females while the grandest girl in the world languished neglected nearly two hundred miles away.

He did not add that what he truly feared was not Miss Desmond's languishing neglected, but quite the opposite. One more peril of Town was the abundance of idle young gentlemen like himself. Instead, the viscount made his papa a curt bow and stalked majestically from the room.

* * *

Mr. Atkins entered not long after. Having given the matter long and painful thought, he'd decided to advise his partner to give up the memoirs as a lost cause. He also gallantly recommended that Lord Streetham dispose of his shares in the firm while there was still time to salvage something from the wreckage.

Lord Streetham smiled as he stepped away to his writing desk briefly. He returned with a handful of pages which he gave to the baffled publisher.

"The memoirs," said the earl—unnecessarily, for Mr. Atkins had already begun reading.

A moment later, Mr. Atkins looked up. The glow of his face was almost beatific. "My Lord, this is extraordinary. How did you do it?"

"Let us simply say I left no stone unturned. Desmond is deep, devilish deep, but even he can be excavated, if one is diligent."

"Devilish indeed," said Mr. Atkins, too filled with wonder to appreciate the earl's puns, though these amused the noble gentleman immensely. "This bit about Corbell—I had not remembered it being quite so revealing."

"Yes, it is a great piece of wickedness, but that is what the hypocritical public demands. I will want a few weeks to complete my review—it goes slowly because Desmond's hand is virtually illegible. Then you may be sure I will personally deliver the work to you. Meanwhile, I suggest you take a well-deserved vacation, Atkins. I would recommend a location some distance from London."

Small drops of moisture appeared upon the publisher's brow. "I b—beg your pardon, My Lord?"

"Desmond is not to be relied upon, as you have already learned to your cost. I am concerned he will once again experience a change of heart and demand his work back. If you are not at hand, however, he cannot trouble you. I am forced to go to London on pressing family matters, but you may

159

rest easy on that score. The work can be stored with my solicitor, and I shall take only parts of it to Melgrave House as I need them."

The handkerchief came out and was applied to Mr. Atkins's brow.

"Do not make yourself anxious, Atkins," said the earl with a thin, cold smile. "But do set out at once, and be sure to keep me apprised of your direction so that I may contact you when the time is right."

13

With the rising of Parliament and the coincidental rising of the stench of the Thames, London becomes a vast wasteland. Though the City itself may appear to be teeming with life, the West End acquires a funereal air, for the majority of the upper classes have departed. Some go to their country estates and others to any of several resorts, of which the Prince Regent's architectural whims have made Brighton the most fashionable.

Mr. Beldon, to his unspeakable frustration, was not a participant in this exodus. He was temporarily confined to London due to a misunderstanding with his tailor, vintner, boot-maker, and landlady which could not be resolved until he first came to an amicable arrangement with a money-lender. This, to Mr. Beldon's great astonishment, had proved exceedingly difficult.

As he wandered listlessly up and down Bond Street, Mr. Beldon was weighing a future in King's Bench Prison against exile to whatever godforsaken spot of the continent was not in the greedy grasp of the Corsican monster. These meditations came to an abrupt halt, as Mr. Beldon did, when a far more animate and spellbinding vision appeared before him. He blinked, rubbed his eyes, blinked again, and pinched himself. Then, being a true patriot, he hastened to alert the kingdom.

Within hours, the few benighted souls remaining in London were apprised of the startling circumstance that Devil Desmond was in Town, and with him a black-haired beauty who must be Cleopatra or Helen of Troy reincarnated.

By the time the news reached Brighton, it was enhanced by more intriguing information: The beauty was none other than the Devil's own daughter, an even more exotically gorgeous creature than her infamous mother. Upon seeing her, it was said, Lord Argoyne had driven his phaeton into a hackney. Sir Matthew Melbrook had tripped over his own walking stick and fallen face down into a puddle. In short, every time London's gentlemen spotted Miss Desmond in public, they fell to pieces.

Fortunately, these occasions were exceedingly rare, because Lady Potterby, for some reason—possibly to whet appetites—seemed determined to keep the girl under wraps.

Mr. Langdon was surprised by neither the stir the Desmonds' arrival caused in London nor the rapid influx of previously rusticating members of the Beau Monde. In fact, he might have predicted with precision which gentlemen would be camped upon the doorstep of Potterby House—if, that is, Lady Potterby had permitted such an outrage. She did not. Neither she nor her grand-niece was at home to any of the gentlemen, which was only to be expected.

It would do Miss Desmond's reputation no good to be receiving a lot of idle rogues when none of the ladies wished to have anything to do with her. As Jack learned from the gossips, not one of Lady Potterby's numerous feminine acquaintance had deigned to call.

Though he, like all the rest, had been denied every time he had called, Jack persisted. Finally, after he'd been in London nearly a fortnight, he had the luck to meet up with Mr. Desmond in St. James's, and that gentleman was gracious enough to escort Jack to Potterby House himself.

The visit was a distressing one. Miss Desmond strove mightily to appear untroubled, but anxiety was writ plain in her shadowed eyes.

As he was leaving, Jack could not help taking Mr. Desmond aside to express his concern.

"Yes, I know she looks ill," said the parent. "She worries too much. I have not been able to locate Atkins, though I've had both his house and his office watched day and night. Then, of course, there's the Great World. They don't want her, it seems."

"Would it not be best," Jack suggested hesitantly, "if she were to return to Scotland—temporarily at least?"

"It would be best, but she's stubborn, and I'm afraid her great-aunt abets her in this. Neither will admit defeat. I tell you, I'm greatly tempted to tell her ladyship the truth about the book. I have threatened to do so, to make Delilah go back to her mama, but my heart is not made of stone, Mr. Langdon. How am I to resist my daughter's tear-filled entreaties? Really, sometimes I think we have all lost our minds. Perhaps I should have shackled her to the blacksmith after all."

"Of all the unjust, narrow-minded, un-Christian, hypocritical, perfectly beastly—why this is infamous!" Lady Rand cried. "There, Max, did I not tell you it must be so? When every time I asked what ill they knew of Miss Desmond, those nasty creatures would only tell me tales of her mama and papa. Where should I be, I ask you, if the world judged me by my papa?" She jumped up from her chair. "Oh, I have been much amiss. I *knew* I ought

163

to do something—but I let a lot of horrid prigs intimidate me. Where is my bonnet?"

"Settle down, Cat," said the lady's husband. "You can't go off slaying dragons at this hour. Besides, if you go rushing to Potterby House looking all wild-eyed, they'll pack you off to Bedlam."

"Certainly the matter will keep until tomorrow," said Jack, taken aback by his hostess's sudden tempest. "I only wanted to make sure—"

"Of course you did," Lady Rand interrupted, rushing back to him to take his hand in a firm clasp. "You were quite right to tell us. Only I do wish you had done so sooner. That poor girl—to endure such humiliation—and how poor Lady Potterby can bear it—to see her so-called friends all turn their backs on her. Really, it makes me so angry I can hardly see straight."

Mr. Langdon was not sure at present whether *he* could see straight. He had not remembered Catherine's being so volatile. Sympathy for Miss Desmond's plight he'd expected, for Lady Rand had a powerful sense of justice. He had not, however, expected an explosion of outrage, and certainly not that the viscountess would contemplate dashing into the streets to right Society's wrongs on the spot.

The Catherine Pelliston he had known had always been coolly intellectual and quiet-mannered. Except once, he recalled, when a villain had attempted to wrong *her*. He and Max had posted off to her rescue only to find that the small, fragile-looking creature had rescued herself by dint of crippling her adversary.

"Of course you're angry, sweetheart," said Lord Rand. "But if you can't see straight, you dashed well won't think straight. Can't be going off into fits. Also, I wish you'd leave off clasping Jack's hand to your bosom," he complained. "It's starting to make me see red—or maybe that's only the colour

164

his face is turning. Have a heart, will you, Cat, and leave the poor chap alone. Ain't he got enough on his mind without you trying to seduce him in front of your husband?"

Mr. Langdon's hand was abruptly dropped as the lady rounded on her lord.

"You," she said, "are a low-minded wretch. Here we are talking about an innocent female driven from pillar to post and you—"

"My apologies, madam. You were only trying to comfort him, I suppose. Still, you must remember we were rivals once."

"And you are monstrous tactless to say so." Lady Rand reverted to Jack, her face reddening now as well. "Really, I wonder you continue friends with such a clodpole. Please forgive us both."

"Actually," said Jack, "I'm flattered that such a dashing fellow still considers me a rival. I suppose," he added, glancing down at his cravat, "it is this handsome waterfall arrangement of Fellows's."

Thus the awkward moment passed. In fact, as he left his friends some time later, Jack was surprised at how very unawkward their reunion had been. Though he liked Catherine no whit less than he'd always done, he had felt no stir of envy or regret for what might have been.

Until he'd met her, he had never been able to carry on an easy conversation with a woman of his own class. But she'd understood him from the first, had never been puzzled or irritated by his bookish ways. She had taken him just as he was, and in her company he had discovered the delights of feminine conversation. Those glimpses into a woman's mind, so different in such surprising ways from a man's, had been glimpses into a new and fascinating world. He had been sorry to lose that.

Now he perceived he'd been unforgivably foolish to believe either Catherine or Max would drop him simply because they married. They were so far from doing so that they'd leapt at the opportunity to do the favour he asked.

The following day, Lady Potterby was stunned by Bantwell's announcement that Lady Rand was at the door.

"Good heavens, show her in!" she cried. "What are you waiting for?" As Bantwell was exiting, she turned to her grand-niece. "The Demowerys, my dear. Excellent family. Lord Rand is brother to Lady Andover, a great hostess, and their papa is the Earl of St. Denys—and even his Royal Highness is afraid of *him*. Of, I wish you had taken more trouble with your hair. It is such a jumble I don't know what Lady Rand will think."

Delilah bit back the automatic retort that she didn't care two straws what Lady Rand thought. She did care, very much.

This was the first female visitor they'd had since they'd arrived, and Delilah's heart fluttered with anxiety as she pushed hairpins back into place. If Lady Rand didn't like what she saw, Miss Desmond was doomed.

That she was to be spared social destruction for the time being was evident within five minutes of the viscountess's entrance. Lady Rand began by apologising to Lady Potterby for presuming upon a very distant—perhaps forgotten—acquaintance, but she understood that Lady Potterby had known her mama.

"Of course I have not forgotten your lovely mother," said Lady Potterby. "Indeed, to see you is to see her again, as she was in her first Season."

Lady Rand gave her a gratified smile. "Yes, I believe she and your mama," she said, turning to Delilah, "came out in the same Season. I am very sorry your mother has not come to Town with you," she went on, as Lady Potterby's eyes opened wide in consternation. "I should have so liked to meet her. I am sure she is one of the most courageous women I have ever heard of."

"She believed her presence would reflect badly on me," said Delilah, determined not to skirt the issue, despite her aunt's warning frown. "Men are forgiven everything and women nothing. Courage, you see, is not the quality usually attributed to her."

Lady Rand made an impatient gesture of dismissal. "The world is too often unjust and utterly blind. 'Convention is the ruler of all'—and no one understands that some souls are strangled by convention."

Miss Desmond's rather defensive mien softened. "Yet we cannot each make our own rules or we should have chaos," said she. "So our elders tell us, anyhow. Mama broke the rules. Don't you think that in admiring her you countenance the overthrow of civilisation?"

"Delilah, pray do not be impertinent," Lady Potterby warned.

"*Are* you impertinent, Miss Desmond?" Lady Rand asked ingenuously. "I thought we'd embarked upon a philosophical debate, and I was just beginning to enjoy myself." She turned her enormous hazel eyes full upon Lady Potterby. "Pray let us continue. I was about to quote Ovid."

"Ovid?" Miss Desmond repeated, wracking her brains for the apt quotation, while her great-aunt appeared ready to faint from shock.

"I was about to remind you 'the gods have their own rules.'"

"And Mama is now raised up to Olympus. How immensely gratified she will be to hear of it!"

The exchange following was so rapid, so filled with Greek, Latin, and French, that Lady Potterby threw up her hands in defeat. Still, unbecomingly intellectual as the debate might be, it was a conversation, and both young women seemed happy. The mention of Mrs. Desmond had given Lady Potterby a turn, for she'd instantly expected more unpleasant reminders of the family disgrace, like those they had endured at Rossingley Hall.

Lady Rand was evidently not of the Gathers's ilk, however. Even if she had odd notions, she was one of the few permitted them. An eccentric Lady Rand was still a Demowery, a member of one of Society's first families. If she liked Delilah—and it appeared she did—the rest of the Beau Monde must learn to like her as well.

The Beau Monde received its first lesson the following afternoon, when Lady Rand took Miss Desmond driving in Hyde Park and made short work of any persons who dared show her companion anything less than deferential courtesy.

The second lesson was provided on the evening of the following day, when Lady Andover's dinner guests found the Devil's daughter in their midst.

By the third day, the invitations began trickling in to Potterby House. It had been discovered in the interim that Lady Rand and Miss Desmond were bosom-bows, not to be parted. More important, it had also been learned that Miss Desmond had taken tea with Lady Rand's mother-in-law, the Countess of St. Denys.

If this was rather hard on the ladies, it was doubly so on the gentlemen, many of whom had cherished hopes of making Miss Desmond's acquaintance without the usual restrictions.

"Still, she's bound to go wrong, sooner or later," Mr. Beldon assured his friend, Sir Matthew Melbrook, as they entered Lord Fevis's house together. "It's in the blood. Then they'll drop her like hot coals, mark my words."

Mr. Beldon's opinion represented one faction of Miss Desmond's male admirers. This group was convinced it was only a matter of time before she showed her true colours, committed some social outrage like those her parents repeatedly had, and was ostracised. In that case, she would need a protector. How long until this occurred and the person to whom she would turn in her hour of need were the subjects of intensive wagering.

The other, smaller, camp was more philosophical. These gentlemen secretly hoped Miss Desmond would not fail any of Society's tests or stumble into its many traps. She was a great beauty. Her conversation was lively, which made her company most agreeable. A lifetime of such companionship seemed equally agreeable, especially to those gentlemen sufficiently wealthy and securely positioned to marry where their fancy took them.

Lord Berne found neither camp to his liking, though the latter troubled him a great deal more. He knew that in his case marriage was out of the question. In any case, the notion of Delilah Desmond in another man's arms was insupportable to the point of madness.

He was, in short, boiling with frustration. When he'd finally been allowed into Potterby House, he had confronted a score of rivals, not to mention their frantic female counterparts. The women, except for those of the Demowery family, had no love for their dazzling rival. Still, wherever she was, they had to be as well—otherwise they were in danger of being ignored altogether. Besides, there were advantages to flocking about Miss Desmond: This formed a virtually impenetrable barrier between herself and the gentlemen.

As if there were not barriers enough, Lord Berne sulked as he restlessly prowled Lady Fevis's ballroom. One must be content with a single dance and then subside to the sidelines or else fight the crowd to snatch twenty seconds' meaningless conversation with her.

It was all Langdon's doing, the viscount was certain. There he was, the dratted meddler, politely elbowing Argoyne aside so he could bore Miss Desmond to death with his endless intellectualizing. Which of course the poor girl was forced to endure out of gratitude.

The viscount had no way of knowing it was Mr. Langdon's endurance being tested at the moment. He had just learned that Miss Desmond had promised a waltz after supper to Lord Berne.

"Are you mad?" Jack demanded. "Where the devil was your aunt when you consented? Has she not explained that you can't waltz without permission from one of Almack's patronesses?"

"One, yes," Delilah snapped. "Two, reminiscing with Lady Marchingham. Three, yes, but I forgot."

"Of all things to forget—"

"Because it isn't important," she interrupted. "As you know perfectly well, even Lady Rand cannot get me admitted to Almack's—and if the patronesses will not have me, I do not see why I must abide by their idiotic rules."

"This is the first ball you've attended. You don't even give them an opportunity."

"For what? To judge whether the daughter of an actress is fit for civilised company?"

Miss Desmond might have spared her breath, for Mr. Langdon had stalked off.

Damn her for the pigheaded creature she was, he raged silently as he tripped over the cane of some decrepit roué. As he was apologising, Jack spied Lady Cowper in conversation with Lady Andover. He made for the patroness and, his face crimson, choked out his request.

Emily Cowper was the least forbidding of the Almack's patronesses whom Jack had once incautiously labelled Gorgons. Naturally, the epithet had reached their ears, and they'd never let him forget it—though they'd not gone so far as to ban him from

Almack's. This was not simply because he was too valuable a piece of merchandise in the Marriage Mart, but because most of these ladies found it more amusing to get their own back by tormenting the easily flustered book-worm at every opportunity.

Though she was better natured than the others, even Lady Cowper could not forbear teasing him unmercifully for several minutes, before Lady Andover intervened, asking her friend to take pity on the poor wretch. The patroness considered for another agonising moment before consenting. Then she crossed the room and presented Mr. Langdon to Miss Desmond just as the first notes of the waltz were struck.

Instantly, nearly every eye in the room was upon the couple. Behind their fans, disapproving matrons and disappointed debutantes—all of whom knew of Langdon's feud with the patronesses—clucked and whispered. Half a dozen young ladies who had sighed after Mr. Langdon all last Season in vain gazed with ill-concealed hostility at the black-haired newcomer with her strange, most un-British, tip-tilted eyes. Well, she would disgrace herself sooner or later. It was in the blood, was it not?

The newcomer was oblivious to the enmity she'd aroused. As one gloved hand lightly clasped her waist and the other her hand, her temperature shot up ten degrees. As if that were not bad enough, her heart must also take leave of reason and commence beating erratically. Delilah looked up at her partner in amazement.

"Are you sorry?" she heard him ask through the thundering in her ears.

"Yes," she gasped. "I think I am." She dropped her gaze to his neck-cloth and stared blindly at his diamond stick-pin, which seemed to wink evilly at her.

"They'll stop staring in a moment, Miss Desmond. Only think what it would have been like had you done this without proper permission."

"It isn't them—" She caught herself as she realised what was on the tip of her tongue.

"What is it, then?" he asked, concerned. "What has discomposed you?"

"Nothing. I thought I'd missed a step."

"Impossible. You are the most graceful woman in this room. I'm sure every man here wishes I would be struck by lightning. Tony is glowering, for I have prevented his being first to waltz with you publicly."

True, Lord Berne was staring in a most threatening manner at his friend, but Miss Desmond could not spare any thoughts for him.

At present, she felt rather as though *she* had been struck by lightning. She was monstrous uncomfortable, despite her partner's assured grace. Her limbs felt awkward and stiff, and her heart was rattling along like a poorly sprung carriage. What the devil was wrong with her?

"I—I'm sorry," she stammered. "I seem forever to be causing you trouble."

"It's no trouble, Miss Desmond."

"You cannot deny I was most provoking."

"I should not have been provoked."

She glanced up at him in disbelief, and he smiled.

"I'm glad you wanted rescuing," he said, his eyes unusually dark. "I only wish I could claim every other waltz as well."

His hand pressed her waist more firmly, drawing her closer.

"Mr. Langdon," she feebly protested.

"Trust me, Miss Desmond. I am an accurate judge of distance." He spun her into a turn that brought her, for a moment, against his chest. But in the next they were the requisite twelve inches apart.

"You're very daring," she observed breathlessly.

"No," he said. "It only wants practice, and a naturally graceful partner. To be able to skirt the bounds of propriety, I mean."

"Only just, I think." Her eyes were once more upon the stick-pin.

"A few minutes ago you were prepared to flout convention altogether," he reminded with a smile.

"Are you trying to teach me a lesson, sir?"

"Oh, no. That is a prodigious waste of time. You will not be led, except in dancing. But we men are determined to lead in something, and I could not resist exploiting the rare opportunity."

It was the dance, she told herself. Waltzing was too much like embracing to music. It was too giddy-making, all this whirling about with everyone else whirling round you as well, in every colour of the rainbow—though yellow seemed glaringly predominant—and all that glitter of precious jewels. The room was too hot and too bright because there were too many candles and too many people.

Also, Mr. Langdon was much too close, or she would not have been so conscious of a crisp herbal scent, so light, yet decidedly *male*. Still, to increase the distance between them was to appear missish, which Miss Desmond most certainly was not. She only wished her brain would settle down so she could think.

Her brain refused to settle down, however, even after he returned her to Lady Potterby, who promptly commenced the lecture Delilah knew she deserved. Being genuinely sorry, she tried to attend and make properly penitent answers, but her mind was elsewhere.

Repeatedly, Delilah's attention was drawn to one masculine figure. Her gaze followed Mr. Langdon as he made his way with easy grace through the crowd, pausing now and again to chat—usually with the gentlemen.

As she watched, she gradually became aware that she was not the only one. Countless young ladies were surreptitiously following his movements. Several even attempted to engage him in conversation.

Good heavens, they batted their eyelashes and fluttered their fans just as though he were . . . well, Lord Berne, for instance. And who was that brazen, carrot-haired baggage who dared to touch Mr. Langdon's coat-sleeve and treat him to that simpering smirk? As she watched him smile in that absent way of his and drift away from the coquette, Delilah drew a sigh of relief. Then, vexed with herself, she fanned her hot face furiously.

She was not left long to agitate herself, for her partners did now allow her to catch her breath again until supper was served. Then Miss Desmond had all she could do to keep from swatting her supper partner with her fan. Lord Argoyne was so dull, prosing on endlessly about his tiresome crops. Luckily, Lady Rand came to her rescue and very neatly rechannelled his grace's discourse in Lord Rand's direction, while the two ladies took up their previous discussion of Madame Germaine's prejudices against French silks.

The conversation grew more one-sided when they reentered the ballroom, for Delilah immediately began seeking Mr. Langdon's figure in the crowd once more.

"Miss Desmond?" said a familiar masculine voice. "I believe you had promised me the honour."

Delilah wrenched her mind and gaze back to meet Lord Berne's winning smile.

The smile was the product only of years of practice, for he was at the moment thoroughly enraged. He had not at all appreciated Miss Desmond's pink confusion as she danced with Langdon—or Langdon's smirking satisfaction. Why the devil couldn't the fellow leave well enough alone? Bad enough he'd got the Demowerys to countenance her, but he must bring Emily Cowper in as well. Next you knew, Miss Desmond would be tripping about the hallowed halls of Almack's, and so filled with gratitude to Jack that she'd fall into his arms—where she'd already seemed a deal too comfortable by half.

Her eyes had been too much upon Jack all night, the viscount reflected in vexation. Even now, as she apologised for woolgathering, her smile was annoyingly preoccupied.

"Only woolgathering?' he asked, leading her out. "That's a relief. I'd feared you and Lady Rand had been debating the Greeks, and that I'd interrupted your philosophical meditations."

"Not at all, My Lord. We were talking of French silks."

"Whatever you speak of, you make a lovely picture with your two heads bent close, one like amber and the other like jet. What makes the sight more agreeable still is the evidence of genuine friendship. That is rare between ladies."

Delilah rose to the defence of her sex. "We can be as staunch friends as the gentlemen, sir."

"Do you think so? I wonder. Look at the lady's husband. But a few months ago he and Langdon were rivals for her hand. Yet there is no enmity between them. Jack was his groomsman, in fact, and the two remain as intimate as ever. How many feminine relationships could withstand such a test, Miss Desmond?"

She looked up at her partner with clouded eyes. "You have me there, My Lord," she answered in a subdued voice. "Still, love is reputed to be a woman's whole life, while it forms only a fraction of a man's. Perhaps we're less forgiving in such cases because they are of more significance to us."

Lord Berne registered her dismayed surprise with satisfaction, though he took care to appear hurt. "You underestimate the strength of a man's affections," he reproved. "For some fortunate men there does come a love that consumes all else. Some of us give our hearts completely—and only once, for all eternity."

14

If Miss Desmond had begun to suspect what her
trouble was with Mr. Langdon, Lord Berne's enlightening comments put an abrupt end to this species of self-examination. Delilah had not required
the viscount's additional heavy-handed hints to
grasp the facts of the case: Mr. Langdon had been
and evidently still was in love with Lady Rand.
That was unfortunate, considering the lady had
given her own heart and hand elsewhere and
seemed ecstatically happy with her choice.

Still, that was Mr. Langdon's problem. Human
beings had been disappointed in love since the beginning of time, yet the human race continued. She
need not go into mourning seclusion just because
he was unhappy.

All the same, in the following days, her social life
seemed to lose its sparkle. Potterby House was
crammed with callers and the same glittering group
of Fashionables surrounded her at every affair.
They only made her weary.

She felt she never would fit in this world and began to understand why her parents had been as
pleased to shun Society as it was to shun them.
With the rare exception, such as Lady Rand, every-

thing seemed so false about these people. Their excessive politeness barely masked a great deal of bored discontent, ill nature, and varying degrees of treachery to relatives and friends alike.

Caroline Lamb was only the most glaring example of the immorality that all was too commonplace, and she was castigated mainly because she had been indiscreet. Not that Delilah wished particularly to contemplate Lady Caroline or the lady's abused husband. Miss Desmond saw too many similarities to her own temperament and wondered if she, like poor William Lamb's temperamental wife, must be one day goaded by boredom, frustration, and hunger for sensation to cast discretion to the winds.

Certainly the world seemed to expect it. Delilah could not shake off the feeling that the Beau Monde was waiting for her to fail . . . and fall.

There was as well her own mounting anxiety about the manuscript. Papa had been unable to locate either it or Mr. Atkins. Until that business was settled once and for all, how could she possibly feel at ease among the victims of her papa's pen? Even if the matter were settled at last, how long before she could settle her own business and get a husband? It seemed she would have to be a paragon of rectitude for ages before anyone would be sufficiently convinced of her virtue to marry her—and by then she would be too old. She'd never dreamed she'd be tested so. This might have been expected, since it was the way of the world, but she could not help feeling profoundly discouraged all the same.

Nonetheless, Delilah was not sufficiently weary of life to reject Mr. Langdon's invitation to drive with him, a few days after Lady Fevis's ball. His proposing an unfashionably early hour only added to his offer's appeal.

At least, she thought as he guided the horses into Hyde Park, the entire Beau Monde would not be there to gawk at her. For all that she was tired of being ogled, she had spent two hours fretting about what to wear. She was still fretting. She knew her green frock became her very well and her new capote was entirely *à la mode*, yet her companion appeared utterly oblivious. Or perhaps, being too honest to lie and too tactful to tell her she looked a fright, he had simply decided to hold his tongue altogether.

That he was the epitome of sartorial elegance—his linen crisply immaculate against the form-fitting brown coat—only irritated her. Perhaps this was why she did not behave, as she'd intended, entirely carefree and delighted with her recent popularity. Surely this must be why, instead, all—or nearly all—her pent-up frustrations came spilling out of her, and she found herself confiding in Mr. Langdon more freely than she had even her father.

Papa was never home, she complained, and for all his investigations, day and night, could obtain no word of his manuscript. Aunt Millicent still scolded at least a dozen times a day, until the grandniece despaired of ever pleasing her. Not a single occupation in which Delilah was truly skilled was she permitted. If she played cards, it must be for chicken stakes—and with idiots. She couldn't go anywhere without a chaperone. She could not go to gaming hells, Manton's, or Tattersall's at all. She was, in short, bored to tears.

"At least you have your routs and balls," said Mr. Langdon, after sympathising with these trials. "And, of course, all your beaux. That must be some compensation."

"I didn't come to London just to dance and flirt," she said crossly. "I came for a husband. I'm denied everything that might be pleasure and then I can't even get my business done."

He threw her an odd glance. "That is plain speaking."

She sighed. "Mr. Langdon, if I cannot be frank with you, then there's no one. Except for Lady Rand, the ladies do not invite confidences. If I were frank with most of the gentlemen, they'd get an earful, I promise you. But I must be unspeakably proper and pretend they're properly respectful, even when they stare at me in that disgusting way."

"They're bound to stare, Miss Desmond. But disgusting?"

"They *leer*, and I assure you it is not at all agreeable."

"I'd have thought you'd be accustomed to attracting attention," he said philosophically. "If the men do leer sometimes, you must understand that they may be unable to help themselves."

"They ought to help it. They could if they wished to. They don't treat other young women so. Imagine any of them *daring* to ogle Miss Melbrook."

"Miss Melbrook is not as beautiful as you are."

"She's accounted a diamond of the first water—and I am not begging for compliments, Mr. Langdon," she added, though to her distress she did feel unspeakably gratified. "They look at me the way they do because they're all waiting for my wicked character to reveal itself."

"That is a grave error on their part," he said. "You're not at all wicked. What you are is dangerous. I only wonder you haven't shot anyone so far, if you're so displeased."

She could not help smiling. "I cannot shoot them, since I cannot carry my pistol about with me," she said. "Evening dress is a tad too revealing, and a weapon does weigh down one's reticule."

"Still, if this behaviour distresses you so, we must put a stop to it. I could, I suppose, call the fellows out—but there seem to be a great many of them, which means a lot of rising at dawn and spoiling my boots in some muddy field. No," he said gravely, "Mr. Fellows would never countenance that."

"I suppose he would not," she sadly agreed.

"You'll have to fight the duel yourself," he said as they approached the Serpentine. "But instead of swords or pistols, you must use a more formidable weapon—your eyes."

He drew the carriage to a halt.

"Now," he went on, "look at me—not at my cravat, Miss Desmond, though I admit it is an astounding sight. Full into my face."

Puzzled, she obeyed, though the instant she met his gaze she felt so uneasy that it took all her concentration not to look away. She'd never noticed before how thick and dark his lashes were or the faint beginnings of laugh lines at the corners of his eyes.

She grew more uncomfortable still when the dreamy grey eyes abruptly became those of a stranger. An exceedingly wicked stranger, moreover, whose bold survey began at her bonnet and continued appraisingly down to her neckline, at which point she felt she might as well not be wearing anything at all. He had not touched her—had not moved a fraction closer, yet it seemed as though his mouth and hands had been everywhere his glance had been.

An eternity later, it seemed—though it had been but a moment—the feral expression vanished.

"Was that the way of it?" he asked, quite as though he had merely recited a verse from the *Iliad*, instead of practically *ravishing* her with his gaze.

"Y—yes."

"I thought so. You nearly turned purple, Miss Desmond." Heedless of her sputter of indignation, he continued, "What you must do is immediately fix your mind elsewhere and stare right through the fellow."

180

"Elsewhere? How in blazes am I to do that with you—you leering so?"

"If you concentrate on what he's doing to you, you're bound to blush and appear discomfited, which will please the chap no end. If, however, you appear coldly indifferent, both to the stare and to him, you'll discomfit and confuse *him*. It does work, I assure you," he added. "I've seen Gwendolyn do it countless times, on far less provocation."

Whatever Gwendolyn could do, Miss Desmond must obviously be twice as capable of doing, she adjured herself as her companion once again commenced his visual assault. Though her pulse rate had apparently quadrupled and her entire body seemed to be burning up under his impudent appraisal, Delilah did as he ordered.

She stiffened her spine, adopted an expression of ineffable ennui, and let her own gaze flicker coldly over his face, as though instead of beholding a disturbingly handsome countenance, she were regarding a slug.

Since they were only playacting, it was with some surprise that she observed his colour deepening. A muscle twitched under his left cheekbone.

"Well done, Miss Desmond," he said rather stiffly. "Not that I'm surprised. I've been subjected to that withering expression before."

"That's impossible. You've just instructed me."

"Actually, it was more in the nature of the reminder. The skill you already possessed. You simply didn't realise it would be as effective on these occasions as on others."

"So long as it does work," she said, "I don't care whether I just learned it or knew it all along."

"I assure you it works admirably," he answered as he gave the horses leave to start. "That particular brand of aristocratic disdain cannot be learned. One is born with it. Keep that in mind the next time anyone tries to make you feel like—" he hesitated.

"A trollop, I think you mean."

He uttered an exaggerated sigh. "Madam," he said sorrowfully, "have you never heard of euphemism?"

Delilah was able to put her lesson to practical use that evening at a ball given by Lady Rand. The technique was unfailingly effective, giving Miss Desmond the satisfying assurance that without uttering a syllable she could make a rogue just as uncomfortable as he made her. This made the affair more enjoyable than any she'd attended previously. The ball was sheer pleasure from start to near-daybreak finish, and not a little of her joy, she admitted ruefully, was attributable to Mr. Langdon's lingering nearby for a sizable portion of the evening.

He must like me, she thought later, as she sat at her dressing table, making a vague pretence of brushing her hair. He wasn't a saint. He would not be so kind and . . . protective . . . if he truly despised her. Certainly he would not have encouraged his friends to rally round her if he did. That she knew he had done for her—had perhaps known it in her heart even before Aunt Millicent had pointed it out during a lecture about ingratitude.

There was something else in her heart, Delilah was forced to acknowledge as she put down the hairbrush. When he'd eyed her in that insolent way this afternoon, he'd shocked her to the core. Yet at the same time, his look had conjured up other confrontations—one kiss in particular. And within she'd felt . . .

She shook her head and rose to remove her dressing gown, but as the silk slipped from her shoulders and fell, unheeded, to the carpet, the feeling came to her again. It had been, she realised with dismay, *anticipation.*

Mr. Langdon did not rise until early afternoon. He had not expected to rise at all.

He'd always prided himself on his cool detachment. He'd even managed in the past few weeks to keep his head—more or less—during the hundred mutinies his baser instincts had attempted against his reason. Yet this same philosophical Jack Langdon had fled Lady Rand's ball shortly after midnight in a state bordering on insanity. He'd been seized with a fit of possessiveness so fierce that he must leave the place or commit mayhem.

The fit had come upon him the instant Delilah Desmond had entered. From that point on, it was all he could do to keep from swooping down on her and dragging her away. As it was, he'd planted himself at her side for at least half the evening while he scoured every masculine countenance for a hint of insult towards her. When he discovered what he sought, he could only seethe with impotent fury because he had no right to do anything about it. That she'd defended herself well, just as he'd known she would, had not improved his state of mind—or mindlessness was more like it—one iota.

He did not want them looking at her in any way, let alone talking or dancing with her. She was *his*.

Instead of pretending to be a civilised gentleman of the modern world, he should have been attired in filthy animal skins, grunting as he dragged his knuckles along the ground. That was what he'd felt when he'd danced with her the first time. She had remarked his sleek black coat and told him, in her light, practised way, that he looked rather dashing—and he had practically growled in answer.

When he'd felt his last vestiges of self-restraint deserting him, he'd made his exit. After attempting to relieve his feelings by kicking an unoffending lamppost, he had marched off to White's, to gamble away all his money and drink himself to death.

That he'd failed in the latter was evident when his eyelids scraped open and searing pain pierced the tender organs beneath. He shut them and struggled up very slowly to a sitting position. When he opened his eyes again, he saw Mr. Fellows, tray in hand, gazing down upon him.

"Good grief," Jack groaned. "No breakfast, I beg of you."

"Breakfast today comes from the chemist's shop, sir," said the valet as he placed the tray on his master's lap. "You had better drink it before you try the coffee."

Jack eyed the tray with revulsion. "What is that?" he asked, nodding painfully at the rolled-up newspaper lying next to the coffee cup. "Where is the *Times*?"

"I think, sir, you will find this particular organ of communication more enlightening today."

Less than an hour later Jack was at Potterby House, a torn sheet of newspaper crushed in his hand as he stammered a reply to Mr. Desmond's greeting.

The Devil glanced down at the crumpled paper. "Ah, you have seen it, Mr. Langdon. It seems I was mistaken in my surmises."

He took the paper from Jack and read aloud in mincing tones, " 'Rumours are afloat that Society will be set rocking one month from today, when the first installment of the long-awaited, much-feared Reminiscences of Mr. Darryl "Devil" Desmond are scheduled to appear.' Lurid, don't you think?" said the Devil, with a cynical smile. "Buonaparte earns from the British public little more than a disdainful sniff—while my paltry tale is to trigger an earthquake. Really, one does wonder whether these journalist fellows would not be more profitably employed by the Minerva Press."

"Of course you don't mean to let them get away with this," said Jack. "We'll go to Atkins now. I'm sure we can stop him."

"My dear young man, what is the point of that? The damage is done, don't you see? You and I are not the only persons in London who read the newspapers—if one can dignify this tattle-rag with such a title."

He studied his guest's face for a moment. "Come sir. You look to me a man in need of the hair of the dog." He steered Mr. Langdon into the late Lord Potterby's luxurious study and sent a servant in search of proper refreshment.

The servant had just appeared with the tray when Miss Desmond burst in and pushed him back out.

"Oh, Papa," she cried, running towards him.

Jack considerately closed the door.

What followed was not altogether coherent, though the language with which Miss Desmond denounced Mr. Atkins was plain enough, being composed of nearly every oath Jack had ever heard, in more than one language. She was, he was surprised to discover, more angry than alarmed. The only alarm she expressed regarded her father's safety.

"The hypocrites would say nothing to my face," she raged. "They only pretended they could not see me. But Joan heard plenty as we shopped, from the servants—and Papa, it's just as you said. The members of Parliament are already talking of sedition. It appears," she said scornfully, "your revelations will stir the masses to revolution."

"That's absurd," said Jack. As he caught her startled look, he realised—not with any great surprise—that she'd been unaware of his presence. Stifling a sigh, he continued, "The worst we can expect to happen is that a few noble wives will be angry with their spouses. A very few," he added. "Only those who take any notice of their husbands' existence. Good grief—it's all ancient history."

Mr. Desmond raised an eyebrow.

"I beg your pardon," said Jack. "I did not mean to imply—"

"But I *am* ancient, Mr. Langdon. I will be sixty years old in November. And while I have been irresponsibly racketing about these last thirty or forty years, Marchingham and Corbell have risen to unspeakable heights of political consequence. They and my other old friends are doubtless terrified my book will make fools of them. Your upper classes, sir, have but two fears in this world: appearing foolish and being murdered by a revolutionary mob. Naturally they believe it is all one thing. It is very difficult for the British gentleman to develop and retain more than one idea in his lifetime."

"In other words, your powerful friends mean to work up some trumpery charges to throw you into prison and suppress the book," said Delilah. "Though how they are to stop odious Mr. Atkins when you have been unable, I cannot think. Not that I mean us to remain and see how they'll manage it. We must return to Scotland."

"I had rather go to prison, I believe," said Mr. Desmond unperturbedly. "One meets all one's old chums there—those at least who are not currently running the nation. Scotland is needlessly cold and damp," he complained. "Besides, I can never make heads or tails of what those fellows are saying—"

"Papa!"

"My dear, I know your mama is there, and I do miss her grievously—but she would be appalled if I came slinking back with my tail between my legs. I could never look her in the eye again. Such fine eyes she has," he added dreamily. "You know, Mr. Langdon, I never grow tired of gazing into them,

though we have been married nearly five and
twenty years."

In vain did Miss Desmond try to awaken her father to a sense of his peril. Reason, threats, rage,
and tears were all futile. The Devil had never been
a coward, and he did not propose to begin now. His
daughter may return to Scotland if she liked. He
certainly would prefer that, as he was sure Lady
Potterby would. He, however, would remain. Besides, he had an engagement this evening.

"Speak to him, Mr. Langdon," she entreated.
"You're always so sensible. Make him understand
that a man of sixty cannot long survive imprisonment, and Mama and I will not wish to survive if
anything happens to him."

Mr. Langdon dutifully did his best, though he
found it monstrous difficult to concentrate. Not
once, he thought—not one word about *her* hopes, of
the destruction of her plans. Not a hint of alarm at
the formidable displeasure she must confront if she
remained. It was all her parents.

Was it all? Was that why she was here—for her
parents' sake? Had she not told him once that her
father's skill at cards was their only source of income? What had she said? Something about her
parents not getting any younger. Was her cold-
blooded resolve to marry well solely determination
to provide for them?

That his arguments were disappointingly weak
soon became apparent.

"For heaven's sake, Mr. Langdon, you do sound
as if you take his side," she exclaimed in exasperation. "Must you men always stick together, ranting about honour?"

"Miss Desmond, I can't believe your father is in
genuine danger," Jack answered mollifyingly. "The
work will not be made public for a month. He cannot be imprisoned on mere rumours. Actually," he
went on, "it's you who can most expect to suffer in

the immediate future. Mere rumour is enough to make a social outcast of you. Your father is quite right in his advice. You ought to return to Scotland."

"Yes, my dear. I fear the news will frighten all your beaux away—which, may I remind you, was the reason in the first place we decided against publishing."

"Then who wants such paltry fellows?" she retorted. "I shall certainly not run away on their account—or on account of a lot of hypocritical females, either. I have some pride too, Papa. You did not bring up your daughter to be a coward. I shall never desert you," she concluded rather melodramatically.

Melodrama or no, she had looked very fine, Jack reflected as he left the house some time later. Proud, noble—and obstinately wrong-headed, of course—but that was why he loved her.

Mr. Langdon paused, thunderstruck, as he reached the corner of the square. Then he turned to stare at the house he had just left. *Loved her?*

" 'How sweet, how passing sweet, is solitude,' " quoted Mr. Stoneham. "But—to make a proper shambles of Cowper—do you mind a friend in your retreat?"

Jack shook himself out of his unhappy reveries to welcome the scholar. Stoneham, at least, would not weary him with the current scandal.

"It seems you've found the only quiet corner of White's," said the gentleman. "Perhaps the only quiet corner of the kingdom. All London is buzzing over this impending publication of Desmond's memoirs. What is your opinion? Will the tales of Society's excesses stir the mob to revolution?"

"It's all idle gossip," said Jack, for what must have been the hundredth time this afternoon. "Desmond's appearance in Town is a nine-days' wonder, and everyone is convinced he's come with a purpose other than the entertainment of a marriageable daughter. Naturally some fool has decided it must be a book of reminiscences and that fool tells another and soon the newspapers print it as solemn truth."

"So I had thought," was the complacent answer. "Now we've had our obligatory discussion of Mr. Desmond, I am eager to pursue the matter we were debating the other day."

Jack smiled. "We've said all there is to be said, I think. You may argue until you are blue in the face, Stoneham, but you will never convince me any mortal is capable of 'improving' the Bard."

Mr. Stoneham promptly asserted that the issue was not improvement. "Is it not better that young ladies read the work in diluted form than never read it at all for fear of being put to the blush?" he asked, warming to the debate.

"Young ladies read whatever they please, in spite of their mamas and teachers. To trick them with a work of art mutilated beyond recognition is criminal."

"Bowdler doesn't mean to mutilate, I am sure. A passage here, a change of phrase there. The meaning would remain, but in more palatable form for the innocent."

"Dr. Bowdler is a meddling, officious old busybody who, if he had a grain of wit, would write his own work instead of attempting to rewrite—" Mr. Langdon stopped to gaze blankly at his companion.

"Emendations merely," Mr. Stoneham insisted.

"Emendations."

"Nothing more—and all to a very good end, I must in—Langdon? Where are you going?" the scholar asked in some bewilderment, for his adversary had bolted up from his chair, a wild look in his eyes.

"So sorry. A thousand apologies," Jack muttered. "Just recollected an appointment."

With that, he was gone, leaving a rather affronted Mr. Stoneham to stare after him.

15

HAD HE BEEN a less selfish young man, Lord Berne would have been deeply distressed by the chilly reception Miss Desmond received that evening at Miss Melbrook's birthday gala. Since, however, this only cleared the field of all other rivals, Lord Berne was most selfishly ecstatic.

Still, he made a creditable show of gentle attentiveness as he hovered by her, making conversation and helping her pretend the rest of the company was not keeping its distance. If he expected this thoughtfulness to soften her hard heart, he learned he was much mistaken. Miss Desmond held her head high, and though her smile was brilliant, it was unpleasantly cold.

He bided his time until they danced. Since her card was as yet nearly empty, he'd had no difficulty in obtaining a waltz. Not until they danced did he allow himself to touch upon her difficulties, express indignation with all of Society, and beg her to make use of him.

"The services of a libertine are scarcely what I require," was the unpromising answer. "Besides, they are all afraid of a little book, nothing more. It's not my trouble, but theirs."

Inwardly excusing her unflattering language as emotional distraction, Lord Berne answered gently, "You are a convenient scapegoat. I cannot tell you how my heart aches to see this injustice to one so innocent. You are a national treasure, a splendid jewel in the crown of English womanhood."

"My Lord, I am not in a poetical humour this evening. You would be better served, I think, in returning me to Lady Potterby and addressing your pretty metaphors to some other lady. I am bound to put you out of temper."

"You are distraught," he said, "though no one else would know it, you disguise your feelings so well. Only because your smallest gesture speaks volumes to me do I discern your distress. Miss Desmond, may I speak frankly?"

She shrugged, inadvertently calling his attention to the smoothness of her neck. One part of his mind speculated upon the silken attractions closely connected to that neck, while the other framed his speech.

"I confess I was rather surprised when I first heard of this memoirs matter," he said cautiously. "Your father is a man of vast experience, Miss Desmond. Naturally I was puzzled why he should wish to publish his recollections at this time, when you've so recently entered Society. Was he not aware of the repercussions that would follow? Or was the reason so pressing—"

"Good grief, can you believe my father has had anything to do with this provoking situation?" she asked incredulously.

"Then he hasn't written the story after all?" was the innocent response.

"Yes, he wrote the curst thing—ages ago, when he was ill, and concerned lest Mama and I be left destitute if he died. Since he survived the illness, there was no longer any urgent necessity to publish."

"Yet he did not destroy it."

With some impatience, Miss Desmond explained why not. Not until she was concluding did she reflect that perhaps she was unwise to tell Lord Berne so much. Aunt Millicent had insisted on denial. They must all maintain that the memoirs did not exist and the rumours were unfounded. Still, Delilah thought wearily, what was the use? In another month or so the world would only add the epithet "liars" to all the rest.

"Miss Desmond, are you telling me this work is being published without your father's permission?" He was genuinely surprised. Hadn't his father told him he'd gotten the memoirs from Desmond himself? Why, then, had the earl not destroyed them?

"Without his permission, against his wishes—and no one can find Mr. Atkins or the manuscript to make him give it up."

"No one *else*," Lord Berne corrected. "I will get the memoirs back for you, if that is what you wish."

The music had stopped, but Delilah scarcely noticed. She was not certain whether to laugh at him or hit him, so exasperatingly confident he looked.

"You make promises too easily, sir," she reproached, "I do not care to be sported with in this way."

"You've never believed my concern for your well-being is genuine, Miss Desmond. I cannot blame you. Nor will I bore you with protestations and promises. My actions must speak for me in future," he said, his blue eyes ablaze with fervent sincerity.

Mr. Langdon was rather late in arriving, having spent some hours in conference with Mr. Desmond, then a few more in consultation with his friends. All had agreed that, whatever the upshot of his current plans, the rumours must be squelched in the meantime. Accordingly, members of the Demowery family immediately set about laughing the story off. Their dismissal of the scandal sheet was sufficiently scornful to raise doubts in the minds of many of their acquaintance, some of whom—though naturally they could not admit it—were made to feel ridiculous indeed.

Thus the mood of the crowd at Miss Melbrook's party gradually softened, and soon Delilah had most, if not all, her partners back.

Though she remarked this change, she assumed Lord Berne's dancing with her had somehow brought it about. Consequently, she felt obliged to think more kindly of him. Whatever foolish promises he might make and break, he had done her a service. That was why, when he returned a while later to beg for a second dance, she acquiesced, though she had made it a rule never to dance with any known rake more than once in an evening.

Mr. Langdon, who had kept count, was instantly outraged when he saw Lord Berne claim her a second time. Had she taken leave of her wits? All the guests were sure to remark this aberration and speculate upon it—as if they did not already have more than enough to say about Miss Desmond.

Accordingly, Jack took up a martial stance by Lady Potterby. When Delilah returned to her chaperone and her next partner appeared, Mr. Langdon curtly informed the bewildered major that he had made a mistake.

The soldier wisely retreated before Mr. Langdon's baleful glare, and an irate Delilah found herself being hauled to the dance floor.

"What do you think you're doing?" she fumed.

"Confounding the enemy," he said. "And if you have any *nous* at all, you'll endeavour to appear as imbecilely fascinated with all the rest of your partners as you did with Lord Berne."

"Imbecile? How dare you?"

"You were hanging on his every word," her partner answered.

"Because he was talking sense."

"Tony has never talked sense in his entire life."

The dance separated them briefly, but when she returned to face her partner, Miss Desmond's eyes were blazing.

"Evidently," she snapped, "Lord Berne has been saving up all his sense for when it was most wanted. He has a plan to get Papa's memoirs back," she went on, her voice taunting. "A *plan*, Mr. Langdon. Not just pretending nothing's happened and keeping a stiff upper lip."

Mr. Langdon's upper lip, along with the rest of his countenance, did stiffen at this. He'd altogether forgotten Tony's aspirations. Naturally he'd want to dash to her rescue—and he had the necessary resources. His father had tremendous influence, and being a book collector, was sure to have useful connexions—which Miss Desmond was pointing out when the dance required they separate once more.

Abruptly Mr. Langdon's own plans seemed pathetically inept. When they came together again he felt honour bound to agree with her.

"I'm sure Tony has an excellent plan," said Jack, "as well as the means to carry it out, as you said. I do beg your pardon. My remarks were most unjust. I ought to beg his pardon as well. If he's promised to help you, he will. He would not—no gentleman of honour would—make a promise he wasn't sure he could keep."

Since the day he'd made his dramatic exit from his father's study, Lord Berne had really not given the memoirs any thought. The manuscript was his father's problem. The son's was Miss Desmond, and she had become even more of an obsession with him than the memoirs seemed to be with everyone else.

Nothing would move her. She was indifferent to

195

the viscount's beauty and unresponsive to his irresistible charm. He'd pursued her for more than a month and was no nearer to achieving his aims than he'd been at the start. Nonetheless, he refused to believe the situation was hopeless. She was only more difficult and demanding than other women. Looks, charm, and speeches were not enough for her. At the gala he'd discovered loyalty wasn't enough, either. He would have to be heroic as well.

In the heat of the moment, heroics had seemed reasonable enough, but by the following morning, Lord Berne found himself reflecting unhappily upon the reckless promise he'd made.

He'd assumed his father had destroyed the manuscript as soon as he got it. Now the viscount had no idea what his parent was about, nor did he wish to know. Whatever Lord Streetham's intentions, they were bound to be at odds with his son's.

Instead, therefore, of beginning with his father, Lord Berne began with Mr. Atkins. Or tried to. Mr. Atkins, as Miss Desmond had told the viscount, was not to be found.

At the publisher's office, Lord Berne heard only complaints from the assistant left in charge.

"My Lord, I must tell you I begin to doubt there is such a book," said Mr. Black in aggrieved tones. "Mr. Atkins has written to me, telling me only to have the printer prepared to start on a work at a moment's notice, and to have the first installment complete in a matter of weeks. You should hear what the printer has to say about *that.* Yet my master never says what the work is, so I cannot tell you whether it is Mr. Desmond's memoirs or Dr. Cablebottom's anatomy manual. It is most vexing. I am daily plagued with enquiries—not to mention a lot of threatening letters—and we have lost three of our best people—and Mr. Atkins will not stay in one place that one might write to him."

Lord Berne did not wait for more, but hastened

instead to the printer's. That interview proved equally unprofitable. At the mention of Atkins, Mr. Gillstone only looked hostile and muttered about overdue bills and wondered how an honest businessman could be expected to survive in a world filled with cheats, liars, and frauds.

Over the next few days, Lord Berne spoke to virtually every human being connected with the business, down to clerks, errand boys—even the charwoman. He learned nothing, though he spent a lot of money doing so. A visit with Mrs. Atkins produced two fits and a flood of weeping.

In short, all the viscount could discover was that half the world was trying to find Mr. Atkins, with the same result.

A week after he'd made his foolish promise, Lord Berne had no more information than he'd had at the start. This left his father, and the young man was more loath than ever to even hint what he wanted from the earl. So much secrecy, the disappearance of Mr. Atkins—well, it looked ominous. Whenever Lord Streetham became deep and secretive, it was best to keep out of his way.

Still, the prospect of his father's rage was not nearly so daunting as that of Miss Desmond's. Tony had made too many easy promises, as she'd reminded him. If he failed in this—abandoned her in her hour of greatest need—she'd never forgive him. She'd turn elsewhere for comfort. To Jack most likely—and the viscount had rather be flogged publicly than endure the humiliation of losing her to a poky book-worm.

Accordingly, as soon as his father had left Melgrave House, Lord Berne commenced a desperate search of the premises, which yielded, as he might have expected, nothing. All the earl's important papers were kept locked in his writing desk, and the viscount knew nothing whatsoever about locks.

He sat in his father's chair a long while and

stared at the keyhole in frustration. He would have to break it, and this obviously was not the time. It must be done at night and blamed on intruders.

Since it was scarcely noon, Lord Berne decided he might as well make some use of the eternity stretching before him. He had not been to Atkins's shop in three days. He might as well go again. Perhaps there was some word.

There was more than word. The viscount found Mr. Atkins himself, crouched over his cluttered desk, tearing at his hair.

Lord Berne's face immediately became a mask of sympathy as he apologised for intruding. "I heard you were back," he said. "Being in the neighbourhood, I thought to stop and congratulate you. It appears you have achieved quite a coup with Desmond's—"

"My Lord, I beg you will not speak that name," the publisher cried. "It is cursed, and everything it touches is cursed."

"Surely not," said Lord Berne. "By now I daresay you are inundated with advance orders. This book will be the making of you, sir. Murray and Lackington—not to mention all your other competitors—will be grinding their teeth in envy. I applaud your perspicacity. Indeed, I cannot but regret my ill-chosen words at our last meeting."

"You were right," was the doleful reply. "It ought to have been buried, deep, deep beneath the earth. Where I might as well be. No wonder he has not troubled himself to come and kill me. He has no need. I am ruined. He's poisoned everything."

The publisher lifted a stack of letters and flung it to the floor. "Warnings, threats, all of them. The House of Lords wants me hanged. And that is not the half of it," he went on querulously. "My colleagues, my employees all run from me as if I had the plague. Black has given notice of quitting. Gillstone will not take it—he claims his presses are too busy. Nobody else will take it. Nobody will do business with me. I cannot even buy paper."

"Because of the threats?" Lord Berne asked, barely controlling his eagerness.

"Because the Devil has set rumours abroad that I am bankrupt. The fact is, I am short of cash at the moment—but I am not bankrupt. Yet no one will extend a farthing's credit. I know it was he," Mr. Atkins went on darkly as he drew out his handkerchief and mopped his brow. "No one will say so, but I know it was he."

"Indeed? Well, that must be most disagreeable for you," said Lord Berne, thinking furiously. "What becomes of the manuscript now? Do you admit defeat and return it to Desmond?"

"If only I could. But your father berates me for being superstitious. He is suddenly determined the book must be published, despite everything—and upon the most impossible schedule. Three weeks. Who ever heard of such a thing, even in the cheap paper cover? Does he think I have all the copyists of the *Times* working for me?"

"Pray do not overset yourself, sir," said Lord Berne reassuringly. "My father is a man of influence, which he is bound to exert on your behalf."

"Heaven help me, I wish he would not. The thing is cursed, I tell you, bringing nothing but trouble from the start. But Lord Streetham says we must go forward, and so we must—though I know it is to ruin." Atkins wiped away a tear. "At any rate, I have persuaded him to take it back until the work can begin. I would not have that wretched manuscript in my keeping an instant longer than I can help it."

Lord Berne's heart sank. His father had the damned thing *yet*. Forcing heartiness into his voice, he said, "You must not be cast down, Atkins. My father is a careful man. All will be well, I promise you. You must banish these dark thoughts, and think of your golden future. You will make ten times what Murray has on Byron's *Giaour*."

Mr. Atkins only groaned in reply and dropped his head to his desk.

Lord Berne politely took his leave.

"Naturally they speak of sedition," Lord Streetham impatiently told the son who trailed him into his study. "All the Hunts did was call the Regent names. Desmond has told unflattering tales of half the peerage. He's certain to be tried."

"But if such a matter goes to the courts, will not your connexion be revealed?"

"You know nothing of these matters, Tony, and I wish you would tax neither your brain nor my patience by quizzing me about them."

"You are my parent. I cannot help but be concerned," said Lord Berne piously.

"I had rather," said the parent, glaring, "you concerned yourself with Lady Jane. She is arrived in Town and it would behove you to call on her. Atkins and I can manage our business well enough."

"I don't see how I'm ever to learn anything if you persist in treating me like an ignorant schoolboy," the son complained. "I am trying to understand how you expect to proceed safely in this, when the world is in such an uproar."

Lord Streetham sighed and sat down at his writing desk. While he son watched with suppressed eagerness, the earl took out a key from his pocket and unlocked the desk. "I have a great deal of neglected correspondence to attend to," said Lord Streetham. "But if you must know, it is a question of ownership. We took pains to ensure that the manuscript remained, legally, Desmond's property. It is only his word against Atkins's that the book is published against the Devil's will, and Atkins's solicitor will make short work of that claim, should

Desmond dare to make it. If he does, there is not a solicitor in London, reputable or not, who will agree to take up his case."

"I see," said the viscount, not in the least taken aback by this arrogant abuse of power. "But how is Atkins to publish when no one will trade with him?"

"A temporary setback. I'll settle *that* in short order," said the earl ominously.

"And the manuscript? You have it yet? Are you not concerned Desmond will trace it to you?"

"Do you take me for an idiot?" the earl exploded. "The dratted thing is safely locked up with our solicitor. Now will you go and let me do my work? The nation has some claim on my attention, I think."

Much perturbed, Lord Berne went, cursing his recklessness in making so impossible a promise to Miss Desmond. He could not face her now. He could not possibly go to her and admit he was helpless to assist her.

Therefore he did not go to the theatre that evening, because she would be there. Instead he took himself to a gaming hell and, after signing a year's allowance worth of vowels, proceeded to York Place, to a late-night gathering at the cramped house of Mrs. Sydenham, Harriette Wilson's ill-natured sister, Amy.

Restored, no doubt, by a friendly interlude with one of Amy's attractive rivals, Lord Berne awoke the next day with new resolution. If he did not wish to alienate his adored Delilah entirely, it were best to be at least partially honest. He would admit to being delayed—but only temporarily. If he chose his story carefully, she must in all fairness agree to be patient. After all, no one could get the manuscript now, not even her father.

Which meant that no one else could aid her. Surely, as the days passed, she must come to understand that only the Viscount Berne could protect and care for her properly.

He'd scarcely entered Lady Potterby's parlour when her ladyship was summoned out of the room by an agitated servant. Lady Potterby, whose nerves had over a week ago received a jolt from which they had not entirely recovered, was sufficiently distracted by the servant's panic to hurry out of the room with no thought for her grandniece's lack of chaperonage, though she did have sense enough to leave the door ajar.

The grand-niece was quick to seize the opportunity.

"You have news of the memoirs, My Lord?" she asked, her grey-green eyes bright with hope.

That brightness, the low, throbbing eagerness in her voice, the sweet vulnerability of her entire mien, was Lord Berne's undoing. How sweet, how unspeakably delicious to have her so, lying in his arms! When Paradise seemed so close, how could he wait days, weeks, and in the end perhaps lose her after all—because of some ridiculous book and a lot of stubborn, greedy men.

He had not only word, he lied, but a plan. "It will be difficult, Miss Desmond, and I hesitate to impose upon you after promising to see to it myself."

"Impose?" she whispered, glancing towards the door. "What do you mean?"

The whisper finished him. He could almost feel her warm breath at his ear as he pictured her, snuggled close to him, murmuring shyly in those same soft tones.

"I need your help," he said. "The matter must be handled discreetly and with dispatch, but it will require two people. I have friends I can trust, but—"

"No! I will do it, whatever it is," she interrupted excitedly. "You cannot know how vexatious it is to be a woman, always forced to wait, being told nothing—except that one's help is not wanted. I'm no empty-headed, helpless miss, My Lord, and I'm not afraid."

"I've seen enough of your courage to know that," he answered. "You've been splendid all this time, when another woman would have been weeping and fainting and making a pitiful spectacle of herself. But there's nothing of the helpless victim in *you*. You ought to have been born in another age, when womanly bravery and intelligence were better appreciated."

Delilah flushed with pleasure. Everyone else had called her foolish and obstinate because she would not run away. He understood. Rake he may be, but he treated her as an equal. He asked her to help, to be a partner in this, while everyone else had only told her endlessly to keep out of men's affairs.

"What must I do?" she asked.

"Can you come away? My carriage is waiting."

"Now?"

"There is no time like the present. Surely you will not wish to remain on tenter-hooks another day."

Delilah jumped up from her chair. "Not another minute," she answered, shrugging off a chill of apprehension as excitement. "Only wait while I get my bonnet and shawl."

The words were hardly out of her mouth when she heard voices approaching. In the next moment, an elegant figure in blue satin sailed through the door.

"Mama!" Delilah cried.

"My love," said Mrs. Desmond, taking her daughter in her arms for a brief embrace. Then she drew back to examine Delilah critically. "Your hair is inexcusable," she said. "What on earth was Joan thinking of?"

In the next instant Lord Berne felt the same critical scrutiny, and was oddly unnerved. One might

203

have taken the two for portraits of the same woman, but in different tints. Mrs. Desmond's dark hair partook more of mahogany, while her daughter's was nearly blue-black, yet the mother's skin was the same clear alabaster, scarcely lined.

It was her eyes, though, that most disconcerted Lord Berne. More grey than green, though also with that exotic slant, Mrs. Desmond's eyes were hypnotic, fixing him as a pin fixes a moth, and piercing straight through his brain. He immediately felt guilty, and to his chagrin, found himself stammering as he introduced himself.

"Ah, you are Marcus's boy," she said. "What a naughty fellow he was. But you must save your own naughtiness for another time, My Lord. I have not seen my child in months, and we have a deal of gossiping to do."

She swept the bewildered Delilah from the room, leaving Lord Berne to find his own way out.

16

"WHERE IS YOUR papa?" Mrs. Desmond asked as she led her daughter down the hallway towards the stairs. "And what were you doing unattended with that wicked boy?" Without waiting for an answer, she went on, "He is amazingly beautiful. One would think that Botticelli's paintings had come to life, but I must tell you, when they do so, their sole aim appears to be—"

There was a small commotion in the hall behind them, and the two ladies stopped and turned.

"*Cara*," cried Mr. Desmond, hastening towards them, Mr. Langdon following close behind.

The Devil took his wife's hands and pressed them to his lips.

"My dear," she said composedly, "you are looking well."

"Better now, I am sure. This is a most agreeable surprise. I had not expected you so soon."

"I came by mail coach," said Mrs. Desmond. She turned her attention to her husband's companion. "This must be Mr. Langdon," she said, smiling warmly.

Delilah, baffled, looked from one face to the next. What was Mama doing here? What did she know of

Mr. Langdon? And why must this all happen now, when the daughter might be out rescuing the manuscript from the evil grasp of Mr. Atkins.

"Mama," she began.

Her mama did not hear her, being engaged in issuing commands to the butler.

"Aunt Mimsy is overset by the excitement," she explained when Bantwell had exited. "I have sent her to her room to rest, but someone must see about dinner. You will join us, sir?" she asked Mr. Langdon.

He pleaded a previous engagement.

"Then you will have a glass of wine at least." Angelica led the group to the parlour.

"Mama, what are you doing here?" Delilah demanded as soon as the door was closed. "Aunt Millicent must be in paroxysms."

"If this is how you normally behave before company, my dear, then I daresay she is experiencing paroxysms of relief that I am here. Mr. Langdon, you will ignore my daughter's outbursts, I hope. She *meant* to say how delighted she was to see me. Sit down, Delilah, and stop fidgeting."

Delilah sat, fuming.

The servant entered with wine. Accepting his glass, Mr. Langdon took up a neutral position by the fireplace.

"You might have explained to her, Darryl," Mrs. Desmond began reproachfully.

"I might," was the unperturbed response, "but there has been no proper opportunity. She is rarely at home when I am, and at those infrequent intervals Millicent is inevitably about. Since she was certain to object, silence seemed the wisest course. Besides, as I mentioned, we had not looked to see you so soon."

Miss Desmond glared at Mr. Langdon. He knew whatever it was that had not been explained to her, else her parents would not have spoken so before him.

Mr. Langdon coloured under the glare and said apologetically, "I beg your pardon, Miss Desmond, but I hesitated to discuss the matter with you before I felt more confident my proposal was workable."

"What proposal?" Delilah cried. "Why do you have all these secrets and tell me nothing?"

"You just heard why," said her mama. "There is no need to raise your voice, Delilah. Count to ten."

Miss Desmond reddened. It was not to be borne. To be spoken to as though she were an ill-behaved child—and before this irritating man. She would like to dash Mr. Langdon's head against the mantelpiece, she thought, automatically focusing all her anger on him. That agreeable prospect soothed her sufficiently to allow her to attend her mother's explanation.

"Mr. Langdon has very kindly undertaken to help us prepare a case against Mr. Atkins," said Mrs. Desmond.

"Not that there's any certainty," Mr. Langdon put in, "we have a case. Yet there seems to be a question of ownership, and as far as I can ascertain, no concrete evidence of your father's consent to publication."

"That is why I am here, my love," said the mama. "All your papa's notes for the story as well as his correspondence with Mr. Atkins were in Scotland with me. I thought it wisest to bring them with me, rather than send them. It is a very large package," she said, turning to her husband. "I believe I have everything."

"I know you have, my precious. Though best of all you've done was to bring yourself. I have missed you frightfully."

Mrs. Desmond smiled. "And I you," she murmured, drawing closer to him.

In a few minutes, they had apparently forgotten everything else in this world but each other, for, arm in arm and talking in very low voices, they soon quitted the room.

They might as well have been in their bedchamber, Delilah thought as she watched them leave. Her cheeks pink once more, she turned to Mr. Langdon and was annoyed by the faint smile on his face.

"You might have told me," she said curtly, oddly embarrassed by her parents' indiscreetly amorous behaviour, which had never bothered her before.

"I didn't want to raise your hopes needlessly, Miss Desmond."

"Well, you've got *their* hopes up, and it is very bad of you," she snapped. "You said yourself it was a weak case, and you know how long these lawsuits drag on. It could be years before it goes to court, and by that time my poor father could be dying in prison. What good is it to sue that odious Atkins after the book is published and the damage done?"

Mr. Langdon very carefully placed his still nearly full glass upon a table.

"I have not observed," he answered stiffly, "that Lord Berne has provided for your parents any better solution. To my knowledge, he has not said a word to your father. At least my plan keeps Mr. Desmond safely occupied. I was concerned he might resort to needless risks—"

"Papa is not in his dotage yet, sir. Furthermore, there are times when risk is exactly what's needed—times when it's wiser to *act*, instead of creeping about cautiously."

She rose from her chair and marched to the window, where she stood, fretfully staring at the passing scene.

"If you had not gotten my mama involved, I might have been gone by now," she went on. "I might even have had the manuscript in my hands."

She whirled round to face him. "Lord Berne was just here—and he had a plan—and I was to help him. But you must come and spoil everything—and now the chance may be lost forever."

Mr Langdon's face darkened. "Tony was here? And you remained alone with him?"

"Yes, and he did not ravish me on the spot, for your information."

"I should think not. Not when he could so easily persuade you to go away with him—to God knows where. Have you taken leave of your senses, Miss Desmond? What sort of scheme could he have that required a lady's assistance?"

"Not all women are helpless—"

"You would be, if you went off with him."

"We were not planning to elope, Mr. Langdon," was the tart reply. "Nor do I see why I should not believe him. Did you not tell me but a week ago that no man of honour would make a promise he couldn't keep? Or do you now tell me your friend has no honour?"

"When a woman is so careless of propriety, even a man of honour may be tempted too far," he said, his voice ominously quiet.

"Indeed!" She tossed her head, heedlessly scattering pins. "You are outraged because I spoke privately with him for scarcely two minutes, yet it is quite correct that you remain here forever. Dear me, I forget. Mr. Langdon is the soul of honour. Wise, cautious, and pure of heart. Everyone knows he would do nothing that was not exceedingly correct, for he is above all temptation."

The words had no sooner spilt from her tongue than she regretted them. This was monstrous unjust and ungrateful, when he was only trying to help, and when he had said nothing that Aunt Millicent had not already told her dozens of times already. What on earth drove one to taunt him so? Delilah could feel the tension in the room. As she met his steely grey gaze, she found herself backing towards the window. He was furious.

"Mr. Langdon," she began as he advanced upon her, "I do beg your—"

That was as far as she got because she couldn't breathe. He stood only inches from her, his face taut with suppressed rage, and her heart was pounding so she thought it would choke her.

"You hell-cat," he growled.

She felt his hands close around her throat, but she was immobilized. She could only gaze helplessly into the pitiless depths of his darkened eyes. Then his mouth crashed down on hers and all was darkness.

Darkness and violence, as his mouth moved punishingly over hers until he'd forced her lips open. She was dimly aware of his hands moving from her shoulders to her back as his tongue pushed itself between her teeth. The invasion made her tremble, and she struggled against him, futilely. He only crushed her hard against him so she could scarcely move at all.

Then, to her dismay, she felt the heat well up within her, washing over her in wave after wave, and bringing with it a sweeping need, like hunger ... and a greater need still as his mouth left hers to trail kisses along her cheek and down her neck. She moaned softly, the sound drawn from her in spite of herself.

Dear heaven, she thought wildly, why could she not make it stop? His embrace was gentler now and she might have broken free. Instead, her hands crept up along his coat to his crisp neck-cloth, and on to bury themselves in his hair. She held him so, a moment, then, impatient, drew his face, his mouth back to hers.

She had scarcely tasted his lips again when, without warning, he put her away from him. The world instantly chilled. His gaze flicked briefly over her hot face and he smiled an odd, small, bitter smile.

"Let that be a lesson to you, Miss Desmond," he said, his voice low and harsh. "Even a book-worm can be pushed too far."

Without another word, he left.

Delilah stared blankly at his retreating back, and was still staring as the door slammed behind him.

"Jack?" she said, very softly. Then heat flooded through her once more and she tottered, thunderstruck, to a chair.

She sat for a long while, her eyes wide open but seeing nothing amid the churning sensations assaulting her, nearly as strong as they had been a few minutes before. Once more she experienced the pressure of his hands upon her back, the warm touch of his lips upon her neck, the clean, masculine scent of him ... and the barely leashed rage that had frightened and excited her at the same time—and against which she had been utterly powerless.

Powerless? That wasn't the half of it. All her will had turned into craving ... and she wanted him still, wanted him to come back and torment her again, endlessly.

Yet she could not possibly want him. He was not the dashing scoundrel of her fantasies, the younger version of her adored Papa she'd always hoped for. This was a quiet, provokingly conventional, irritatingly muddled *book-worm*! How could she be attracted to a man who must be thoroughly enraged in order to show a spark of passion?

A lesson, he'd said. Damn, and it was—a humiliating lesson. Book-worm or no, he evidently knew as well as any other man how to stir a woman's senses, and had proceeded to prove it. He'd shown her how little she knew of him, of any man, despite all her so-called worldly wisdom. He'd shown that

Delilah Desmond was as susceptible as any naïve schoolgirl to practised lovemaking.

Only it wasn't love, but anger. He despised her. She wanted to weep when she recollected his cold, contemptuous expression when he'd thrust her away. He'd made her feel like a whore—and certainly she'd behaved like one—after, that is, acting like a Billingsgate fishwife.

Miss Desmond had scarcely made a decent start in flagellating herself when she received Lord Berne's note half an hour later. It was filled with apologies. He'd been too hasty, he wrote. His plan was ill-advised. He'd since learned that Mr. Atkins was temporarily prevented from publishing by circumstances too complicated to tire her with. When, however, the time was right, the viscount promised to consult with her. Until then, they must be patient.

Delilah tore the note into very small pieces. Let him get the manuscript himself, if he could. She would not go anywhere with him or any other man—not without a bodyguard. She'd already had one sample of the viscount's ardour. Suppose, today, he'd been the one to kiss her in that violent way? She might not have escaped so easily. She had never imagined how easily-roused a beast lurked within one.

Delilah was not altogether surprised when Mr. Langdon appeared late the next morning to ask her to drive with him. If she'd had second thoughts about her behaviour, obviously the Soul of Honour must have had some fit of conscience as well.

The conversation was exceedingly polite until they reached the park. Then Mr. Langdon slowed the horses and, without looking at her, apologised.

Delilah had not thought she could possibly feel more vexed with herself, but she did. His countenance was so rigidly unhappy that she couldn't bear to let him finish his speech.

"I beg you, Mr. Langdon," she said, flushing, "not another syllable. It's I who ought to apologise. My behaviour was perfectly beastly."

"That does not excuse what I did, Miss Desmond. Nothing would excuse it. I—I am aware," he went on, each word sounding as though it were being torn bodily from him, "of the abhorrence in which you must hold me. All the same, there are certain rules about these matters—"

"Oh, no," she cried. "You're not going to propose, are you? Please don't. You only heap coals upon my head. In the circumstances, that rule makes no sense at all. It would be far more reasonable to beat me, I think."

He sighed—with relief, no doubt. That was not at all flattering, but she could hardly blame him. Anyhow, he'd done the honourable thing and, much as it would cost her pride, she'd prove she too knew something of honour. She would admit her error.

"Actually, you did me a favour," she went on, watching his eyes widen in amazement. "You did teach me a lesson. If the method was improper, it was probably more effective than words—at least in my case," she added ruefully. "Because you know I always lose my temper first and listen and think after."

He sighed once more. "Are you sure you're thinking now, Miss Desmond? By my count, I have three times crossed the bounds of propriety with you, and you persist in excusing me. Yesterday you didn't even hit me. Aren't you concerned I may interpret this as encouragement?"

"Yes. That's what I meant about learning my lesson. You've made me painfully aware of how ignorant I am. I was utterly incapable of coping with—the situation."

"I see," he said quietly. "No wonder I'm still alive and in one piece."

She winced, but went on determinedly, "Since I'm now acutely aware of my ignorance, you may rest assured I will take great care not to find myself in such a predicament again—with anybody."

He had gone about it all wrong, Jack reproached himself later, putting down his pen and gazing in despair at the heap of papers before him. That he'd never attempted to propose marriage to anyone before in his life was no excuse. Many men did it only once.

He had been reasonably composed. He'd even felt a surge of confidence when he'd first set out for Potterby House. She'd hardly put up a struggle. She'd actually responded to his caresses, ungentle as they were. She'd responded so passionately that he'd had to thrust her away and flee or else he'd surely have dishonoured her—in her great-aunt's parlour of all places!

Yet he wished he'd not been so maddened. Then he might have stopped it more gently ... might have even dared admit what was in his heart. He should have offered then, instead of covering up with that insulting bravado. What had possessed him to say such an unforgivable thing—after assaulting her, no less? Why had he been so craven today and allowed the horrified expression in those grey-green eyes to unman him?

Max wouldn't have taken No for an answer. Certainly not before he'd said his piece—or swept her into his arms and banished all her anger with kisses.

But it wasn't anger, Jack thought despondently. He'd humiliated her and lost whatever trust she might have once reposed in him. His ill-worded offer today had only added insult to injury. Why could he not say the right words, he who had read hundreds of volumes in half a dozen languages?

Because he had only to look into that devastatingly beautiful face and Reason and Sense abandoned him altogether. He became an inarticulate, tormented brute.

Amantes amentes, he reminded himself. Lovers are lunatics, as Terence had observed centuries ago. Now there was all this curst paper and ink. And so little time. So little, when it seemed he would need three eternities to learn to woo her properly and another ten to win her heart.

Mr. Langdon would have been much comforted to learn that Miss Desmond was suffering her own harrowing reflections, but as she confided these to nobody, he was denied such solace.

Delilah only told her great-aunt she was overset by the excitement of her mama's arrival and had rather not go out this evening.

Lady Potterby was vastly relieved. Though she prided herself on her fortitude, the shock of Angelica's arrival, coupled with the strain of the days following the newspaper announcement, had been rather more than her nerves could comfortably sustain. Though she was not a timid, weak creature, and though she did not mind a little excitement in her life and had a taste for a challenge, her relatives were beginning to wear on her. The prospect of one quiet evening at home and an early bedtime was altogether delightful.

Delilah did not take to her own bed very early. She tried to read, but the *Giaour* only irritated her with its romantic histrionics. She found herself conjuring up instead one handsome, serious countenance with dreamy grey eyes and one gentle, thoughtful voice. How desperately unhappy and trapped Mr. Langdon had looked today. Trapped by his own chivalry, by the rules that were so important to him, by the Honour that demanded what his very soul must recoil at.

That she'd spared him was not, she knew, entirely attributable to noble self-sacrifice. How could she possibly have allowed him to make his offer— let alone have accepted it?

She put her book aside and rose from her chair to stand by the window. Even in Town Lady Potterby must have her garden, more elaborate yet than the one at Elmhurst—perhaps to compensate for the lack of acreage.

As she gazed out into the shadows, Delilah remembered one late-night meeting in another garden . . . the looked-for kiss that never came and her embarrassed retreat. She shook her head. Of course she could not marry him, she who was prepared to accept the first respectable offer that came her way. Her cynical heart was not quite cynical enough. It was not quite hard and cold enough to bear rejection, regardless how courteous a form it took.

In the following weeks there were few opportunities to be rejected, politely or otherwise, for Mr. Langdon was rarely to be seen. Of a half dozen events, he might attend one, and then came and went so quickly that their conversations were little more than greeting and farewell.

Delilah did not see much more of her parents. They spent a great deal of time away from the house, though they were never seen at any fashionable gatherings. When they were at home, they were generally in the study, poring over papers.

Though for the first time in her life Delilah felt shut out, she was not altogether sorry. Her parents were far too perceptive, and she did not wish to be closely examined by either of them. They would know immediately something was wrong and would not rest until they'd teased it out of her. Delilah did not want to think about what was wrong if she could help it. Certainly she did not wish to voice any of her unhappy thoughts, even to her beloved parents.

Instead she kept busy, which was not at all difficult. When no more was heard of the memoirs, the Beau Monde quickly turned its attention to other matters, while its members assured one another they had known all along the announcement was nothing but a hoax. Even Angelica Desmond's arrival scarcely caused a stir. For one, she was almost never seen; for another, she was old news.

In mid-August, following the breakdown of the Prague conference, hostilities had resumed with Napoleon. Though his army was rapidly dwindling, the allied forces were behaving so indecisively that Britons at home devoted considerable energy to expressing their exasperation.

On the non-political side was Byron, who had recently embarked upon an affair with Lady Frances Webster. These and other current sensations were a deal more interesting than what one woman had done more than twenty-five years ago.

Thus the invitations continued to arrive at Potterby House. In addition to Society in general was Society in particular—that is to say, Lady Rand. She and Delilah spent their days shopping for books as well as more frivolous items, or visiting galleries, or seeing London sights. In the evenings they danced their slippers to shreds or got crushed at routs or stifled their yawns at rather mediocre musicales. Occasionally they went to the theatre or opera, and would rant happily at each other on the way home about the audience's boorish behaviour.

Through all this activity, Lord Berne was very much in evidence, the most prominent of Delilah's beaux. Oddly enough, he had also become the most kind, courteous, and altogether well-behaved of the lot. He seemed to be a changed man, for he behaved with a discretion Miss Desmond would not have thought possible. Though he was frequently at her side, there were no more languishing looks and ardent speeches. Instead he treated her with gentle affection and polite solicitude. He contented himself with one dance of an evening, and though he hovered before and after, he was so amusing and made himself so agreeable that Delilah could find nothing whatever to fault him with. He was so decorous a suitor, in fact, that his mother threw up her hands in despair.

Lady Jane, for her part, had too much pride to acknowledge his preference for another, and soon stopped wasting her hostile looks and innuendos on what everyone had begun to perceive as a lost cause. She took up with Lord Argoyne, much to the delight of that gentleman's mama, who had been in agonies all year because he persisted in throwing himself at nobodies.

Since these two enemies seemed to believe Lord Berne was finally, seriously, in love, Delilah was cautiously inclined to believe so as well. All the same, she was determined not to be overly confident again and made a point of giving all her admirers equal attention. Unfortunately, Lord Berne was so assiduous and so formidable a rival—being, perhaps, the most beautiful young man who had ever been seen in London—that gradually the others withdrew in defeat. While she still had dance partners and riding and driving offers, Delilah soon perceived that no other sort of offers would be forthcoming. Like it or not, Lord Berne seemed to be her only solid prospect.

She did like it, she told herself. He was extremely handsome. He admired her, amused her, and treated her kindly. He actually did seem to love her. That she didn't yet return the sentiment was no great obstacle. If he was a good husband, she would learn to love him. If he turned out a bad one—which was a risk everyone must take—at least he could not hurt her, and certainly she would have every comfort for herself and every means of caring for her parents.

Was this not the reason she had dragged her family back to England? Had she not told her father months ago that love had nothing to do with it?

17

Miss Desmond succeeded in convincing herself that matters were as well as she could have wished—until one morning in early October when she met up with Mr. Langdon as he came out of her father's study.

His hair was as rumpled as an unmade bed and his coat looked as though he'd slept in it. She felt a queer tugging inside as she looked at him, and wished she had a comb at least.

"You are about early, sir," she said, keeping her voice light. "Or have you spent the night with Papa, poring over your papers?"

How odd his eyes looked. There was a peculiar light in their grey depths, a glitter of something, like suppressed excitement.

"Actually, I have," he said nervously. "Please excuse my appearance, Miss Desmond."

"You've been hard at work. You needn't apologise for that, when you work on my family's behalf." Resisting the urge to straighten his cravat, she forced a bright smile. "I only hope Mr. Fellows will understand."

"No, he won't," was the rueful answer. "He's already out of all patience with me. I daresay he'll

give his notice as soon as he catches sight of me—
or at least when he finds out how little time I can
give him to make repairs."

Delilah retreated a step. "I beg your pardon.
You're in a hurry and I keep you."

"Not at all," he said. "That is, I am in rather a
hurry—but then it seems I have been for weeks—
and I do regret I cannot stop—"

"There's no reason to regret, Mr Langdon. I'm
sure we're all most obliged to you."

"Not at all," he mumbled, turning away.

She meant to turn as well, to let him go his way.
Instead she moved towards him and touched his
coat-sleeve. "Mr. Langdon—"

He stopped abruptly and her cheeks burned as
she met his puzzled look.

"I—I hope you will try to get some rest, sir. Papa
is indefatigable, you know," she went on hurriedly,
"and because he rarely sleeps, he thinks no one else
does." She remembered her hand, then, and tried
to draw it away, but his absently closed over it.

He smiled. "In my case, he's quite correct, Miss
Desmond—but you're kind to mention it. Thank
you." He hesitated an instant, pressed her hand
briefly before releasing it, then walked quickly
away.

Shortly after noon, a very curious figure was seen
making its way down Dean Street. Though the day
was mild, the figure was attired in a great coat,
round the collar of which was wrapped a thick
shawl that covered all but its eyes, and these were
shaded by the stove-pipe hat tipped low over its
forehead.

The singularity of the figure's appearance was
matched by its behaviour. Instead of walking
straight on in a forthright manner, it darted from
doorway to doorway, glancing furtively over its
shoulder from time to time—rather in the way of a

criminal pursued by the forces of law and order than that of an honest publisher attempting to do an honest day's business.

This was, nevertheless, none other than Mr. Atkins, who, his heart filled with dread and his teeth chattering like a monkey's, was on his way to the printer with the bane of his existence, Mr. Devil Desmond's memoirs.

Mr. Atkins was so terrified that he scarcely dared breathe the entire way. Fortunately, the distance was short. When, his face nearly blue with strain, he reached the entrance he sought, he drew a badly needed breath and thus had sufficient strength to make a mad rush at the door.

Unfortunately, his hat chose just this moment to fall over his eyes and become entangled with the shawl, which prevented his seeing the obstacle in his path.

The obstacle was a gentleman who was at that moment hurrying out of the shop. The resulting collision threw Mr. Atkins back upon the doorstep.

As he frantically pushed the scarf and hat away from his eyes, Mr. Atkins discerned with no small alarm that the man in his way was Mr. Langdon.

"Good heavens, sir! I do beg your pardon," said a greatly flustered Mr. Langdon. "I was not looking—most careless of me. I hope you have taken no harm, Mr. Atkins."

Mr. Atkins clutched his package to his bosom.

"N—not at all, sir. I—I fear I was at f—fault. Excuse me." He tried to get by, but he could not, for Mr. Langdon had bent over in the doorway to retrieve the parcels he had dropped. When he straightened, he apologised again profusely before moving out of the way.

Mr. Atkins, his face soaked with perspiration, edged through the door . . . and came up short against a large, hard figure. Swallowing, he looked up into the glittering green eyes of Devil Desmond.

Mr. Atkins turned white and began to sway.

Mr. Desmond called for assistance, and an apprentice hastened in to help him lead Mr. Atkins to a chair.

"My dear fellow," said Mr. Desmond after the publisher had been made to swallow a few gulps of gin. "I'm afraid I gave you a turn."

"Don't kill me," Mr. Atkins whimpered. "It isn't my doing, I swear to you. I never wanted—"

"Pray do not distress yourself, sir," came the solicitous reply. "I have no wish to cause you any trouble. I've only come for the rest of my money."

"Y—your what?"

"The money, sir, you promised me." Desmond glanced around at the gathering crowd of onlookers. "But perhaps you would prefer to discuss these mercenary matters in a less public place."

A short time later, Mr. Atkins was sufficiently in possession of his wits to believe he was not dreaming. This was Devil Desmond, sitting calmly across from him in a cramped room, claiming to be perfectly content to have his work published after all.

"Much ado about nothing," the Devil confided to his stunned listener. "What is Woman if not changeable? My daughter, sir, is bored to extinction with London Society and wishes to go abroad. Immediately, of course. She has no patience, you know. I have been trying for days to speak to you, but you have been unavailable." The Devil's teeth gleamed as he grinned. "Press of business, I daresay. You could not possibly have been avoiding me. You are not so poor-spirited a fellow as that."

Mr. Atkins was sufficiently poor-spirited to tremble, though he still maintained his fierce possession of the manuscript. Even when he had swooned, he had not loosened his grip. His fingers had apparently long since frozen permanently in position.

"My good man," said Mr. Desmond. "I assure you there is no reason for suspicion. Please, do what

223

you must with that package. I shall wait here patiently. I suppose there are papers to be signed?"

"Y—yes," said Mr. Atkins. "But they are at my office."

"Then by all means let us go there. I shall be confounded relieved to have done with this tiresome business."

Not many minutes later, the printer had the package and his instructions, while Mr. Atkins, still nearly speechless with amazement at this turnabout, was accompanying his author back down Dean Street.

When the two had turned the corner, Mr. Langdon stepped out of the nearby chemist's shop and disappeared into the printer's. He re-emerged ten minutes later and glanced furtively about him before hastening down the street.

Lord Berne, who had been watching events unfold from the shadows of a doorway across the street, broke into a smile. No wonder Desmond had got the word so quickly—even before himself. The Devil had had Langdon—innocent, honest Jack—do his spying for him. And Langdon had probably got all his information just by appearing muddled and forgetful. He had likely not paid a farthing in bribes.

"Ah, Jack," he murmured, "How it saddens me to see you take up these wicked ways. Yet I do believe you have spared me a great deal of trouble."

Mr. Langdon managed to restrain himself until he was safely home. He had walked slowly, looking, he hoped, as innocently preoccupied as ever, and suitably inept as he hailed a hackney.

He even managed a semblance of calm as he entered his library. Then he shut the door and began ripping open one of his packages. Not until he'd checked the pages and assured himself this *was* the manuscript did he sit down and allow himself a sigh of relief.

Thank heaven he looked so muddled. Even the printer, harassed as he was, had felt sorry for him. He'd never doubted for an instant that Mr. Langdon had picked up Mr. Atkins's package by mistake and given the publisher his own.

Jack had just rung for a well-deserved glass of brandy when Lord Berne was announced.

"Two glasses, Joseph," said Mr. Langdon. "Only give me a moment before you show him in."

As soon as the servant left the room, Jack slipped the manuscript back into its wrapper and placed it underneath the other parcels.

"Jack! How glad I am to find you at home," Lord Berne cried as he entered. "One sees so little of you these days. No doubt you've reverted to habit—buried in your books again." He glanced at the stack of packages heaped on a chair. "Are these additions to the collection?"

Jack nodded. "With Madame de Stael in residence, I thought I ought to familiarise myself with her work."

Joseph entered with the brandy. Mr. Langdon poured. His hands were surprisingly steady, considering he was beside himself with impatience. If only he could be rid of Tony quickly, so he might go at once to Potterby House with the book. He should have gone directly, but he could not trust his luck, and had to check his treasure first—without Miss Desmond's scornful eyes upon him.

"Ah, just the thing," said Lord Berne. "For now, that is. Perhaps later today I may return the favour with champagne, when I solicit your congratulations."

Jack paused in the act of lifting his glass.

"I'm going to do it, Jack. I mean to be riveted at last—if she'll have me." Glass in hand, Lord Berne sauntered away from his friend to gaze at a small

225

marble bust of Caesar Augustus that stood upon the mantel. He smiled. "I think she will. She has at least given me reason to hope."

He turned his innocent blue gaze upon his friend. "Will you wish me luck, Jack? Though she has been kind, I find my courage repeatedly deserting me. I have twice set out for Potterby House today and twice turned back. I was so agitated I feared I should be incapable of speaking at all."

"Potterby House," Jack said weakly, his one frail, mad hope that Lord Berne referred to another woman dashed. Then, catching himself, he went on. "You mean to offer for Miss Desmond? Have your parents yielded at last?"

"No, they have not," was the composed answer. "Yet I am no babe, to have my life managed and manipulated by my parents. They would consign me to Hell—to Lady Jane—which is quite the same thing. 'But when I became a man, I put away childish things.' I've learned there is only one woman I love, can ever love, and that is the woman I will have. No other course bears contemplation."

Jack Langdon was too much in the habit of putting himself in the other's place to leave off now. He had dreamed and hoped for months. He had laboured all these past weeks with one aim. It was not inconceivable that Tony, in his own way, had been doing the same. Less inconceivable was that Tony had been doing so to better purpose.

While Jack was not sufficiently unselfish to keep from hoping desperately that his friend would fail, he knew the hope was not only futile, but absurd. What woman in her senses could ever resist Tony? Countless women had abandoned the path of virtue because he smiled upon them. Though Miss Desmond, unlike the others, had resisted ruin, that was just barely. Certainly she would not decline his honourable offer of marriage.

Jack suppressed a sigh, scarcely attending his

friend's impassioned declarations of love, loyalty, fearlessness, and heaven knew what else. Really, it was beginning to grow tiresome. First Max with Catherine, now Tony with Delilah. All in the space of a few months.

This time was worse than the one before, far worse. Jack could not imagine what the next time would be like. Perhaps there would be no next time. Perhaps he would simply withdraw from the world as his Uncle Albert had and spend his remaining days as a reclusive, confirmed bachelor, his sole passion lined up neatly upon the shelves of his library.

Jack swallowed his brandy in one long gulp and raised the decanter once more. He might as well get drunk. He was entitled.

That was the last complete thought he had, for as he was refilling his glass, there came a sharp, blinding pain . . . and then there was nothing at all.

Lord Berne gazed sadly down upon the unconscious form sprawled upon the carpet.

"Frightfully sorry, old chap," he said softly, "but we can't have any more of that misplaced gratitude now, can we?"

He coolly began unwrapping the packages piled on the chair until he found the one he wanted. Then he sat down at his friend's writing desk, scrawled a brief note, and left.

Having had an unsatisfactorily short and not altogether enlightening conversation with her mama, Miss Desmond was at the moment wearing a circular path in the parlour carpet. She was not fitted by nature to endure suspense with her mother's tranquillity. That lady had, to Delilah's utter incredulity, retired to her chamber for a nap. She had been up all night, like everyone else, it seemed, while Delilah and Lady Potterby had slept in blissful ignorance of the plots being hatched below.

Delilah was still not altogether clear on just what the plot was, because her mama had looked ready to drop from exhaustion. Baffled as Delilah had been, she'd tried to be considerate, and refrained from demanding lengthy details. At any rate, Papa and Mr. Langdon would explain when they returned, her mother had promised. For now, it was enough to say they'd gone for the manuscript and had no doubt of success.

Still, that was hours ago. Surely they ought to be back by now . . . unless they had failed. The thought was most alarming. Though Delilah had more than once taunted Mr. Langdon with his excessive caution, she did hope he had not been reckless. Papa was accustomed to skirting the boundaries of the law and adept at wriggling out of awkward situations. Mr. Langdon had no such experience. Oh, where *was* he?

She heard the door knocker then and abruptly sat down. Whatever else happened, she would show Mr. Langdon she had as much poise and self-control as any other lady. She folded her hands tightly in her lap and waited.

To her disappointment, Lord Berne was announced. As he entered the room, she struggled mightily to erase all evidence of vexation from her countenance.

Fortunately, Lady Potterby had accompanied him and, during the interval of greetings and small talk, Delilah took herself in hand. She was pleased to see him, she told herself. How could she not be, when he looked so impossibly beautiful, his golden curls slightly windblown, but all else so elegant, sleek, and graceful.

"Indeed, the weather is fine today," he was agreeing with his hostess. "There is not a whisper of a cloud in the heavens. Since these opportunities will be too rare in the coming weeks, I hastened here in hopes Miss Desmond would consent to drive

with me—if she will forgive the short notice," he
added, bestowing an affectionate glance upon the
young lady.

Lady Potterby was even less informed of the latest memoir-connected events than her grand-niece
was, for her family had naturally supposed her
nerves could not bear more anxiety. She was, furthermore, waiting for Lord Berne to come up to
scratch. There was no other possible way to interpret his behaviour of the past three or four weeks,
regardless what Angelica said. At the moment, the
viscount looked as though he were about to burst
with something, and Lady Potterby was not slow to
guess what that was. Today. He'd offer today.

To her surprise, her grand-niece appeared most
hesitant. Still, her ladyship reflected, that was the
way with girls. Bold as brass one minute, then,
when matters grew serious, overcome with modesty. Delilah wanted nudging, that was all.

"You could do with some exercise, my dear,"
Lady Potterby urged with unusual firmness. "You
have been too pale these past few days, which I am
sure is because you do not take the air. His lordship
is most kind to invite you. Though I must ask you,
My Lord," she added, dropping him a knowing look,
"not to keep her long. She has an appointment with
her dressmaker."

Lord Berne solemnly vowed that Miss Desmond
would be returned in good time for her appointment.

Miss Desmond smiled weakly and consented.

At least, Delilah thought as the carriage reached
the park gates, this was something to do. Better
than pacing, certainly, and far better than working
herself into a pet because her parents and Mr.
Langdon had kept secrets from her. Not that she'd
given her parents much opportunity to do otherwise. For nearly a month she'd scrupulously

avoided them. As to Mr. Langdon, why should he tell her anything, when all she ever did was pick on him.

She was abruptly jolted from these reflections when Lord Berne, who had been uncharacteristically mute, stopped the carriage and found his tongue.

"Miss Desmond, a few weeks ago I made you a promise," he said, his voice low and rather unsteady. "I have kept it."

She turned a baffled glance upon him. "I beg your pardon?"

"The memoirs. I've got them at last."

He shifted the reins to one hand and reached under the seat. As he drew out a thick package, Delilah experienced a curious sinking sensation. More curious still was the reluctance with which she took the parcel from him and began to undo the wrapping.

"I don't understand," she said, as her eye fell upon the title page. "This is not possible. How—" She broke off as she flicked through the pages and saw this was indeed her father's work.

"It was very nearly impossible, Miss Desmond," said her companion. "I'm afraid I've gotten myself in a—a bit of trouble as a consequence."

What was wrong? she asked herself. She'd been certain she'd never know a moment's peace until the work was back in her possession. Here it was, and she felt nearly ill. This was undoubtedly her father's hand—though the lines seemed uncharacteristically shaky. Or was that her vision? To her chagrin she discovered her eyes were swimming. She blinked back the tears and made her belated answer.

"I'm sorry. I didn't know what to say. I was just so—so surprised," she murmured. "My Lord, this is—this is exceedingly kind of you. Thank you. I cannot tell you what a relief it is." Then his last words penetrated. "Trouble?" she asked, making herself meet his gaze. "What do you mean?"

"I had to use my father's name to get them," he answered. "Atkins has dealings with him on occasion, you see. He'll be expecting to hear from my father by now, and when he does not, he'll seek him out—and I shall be found out."

Lord Berne's face seemed composed, but the feverish light in his eyes made Delilah uneasy.

"Your father will be very angry, My Lord," she said. "I never meant—I'm sure I never wished—"

"It's of no consequence, Miss Desmond," the viscount replied with a shrug. "My sire and I have already quarrelled bitterly. He's told me in no uncertain terms that I must cease my pursuit of you." He nodded towards the manuscript. "There is my answer to him." He paused a moment. "It's also my question to you, Miss Desmond," he continued in lower, caressing tones. "Will you believe now that mine is not some fickle fancy? I have stood your friend all these weeks, asking nothing in return. I have kept the promise I made you. Will you believe at last that I love you?"

He reached to take her hand and bring it to his lips. "Because I do love you," he went on softly. He kissed each finger. "More than life, more than honour. Ask me anything and I will do it. Tell me how to go away forever, and I will."

He turned the unresisting hand over and kissed the palm. Then he raised his head, and his blue eyes seemed to burn into hers. "But you must tell me now—and it must be forever," he said, more softly still. "I cannot wait any longer, my dearest."

Miss Desmond knew an ultimatum when she heard one, and like it or not, she had to see the reason in it. She could not expect to keep him dangling forever. However he'd gotten the manuscript, he had done it, and saved her father as a result. To spurn the viscount now would be the height of ingratitude—not to mention stupidity. Where would she ever again find so heartbreakingly handsome, so charming, so compelling a lover? Still, he had better understand he must be more than a lover.

"Before I answer, My Lord, you must be more specific about what you are asking," she said, her own voice as soft as his.

He smiled faintly. "Even now you don't trust me, though I understand your reasons. I'm asking you to be my wife. Will you come away with me—now—and marry me?"

She drew back a bit. "Now?"

"It must be. When my father discovers what I've done, he'll know immediately for whom I did it."

"But you did nothing wrong," she cried, apprehensive now. "The book is my father's. You were only returning his property."

"The book is of no consequence. It's *you*. Are you prepared to tell my sire that after obtaining the manuscript from me, you gave me my *congé*? No other answer will appease him, you know. If you can't assure him you've cast me off, he'll do all he can to be rid of you—even if it means destroying your family."

"I don't understand," she said stubbornly. "I must either marry you at once or never see you again? That makes no sense."

"There is no other way I can protect you from my father's rage. Don't you see?" He squeezed her hand tenderly. "Please, my dear, come with me now. We'll go far away. By the time he finds us—if ever he does—it will be too late. He'll have to accept you then, because the alternative is an ugly scandal."

"What of *my* parents?" she returned. "They'll be beside themselves if I don't come home."

"We haven't time. We'll send a message once we're well upon the road. My love, I beg you, no more delay." He released her hand to reach into his pocket. He took out a document and gave it to her.

232

"A special license," he said. "After the last row with my father I saw there was no alternative. If you were generous enough to consent, I had to be ready to make it right immediately. I'm ready. Will you continue to delay, when every moment is precious, when every second keeps us from our vows?"

Naturally, Delilah wanted to delay, to ask another hundred questions. This was too sudden. She hadn't had time to prepare her mind and heart to accept him fully. Besides that, she was skeptical. Even though he'd behaved well for weeks, perhaps he'd only wanted to give her a false sense of security. He could not suppress the passion in his voice now, any more than he could mask the hot gleam in his eyes.

Still, lust was not a terrible thing—not to her. She could never be happy with a passionless man, she told herself, thrusting another image from her mind. Even if bedding her formed the greater part of Lord Berne's wishes, she sensed there was sufficient love in him as well. That would serve—so long as he did marry her.

That he would do, she vowed inwardly, whatever he truly intended. She was no green schoolgirl. A special license was all very well, but she had her pistol in her reticule, and that was better.

18

At about the time Miss Desmond was agreeing to run away with her desperate swain, Mr. Langdon was being recalled to consciousness by his valet, who had been summoned by a hysterically babbling Joseph.

Though Mr. Langdon was confused and in great pain, he was in sufficient possession of his wits to know he had not passed out from drink. Nor did Mr. Fellows need to point out that his master must have been struck on the back of the head with the bust of Caesar Augustus. The bust, being made of marble, lay undamaged upon the carpet. Mr. Langdon's head, being made of more delicate material, was in the process of producing a large, throbbing lump.

Mr. Fellows expressed his disapproval. He could not think what the world was coming to when young gentlemen must behave like the veriest ruffians, engaging in brawls in respectable households and bashing one another's skulls.

"Damn it, man, it wasn't a brawl," Jack growled as his valet helped him to his feet. "He came up on me from behind and—" He broke off as his gaze fell upon the disorderly heap of wrapping paper and books on the floor by a chair. Thrusting his valet aside, Jack tore into the heap, flinging away paper and books in a perfectly demented manner and leading Mr. Fellows to observe aloud that his master was suffering from concussion.

"He's taken it," said the unheeding Jack in stunned disbelief. "He knocked me unconscious and *stole* it."

"Inbreeding," Mr. Fellows pronounced. "That is the trouble with the aristocracy. In another generation, mark my words, they'll all be precisely like His Majesty."

That he was nonetheless moved by the present situation was apparent, for Mr. Fellows immediately set to restoring order himself, instead of requiring the dumbfounded Joseph to do so. The valet picked up the books and placed them neatly on a nearby table—which was when he saw the folded piece of note paper.

He handed it to his employer, saying, "I suppose there is some delirious explanation in it." He turned to Joseph. "You needn't stand there gaping like an imbecile. Go find some ice."

Mr. Langdon staggered to a chair and sat down to read the note, though the letters seemed to dance before his eyes. Fortunately—and uncharacteristically—it was brief. No more than five apologies and a dash of purple prose clouded the main point, which was that Tony had relieved his friend of the manuscript because he had a greater need for it, Love taking precedence over all other human concerns.

When Jack arrived at Potterby House, he found Mrs. Desmond, who'd only moments before come downstairs, standing in the hall upbraiding her aunt.

"Unchaperoned, Aunt Mimsy?" she was saying,

her voice deeply reproachful. "With *him*, of all men?"

Lady Potterby was opening her mouth to defend herself when Jack hurried forward.

"She's gone?" he asked, too agitated to remember his manners. "Miss Desmond has gone out?"

Mrs. Desmond's glance took in his ashen face, the wreck that was once his starched neck-cloth, and the ruin of his frantically-raked hair. "The parlour," she said quickly. "Aunt Mimsy, go to your room."

Mr. Langdon spent no more than five minutes in the parlour—only enough time to make Mrs. Desmond promise to say nothing to her husband. Or, if this was impossible, she must at least do all she could to keep him at home.

"Then I must lie to him, Jack," she said, "and I've never done so before."

"This is no time for scruples, ma'am. Tell him she's with me. She will be, I promise you."

From Potterby House Mr. Langdon rode directly to Hyde Park. The hour being relatively early, the place was not yet jammed with vehicles. He did not therefore require too much time to ascertain that Tony's curricle was not there.

With increasing sense of foreboding, Jack left. He had no idea where Tony could have taken Miss Desmond. There was only one hope of discovering a clue.

Not long after he'd left the park, Jack was at Melgrave House, crashing the knocker against the door.

"Lord Berne," he demanded of the stony-faced servant who opened the door. "Where is he?"

"His lordship is not at home, sir."

"Damn it, I know he's not home. Where's he gone?"

The porter retreated a step from the wild-eyed

figure before him, though he maintained his frigidity.

"An extended trip, Mr. Langdon," he answered curtly as he attempted to close the door.

Jack pushed him aside and stormed down the hallway. "Where is Lord Streetham?" he shouted.

The shout brought out the butler and several other curious servants, none of whom seemed inclined to cooperate with this madman. That he was not taken up and thrown out bodily was attributable only to his being considered more or less part of the family. Thus, though unhelpful, no one attempted to prevent him as he stomped towards the earl's study, where he met the gentleman at the door.

"What a devil of a noise you're making, Jack," the earl reprimanded. "Don't tell me you and Tony have taken to quarrelling again as you used to."

"Where has he gone?" Jack demanded. "You would know. You know all his hideaways. Where has he taken her?"

"My dear boy, I haven't the least idea what you're raving about."

"Tony has run off with Miss Desmond," said the dear boy in some heat.

Lord Streetham's lip curled in contempt. "Is that all? He's run off with a wench. What of it? This would not be the first time."

"All?" Jack echoed incredulously. "This is not some ballet dancer we speak of, but Mr. Desmond's daughter. Lord Stivling's grand-niece—"

"I know who her relations are," said Lord Streetham. "Most of them do not acknowledge her existence—and rightly so, if what you announce is true. She has bewitched my son and he has made her his mistress—as she no doubt has schemed for from the first. Well, I wish her joy of the transaction, for not a penny will I give that stupid boy to throw away on *her*."

237

Upset as he was, Jack could see that pleading Miss Desmond's innocence would be futile. Though certain she'd been deceived—may even have been rendered unconscious, as he had—Jack could never convince the earl of that.

Only one prospect might rouse Lord Streetham from his sneering complacency.

"I think, My Lord," said Jack, "you underestimate how thoroughly 'bewitched' Tony is. Not two hours ago he was at my house, informing me he intended to marry her." He went on to repeat as much as he could remember of Tony's speech, with particular emphasis on his friend's expressed defiance of his parents.

"All talk," said the earl at the end of the recital. "More of his absurd speeches. I am sure he believed himself—for at least ten minutes."

Nonetheless, a flicker of uneasiness had crossed the older man's face. That was the only hint, but it was all Jack had. A few minutes later, he'd taken his leave.

Mr. Langdon waited in the mews until he heard, with unspeakable relief, the summons for Lord Streetham's carriage.

After another endless wait, the carriage was readied. A short while later, it was on its way, with Mr. Langdon following at a discreet distance. Not until night had fallen did Jack feel sufficiently sure of its direction to dash ahead.

They were headed north, which could mean Gretna Green. Unfortunately, it could also mean Lord Streetham's hunting box in Kirkby Glenham. Still, the earl could not be certain either, unless Tony had been unusually confiding in his valet. At any rate, Jack told himself, his lordship must stop to make enquiries along the way, and it would be wisest to precede him.

* * *

Darkness had descended and the air, consequently, had grown chilly. Miss Desmond, wrapped in a thick rug her thoughtful spouse-to-be had provided, was only uncomfortable inwardly. The farther they retreated from London, the more she repented her decision, and the harder it became to understand why she had made it, why she had so little considered the pain her act would cause others.

Her parents must be beside themselves with worry—or, in Papa's case, rage—and she hated to think the condition Aunt Millicent must be in. Delilah could only hope her father was not yet in hot pursuit. At least he had no clue to her direction. Though at present she wouldn't mind being caught and taken home, she would mind very much what Papa would do. The Devil was not short-tempered, but even his patience could be tried too far, and the result would be deadly. If he found them, he'd be certain to kill Lord Berne first and ask questions after. Then Papa would be hanged—and it would all be her fault.

If she had been more discreet, Lord Berne would have known nothing about the manuscript but what the gossips said. Then he would not have stolen it. It was a stupid thing for him to do, and so clumsy. Papa would have had a much cleverer scheme, untraceable to himself. Still, she was to blame for the viscount's foolhardiness. She'd demanded heroics and Tony, romantic fool that he was, had performed them.

Even Mr. Langdon had tried, in his way, to be heroic. Only he'd failed, poor man. How embarrassed he must be. She could picture him, his hair all rumpled and his cravat limp and wrinkled and his face flushed . . . and she wanted to weep, because she would have given anything if, at this moment, she might have smoothed his hair and straightened his cravat . . . and covered his flushed face with kisses and told him she loved him anyway.

This last reflection resulted in an urge to weep so violent that she had to focus all her energies upon resisting it. Being so occupied, she did not at first comprehend the sudden halt of the carriage, or the meaning of the hoarse shout, "Stand and deliver!"

Not certain she had heard correctly, Delilah raised her head—to behold a masked figure astride a dark horse. The figure was pointing a pistol at Lord Berne's head.

Delilah's heart seemed to shoot up into her throat, but her brain instantly cleared. Under cover of the rug which wrapped her, she drew her reticule closer and opened it. Her hand had just clamped round the handle of her pistol when the harsh voice rang out once more, making her start.

"No, madam. Throw it down—now—or your lover dies."

"For God's sake, Delilah, do as he says," Tony whispered.

Delilah threw her reticule into the road in front of the robber's horse.

"Now you," he said hoarsely to Lord Berne. "Give the lady the reins and down into the road with you."

Tony scrambled down from the carriage.

"Off with your coat—and your waistcoat—and your boots. And be quick about it."

Though Lord Berne promptly obeyed, Delilah could see, even in the weak moonlight, that his face was contorted with rage. She could not think what to do. She dared not whip up the horses. The highwayman might shoot Tony—not to mention *her*. Her reticule was now far out of reach, and she could hardly expect to overcome their assailant by throwing the manuscript at him—even if she could get to it without attracting his attention.

She wracked her brains for some comparable experience of her father's to guide her. But Papa would never have been so careless. Gad, how could Lord Berne have been so foolish as to continue travelling after dark? Why was he not armed? Why had he not suggested they spend the night at the inn where they'd stopped earlier?

While Delilah was plaguing herself with If Onlys, her companion had completed his undressing.

Keeping his pistol trained on the viscount, the robber dismounted and collected Lord Berne's belongings and her reticule. He tied his horse to the carriage, then climbed up onto the seat beside her.

"Turn the carriage," he growled, his pistol now aimed at her.

"I can't," she lied. "I don't know how."

"Turn it!" the thief hissed.

"Don't argue with him, Delilah," Tony pleaded. "He'll hurt you."

Muttering a most unladylike oath, and certain she would be hurt regardless, Delilah turned the curricle. With the pistol pointed at her, she could do nothing else but drive on as ordered, leaving Lord Berne behind in his silk-stockinged feet, in the dust.

Considering her peril, Miss Desmond ought to have been frightened out of her wits, but she was too furious to be afraid. To be at the mercy of a common thief—she, the daughter of Devil Desmond—was the outside of enough. At the first opportunity, she vowed inwardly, she'd drive the carriage into a ditch. At worst, they'd both be killed. At best, she might make an escape. In any case, she would not wait quietly to be raped by this low ruffian.

Rape seemed inevitable. Why else had he not left her behind with Lord Berne?

They were rapidly approaching a fork in the road. The highwayman told her to take the right turning—which was odd, she thought. This was the way she'd come from London—but no, there were other turnings. He must be heading for some out-of-the-way spot. His hideaway, no doubt. Some thieves' den.

Her mouth went dry. He must have accomplices. Lud, what would Papa do? The odds. Weigh the odds first. One man, one pistol, versus one woman. Later, who knew how many cutthroats, or how soon she'd be in their midst? It must be now.

Delilah slowed the carriage, ostensibly for the turn, then pulled hard on the reins. As the horses reared in protest, she threw herself at the robber.

The sudden attack took him by surprise, and the pistol fell out of his hand to the floor of the carriage. Delilah lunged for it, but was taken up short when he grasped the hair dangling at her neck and yanked her back.

He tore the reins from her hands. "Damn you," he rasped as the horses settled down. "Are you out of your mind?"

Somewhere in the periphery of her consciousness was a jolt of recognition, but Delilah was in too violent a state to pay attention. Her fist swung towards his face, only to be grabbed and wrenched aside. Then a hard chest pressed upon her, pushing her back hard against the carriage seat. She could scarcely breathe, but with what little breath she had she informed him in Arabic that he was the product of an interesting relationship between a camel and a dung beetle.

As she tried to twist away from the menacing masked face lowering to her own, she thought she heard him snicker.

Startled, she looked at him. Behind the narrow slits of the mask were glittering eyes. In an instant, the glitter turned to darkness as his mouth descended upon hers.

Though she twisted and struggled, she found herself slowly, inexorably sinking back onto the seat under the relentless pressure of her attacker's body. Unable to budge him, she shut her eyes tight and willed herself to be rigidly unresponsive. That much control she had at least.

Unfortunately, her position was awkward and painful to begin with. Maintaining a stiff posture made it more so. Her body ached horribly, and she was badly winded. Even her will was rapidly deserting her. Struggling had done nothing, evidently, but drain all her strength, for her stupid body was weakening, warming, succumbing to the brutal, seeking kiss. Sick and miserable, she gave up battling because she simply couldn't continue. Later, she promised herself . . . later she would *kill* him.

In the next instant, to her astonishment, the weight was lifted off her. She opened stunned eyes to meet her attacker's serious gaze. Serious? It could not be, she thought hysterically.

He'd started to move away from her, but in a flash she caught hold of the scarf covering his face and yanked it down, unmasking him.

"You," she gasped. "Good God, Jack, I nearly killed you. Why didn't you say right off it was you?" Joy, relief, welled up inside her, and she was about to hug him when he moved hastily away and gave the weary cattle leave to start.

"I was about to," he answered irritably, "when you attacked me. What on earth possessed you, Miss Desmond? We might have both been killed. If the horses hadn't been so tired, they might have taken off and overturned us."

Miss Desmond? Delilah squelched a sigh of vexation. "I thought I was being abducted by a highwayman," she said, striving for patience. "What did you expect me to do? It's the middle of the night. You were wearing a mask. How was I to know it was you?" Her lower lip quivered. "I think you're

243

monstrous unfair to scold me," she went on unsteadily, "after you've frightened me half to death. You might at least have said something, instead of—of assaulting me."

"As I recollect, it was you struck first," he shot back. "Since I could not hit back, I tried to restrain you. When that didn't work, I resorted to the only response that ever does seem to work with you. I'm sorry I frightened you, but really, you left me no choice."

She threw him a reproachful glance, but he was staring stonily ahead, his posture rigid. She could not comprehend how a man could kiss one so passionately one moment and be so coldly indifferent in the next.

Yet she did understand. He'd only wanted to subdue her, and he'd succeeded because, as he'd said, that way always seemed to work. Without answering, Delilah turned her mortified gaze to the trees that lined the road. She heard a bird cry somewhere in the distance and another cry answering it. She wanted to cry out too.

They rode on in tense silence for a few minutes. Then he spoke. "You're shivering," he said, his voice gentler.

She pulled the rug up over her.

Mr. Langdon drew a long breath. "Miss Desmond, have I made a mistake?" he asked. "Did you truly wish to go away with him?"

"I don't know if you've made a mistake, Mr. Langdon. You still have not told me why you came," she hedged.

"Why I came?" he repeated in amazement. "I thought he'd made off with you. I couldn't believe my eyes when I saw you sitting so tamely beside him. I'd thought surely to find you trussed up and unconscious. I could not believe you'd go away with him of your own free will."

Delilah's face began to burn. "So now you conclude I was going passively to my ruin—is that what you think?"

"Not *passively*," came the meaningful reply.

"I see," she said, turning away so her face would not betray her. "You thought I was ready to throw my cap over the windmill. Indeed, why shouldn't you assume what everyone else does? Licentiousness is in my blood, of course. I could not possibly be running away to be married."

"If that's what he told you and you were naïve enough to believe him—"

"I did not believe *him*, Mr. Langdon. I believed a piece of paper signed by a bishop." She rubbed away the traitorous wetness on her cheeks, though she still would not look at him. "It's in my reticule," she added with cold dignity, "if you care to read it."

The carriage stopped.

"He showed you a license?" Jack asked, his voice uneasy.

"Not only showed it, but gave it to me for safekeeping. In my reticule—somewhere in that heap with all his things. He'll probably take a terrible chill and die, and he has his friend to thank for it," Miss Desmond continued while her companion bent to search.

He found the reticule and offered it to her, but she shook her head.

"You can't be so careless as to trust me with that," she said. "As you must have guessed earlier, my pistol is in there, too."

He opened the purse and drew out the folded document.

"It's too dark to read it," he said.

"How thoughtless of me not to bring a tinder-box and candles."

Mr. Langdon considered briefly, then drew a sigh.

"I'd better take you back to him," he said wearily. "I won't even attempt to apologise." He paused to gaze at her unmoving profile, then blurted out, "Damn, Delilah, but I'm sorry. Only I thought—well, you know what I thought—but I was so—I was half out of my mind with worry," he went on hurriedly. "I was sure he'd hurt you. He wasn't himself—I mean, he knocked me on the head with Caesar Augustus and ran off with the manuscript and I was sure he'd gone mad—"

Miss Desmond's head whipped towards him. "He *what*?"

Mr. Langdon must have recollected himself, because he turned away from her horrified gaze. "Nothing," he said quickly. "He was beside himself, and I suppose I can understand. His father was perfectly beastly, and Tony must have felt desperate. I mean, he'd *promised* you, hadn't he? He wanted to help you, to be your hero, I expect—only I was in the way."

"*You* had the manuscript?" Delilah asked shakily. "He stole it from *you*—not Mr. Atkins?"

"Evidently, I got there first."

"Are you excusing him? He attacked you—stole the memoirs from you—and you make excuses?" Delilah blinked, but it didn't help. The world was still hopelessly askew.

"I cannot decide," she said slowly, "which one of you is more insane. But one thing is certain. I am not going back to him this evening. You will take me home, Mr. Langdon. I am not in a humour at present to be married—and certainly not to a lunatic."

Nonetheless, the lunatic was not altogether abandoned to his fate. Jack insisted upon leaving messages at the tollgates for Lord Streetham, describing where he might collect his son. Luckily, they were able to pass the earl's carriage unnoticed half an hour later. He had stopped at an inn and was inside, probably making enquiries, when Jack and Delilah drove by.

* * *

To neither Delilah's nor Jack's very great surprise, they were received by her parents with complete composure. Lady Potterby, succumbing to the welcome enticements of laudanum, had gone to bed. Thus, there were no shrieks, tears, upbraidings, nor any other sort of carryings-on. Even after Mr. Langdon had departed, the parents only gazed upon their daughter as though she were an exceedingly intricate and difficult puzzle.

"You and Mr. Langdon were rather cool to each other, I think," said Mrs. Desmond at last, as her husband refilled her wine glass. "Did you quarrel the whole way back?"

"Not the whole way, Mama. For the last two hours we did not speak at all."

"Oh, Delilah," her mother said reproachfully.

"Well, what would you have me do, Mama? He made me feel a perfect fool. I thought—well, I could not believe he'd go to so much trouble—disguising himself as a highwayman, no less. I thought—" Delilah's eyes went to her father then, and she flushed. "I thought he cared for me—but all he did was scold. And then the provoking man must commence to defending his friend. He even offered to take me back to Lord Berne. Can you believe it?" She sighed. "I can do nothing with him at all. It's perfectly hopeless, which I knew it was all along. It's all hopeless," she went on drearily. "I wish he'd never come. I wish I'd gone back and married Lord Berne after all. He at least I can manage."

"Good heavens," said Mr. Desmond. "Why did you not tell me you wanted someone manageable? I might have ordered Lord Berne at swordpoint to marry you at the outset, and spared us all a great deal of aggravation."

Delilah blinked back a tear. "I am not in a humour to be teased, Papa," she said. "I am very tired."

247

Her father gazed blankly at his wife. "My dear, I am certain she has told me a dozen times at least that she could only be happy with some sort of deceitful, unpredictable scoundrel like her poor papa."

"Indeed, she has said as much to me countless times," the mama agreed.

"Am I manageable, Angelica?"

"Not in the least. There is nothing to be done with you." Mrs. Desmond sounded resigned.

Their daughter, who had been trudging dispiritedly about the room in pale imitation of her usual energetic pacing, now flung herself into a chair. "I had rather be punished, you know. You might as well scold me and be done with it. Or lock me in my room for the rest of my life. I really don't care. I'd prefer it, actually. Obviously there's no other way to make me behave properly." She stared glumly at the carpet.

Her father paid her no mind, but went on addressing himself to his wife.

"I do not understand," he said. "I thought he was exactly what she wanted. He has a perfect genius for skullduggery. Who was it finally unearthed Streetham's connexion with Atkins? Who learned the precise hour Atkins would deliver the manuscript to the printer? Who suggested exchanging one package for another, so that Atkins would not know what had happened until it was too late?"

Delilah looked up. "Are you telling me, Papa, this was all Mr. Langdon's doing, not yours?"

"Not *all*," the father corrected. "Let me see. It was he who asked Lady Rand to take you about—but you were aware of that, I think. He also asked the Demowerys to help us by denying all existence of the memoirs and persuading the gossips the newspaper article was a hoax. Then there was his idea of spreading rumours better suited to our purposes—such as the legal case I was preparing against Atkins and the sad state of the man's finances." Mr. Desmond reflected a moment as he sipped his wine. "Oh, yes, and the matter of luring away employees, so that certain businesses could not function with their usual efficiency. Well, there's more, I suppose, but Mr. Langdon prefers to keep some matters to himself. Very close he is, and sly. Not at all to be trusted, now I think on it."

"Certainly he was not open and aboveboard in disguising himself as a highwayman," Mrs. Desmond concurred. "I'm afraid he was not altogether frank with Lord Streetham, either. Mr. Langdon must have tricked him into betraying his son's direction. Moreover, though Delilah is too delicate to mention it, I feel certain Mr. Langdon's behaviour this evening offended her modesty."

The delicate daughter flushed.

"She is quite right," said Mr. Desmond. "The fellow is altogether incorrigible."

"We should have paid more attention, Darryl. Poor Delilah is obviously no match for such a scoundrel. He would only run roughshod over her," said Mrs. Desmond.

Mr. Desmond shook his head sadly. "I'm sorry I did not see it sooner. Of course she will do far better with Berne. She will do, in fact, anything she likes with him."

The pair turned apologetic gazes upon their daughter. "We do beg your pardon, dear," said her mama. "We have sadly misjudged the situation."

Delilah glanced from one compassionate countenance to the other. Then she gave an exasperated sigh, rose from her chair, and stomped out of the room.

19

Being a man of honour and possessed of a powerful sense of justice, Mr. Langdon knew where his duty lay. He had a most disagreeable task to perform, but he did not shrink from it. He would do what honour required of him . . . and then he would hang himself. It was quite simple, really. All would be over within a matter of hours.

Accordingly, after he had lain in his bed long enough to call it rest, he arose, dressed, and taking up the neat bundle Mr. Fellows had made of Lord Berne's clothes, took himself to Melgrave House.

Though the butler admitted him with some reluctance, he did admit him, no orders having been given to the contrary, and directed Jack to the viscount's dressing room.

Lord Berne glanced at his friend's face, then at the bundle he handed the valet.

"Leave us," the viscount told his servant.

The valet exited.

"There is no point in calling me out," said Lord Berne before Jack could speak. "If you force me to a duel, I promise to delope. You may kill me if you like. I cannot blame you. You'd be doing me a great favour, in fact. I wish I was dead." He said all this without his usual dramatic vehemence, though his face was white and rigid.

Jack looked at him in incomprehension. "I don't think you understand, Tony. It was I last night—"

"I know. I guessed it when my father told me how he found me so speedily. He told me you'd been here looking for me earlier."

He turned from his friend's gaze. "I should not have hit you. I might have killed you. I should not have done a great many things, as my father has pointed out at length. He says I'm to offer for Lady Jane today," Tony went on bitterly. "If I do not, he'll cut off my allowance and forbid every tradesman in the kingdom to extend me credit. If he had another son, I'm sure he wouldn't hesitate to have me transported."

Jack thought that if Conscience had been a living creature, it would have risen up and throttled him on the spot.

"This is all my fault," he said. "I misjudged you horribly. You've told me repeatedly how much you cared for Miss Desmond and I refused to believe you. I persisted in thinking this was like every other passing fancy, when naturally it couldn't be. You've never spoken so of other women, never persisted so long."

The viscount smiled faintly. "An hour, Jack. Maybe a day. Certainly I never nearly murdered my friends on such an account. Yes, it was—is—different, but—"

"And you might have been married by now, if I hadn't jumped on my charger. Gad, I shall never forgive myself. Lady Jane—Tony, you cannot do it."

"I must. I am not equipped to live modestly, and, being a perfect gentleman, I have no productive skills by which to earn my keep. I'm not even a good card player." The smile turned bleak.

Jack considered a moment. "Miss Desmond is," he said absently. "Her father taught her a great

251

many things, including how to use a pistol." Noting his friend's bafflement, he added, "You knew she had a pistol with her, didn't you, Tony?"

"No," came the stunned reply.

"That's why I made her throw down her reticule. She would have shot me without turning a hair."

Lord Berne found a chair and fell into it, his face working strangely.

Jack moved to the dresser. Jewelled tie pins, rings, watchchains, and seals lay strewn about in gay abandon. Idly he began arranging and rearranging these in tidy lines.

"How idiotic I was," he said, "to think you could dishonour her, even if you'd meant to—though I do apologise for thinking you would. You know enough of women to know she's a treasure."

He placed an emerald tie pin next to a diamond ring, frowned, and moved it next to one of the seals.

"There's no one, there never will be anyone like her," he went on. "You saw that, and told yourself you could never settle for anything less."

Lord Berne was staring at the carpet.

"It's more than beauty, isn't it?" said Jack. "Even though it's a beauty that breaks your heart. When she's near, you feel you're in some wild, primitive, very dangerous place. Yet there's something so tender and fragile about her, as well. She *will* strike out and wound you, and even as you're reeling from it, you ache to protect her—perhaps from herself."

He drew a deep breath and moved away from the dresser. Tony looked up, and there was dawning respect in his blue eyes.

"How do you know so much, Jack," he asked.

Jack shrugged. "She's the Devil's daughter," he answered lightly enough. "She makes every man a little mad, I think, and so to some extent, every man must understand."

"You love her." It was not a question.

"I love quiet and peace, everything in its proper place. When one is forever muddled, you know, one prefers that everything else not be so."

"That's no answer," said the viscount quietly. "But I won't plague you. I've done enough of that—more than I knew. If it's any comfort to you, I shall be paying, all the rest of my life. Lady Jane will see to it."

"In that case," said his friend, "you're a great fool."

And without another word, the friend was gone.

An hour after his conversation with Jack, Lord Berne was at Potterby House. To be precise, he was in the study with Mr. Desmond, under whose withering, green-eyed scrutiny the viscount struggled in vain not to quail. The viscount seemed to be shrinking smaller by the minute under that gaze, until he felt he was looking up at the Devil's boot. At least, the young man thought wryly, it wasn't a cloven hoof.

"Marry her?" Desmond was saying in the most affable way. "Why the deuce should I give my daughter into the keeping of an ill-gotten, lying, sneaking, idle wretch of a pretty boy like yourself? Even if I didn't think you were mad as a hatter—which I do, incidentally. Even if I were not convinced you were a prime candidate for Bedlam, why should I give her into the custody of one whose father has done everything possible to destroy my family?" He turned away and sauntered to the window. "I only ask for information," he added.

"When you put it like that," said a thoroughly crushed Lord Berne, "I really cannot imagine any satisfactory answer."

"Then perhaps you are not quite so deranged as I thought. You are correct. There is no satisfactory answer."

Mr. Desmond continued to gaze out the window.

After an agonisingly long minute he said, "She tells me you never touched her. Is that so, or was she protecting you?"

"It is true, sir." The green eyes fastened on him again and Lord Berne, to his horrour, heard himself adding, "I did not have the opportunity."

"That's just as well," was the cool reply. "She would have shot you."

The viscount wondered wildly if what he'd heard was true: that the Devil was a mesmerist. Certainly one could not possibly tear one's gaze from those glittering eyes. No more had Lord Berne been able to keep back his ghastly confessions, for it seemed as though that control too had been given over entirely to the Devil's keeping.

"Moreover," Desmond went on, "it would give me the greatest pleasure to shoot you myself. Unfortunately, that would only play into your father's hands. He would like to see me hanged. He's longed for such a conclusion these five and twenty years. Do you know why?"

Lord Berne shook his head.

"Because my wife would not have him." He smiled faintly. "They say Hell hath no fury like a woman scorned. How little they know. How little *you* know, My Lord. But you have a beautiful face and a fine figure, and perhaps Delilah will take those into account. At any rate, I'm confident she'll provide you a most stimulating education."

Lord Berne required a moment to digest this speech. "I beg your pardon, sir. Are you giving me your permission?" he asked, astonished.

"I have no choice. I am so overcome by your audacity that I have not the strength of mind to resist you."

"But you hate me," said Lord Berne.

"My dear young man, you are scarcely worthy of so much energy. I do, however, pity you, for a number of reasons—your obsession with Delilah being

254

not the least of these. Whether she accepts you or not, she will make you thoroughly wretched, and there is some satisfaction in that. She will make your father even more wretched, and to be perfectly frank, I find the prospect irresistible."

"My father can have nothing to say to this. I explained the situation to you, I thought."

The Devil waved this away.

"You are merely his son," he said. "He does what he likes with you. He will not find me nearly so malleable. If Delilah weds you, it will be in St. George's, Hanover Square, and all the world will be obliged to think it a very good match, indeed. Rely upon it."

Mr. Desmond returned his cynical gaze to the window. "You may go to her now," he said. "After you've had your answer—whatever it is—my wife and I will have something more to say to you."

Mr. Langdon had proceeded from Melgrave House to that of Lord Rand, in order to see his friends one last time before he hanged himself.

He had devoted the walk to convincing himself he had no need to see Miss Desmond one last time because she would only break his heart again. It was wounded in so many places already that one more blow would surely collapse it altogether, and he did not wish to die in front of her. Hanging himself was more dignified, and certainly more discreet.

All of which he knew was ridiculous, but he was lovesick and his case was hopeless and, in the circumstances, being ridiculous was virtually an obligation.

Peace, he thought, eternal peace. Never again need he struggle to preserve the mask of a civilised gentleman while a ravening beast within fought wildly to overpower him.

In the end he'd be quiet, just as he'd told Tony—

in a cool, tranquil vault where she could never get at him and rattle him. Never again would he look upon her maddeningly beautiful face or hold her in his arms. Never again would she run her willful hands through his hair ... and pull his mouth to hers ... and moan so softly, her breath warm on his face. ...

He had just turned the corner into Grosvenor Square and had to stop and lean against a railing because all the breath seemed to have rushed out of his body at once. He stood there, clutching the railing, oblivious to the curious stares of passersby, a long while. Then he straightened, tugged at his cravat, and turned back in the direction of Potterby House.

The butler was just explaining that Miss Desmond was busy at the moment, when Lady Potterby fluttered out, all smiles, and led Jack into the drawing room.

Ten minutes later, Jack was on his way home. He saw no need to linger. Tony was in the parlour with Delilah and they were unchaperoned because Tony was proposing, as Lady Potterby had been stubbornly assuring one and all he would. He had even, her ladyship announced triumphantly, gone about it in the proper way, speaking first to the young lady's papa.

Oddly enough, Jack felt calm at last. This was the end of it. He would not hang himself—not yet. No doubt Tony would want his friend as groomsman, and it would be churlish to commit suicide before fulfilling one's obligations to one's friends.

Meanwhile, Jack would go back to Rossingley. He would not, however, stop at any inns along the way, not even if overtaken by a hurricane.

Lord Berne made the most moving proposal any young lady was like to hear in this century. Following his interview with her father, Tony had decided he'd be wisest to commence with a clean state. He admitted he'd been driven by lust and had intended only to make her his mistress. The special license, he explained with some shame, he'd had for ages, and had used twice before to deceive his victims.

Delilah did not appear at all surprised. She listened quietly, in a vaguely bored manner that made her suitor feel even more like a worm than he'd been made to feel by everyone else.

Nevertheless, he went on determinedly, "Even today I thought only of myself, and felt sorry for myself because I had failed and would not have another chance. I was even prepared to wed as my father ordered, because I was afraid of the consequences if I didn't. Luckily, I have a friend far more loyal than I deserve, who helped me see my error. I tell you all this to make an end once and for all, of deception. I only hope you will be more generous than I deserve. Will you forgive me, my dear, and allow me to begin fresh? Will you do me the very great honour and give me the great happiness of consenting to be my wife?"

Delilah was certain she'd meant to say Yes. The words came out as No, however, and she thought her heart would break when she saw the shattered look on his beautiful countenance. More beautiful, she thought, than it had ever been before, perhaps because for once in his life he had told not his fantasy truth but his heart's truth.

Yet as he'd spoken, he'd somehow revealed her own heart's truth as well, and that crumbled all her carefully built defences, her cynical rationales, and her assurance.

"I'm so sorry, Tony," she said. "I really am sorry to hurt you. I meant to marry you, you know. I would have made you do it—you don't know me— and then we would have been so unhappy."

"Why? How?" he asked. "You could never make me unhappy—except now, to tell me you will not be my wife. I love you, Delilah. I would die to make you happy."

Even as he spoke the words, he knew they were futile. Though she sat quietly enough, gazing down at her folded hands, he sensed this was not the world-weary repose it seemed to be. With a jolt he remembered what Jack had said.

Tony lifted her chin so he could look into her beautiful eyes. "It's Jack, isn't it?" he asked. "You're in love with him. That's why." There was no reproach in his tones. He saw it in her eyes, a fact, and like the others he'd confronted today, this would not go away for wishing or pretending.

She smiled, rather cynically, he thought, but that was not the truth. That was pose. What she said was pose as well—pretending, wishing.

"Oh, Tony," she said. "You look for a rival instead of listening to what I say."

"It's what I see," he answered.

"Your vision is clouded," she said, "if you see Delilah Desmond in love with a book-worm."

He'd risen, intending to leave, but something nagged at him. He struggled for a moment, then sat down beside her on the sofa and, taking her hand, began to speak once more.

"What is this?" Mr. Atkins screamed. "Where did you get this?"

Mr. Gillstone gazed down in bewilderment at the sheets the publisher was clutching in his hands. "From you," he said, wondering if the man had at last gone completely mad. Atkins was too high-strung for the business. It wanted a less sensitive nature.

"This is not the manuscript I gave you," the little man cried. "Do I not know the curst thing by heart? Where did you get it? Who bribed you to take it?"

A heated argument ensued, Mr. Gillstone being much offended by the accusation.

They shouted at each other for twenty minutes. Finally, when Mr. Atkins's face had turned purple and the blood vessels were visibly throbbing in his temples, the printer recollected the muddled, flustered, apologetic young man who'd come to him yesterday. Then he dragged Mr. Atkins to his office, made him swallow a tumbler of gin, and told him what had occurred.

The soothing effects of geneva notwithstanding, Mr. Atkins bolted from his chair, snatched up the manuscript, and dashed out of the shop.

Two minutes later he was back again.

"Print it," he said.

"Print it?" Mr. Gillstone echoed.

"Yes. This is the only book we shall ever get from that fiend without trouble and I shall never see my money again, so we might as well salvage what we can. Just don't show it to me when it's done. Deal with my assistant. I never want to see the curst thing again as long as I live."

20

Mr. Langdon had ordered his bags packed so that he might leave first thing in the morning. He'd had enough of dashing about like a madman in the middle of the night.

All the same, he did not expect to spend the night in repose, so he did not even attempt to go to bed. He sat in the library, staring at a volume of Tacitus for two hours before he noticed he had not turned a page. He slammed the book shut and flung it aside.

Then he put on his coat and went out for a walk. A long walk. Perhaps he would be set upon by ruffians and savagely beaten. That would be a profound relief.

He circled the West End endlessly, passing houses where drawn-back curtains and brilliant lights boasted of festivities in progress. Occasionally a carriage clattered past, but it was too early for great folks to be heading home, and the streets were relatively quiet. At midnight the watchman's voice rang out, informing the interested public not only of the hour, but of the circumstance that the world, at present, was well, the moon in the sky where it belonged, and the sky itself gradually clearing.

That was when Jack's mind must have snapped, because the watchman had scarcely completed his observations when Mr. Langdon's legs, no longer controlled by a brain or anything like it, blithely took him to Potterby House.

The house was dark, in the front at least. Facades, however, can be deceiving, and ever a seeker of Truth, Mr. Langdon slipped round to the back. There on the second floor, one window remained faintly lit. He stood at the gate for a moment. Then he climbed over it and dropped into the pathway leading to the garden.

His eyes went up to the window once more, and his heart began to pound because he saw a movement by the curtains. A figure in a gauzy negligée passed quickly—though not quickly enough to prevent his catching one tantalising glimpse of the form outlined in the candlelight.

" 'But soft! what light through yonder window breaks?' " he murmured, though he had sense enough left to smile at his folly. " 'It is the east, and Delilah is the sun. Arise, fair sun, and kill the envious moon—' "

The light went out.

"Oh, Delilah," he whispered. "You'll be the death of me."

Twenty times in the next half hour he turned to leave, and twenty times he turned back, because the window held him. Though it was painful to remain, he could not go—not while his mind persisted in reviewing every element of her being. The black, unruly hair that fell so easily into disorder and always made him yearn to see her tumbled among thick pillows in the flickering light of a single candle ... to see the shadows playing upon the fine bones of her face and the soft light reflected in her lustrous eyes, like moonlight on a lagoon. He longed for so much more. To touch her . . . to feel her touch . . . those restless hands in his hair . . . and so much more still. He wanted to scream.

His heart commenced to crashing against his ribs because he knew what he was going to do even as he was commanding himself not to consider it. He knew what he was going to do because Max had told him how to do it, had described a dozen times how he'd done it himself.

Not to put too fine a point upon it, Mr. Langdon proceeded to scale the walls of the house. The window was open, after all, practically shouting at him. So, like a common thief, he climbed up to it.

One kiss, he promised himself as he paused halfway over the sill. Just one chaste kiss. He would not even waken her—good grief, he'd better not—and then he would go.

He crept noiselessly across the thick carpet towards the bed. Though there was no flickering candle, there was sufficient moonlight to outline the form: a dark head upon a white pillow. He bent over her face.

Instantly, a hand seized his wrist, jerking him close. Simultaneously hard metal thrust against his chest. Jack cautiously tried to pull away.

"Another move and you'll find yourself a grave man," she whispered.

He froze.

The hand on his wrist tightened, and the pistol tried to force its way into his lungs.

"Don't," he said.

"Jack," she whispered. "Why it's only you."

Nonetheless, the weapon remained where it was. Jack began to perspire.

"Yes," he said edgily. "Will you please put that away?"

"And leave myself defenceless? Certainly not."

"It's only me, Miss Desmond. You know I mean

you no harm. And you're digging your nails into my wrist," he complained.

He heard a derisive sniff.

"No harm?" she repeated scornfully. "From a notorious highwayman, an abductor of innocent maidens? Papa was right. You're a blackguard, Mr. Langdon. I really can't understand how I let myself be so deceived in you."

Actually, he thought, it was better to have the pistol jammed into his chest. Otherwise he might mean harm in spite of himself, because he was too close to her. He was acutely conscious of a faint fragrance which reminded him of roses after a rain.

"Miss Desmond, this is an extremely uncomfortable position. In another moment, my spine will snap."

"Just as well. That will be much less untidy than bullet wounds. The maids would never get the stains out of the bed-clothes."

He tried to shake off the viselike grip. "You won't shoot me," he said firmly.

"I don't see why not. The world rather expected something of the sort, and I should so hate to disappoint them. Why are you here?" she demanded.

There was no point in pretending—even if he'd been capable of formulating a single decent excuse. He sighed. "I only wanted to kiss you," he said, though he was embarrassed as soon as he'd said it. "Just once, before I leave To—to say good-bye."

"Only to say good-bye?" she asked. "Why, you must have had to climb over the gate. I know it's locked. Then up the house—and there is not much foothold because they've cut back the ivy. Really, that was reckless of you, though quite romantic. But you are a desperate villain, and I suppose I have no choice but to let you kiss me."

A kiss? What the devil had he been thinking of? He could never leave contented with a single kiss.

He could probably never leave at all—unless he did so now.

"I—I had better not," he said, panicking. He needed to pull away, but he was concerned the pistol would go off. At the moment, he was not certain whether he'd prefer to be shot, but the noise would arouse the household, and that would never do, he thought wildly.

"If you do not kiss me now," she said slowly, "I will shoot you, and you'll never have another chance. 'The grave's a fine and private place,/ But none, I think, do there embrace.' That is Marvell, is it not?"

Mr. Langdon had had enough. He yanked the pistol from her hand and dropped it on the carpet. Being a small weapon, it made only a small thud.

"Not so much noise," she warned. "Do you want to wake everyone?"

"Delilah, don't make a game of me."

"Jack, don't be such a damned, thick-headed fool. Kiss me at once or I'll scream my head off."

He kissed her. It was not the chaste kiss on the cheek he had intended but he knew now that was never what he'd intended. His lips touched soft, cool ones and he was lost, caught, helpless, because her hands came up to caress his face, then wandered into his hair. He wondered if he'd been killed after all and had flown up straight to heaven.

Several devastating minutes later, he drew away. "I can't stay," he said. "You're driving me crazy, and you don't know how much danger you're in."

"I know," she said wistfully. "I hate being respectable. Oh, Jack, I wish you would kiss me forever."

Being an exceedingly courteous fellow, he instantly set out to oblige her, which was a great mistake, regardless how polite. He soon found himself on top of the bedclothes, and the need to slip under them was becoming painful. He shuddered and pulled himself away.

"You are impossible," he said, his voice rough. "You know I can't stay, yet you do all you can to keep me here." Then an awful thought struck him. "Tony," he breathed. "You're engaged!"

"Not at all. You haven't asked me." Her voice was soft and languorous. "You'd better, you know. There's no getting out of it now."

Jack grasped her shoulders to shake her back into the real world. "Tony," he said. "What of Tony?"

"There's no need to be so ferocious, Jack. I declined his offer. Really, do you think I would be entertaining you now if I hadn't? Though it would have served you right if I had," she went on petulantly. "You and your dratted honour and loyalty and I don't know what else." Her hands reached up to bury themselves in his hair once more. "Oh, Jack, how difficult you've been."

"I?" he answered indignantly. "I've been getting slapped and screamed at and insulted and—"

"How else was I to get your attention?" she interrupted. "Do you have any idea how hard it is to penetrate that wall of politeness of yours? How frustrating—" She broke off abruptly.

He brought her hand to his lips and kissed the palm. "If you only knew," he said softly, "how very difficult it's been to be polite and gentlemanly. I've wanted you from the moment I knocked you down. Wanted you desperately. And no matter what I did, it only got worse."

"Then you should have offered right off. That would have been the proper thing." She paused. "Or were you appalled at the prospect of shackling yourself to a wanton adventuress with a beastly temper and unspeakable manners? That must be it. You wanted a ladylike, intellectual, sweet-tempered woman like—like Catherine."

265

He drew back a bit, much surprised. "What about Catherine?"

"You loved her—love her. That's what everyone says," came the rather wistful reply.

Jack considered briefly. "I see," he said. "You're jealous."

"Yes. If I didn't like her so much I would have throttled her long since, I promise you."

He smiled. "Good. I hope you remain insanely jealous of her all the rest of your life. Perhaps that will make you a tad more manageable."

"You are a coxcomb, Mr. Langdon." Her hand slipped to his neck-cloth to pull him closer. "I will not be manageable at all, and I will make you forget her. Rely upon it."

Evidently, she planned to begin this task immediately, for a most passionate embrace ensued.

Mr. Langdon did not wish to discourage his companion's efforts to extract Lady Rand's image from his heart. On the other hand, he had a ticklish conscience and a powerful sense of honour. These won the day, and he managed to extricate himself before he committed any grave impropriety—though he could not help cursing propriety in the process.

"That is quite enough," he said thickly. "I had better go—*now*. Tomorrow I'll speak to your father."

He got up from the bed and turned to leave.

"Jack."

"No."

"Jack."

He clutched his head and turned back towards her. "What?"

"You haven't said."

"What?"

She hesitated. Then, "That you love me," she said very softly.

He moved back to the bed. "I love you. I've loved

266

you for ages. I adore you. You make me crazy. Please, Delilah, let me go."

"I love you, Jack," she whispered. "I've loved you forever."

He groaned, and kissed her once, quickly. Then he did go, though of all the difficult tasks he'd ever undertaken, this was the hardest by far.

Having given up all hopes of ever sleeping again in this lifetime, Mr. Langdon's return home was occupied primarily in pacing until the servants began to stir, when he could at last order a bath. Despite the time consumed in having hot water hauled up the stairs, not to mention shaving and then changing his clothes some half dozen times—which elicited a sharp lecture from his valet—it was only a bit past nine o'clock when Jack arrived at Potterby House. Luckily for the aspiring son-in-law, Mr. Desmond was congenitally incapable of sleeping more than three or four hours a night, and was swallowing the last of his breakfast ale when Jack was shown in.

"You had better not do that again," said Mr. Desmond before his visitor could do more than wish him good morning. "There is hardly any foothold at all, and you might have broken your neck."

There was no point pretending incomprehension when one's red, burning face had already given one away. Nor could Mr. Langdon feel in the least amazed at Desmond's powers of perception.

"Sir, I really cannot express to you how deeply—"

"Then don't. You had better marry her while you are still in one piece. As it is I cannot understand how you've survived the courtship—or whatever it was, exactly." Mr. Desmond gestured towards the sideboard, which was heavily laden with covered dishes. "Take some breakfast, Jack."

Jack could not consider anything so mundane as food. He was frantically in love, and he was *loved*, which was inconceivable. All he wanted at the moment was to see his maddening darling. Unfortunately, he could not think of any acceptable excuse for dashing up to her bedchamber.

A swish of soft fabric and light footsteps made him stiffen suddenly, in the way of a setter that has caught scent of its prey. But the figure pausing in the doorway was Mrs. Desmond. As she entered, Jack crushed his impatience and made his bow.

She smiled, then bent to drop a kiss on her husband's forehead.

"I have news for you, my love," the husband said.

"Do you, dear?" She was moving towards the sideboard, but Jack gallantly offered to do the honours.

"Yes," said Mr. Desmond. "Jack is to marry Delilah."

"Are you, Jack?" said she, taking her seat. "I'm glad to hear it. I hope you took no hurt last night." She did not appear to hear the cover crash against the coffee urn. "I cannot think why Aunt Mimsy had all that lovely ivy cut back."

With studied composure Jack placed her plate before her, then took a seat opposite. "I hope Lady Potterby is fully recovered from recent events," he said politely.

"Oh, quite. She is surprisingly resilient. She has managed to confront each catastrophe with a minimum of sal volatile and burnt feathers. Then she immediately puts the whole matter from her mind. She is a lady to the core." Mrs. Desmond spooned a dab of preserves onto a small piece of toast. "Actually, I'm more concerned about your friend, Lord Berne," she said with a brief glance at her husband.

"So am I," said Jack, frowning. He met Mr. Desmond's enquiring look and added, "Not that I intend to make any stupid sacrifice on his account. He had his chance—and I've done quite enough for him. Practically ruined my life. But that's done with." His eyes went to the door.

"Is she never coming down?" he asked plaintively.

Though Delilah had believed sleep quite impossible, she must have slept nonetheless, for the sun was shining brightly as she opened her eyes and stretched, just like the laziest, most self-satisfied feline in the world.

She had a right to be satisfied. She was madly in love with Jack Langdon and he was madly in love with her. She'd realised this stunning fact as soon as she'd heard the rustling in the garden under her window. It might have been any villain, and she ought to have been afraid, but villains did not daunt her—not when she had a pistol under her pillow. Besides, she had known—there was no question—it was he.

Joan entered. "If you please, Miss, your mama sends her compliments and when will you be down or should she tell Mr. Langdon to come back 1—"

Delilah leapt from the bed, tore off her nightgown, and flung herself at the wash basin.

Fifteen minutes later, she was in the breakfast parlour, sublimely unconscious of the fact that her hastily-arranged coiffure was already tumbling to pieces and one of the buttons at her wrist was as yet undone.

Jack rose as she entered, then was nearly knocked back down again, for she threw herself at him and kissed him so soundly she nearly dislocated his jaw.

"Stop that, Delilah," said her mother. "A young lady does not leap upon her beau like a savage upon the poor beast he's just trapped."

Delilah reluctantly retreated to the seat her mama indicated beside her.

Mr. Langdon dropped back into his own chair and

took a deep, steadying breath. When he dared to look up again, he found a pair of tip-tilted grey-green eyes fastened upon him, conveying a message that set his poor, abused heart thumping like Mr. Watt's steam engine.

"This," said Mr. Desmond, glancing from one to the other, "will never do."

"Certainly not," his wife agreed. "They cannot go out in public together. What would Mrs. Drummond-Burrell say if she saw Delilah wrestling her fiancé to the floor at some elegant society affair?"

"Bother Mrs. Drummond-Burrell," said Delilah. "Jack *likes* to wrestle with me, don't you darling?"

"Yes, I'm afraid I do," said Jack. He looked for a moment as though he would leap over the table to prove it.

"Am I delirious, Angelica?" Mr. Desmond asked. "Are parents not present? Is this conduct—or conversation—at all becoming in a newly betrothed couple?"

"Not at all, particularly at breakfast. I'm certain my digestion will be adversely affected," said Mrs. Desmond. "They had better adjourn to the parlour."

As the couple hastily arose, she fixed Jack with a basilisk look. "I am counting on you, sir, not to abuse a parent's trust. Obviously it is pointless to rely on my daughter's sense of decorum, as she hasn't any."

While the two besotted lovers were struggling to maintain a pretence of decorum in Lady Potterby's parlour, Lord Streetham was having a most disquieting conversation with his son. That son, having apparently lost his mind at last, was demanding a commission in the army. The earl's only offspring was insisting upon joining the military—now, of all times, when the nation was at war on virtually every continent—and promising bitter consequences if his father would not help him.

Since it is often considered wise to humour the insane, and since moreover the earl was thoroughly alarmed—though he never showed it—he quietly agreed. When his son had left the house, Lord Streetham ordered his carriage.

"Ah, Marcus," said Mr. Desmond as the earl was shown into the study. "I have been expecting you."

"I daresay," was the curt reply. "Well, what is it you want?"

"I?" the Devil innocently enquired. "I rather thought there was something *you* wanted."

"You know what I want—my son. You know what he plans. I expect it was you suggested it. You are quite in his confidence, I understand. His mentor, perhaps," Lord Streetham said sarcastically.

"Perhaps."

"Very well. I see you have bested me in this—you and that conniving girl of yours. I must have her as a daughter-in-law or send my only son off to be killed. State your demands, then. What will it cost to make the young lady change her mind?"

"My dear fellow, Delilah will not change her mind," said Mr. Desmond in mild astonishment. The earl must have looked like contradicting him, because he added, "Before you say anything you might regret, Marcus, I must assure you this is no invidious plot. My daughter has fixed on Jack Langdon, and I should have to sever her arms to pry her loose."

Though warned, Lord Streetham went on to say a great many reckless things. Mr. Desmond, being a patient man, calmly allowed his guest to rant until exhausted, at which point the earl was obliged to take the chair courteously offered him.

"I am aware that Lord Berne is rather distraught at present, and I appreciate your alarm. All the

271

same, you cannot buy off this trouble from your son," said Mr. Desmond as he seated himself opposite. "Indeed, you have done him a great injury in doing so repeatedly, all his life. My wife tells me she could hardly bear to look at him, for it nearly broke her heart to see what a pathetic, undisciplined creature you have made of your fine, handsome boy."

"It's you who've done this to him," said the earl hoarsely.

"I, to my infinite regret, have done nothing to him. It was you set him after my daughter," Desmond answered calmly. "Really, it is a wonder to me how a man so clever in so many ways can be so blind in what most nearly concerns him. I must give you credit for cleverness, Marcus," he added with a faint smile. "It required weeks to uncover your connexion with Atkins, though I suspected you from the first. However, I must admit I did not exert myself overmuch. You see, I thought you intended to destroy the manuscript."

The colour drained from Lord Streetham's face. Still, he managed to collect himself sufficiently to answer coolly that he hadn't the least idea what his host was talking about.

"Not until the newspaper announcement appeared," the Devil went on, unheeding, "did I suspect otherwise. I had been quite certain you had not even looked at the work before consigning it to the fire. But you did. Were you surprised?"

The earl only glared at him.

"Not a word about your fanatical pursuit of Miss Angelica Ornesby, who had declined your offers some half dozen times. Not a word about the abduction you'd planned, bribing her friends in the theatre company to help you. No mention of the actress who took her place that night, while Angelica and I were in Bristol, being wed."

Mr. Desmond appeared to gaze off into some great

272

distance. "Now I wonder why I left that fascinating story out?" he asked thoughtfully. "Something to do with not kicking a fellow when he's down, I expect. I had won the angel. It seemed base to rub your nose in your failure—especially after all these years."

Lord Streetham drew back ever so slightly as the glittering green gaze flickered to his face.

"But you have not forgotten, have you, Marcus? Your failure still gnaws at you. I suppose that is why you chose to enhance my tales with your own bits of filth. Quite a coup, you must have thought: Confound and humiliate your political rivals, destroy the Devil, break his wife's heart, and ruin his daughter, all at once. Your son, of course, would see to the last. You were certain you could count on him for that, if nothing else."

"This is monstrous," the earl gasped, rising from his chair. "I will not remain to hear another word. You will regret this, Desmond—"

"You will remain, My Lord, and I will regret nothing, because I hold the tainted manuscript. Or actually, Lady Potterby's solicitor has it," Desmond corrected. "In a carefully sealed package. A letter is enclosed, addressed to Lord Gaines, to whom the material is to be delivered in the event of my untimely demise."

Lord Streetham sat down. "Gaines?" he croaked.

"That rings a bell, perhaps? Let me refresh your memory, for you must have somehow forgotten when you were hard at work on your revisions. Perhaps because you were so drunk on that evening long ago, you forgot that I and the others had already retired to our entertainments while you and Gaines continued to dicker with the bawd."

"You—and the others—gone?"

Desmond nodded. "The tale was a revelation to me. I suppose Gaines swore you to secrecy. Certain he disposed of the bawd. She was taken up next day, tried speedily, and transported. She did not survive the voyage to New South Wales, I'm afraid. But then few persons ever do survive Gaines's displeasure."

The earl drew out his handkerchief and wiped his forehead. His hands trembled slightly.

"You know," his host continued, "were Lord Gaines to read those pages, I suspect he would have no difficulty believing you had written them. Perhaps, after so long a time, he would see the humour in the episode, perhaps not. What is *your* opinion?"

A strangled sound escaped Lord Streetham's throat, but for a moment or so, nothing else. Then he put away the handkerchief, and with visible effort, drew himself up. "I should have known," he said. "You made it too easy. You were waiting."

The Devil smiled. "My wife tells me I am patient to a fault. I rather think it is sheer laziness. Once I learned for certain you had the work, I was most curious what you were about. Still, I could not produce one good reason for exerting myself to steal it from you when I might have it from Atkins with no exertion at all. From Atkins's printer, actually. Even then it was Mr. Langdon who did all the planning and all the work. But I suppose your son has told you about that."

"Yes, and I was scarcely surprised," the earl grumbled. "You bend everyone to your will. Why not that poor, muddled boy?"

Mr. Desmond rose to ring for a servant. When he returned to his chair he answered, "I really do not understand why everyone insists Mr. Langdon is muddled. From the moment I met him, I was struck by his sagacity. My most terrifying grimaces were utterly wasted on him. He would neither cower nor be distracted. Quite remarkable. Of course, he could hardly see me for Delilah, but that—Ah, Mr. Bantwell," he said as that personage entered. "You are a miracle of promptness, indeed. Will you be kind

274

enough to send in one of your minions with a sample of the smuggled spirits her ladyship keeps in the cellar?"

"That is not necessary," Lord Streetham said hastily as the butler was leaving.

"Oh, but it is," said Mr. Desmond.

Bantwell left, closing the door behind him.

"We have not yet discussed your fervent desire to make amends," the Devil explained.

"I knew it was too easy."

"Certainly. You have not yet spoken with Angelica."

The earl turned startled eyes upon his host.

"I thought it best," said Mr. Desmond, "that the brandy be near at hand when you did."

21

Mr. Langdon's mama, with her youngest daughter in tow, burst upon London a few days after the earl's conversation with Mr. and Mrs. Desmond. She made direct for Melgrave House, where she launched into a fit of hysterical grief that would have done Mrs. Siddons proud.

Lord Streetham, however, knew he had far greater reason for hysterical grief. Her only son was merely getting married, not going off to some filthy battlefield to be killed by barbarous Frenchmen. This made an extremely distasteful task somewhat less offensive than it might have been, and he was able to call her to order with a respectable show of his usual imperiousness.

"My dear Edith," he said coldly, "you are quite absurd. The young lady is—" He paused to clear his throat of some obstruction. "She is utterly charming, beautiful, and intelligent. She will be"—there was another moment of difficulty—"one of the foremost hostesses of the Ton."

"A hostess!" Mrs. Langdon screamed. "The daughter of an actress. Devil Desmond's daughter. The mortification will kill me. Oh, how *could* my son—but I cannot blame Jack," she added with a sob. "What does he know of women—of anything but his stupid books? The minx has tricked him. You must put a stop to it, Marcus."

"Certainly not," said the earl. "I have already given them my blessing."

Mrs. Langdon promptly fainted dead away. When she revived, the world still had not got to the right-about, for Lord Streetham only told her to take herself in hand and be sensible.

Thus began the making of amends. In the two months preceding the wedding, Lord Streetham found the amends he was obliged to make not unlike the labours of Hercules, though he was certain that cleaning the Augean stables was nothing to what he had to do.

When Mrs. Langdon's attitudes had been satisfactorily rearranged, the earl proceeded to those of Lord Stivling. This was a more formidable task, but Lord Streetham was formidable himself. Within a week, Lord Stivling had not only condescended to acknowledge his young relative, but agreed to provide her an extravagant betrothal celebration. By the day of this ball, the Baron Desmond had likewise been seized by a fit of Christian forgiveness. By the time the ball concluded, Miss Desmond's position, not only in her family but in Society as well, was as secure as she could have wished.

More important, both a comfortable annuity for her parents and a generous dowry for herself had very recently been arranged by the two families—and miraculously enough, without any prodding from Lord Streetham. Not only need she not ask her prospective spouse to support her parents, but she need not go to that spouse empty-handed. Though Mr. Langdon did not care two straws what she might cost him or what she brought him besides herself, Delilah was half Ornesby and half Desmond, after all, and had all their combined pride. As it turned out, she also had Gwendolyn Langdon, with whom, to Jack's great amazement, she had become fast friends. Gwendolyn had even agreed to be Delilah's bridesmaid—primarily, the young lady told her brother, to assist Delilah should she come to her senses at the last minute and need to make a speedy getaway from the church.

A few days before the wedding, the two women were sitting together in Lady Potterby's parlour, inspecting a deck of cards.

"Now, run your hand along the back of the card," Miss Desmond was saying. "Do you feel the tiny pin pricks? It's a stupid trick, not subtle at all, but I promise you Lady Wells had such a deck—and everyone believes her such a high stickler."

Gwendolyn laughed. "Good heavens, no wonder Mama came away so cross from that party. And I had thought you refused to play because you wanted only to gaze at Jack in that perfectly revolting way. You really should not, you know. It makes him conceited, and so high-handed with Mama that I scarcely know him anymore."

"So," said Mr. Langdon, who had noiselessly entered the room. "You are teaching my sister to cheat at cards. That is very bad of you, Delilah. How will you face the minister in two days?"

"With resignation, I daresay," his sister answered. "I have been trying to open her eyes to her error, but she will not attend. She'll learn her mistake soon enough, when she tries to get your attention—for instance, if the house takes fire—and you will not look up from your book. Then it will be too late."

She turned to Delilah. "He'll never notice your new bonnets, you know. And he will not sympathise if the parlour maid is saucy, not to mention—"

"Go away, Gwendolyn," said Jack. "I have something particular to say to my affianced wife."

Gwendolyn eyed the package in her brother's hand. "A present—and you will not let me stay to

278

see her open it. That is very bad of you," she said, though she did rise to leave. "But of course it can only be another book. Really, Jack," she added as she moved towards the door, "you are so *unromantic*."

When she was gone, Delilah reached out to take her husband-to-be by the hand and draw him to the sofa beside her.

"You had better kiss me," she said coaxingly, "or I shall be forced to believe your sister."

"I had better not," he answered, moving primly several inches away. "It always starts as but a kiss and ends by my having to put my head under the pump. Don't pout," he added, as her lower lip began to protrude. "Open your present. Perhaps I shall kiss you after."

Delilah dutifully untied the wrapping, though she declared herself far more interested in the person who had brought it. Then her eyes widened in amazement as she stared at the book in her lap.

"Papa's memoirs," she said, baffled. She looked up at Jack. "How can this be? I gave them to Papa that night when we returned."

"You gave him the manuscript Lord Streetham had 'amended,' " Jack corrected.

"Yes—and Papa gave it to the lawyer, so Lord Streetham could not give us any more trouble. That's why I don't understand—"

"We had to give Atkins something," Jack interrupted. "We might have given him a parcel of blank paper, but we'd have been found out too soon. I thought he might as well get memoirs, since that's what he wanted so badly. So, we rewrote them."

Delilah reflected as she gazed at the book cover. "I see," she said at last. "That's why Mama came with all those notes and letters. It had nothing to do with a legal case. Now I remember—Papa said something about it that night you brought me home—how you wanted people to think—" The gaze she raised to her betrothed was reproachful. "You let *me* think it, Jack."

"Don't look at me that way," he answered uncomfortably. "I suffered agonies of guilt the whole time. Originally, I didn't want to tell you because the plan was so farfetched. We had no idea whether we'd have enough time, whether we could delay printing long enough. Then, when I realised Tony had got you to confide in him, I couldn't risk it, because he might be reporting your conversations to his father. A lawsuit wouldn't alarm Lord Streetham, but what we were truly up to would—and he'd be quick to act."

Delilah flushed. "I suppose you were right," she admitted, "not to trust either me or Tony. Obviously, I was an idiot to trust him—"

"It's hard not to trust him. I've known him all my life, yet I believed a whole pack of lies—but then, he half-believed them himself."

Reflections upon the unhappy Lord Berne could not but be painful, yet they could not be thrust away so easily either. For a few moments the pair sat in silence—until Miss Desmond recalled that she still had not a satisfactory explanation for the book. She pointed out that the crisis had been resolved some time ago. Jack and Tony were bosom-bows again. In fact, the viscount was to be groomsman, before going abroad with his regiment. His father, moreover, had turned all Delilah's relatives up sweet.

"Everything has been tranquil and relatively sane for two months," she reminded severely, "yet you never once said a word about this." She gestured at the volume in her lap.

"Oh, yes. That." Jack fished out a piece of paper from his pocket and gave it to her. "The reviewer is anonymous," he said, "but I can make a guess who it is. A noted bibliophile of our mutual acquaintance. Member of Parliament, closely connected with the ministry, belted earl—that sort of thing."

Delilah swiftly perused the clipping. " 'Charming, lively tales of bygone days,' " she read aloud. " 'Not at all the prurient trash the public was led to expect. A work to be savoured—' " She broke off to gaze at her fiancé with undisguised admiration. "Oh, Jack—you wrote this book?"

"Hardly. Your father dictated, mainly, and we worked on the rephrasing together. I didn't want to cut the heart out of it, you know—so we went for more humour and less bawdiness. Your father is a genius, Delilah. I hope he continues to write—"

"I know he's a genius," she interrupted. "But I see I have a great deal to learn about *you*. You are even more underhanded than I thought."

"Am I?" He took up her hand rather absently and kissed it. The clipping fluttered to the floor.

She sighed. "Oh, Jack." Then she jerked her hand away. "There—you're doing it again. You still have not answered my question. Two months we've been engaged and you never told me you'd rewritten Papa's book."

Mr. Langdon's countenance assumed an expression of abstraction. "Didn't I?" he asked. "I must have forgot. So much on my mind, you know."

"You did not forget," she retorted. "And I will not be taken in by any more muddled looks."

"But it's true," he said gravely. "For two months I have been unable to think of anything but the night on which I will finally be permitted to slake my savage lust upon your innocent person."

"Slake your savage lust?" she repeated, turning a skeptical smile upon him. "That sounds rather like something you got out of a book."

"Yes. I get a great many things out of books. I got you because of one. I am a book-worm through and through and—" He paused, his eyes very dark now.

281

"And?" She reached up to brush a lock of hair back from his forehead.

"And I think I am about to mistake you for a volume of Ptolemy." He drew her face closer to his. "Make that Ovid," he said. His lips brushed lightly against hers. "Make that *Ars Amatoria*."

"Make it anything you like," she whispered impatiently as she threw her arms about his neck. "Only kiss me, Jack, properly—and *now*."

He did.

Read on for an excerpt from Loretta Chase's
latest historical romance,

Miss Wonderful

now available from Berkley Sensation.

"Wickedly witty, simply wonderful! Loretta
Chase delivers a book that delights and
charms, tempts and tantalizes. Don't miss it!"
—*New York Times* Bestselling Author
Stephanie Laurens

London, late autumn, 1817

The Right Honorable Edward Junius Carsington, Earl of Hargate, had five sons, which was three more than he needed. Since Providence—with some help from his wife—had early blessed him with a robust heir and an equally healthy spare, he'd rather the last three infants had been daughters.

This was because his lordship, unlike many of his peers, had a morbid aversion to accumulating debt, and everyone knows that sons, especially a nobleman's sons, are beastly expensive.

The modest schooling aristocratic girls require can be provided well enough at home, while boys must be sent away to public school, then university.

In the course of growing up, properly looked-after girls do not get into scrapes their father must pay enormous sums to get them out of. Boys do little else, unless kept in cages, which is impractical.

This, at least, was true of Lord Hargate's boys. Having inherited their parents' good looks, abundant vitality, and strong will, they tumbled into trouble with depressing regularity.

Let us also note that a daughter might be married

Excerpt from *Miss Wonderful*

off quite young at relatively small cost, after which she becomes her husband's problem.

Sons . . . Well, the long and short of it was, their noble father must either buy them places—in government, the church, or the military—or find them wealthy wives.

In the last five years, Lord Hargate's two eldest had done their duty in the matrimonial department. This left the earl free to turn his thoughts to that twenty-nine-year-old Baffle to All Human Understanding, the Honorable Alistair Carsington, his third son.

This was not to say that Alistair was ever far from his father's thoughts. No, indeed, he was present day after day in the form of tradesmen's bills.

"For what he spends on his tailor, bootmaker, hatter, glovemaker, and assorted haberdashers—not to mention the laundresses, wine and spirit merchants, pastry cooks, et cetera, et cetera—I might furnish a naval fleet," his lordship complained to his wife one night as he climbed into bed beside her.

Lady Hargate laid aside the book she'd been reading, and gave her full attention to her husband. The countess was dark-haired and statuesque, handsome rather than beautiful, with sparkling black eyes, an intimidating nose, and a strong jaw. Two of her sons had inherited her looks.

The son in question had inherited his father's. They were both tall men built along lean lines, the earl not much thicker about the middle now than he'd been at Alistair's age. They owned the same hawklike profile and the same heavy-lidded eyes, though the earl's were more brown than gold and more deeply lined. Likewise, the father's dark brown hair bore lines of silver. They had the same deep Carsington voice, which emotion—whether positive or negative—roughened into a growl.

Lord Hargate was growling at present.

"You must put a stop to it, Ned," Lady Hargate said.

He turned his full gaze upon her, his eyebrows aloft.

"Yes, I recollect what I told you last year," she said.

"I said Alistair fusses overmuch about his appearance because he is self-conscious about being lame. I told you we must be patient. But it is two years and more since he returned from the Continent, and matters do not improve. He is indifferent to everything, it seems, but his clothes."

Lord Hargate frowned. "I never thought I'd see the day we'd be fretting because he *wasn't* in trouble with a woman."

"You must do something, Ned."

"I would, had I the least idea what to do."

"What nonsense!" she said. "If you can manage the royal offspring—not to mention those unruly fellows in the House of Commons—you most certainly can manage your son. You will think of something, I have not the smallest doubt. But I urge you to think of it *soon,* sir."

A week later, in response to Lord Hargate's summons, Alistair Carsington stood by a window in the latter's study, perusing a lengthy document. It contained a list of what his father titled "Episodes of Stupidity," and their cost in pounds, shillings, and pence.

The list of Alistair's indiscretions was short, by some men's standards. The degree of folly and notoriety involved, however, was well above the norm, as he was most unhappily aware.

He did not need the list to remind him: He fell in love quickly, deeply, and disastrously.

For example:

When he was fourteen, it was Clara, the golden-haired, rosy-cheeked daughter of an Eton caretaker. Alistair followed her about like a puppy, and spent all his allowance on offerings of sweets and pretty trinkets. One day a jealous rival, a local youth, made provocative remarks. The dispute soon escalated from exchanging insults to exchanging blows. The fight drew a crowd. The ensuing brawl between a group of Alistair's schoolmates and some village boys resulted in two broken noses, six missing teeth, one minor concussion, and considerable property damage. Clara wept over the battered rival and called Alistair a brute. His heart broken, he didn't care that he faced expulsion as well as charges of assault, disturbing the King's peace, inciting a riot, and destruction of property. Lord Hargate was obliged to care, and it cost him a pretty penny.

At age sixteen, it was Verena, whom Alistair met during summer holiday. Because her parents were pious and strict, she read lurid novels in secret and communicated with Alistair in hurried whispers and clandestine letters. One night, as prearranged, he sneaked to her house and threw pebbles at her bedroom window. He'd assumed they would enact some variation of the balcony scene from *Romeo and Juliet*. Verena had other ideas. She threw down a valise, then climbed down a rope of knotted sheets. She would be her parents' prisoner no longer, she said. She would run away with Alistair. Thrilled to rescue a damsel in distress, he didn't worry about money, transportation, lodging, or other such trifles, but instantly agreed. They were caught before they reached the next parish. Her outraged parents wanted him tried for kidnapping and transported to New South Wales. After settling matters, Lord Hargate told his son to find a trollop, and stop mooning after gently-bred virgins.

At age seventeen, it was Kitty. She was a dressmaker's assistant with enormous blue eyes. From her Alistair learned, among other things, the finer points of women's fashion. When a jealous, highborn customer's complaints cost Kitty her position, the outraged Alistair published a pamphlet about the injustice. The customer sued for libel and the dressmaker for defamation and loss of trade. Lord Hargate did the usual.

At age nineteen it was Gemma, a fashionable milliner. One day, thief-takers stopped their carriage en route to a romantic rural idyll, and found in Gemma's boxes some stolen property. She claimed jealous rivals had planted false evidence, and Alistair believed her. His impassioned speech about conspiracies and corrupt officials drew a crowd, which grew disorderly, as crowds often do. The Riot Act was read, and he was taken into custody along with his light-fingered lover. Lord Hargate came to the rescue once more.

At age twenty-one, it was Aimée, a French ballet dancer who transformed Alistair's modest bachelor lodgings into an elegant abode. They gave parties that soon became famous in London's demimonde. Since Aimée's tastes rivaled those of the late Marie Antoinette, and Alistair wouldn't dream of denying her anything, he ended up in a sponging house—last stop before debtors' prison. The earl paid the astronomical debt, found Aimée a position with a touring ballet company, and told Alistair it was time to take up with respectable people and stop making a spectacle of himself.

At age twenty-three, it was Lady Thurlow, Alistair's first and only married paramour. In the Haut Ton, one pursues an adulterous liaison discreetly, to protect the lady's reputation and spare her husband tedious duels and legal actions. But Alistair couldn't hide his feelings, and she had to end the relationship. Unfortunately, a servant stole Alistair's love letters, and threatened to publish them. To protect his beloved from scandal and an outraged husband, Alistair, who had no way of raising the enormous ransom demanded, had to ask his father's help.

At twenty-five came his worst folly. Judith Gilford was the only child of a wealthy, newly knighted widower. She entered Alistair's life early in the new year of 1815. He soon vanquished all rivals, and in February the engagement was announced. By March he was in purgatory.

In public she was lovely to look at and charming to talk to. In private she fell into sulks or threw tantrums when she didn't get exactly what she wanted the instant she wanted it. She expected all attention, always, to focus on her. Her feelings were easily hurt, but she had no regard for anyone else's. She was

Excerpt from *Miss Wonderful*

unkind to family and friends, abusive to servants, and fell into hysterics when anyone tried to soften her temper or language.

And so by March Alistair was in despair, because a gentleman must not break off an engagement. Since Judith wouldn't, he could only wish he'd be trampled by runaway horses or thrown into the Thames or stabbed to death by footpads. One night, en route to a seamy neighborhood where a violent death was a strong possibility, he stumbled somehow—and he still wasn't sure how—into the comforting arms of a voluptuous courtesan named Helen Waters.

Alistair once again fell madly in love, and once again was indiscreet. Judith found out, made appalling scenes in public, and threatened lawsuits. The scandalmongers loved it. Lord Hargate did not. The next Alistair knew, he was being hustled onto a ship bound for the Continent.

Just in time for Waterloo.

That was the end of the list.

His face hot, Alistair limped away from the window and set the documents on the great desk behind which his father sat watching him.

Affecting a lightness he didn't feel, Alistair said, "Do I receive any credit for not having had an episode since the spring of 1815?"

"You stayed out of trouble only because you were incapacitated for most of that time," Lord Hargate said. "Meanwhile, the tradesmen's bills arrive by the cartload. I cannot decide which is worse. For what you spend on waistcoats you might keep a harem of French whores."

Alistair couldn't deny it. He'd always been particular about his clothes. Perhaps, of late, he devoted more time and thought to his appearance than previously. Perhaps it kept his mind off other things. The fifteenth of June, for instance, the day and night he couldn't remember. Waterloo remained a blur in his mind. He pretended he did remember, as he pretended he didn't notice the difference since he'd come home—the idolatry that made him squirm inwardly, the pity that infuriated him.

He pushed these thoughts away, and frowned at a speck of lint on his coat sleeve. He resisted the urge to brush at it. That would seem a nervous gesture. He was beginning to perspire, but that didn't show. Yet. He prayed his father would finish before his neckcloth wilted.

"I detest talking about money," his father said. "It is vulgar. Unfortunately, the subject can no longer be avoided. If you wish to cheat your younger brothers of what they're entitled to, then so be it."

"My brothers?" Alistair met his father's narrow gaze. "Why should I . . ." He trailed off, because Lord Hargate's mouth was turning up, into the barest hint of a smile.

Oh, that little smile never boded well.

"Let me explain," Lord Hargate said.